MALCHUS

W.G. GRIFFITHS

MALCHUS

This is a work of fiction. The names, characters, places and incidents are either from the author's imagination or are used in a fictitious manner. Any resemblance to actual persons, living or dead, events, or establishments is purely coincidental.

Unless otherwise indicated, all Scripture quotations are taken from the *King James Version* of the Bible.

Malchus
ISBN 1-58919-967-7
46-607-00000

Published by RiverOak Publishing
P.O. Box 700143
Tulsa, Oklahoma 74170-0143

ACKNOWLEDGMENTS

I MUST FIRST BOW to God before going any further. (Please pause. Really.)

Of God's children, my first thanks must go to Markus Wilhelm. Without his confidence in me and his determination to make it all happen, this book would still be a manuscript.

I am very, very grateful to Michelle Rapkin. Malchus was her baby from the get-go, and she took the work, and me, by the hand through every step of its publication.

I thank the ever-energetic Roger Cooper for his advice, constant encouragement, and friendship. Thanks also to my editor, Pam Strickler, a real pro who has the gift of being able to make the crooked path straight without the reader knowing it. She really had her work cut out for her and accomplished all that had to be done and more. I am also grateful to Barbara Greenman and her staff. All they do is amazing.

I want to thank my uncle, Charles Palmer, for assisting my research and experience in the land of Israel and also the Gardner Scotts and the staff at the Garden Tomb for their generous hospitality.

I am indebted to my hardworking friend, Pastor David Harwood, for his feedback and assistance in the research. Errors or inaccuracies are mine, not his.

I thank Cynthia Sterling and Magen Davidson for their valuable time and professional evaluations.

A very warm thanks to my first readers—Janice Nicolich, Melissa and Dominic Renaldo, Bill and Dorothy Griffiths, Andrew Syrotick, Maryann Griffiths, Bill McCarty, Barry and Beth Mevorach, Shira Harwood, Karianne Stordal, Steve

Hutcher, Debbie Logerfro, and Norman Sorenson—for early feedback after suffering through some truly rough drafts.

A special, special tribute to Mark Eskenazi, and his wife, Linda, for the many hours she gave him up for me. A simple acknowledgment does not seem adequate for my friend who generously took on the grueling job of being the first editor of my first book. His sweat and skills are forever weaved into the fabric of this book and my heart.

Finally, my deepest gratitude goes to my beautiful wife, Cindy, whose daily understanding, enthusiasm, and prayers fueled me and for her crying at all the right places during her many reads. And, of course, I thank my children, Stephen, Robyn, Luke, Willy, Peter, and Summer for their love and for allowing me the time to write when I could have been with them.

PROLOGUE

37 B.C.

The high priest had struggled violently when they ripped him out of his bed. The peace of Jerusalem and the stature of his office had been shattered in the shadows of dawn. Now exhausted, he resisted only with his weight as the Roman soldiers dragged him through the parched dirt street, chains on his neck and wrists.

The arched doors of Herod's palace opened wide before him as the stone-faced soldiers hauled him into the courtyard, his feet plowing the soil behind them.

"What is the meaning of this?" The high priest yelled, thinking Herod or someone in charge must be within earshot. In answer, his captors shoved the priest face-down in the dirt beneath a newly erected wooden beam, which stretched across the confine. Rough posts, sunk every twenty feet, supported the beam. The high priest looked up. "I demand to see Herod," he said, spitting dirt from his mouth. A swift kick to his side left him gasping, gulping for air.

A soldier threw a rope over the beam and tied it to the fetters around the high priest's wrists. Then, with the help of another soldier, he hoisted him up. The priest balanced on his toes to try to relieve his bruised wrists of his own weight. Still gasping for air, he tried to speak, but a commotion behind him drowned out his words. He turned to look over his shoulder and saw one of his chief priests being dragged through the gate, as he himself had been, and dropped to the ground. Then, another priest was dragged in. And another. Any who dared to complain or resist were summarily subdued by a brutal kick to the stomach or groin. The soldiers methodically hoisted up the priests as if they were hanging grape leaves to dry in the sun. Their black robes trailed in the dust.

The high priest realized that each priest hanging beside him was a member of his Sanhedrin. *Is he mad?* he wondered.

After the king, the Sanhedrin was the highest administrative and judicial authority of all Jewry. The Sanhedrin was the law, and its mandates were to be treated as if they were the words of God.

The high priest remembered Herod's ambition. His thirst for power. His need to control everything he touched, and anything that touched him. The Sanhedrin had affronted him once, and Herod apparently never forgot. Who could have seen this ruthlessness?

"Why are they doing this, Antigonus?" the priest beside him asked. His face and beard were caked with dirt.

"I believe it's an answer to yesterday's question." The high priest was referring to the Roman senate's proclamation that Herod was the new King of Judea. The announcement had enraged the Sanhedrin, and they had demanded a further explanation. Judean taxes were paid on time and in full, and Rome had always favored the Sanhedrin to govern the Jews as long as it recognized that Rome held ultimate authority.

Looking down the line of hanging black-robed priests, the high priest counted forty-five members of the Sanhedrin. He could see by their bloodied faces that some had resisted more than others. His own blood was running down his arm inside his sleeve from the cuts inflicted by the rough, hammered chains around his wrists. A soldier stepped before them with a long whip.

Maybe he actually is going to flog us. How dare he! How dare he! Does he think he can break our spirits with a whip?

Herod emerged onto the second-story balcony. As was his custom, he was dressed in royal purple, his hair neatly trimmed and combed. He surveyed the line of captive priests without expression. Antigonus watched Herod's gaze move down the row of priests until it came to rest on him. The high priest stared back. Herod raised his chin, but his eerie gaze held the high priest's eyes without blinking for what seemed like minutes. Finally Herod looked away, emotionless, to the end of the line again. There stood a soldier with a drawn Roman broadsword. Herod looked briefly back at Antigonus, then nodded to the soldier.

The soldier placed the point of his two-foot sword at the midsection of the first priest. The other priests pivoted on their toes and stared in dread and silence as the soldier slowly positioned the blade, then, in one motion, drove it through the priest until the sword's hilt hit his body. The priest groaned in agony, and his life ebbed before his bound brethren.

"Why, Herod? Why?" the high priest cried out.

While some priests began to scream, others were shocked into silence. A soldier with a whip lashed at the ones who dared to say anything, striking them in their faces.

The executioner yanked his sword from the dead priest's body, pushing the man free from the blade with his foot. He moved on to the next priest, found the cavity beneath the man's ribs with the point of the sword, and plunged forward again until the blade could go no farther.

Antigonus squeezed his eyes shut at the death cry of the priest as the soldier yanked hard to retrieve his weapon, then moved down the line to the next victim. The high priest could stand it no longer. He opened his eyes and looked pleadingly at Herod. The man seemed completely relaxed, observing the slaughter without expression.

"What do you want?" Antigonus cried out. "Tell me, please! Take me. I'm their leader. This isn't necessary."

He slammed his head back as the Roman whip slashed across his face. Herod examined his fingernails and looked at the morning sky, as if enjoying the start of the day.

"It's no use, Antigonus," whispered the priest next to him. "We're all going to die today. God will judge him."

The high priest leaned forward slightly to look down the line. The soldier was methodically moving toward him, his weapon dripping red as the bodies suspended from the beam left pools of blood at their own feet.

"God has already judged this man, my friend," Antigonus said quietly, "but God help our people."

Herod spared only the high priest that day, then commanded his soldiers, "Take him to Antony in Antioch. Make sure the people see him leave the city alive. Have him beheaded upon arrival."

As Herod spoke it, so it was done. For the first time in Roman history, a ruler in an occupied land was executed in the name of Rome. Herod then took the liberty of handpicking a new high priest and a new Sanhedrin for his new subjects, the Jews.

And the empire of Herod the Great grew and evolved over the course of the next thirty-three years until it arrived at a place that the prophets had called the fullness of time.

MALCHUS

And Jesus said, "Do what you have come for." Then they came forward to seize and arrest Him.

One of the disciples, having a sword, drew it, and struck the high priest's slave, cutting off his right ear.

Jesus therefore said to him, "Put down your sword; for all those that live by the sword, shall die by the sword." Having said this, He touched the slave's ear and he was completely healed. The slave's name was Malchus.

—Luke 22: 50–51, John 18:10, Matthew 26:50–52

ONE

32 A.D.

Pain shot through Malchus's cupped fingers as he struggled to carry the heavy wooden tables up the temple steps and into the court. He pried each finger straight and shook them until the blood returned.

"Not there," the priest yelled, shaking his head. "They need to be brought closer to the gate. How long have you been doing this?"

Too long, Malchus thought, knowing for certain they had set the table down in this exact spot last Passover—after moving it back from being too close to the gate.

"Malchus!" called a familiar voice from behind. Elias was the oldest of the chief priests, and it was becoming increasingly apparent that the preparation for Passover was too much for him. The workload was as overwhelming as the crush of pilgrims pouring into Jerusalem. The old man's weak voice could barely be heard over the bleating sheep and cackling doves. "These are the wrong ledgers. You need to take these back to Caiaphas's immediately and get me the new ones."

"I'll get them right away," Malchus said, grateful to leave the tables with the carpenters who made them impracticably big, just as they had been ordered to do.

Malchus had grown to dread Passover. The city's population of eighty thousand would swell to over a million before the feast was over, and every last one of them would funnel through the gates and stop at the money changer tables to exchange their money for the only currency the temple would accept . . . its own.

Malchus decided to take the outermost road back to his master's small palace. The west road along the ancient city wall might not be the shortest route, but it was definitely the fastest. Congestion in the center of Jerusalem had been increasing steadily over the last few weeks, and now with Passover just days away, Malchus found the midday crowds overwhelming. But while the crowded streets were an annoyance, Malchus preferred them to the temple.

The day was unseasonably hot and far from over. Malchus passed by the open Damascus gate and scanned the rolling hills beyond, trying to estimate just how many pilgrims had made their camp on the inhospitable terrain. Something in the foreground suddenly caught his eye. Two temple guards on horseback pulled a rope, which had been tied around the neck of a man. The captive, his hands tied before him, desperately tried to keep up with them. When the horsemen came to a stop on the crest of a crossroads that led to the Roman fortress known as Antonia, the man doubled over and dropped to one knee, exhausted. Malchus and a small crowd of pilgrims pressed closer to the gate for a better look. The sound of more hooves drew everyone's attention northward. Two Roman soldiers on horseback galloped toward them, trailing a cloud of swirling dust. The bound man looked up at the Romans and then to his captors and pleaded with the guards.

Malchus could not hear what the man was saying, but the scene was easy enough to figure out. He was begging them to deal with him themselves and not to give him over to the Romans. When it came to meting out punishment, the Jews were constrained by the Law of Moses. There were very specific limitations on what could be done. The Romans were constrained only by how they felt that day or by the stamina of the man administering the punishment. At Roman hands, few survived.

Malchus had a good idea what the man's crime was without ever having seen him before. He had to have committed an offense against a Jew, or the temple guard would not have been involved. The man also had to have committed a crime against Rome in some way, or the temple guard would not be handing him over. And they would not be handing him over if he was Jewish. All of which meant that he was probably a fugitive slave who had tried to stay alive by stealing, probably by stealing from a Jew.

Malchus did not envy the life of a slave on the run. For a slave, running was the way to misery and death, not the way to freedom. Malchus knew this and had never run, though in the early days he thought he might burst from longing.

The guards handed the rope off to the Romans, who promptly turned about and started back to the Roman fortress from where they had come. The huge old doors of Antonia opened as the soldiers approached. The man was unable to keep up with the soldiers. He was now being dragged on the ground by his neck, his hands clutching at the noose to keep from choking. Malchus wondered if the Romans were even aware that he had fallen. He knew they did not care. And he knew that the likely end of this drama would be with the man upon a cross, sentenced to the hideous death that was the cornerstone of Roman punishment.

When the fortress doors closed, Malchus continued on his way home. He tried not to picture what the Romans were doing to the man. More than likely the man was a Gentile. Jewish slaves rarely tried to escape. In fact, Malchus had never even known of such an attempt. He certainly would not try it. Especially now, with his release so close.

Six more months, and his debt to Caiaphas would be paid off, Malchus thought as he walked up the finely chiseled stone steps of the high priest's palatial home. For years the thought of freedom was painfully remote, miles away from where he was. But now, after six and a half years being Caiaphas's slave, he would indulge thoughts of freedom, which was no longer a bitter, distant memory.

The shade provided cool relief as Malchus walked under the main entrance arch. On either side of the massive, heavily hinged olive wood doors stood two members of the temple guard. They were always there, sunup to sundown, and all through the night. Malchus thought of them more as ornaments adorning the doors than real security. The temple guard, or temple police, as they were also known, was made up entirely of Levites. Tradition held that they were once a well-trained, protective army. Now, after decades of Roman rule, they were barely permitted to carry a sword, and not one of the guard would touch the handle of his weapon while in the presence of a Roman soldier. They were far too familiar with Roman punishment dealt out for even anticipated crimes of rebellion. All of this meant they were virtually an unarmed militia, soldiers in name only. But since Rome had spread its empire so far, it permitted occupied territories to police themselves and allowed limited weaponry to be possessed as an aid to local rule.

"Shalom," Malchus said curtly in Aramaic as he pushed open one of the doors to enter. The silent guards surveyed him with a look of arrogance in their eyes. Without looking back as he walked past them, Malchus threw the door shut behind him harder than necessary, registering his contempt. He almost smiled as it slammed closed. He knew they resented him. Although he was not a Levite like them, he *was* the Jewish slave of the high priest and, under the Law of Moses, was to be treated like a son by his master. And in this case, by his master's servants, also. When Malchus first arrived, he found the sonship treatment to be embarrassing. However, as he got to know the guards better, with their own subtle brand of sarcasm and ridicule, he enjoyed flaunting his status as Caiaphas's slave-son, relying on Jewish law to protect him. They could do nothing in response, or they would have to answer to Caiaphas. They had to be satisfied with treating him with contempt, which they did openly, obviously, and frequently—at least when Caiaphas was not looking.

The Law of Moses had other benefits as well. A Jewish slave could not be held against his will for more than seven years. As a result, Jewish slaves were much less expensive than gentile slaves, who were slaves for life. Malchus had the option to stay on of his own free will after the seventh year was complete, and in these times, many Jewish slaves did just that, particularly if the master was kind and the surroundings comfortable. In Malchus's case, the surroundings were more than simply comfortable, they were spectacular, so he was widely expected to stay. Indeed, Caiaphas was counting on it. Malchus had proven invaluable in assisting the oversight of the temple trade. He had an eye for detail and a way with merchants that impressed even Caiaphas. Malchus, however, would have no further part of servitude. He would rather be a poor free man than a palace slave.

Malchus paid no attention to the expensive draperies on the walls as he walked through the grand foyer. Nor did it matter to him in the least that the rug he was walking on was worth more than all his father had ever earned before his death seven years ago. He could remember when he had first entered this same hall on the day Caiaphas had purchased him at the auction stone after the trial. He was awestruck. If only his father could see him now, he had thought.

After a short time of living and working for the high priest, the awe had faded and he started questioning the beliefs that his father had instilled in him his whole life. Now he thought of the teachings as mere fables. His father had taught him that the Lord God was the beginning and end, Jerusalem was the holy city of God, the priests were divinely connected just below the heavens, and the Jewish people were chosen to inherit God's riches. Over the past few years Malchus had gained a different view. God was not the beginning and end, He was a means to an end. Jerusalem was a product. The priests were salesmen. And the Jewish people were consumers who kept the business going with their tithes and offerings. If Jerusalem was thriving, God's will was being done.

He walked down the center hallway toward the study where the records were kept. As he passed the kitchen entrance, he heard a loud crash and a gasp. He turned back and ran into the room. A young woman was bending down to pick up broken pieces of a ceramic bowl. He had never seen her before.

"Are you hurt?" Malchus asked before he realized that she did not know he was there. She looked up, startled.

"I'm fine," she said, then quickly looked back down. "I feel so foolish for letting the bowl slip out of my hands like that. I'm not usually so clumsy," she said, continuing to pick up the pieces. "I shouldn't have put so much fruit in it." Her accent was unmistakable. She was Nabataean.

Malchus dropped to one knee and reached for a pomegranate. "Let me help." Who was this Gentile girl, and what was she doing in the kitchen of the high priest?

The girl's hands were shaking slightly, picking up pieces of ceramic as if restoration were possible.

"Don't worry about that. No one will miss this old bowl," he said reassuringly, knowing it was worth a small fortune and had better be cleaned up quickly or there would be trouble. "What is your name?" he asked, picking up pieces of fruit and cradling them in his left arm.

She barely looked up. "Zara."

Malchus unloaded what he had collected onto a wooden table and took an orange for himself. "Are you here for Passover?" he asked, figuring she was the slave of an early-arriving guest. Before he became involved in temple business and trade, he would travel out from Jerusalem to meet some of Caiaphas's more important guests and formally escort them and their slaves back. Now, as he continued to learn the business of the temple under Elias's tutelage, escorts were less and less his responsibility.

"Yes, I'm here for the feast." Then Zara stood up, the top of her head about even with his chin. She turned and looked directly at him. "Joseph Caiaphas is my new master."

He was stunned silent, not only from what she said but how she looked. She was absolutely beautiful. Not just pretty.

Beautiful. Her nose was softly rounded and straight; her large brown eyes wide apart; and her mouth broad, revealing straight white teeth when she spoke. Her long black hair was pulled back and braided to keep it out of her way as she worked. He could hardly believe his eyes, which were transfixed by hers. She blinked slowly—doelike. She could not be much more than eighteen, twenty at the most.

Malchus realized his mouth was hanging open, so he bent down to pick up the last piece of broken pottery and to compose himself. Where had Caiaphas found her?

"Thank you," Zara said, taking the piece of cracked bowl from his hand. She turned to place it with the other pieces, revealing her profile and, with it, an inch-long vertical scar on her left cheek.

Malchus winced upon seeing it. In sympathy, he reached involuntarily for his own cheek. He was not repulsed by the scar, but he felt bad for her, that her beauty had been marred, even slightly. She looked at him, perhaps catching his stare. He immediately brought his hand up higher and scratched at his short black wavy hair. She smiled, forming a dimple that swallowed up the scar. He was smitten by her, but he couldn't tell if she was being friendly or letting him know that he wasn't fooling her.

"I see you two have already met," came a familiar voice from behind Malchus.

"Hello, Levia," Malchus said, disappointed by the intrusion. But after all, it was her kitchen, Malchus thought, remembering all the times she reminded him of that fact as she chased him out of her kitchen. Levia was another example of Caiaphas's ability to match the right person with the right job. Levia was more than a housekeeper. She ran the house—not Caiaphas's wife, Yardenah, as one might expect. Yardenah was usually at her father, Annas's, house with her mother. She was rarely seen at Caiaphas's house and barely thought of it as her home.

Malchus often thought of Levia as a second mother. In many ways she had adopted him. Like Malchus, she was a slave, but she was a Gentile and was, therefore, a slave for life. He would miss her someday. She was one of the few people he had met here who was not caught up in all the wealth and power of her master. With all the work she did, she was the only one who had a right to boast.

With Levia, there were no surprises, which was just the way Caiaphas wanted it. He would say, "Where there is order, there is peace." Levia provided order. It had been that way long before Malchus had arrived. Caiaphas had trained Levia to be an extension of his will in the affairs of the household. She alone was responsible for the guest schedule. Her job was to know the various whims and peculiar desires of the visiting guests of the high priest—very wealthy and influential guests, who traveled from as far away as Macedonia and Rome. Caiaphas picked his guests quite carefully, if not with calculation. In fact, he often invited a friend or relative of the person he wanted to influence rather than that person himself. He found this to be a most effective approach, and Levia to be a most effective hostess.

"Malchus, this is the third time I've seen you here today," Levia said, taking the fruit from his hands. "Don't tell me Elias has you running again?"

"Actually, Levia, the ledgers he sent me for are the very ones he had me bring back here this morning," Malchus said. When Levia turned to put the fruit in a bowl, Malchus allowed himself to look at Zara again. He did not want to stare, but her beauty was irresistible. Tantalizing. Catching his gaze for certain this time, she smiled just enough to curl her upper lip slightly. He smiled back, his face feeling a little flushed.

"Well, you best bring them, and any other books or accounts he will be needing, tomorrow."

"Why is that?" he said, retrieving the orange from the bowl.

"As you know, your cousin Seth is out on an escort. Tomorrow he will be escorting Evaratus, of the Island of Cos, up from Jericho."

"If Evaratus is coming from Cos, why is he taking the Jericho route? It's so much faster to take a boat to Caesarea than to travel by land."

"Last year Evaratus got so seasick in a storm that he swore he would never do it again," she explained.

Malchus looked at her suspiciously. "So what does that have to do with me?" he asked, sticking a wedge of orange in his mouth.

"Sometime tomorrow their caravan is due to stop at Bethany, where the road levels out. There you will separate Evaratus from the rest of the caravan and bring him here in Caiaphas's private chariot."

"Me?" Malchus almost choked on the orange. The road to Jericho, even a few miles of it, was not a pleasant prospect to Malchus. The road that linked Jerusalem through the Judean Desert to the Dead Sea would be very crowded, and it was in terrible shape. It was never maintained by the Romans, who cared only about the road to Caesarea. He would have to travel it mostly by foot, leading a donkey or horse. Anything with wheels could barely negotiate the terrain.

"Yes, Malchus, you. And be careful with that chariot," Levia said, winking at Zara.

"Careful with the chariot? Look, there's got to be someone else to do this. Elias needs me at the temple."

"Elias has been doing this since before you were born."

"But he's not who he used to be."

"Maybe not, but Evaratus is who he used to be, and that means the job is yours."

That sounded more like Caiaphas than Levia. Evaratus was an extremely wealthy businessman and landowner, who, over the years, had been faithful to bring the tithe for the people of the Island of Cos in Asia Minor, which had a substantial Jewish population as a result of the Diaspora. Evaratus was also a friend of Herod Antipas, the son of Herod the Great.

"Besides, if you run into any serious trouble on the road, Zara will be there to save you," Levia said, pointing to her. "These are Caiaphas's written instructions, not mine. I'll leave them for you in the morning." She turned and walked away with a curious hint of a smile.

"Zara?" Malchus asked himself as he mouthed her name. Suddenly the escort took on a new light. He could not imagine why Zara would be accompanying him, but he was not going to complain anymore. After all, orders were orders.

"You really don't want to do the escort, do you?" Zara asked from across the room.

"It's not that," he said. "It's just that I don't understand why. Caiaphas needs me to help Elias. The workload at Passover is more than the old man can deal with by himself. He's not as able as he was five years ago when I was first assigned to help him. If

I'm not there to sort everything out for him, it will mean twice as much work when I get back." The more Malchus talked, the more his thoughts shifted to the work at the temple. "What's Caiaphas thinking? He hasn't ordered me to do an escort in over two years. And now? During Passover? It's the busiest time of the year!" He began pacing as he continued. "And tomorrow we're scheduled to announce the new exchange rate to the merchants, which means I'm going to have to explain to each and every one of them how to calculate their percentages. When will I get to that?" He walked over to the window and stared for a moment, shaking his head. Then he turned to Zara. "And why in the world does he want you to go with me? It's not like Caiaphas to send a new slave girl on an escort."

Zara looked down at the floor.

"Not that I'm not looking forward to your company, Zara," Malchus said quickly, seeing that he may have hurt her feelings. "And who am I to question the high priest? He wouldn't send me if he didn't have a good reason," he said, wondering what it possibly could be. "In fact, what do I care? It's not my temple. I couldn't work any harder than I already am. This will be a welcome break from the insanity of that place. And with you there, I won't have to talk to the horse . . . I mean . . ." Malchus fumbled, trying to redeem himself.

"Thank you, Malchus," Zara interrupted with a smile. "I'll try to live up to your expectations. And I don't eat much hay."

Malchus wanted to keep talking, but he was afraid he would say something even more stupid. "Well, I guess I'd better get back to work," he said, walking out and still looking at her. "Shalom," he said with a smile and a nod, then walked into the side of the doorway, banging his head.

Zara covered her mouth with both hands to keep from laughing. "Are you hurt?"

"No, no. I'm fine," he said, rubbing his forehead. He looked back as he passed through the doorway. "Wasn't that the first thing I asked you when I came in?"

Zara nodded, trying to look concerned and doing her best to keep from laughing.

"I guess we're even," Zara said to him when he turned down the hall.

Malchus thought he heard her laughing as soon as he was out of her sight. He did not care. *Tomorrow's going to be a very good day,* he thought as he walked down the hall, a new bounce in his step.

TWO

Malchus went out walking. He had just finished one of Levia's dinners. Tonight's meal had included roasted chicken with tarragon, chickpeas, figs, fresh bread, grain, and chicory. No one in Jerusalem, maybe no one in the entire Roman Empire, could cook like her. *Caiaphas clearly had the leading of God when he put her in charge of the kitchen,* Malchus thought. *Perhaps the only time.*

Of course, Levia had the finest vegetables in all of Jerusalem at her disposal. They came from Caiaphas's own private garden, situated on the west slopes of the Kidron Valley, just outside the walls of the temple. The garden always produced a phenomenal crop, regardless of what variety was planted. The floor of the temple was pitched in such a way that the blood from the sacrifices would run down hill and drain through openings in the temple's east wall. That blood and water runoff then irrigated the soil on the west side of the temple. Somehow, sacrificial blood and water had a wondrous, even miraculous, effect on anything planted. The flourishing vegetation on the west slope did not escape Caiaphas's notice. Soon after assuming office, he designated the area "the holy garden for the priesthood," and used his impressive produce to advertise the miraculous power of God's blood-enriched temple water. Local farmers would then obtain blood from the temple to fertilize their own gardens. And, of course, the farmers and gardeners who took such holy fertilizer felt obliged to make the appropriate offering in exchange. Caiaphas managed to turn a profit even from sacrificial runoff.

Malchus hoped he had not made a fool of himself at the table, but he could not keep his eyes off the new slave girl. He went so far as to eat a third helping, just so he could spend time in her presence and look at her a little longer. When Levia finally sent her away on an errand, he felt stuffed and uncomfortable and needed to walk the meal off.

The clear starlit night brought a cool brisk air with it. As was his habit, he walked to a nearby fire on the side of the road, where a few slaves and a couple of Roman soldiers gathered. They were warming themselves around the flames, shifting away from the twisting smoke that seemed able to harass each of them as if it had a mind of its own.

The men hailed Malchus as he strolled near. Men he never saw anywhere but near a night fire. Men who spoke to him like old friends. Men who always seemed to have a wineskin at their side.

"Malchus!" someone called. With the fire behind him, the caller was only a silhouette to Malchus, but nothing could disguise the voice, or attitude. "Did you come out to clear your head of all those mind-numbing numbers you've had stuck to your face all week, or were you feeling cooped up in that little shack you call a home?"

"Judah, Judah. Can't you ever just say hello like any other sane person?" Malchus asked, shaking his head.

Judah was the temple scourge. His job, under the temple jailer, Ben Bebai the Levite, was to administer punishment, or correction, as he called it, among the priesthood. Some thought he enjoyed his job a little too much. He was also Malchus's good friend and occasional coworker. In truth, no one knew Malchus better than Judah. They were both in their early twenties, and over the last six years they had spent many a night around a campfire drinking their masters' wine and swapping stories. Both of their masters highly valued their services and extended certain privileges to them that other slaves would never know, in the hope they would stay on beyond the term of their servitude. And they made the most of their situation.

On the other feast days of the year, the sheep were shorn before they were sacrificed, and the wool went to the priests. In turn, the priests sold the wool, usually to the Romans, and earned additional income from it. During Passover, however, shearing a lamb before sacrificing it was not permitted by law because the animal was required to be unblemished. Perfect. This Pascal lamb, as it was called, was then given back to be eaten. The skin and fleece were now an inconvenience, presenting an opportunity for Malchus.

No one wanted to waste any part of the sacrifice. The fleece would be harvested, as would the hide. First, it had to be skinned off the lamb, then tanned or it would become as hard and rigid as wood. For the pilgrims who had traveled far, it was a messy job of which they wanted no part, nor did they want more to carry around. Malchus and Judah were allowed to furnish a limited service for some of the pilgrims at Passover by preparing the lamb so it could be cooked. They would skin the lambs in an area away from the temple, then sell the fleeces to some Roman soldiers who were, first and foremost, businessmen. The soldiers would then send the fleeces in bulk back to Rome. Everyone benefited.

Given the holiday, the temple could not involve itself in this particular transaction, so it really was not losing any money. In any case, the temple appeared to be providing a public service for the hungry pilgrims, so Caiaphas was agreeable, if only for that. As for Malchus, he would take the money he made and send it to his mother, who had no other means of support since his subjugation. This Caiaphas also knew, and that was another reason why he authorized the venture. He was not being charitable. He knew Malchus would feel indebted. Caiaphas figured Malchus would not be very cooperative if his mother was not provided for.

"I hate to tell you, Malchus. I'm the sanest person you know," Judah said, making a face like a crazy person, scrunching his eyes, nose, and mouth as close together as he could. "And that goes for all of you," he added, addressing the men around the fire, his face still contorted in mock insanity. They responded with both laughs and curses.

"If you're sane, then we're all in trouble," Malchus said. "I don't know about the rest of you, but I'm worn out, and Passover hasn't even started yet," he said, extending his chilled hands toward the fire.

"It's true," said a man with a patch over one eye. "This is the only rest I've had all day, and I'm too tired to enjoy it."

"Yes," said a man sitting near the fire, staring at it with half-closed, bloodshot eyes. "But after the feast you'll get to sleep for a week straight, once your master leaves town, while the rest of us will be working just as hard cleaning up. It's the same thing every year."

"Ah yes, what a pity that will be. You poor men. I'll feel terribly guilty every time I see you. I just hope it won't keep me awake," teased the man with the patch.

"You all cackle like hens," said a Roman soldier over the laughter. "Malchus, you've still got that same stupid grin on your face that you wore as you walked over here. What haven't you told us? Have you been hitting Caiaphas's private wine collection, or do you actually find this chatter amusing?"

"Alexander," Malchus said, addressing the soldier to whom he and Judah sold skins. A number of soldiers, including Alexander, enjoyed the company and unique sense of humor the Jerusalem Jews were known for, but the Jews also knew just how quickly these same soldiers could be ordered to take a life, and just how quickly they would carry out the order. It was an odd relationship, but Malchus and Judah had managed to adapt. "Do you think I would help myself to Caiaphas's finest without bringing you some?"

Alexander gave a half smile. "Yes."

"You're right. But no, I haven't been drinking. I have a better reason to smile."

"Why? Have you figured out a new way to divide fractions?" Judah cracked.

"Not yet, but I'll keep trying just for you. In the meantime, I won't be at the temple tomorrow. I'll be in Bethany with the temple chariot, waiting to meet my cousin Seth. He's escorting a caravan with Evaratus, whom I'm bringing back to Caiaphas's house."

"Well, doesn't that sound special," Judah said. "The road to and from Bethany, like every other road at this time, will be unbearably crowded, especially for an escort as ugly as you."

"Ugly? My mother always told me I was quite cute," Malchus said, smiling.

"Yes, but that was when you were a suckling, and she wasn't talking about your face," Judah said to a roar of laughter.

"Very funny, but you all have a right to be jealous. Tomorrow I won't be alone on the escort. I'll be accompanied by the most beautiful girl I have ever seen."

"A girl? Who is she?" Everyone leaned a little closer. Malchus had their undivided attention.

"Sorry, men," Malchus said to a circle of unblinking eyes. "Privileged information."

"We're privileged," said the man with the patch.

They all laughed, then most went back to their wineskins. Malchus gave Judah a tug on the arm, and the two friends turned away from the fire.

"Her name is Zara. She's Caiaphas's new Nabataean slave," Malchus whispered. The warmth on his face from the fire quickly vanished and was replaced by the chill of the cold darkness before him.

"Caiaphas? A new slave girl?" Judah asked loudly, sounding surprised.

Malchus threw his arms up and turned back toward the fire and laughter. He should have known better than to trust his prankster friend in front of an audience.

"Are we privileged yet?" Alexander said. The circle nodded and bobbed as they all laughed at Malchus.

Malchus had to smile. "Very funny, but tomorrow the joke will be on you," he said, then left with Judah following him.

"Sorry, but I couldn't resist," Judah said.

"Yes, you could have, and you're not sorry."

"Oh, don't be mad, tell me about the girl."

"She arrived today and will be with me all day tomorrow. Just the two of us," Malchus said proudly. "Alone. Together. At the Garden Stable. Waiting all day if need be. Yes, it's going to be quite a day."

"And whose brilliant idea was it to send with you a new Gentile slave, a *woman*—who likely has no escort experience at all—while there is so much preparation to do at the house?" Judah asked suspiciously. "Or is she there to protect you?"

All the men standing there started joking about how she would defend Malchus from marauders. "My hero!" Alexander added, clenching his hands together and pulling them toward his chest.

Everyone laughed except Malchus, who turned to Judah. "I don't have to worry about the timing. The order for her to accompany me came directly from Caiaphas."

Judah paused for a moment, then laughed, shaking his head.

"Now, what's so funny?"

"You don't get it, do you?"

"Get what?"

"You're so easy."

"Who?"

"You."

"What are you talking about?"

Judah held up his hand as he stopped laughing. "Fine. How much more time before you're a free man again, Malchus?"

"Six months."

"And what are you going to do then?"

"Leave."

"Does Caiaphas know that?"

"No."

"I say he does. He's very smart and knows you much better than you think."

"So what are you saying, Judah?" Malchus snapped, annoyed.

"Just this. Anyone can see the job you've been doing for Caiaphas and how invaluable you've become to him. You have a gift with numbers. How can he afford to let you go, especially with Elias on the way out? He can't. So he buys a beautiful Nabataean slave girl, which is coincidentally where you're from, to seduce you into giving up your freedom. His hope is that you'll want her, which apparently is happening, and she can't leave. So you'll stay, too. You'll have to if you want her. It's all in the law. And if Moses wrote it, Caiaphas is well aware of it." Judah feigned sadness, and then, as if offering condolences, added, "I guess she must be something special."

"Why do you say that?" Malchus said, still trying to digest this explanation.

"If she wasn't, I wouldn't have had to tell you. You would have already figured it out and told me," Judah said, giving Malchus a playful push on his shoulder.

Malchus did not know what to feel. He liked this new girl, but Judah did make the whole idea sound rather obvious. Caiaphas certainly was not beyond this type of scheme. In fact, being shrewd and creative and putting plots into action was what he did naturally. But he usually did it to other people. Malchus felt deceived. Still, the thought that Caiaphas might have gone to so much trouble to keep him proved a little flattering.

Malchus wondered how he had failed to figure this out. It was not as if he had never heard of savvy slave owners doing this before. He had always prided himself on his ability to solve problems logically and see the equation when everyone else saw randomness. His gift with numbers was nothing more than an ability to spot all the pieces of the equation, put them together, and add them up. To Malchus, math and life were much the same. In fact, his cynical attitude toward his master's religion was an outgrowth of this approach. All the hypocrisy he had seen the last seven years just did not add up. At least not in a way that pointed to God as the answer. His father must not have done the math or did not have all the facts Malchus had.

"Maybe you can get Caiaphas to suggest an idea like that to Bebai?" Judah said. "I'll give you a list of exactly what I'm looking for so you can pass it on."

"I'll give the list to Zara tomorrow. Maybe she has a sister somewhere," Malchus said. "An ugly sister!"

"I'll have it for you first thing in the morning," Judah said, laughing as they said good-bye and set off in opposite directions.

"Judah," Malchus called to his friend who turned to listen. "Do you think Zara is in on it? Do you think she knows?"

Judah shrugged. "Ask her."

"I can't ask her something like that. I don't even know her."

"So get to know her."

THREE

The man standing before Malchus held something in his hands. He was speaking, but Malchus could not understand him. The man looked angry. He appeared to be middle-aged, with streaks of silver accenting his black beard. His deep-set dark eyes seemed to sink even deeper as Malchus looked into them. The man grabbed Malchus by the arms and held him tightly. Malchus struggled to pull away but couldn't. The man squeezed even harder until Malchus could feel a throbbing pulse. Malchus tried to scream, but no sound would utter from his open mouth. The pain became unbearable, and his breathing became fast and shallow. The man lifted Malchus effortlessly as he commanded with a roar, "Up. Up. Up to the temple! Now!" He screamed, his breath hot and foul, into Malchus's face. Malchus felt sick and turned his face to protect himself. Suddenly there was silence. When Malchus looked back, he saw the man wore the distinctive robes of the high priest.

"Malchus! Malchus, wake up!"

"Huh?" Malchus said, groggily. He opened his eyes wide. He was in his bed. He looked toward his doorway and saw a man holding a lamp. A man in the robes of the high priest. It was Caiaphas. Malchus had been dreaming.

"Finally! I was wondering if you were dead. Put your clothes on. We have to get to the temple early. I need your help with a few things before you go on escort," Caiaphas said, then disappeared.

Malchus was not entirely sure he was awake. Caiaphas's image at the doorway, lamp in hand casting an eerie shadow on the high priest's face, seemed part of the dream, not part of the morning. He rubbed his eyes with the back of his hands. He felt sweat on his face. He wiped the sleep from his eyes and sat up.

The dream had been terrifying, and not the first one he had experienced. He wondered for a dazed moment about his dark, inner perception of Caiaphas. Could he at least be a free man in his sleep without the high priest seizing hold of him in some way or another?

Malchus had gotten in late last night. He had spent much of the night dwelling on the coming day while trying unsuccessfully to will himself to sleep. He had looked out his window just in time to catch a shooting star. There were still stars out. What time was it? The predawn light was barely outlining the eastern city walls and the Mount of Olives beyond. He closed his eyes and fell back to the mattress. Almost as soon as his head hit the bed, the man in the dream returned.

"Malchus!" Caiaphas again called from down the hall.

Malchus bolted upright, jumped from the mattress, pulled on his tunic, and adjusted it as he ran down the hall toward the high priest. Half-dazed, he stubbed his toe hard and fell headlong into the corner of the kitchen doorway. The impact left him stunned on the floor. If his left eye did not hurt so much, he might consider falling back to sleep where he lay. This was not a very good start to the day, he thought.

"Malchus!"

"Coming."

†

The crispness of the morning air went unmentioned as Caiaphas recited to Malchus a long list of meetings and events that would fill his busy day. Malchus knew he would not be around for most of it, but he listened without interruption as he followed the high priest past the posted guards. Caiaphas was probably talking to himself anyway.

Malchus exercised extra caution as he descended the stone steps, now wet and slippery from the early-morning dew. He touched his eye and winced. There was some blood on his finger, and the soft tissue around the eye had already begun to swell. *Wonderful,* he thought.

With the rapidly approaching feast now only a couple of days away, the local craftsmen were already at work on the street. The sound of tools seemed to prod Caiaphas to a quicker pace.

Caiaphas often mumbled aloud to himself, as if Malchus were not there. The invisible life of a slave. Caiaphas always muttered about how time was so fleeting and how the day was slipping away from him. To Malchus, it was the same old thing. Rush, rush, rush. Keep up with the high priest and try to figure out when the man was actually talking to him.

"Bless you, Holy One," called a leathersmith from the roadside after rising from his work and bowing his head. By law, laboring craftsmen were not obligated to rise from their work, but most did for Caiaphas, who would ignore such accolades the same way he would ignore Malchus, seemingly lost in thought and oblivious to anyone who was not the focus of his immediate attention. They would pay him honor, and Caiaphas would rarely even acknowledge them with so much as a nod.

Caiaphas was a holy hero. Like most everything else, the answer could be found in simple math. The locals were making money. Since Caiaphas had become high priest, trade had increased tremendously, as did the cost of doing business in the temple. Caiaphas had shown Malchus the secret to all business success—supply and demand. In the temple's case, there was only one Holy Temple of Jerusalem, so the market was essentially covered. Demand could easily be elevated with either guilt or zeal, the former requiring less energy to perpetuate, though either was welcome. Malchus wondered how holy Caiaphas would appear if the money flow dwindled.

With the Jews, Malchus felt insignificant but privileged, but before the ever-watchful Romans, he felt embarrassed chasing after Caiaphas like an ignorant dog after his master. The Romans held what Malchus considered to be a more realistic view. The soldiers held one of two opinions about the priesthood of which Caiaphas was head. One, they were naive fools of the worst kind, or, two, they were savvy entrepreneurs taking advantage of their historical legacy and taking the crowds for all they were worth. Neither view was very flattering, and Malchus believed both to be true.

Soon though, very soon, he would never have to trail after that black robe again. He would leave, never to return. And if he went back to being a shepherd, like his father had been, his flock would be only for wool and food, not for sacrifice. He would not help perpetuate the temple hypocrisy at the expense of a bunch of helpless animals. As easy as it would be to make money selling sacrificial fodder, he would manage without participating in this holy charade. He might not get rich, but he would have peace. He would be free mentally and physically. Free from Caiaphas. Free from Caiaphas's religion.

"Free in you," Malchus whispered, his eyes looking lazily upward to the sky. He touched his eye again to see if it was still bleeding. It was not, but the swelling had gotten worse.

He said it again, shaking his head. "Free in you." It was a sarcastic comment he made to himself as he struggled to keep up with Caiaphas. That little phrase, *free in you,* was all that was left of a prayer that had begun in faith a long time ago, but was now no more than a cynical comment he oft spoke to the heavens to remind God how He had failed him.

When Malchus first had been enslaved, he used to pray often. Every day. He needed to tell God he still believed in Him—trusted Him—even though he resented Caiaphas and did not believe anything he did was really for God. The prayer began as an apology, letting God know he was not rejecting the Law of Moses, only its use by the priests to exploit God's chosen people. Joined to this prayer was a lament about being unjustly enslaved and a reminder that justice should result in his immediate release, without his serving another day of his seven-year sentence. Waking up as a slave, day after day, getting bitter about the time served and the length of time owed, transformed this prayer into a combative gripe. An argument with God. Almost a diatribe against Him. As a precaution, however, and to avoid incurring God's wrath, Malchus would always end in an apology for complaining.

In the beginning the prayer came as long, meandering discussions with God. After a time, however, he worried God would tire of his persistent and repetitive whining. Or worse, the Lord might actually be roused to anger at Malchus for his impatience and unwillingness to endure and suffer in silence his dispensed portion of hardship. Then, God might not listen to anything he had to say.

With everything God was doing, holding the stars in the sky at night and moving the sun from east to west by day, he could not possibly enjoy the incessant murmuring of a whimpering slave. So considering God's workload, a nagging fear of God's reaction, and his own sense of defeat, Malchus's prayer became shorter and shorter, until by rote, it became, "Lord, I'm still a slave in Jerusalem and desperately need to be delivered from bondage soon. Meanwhile, please give me strength to feel free in your presence and to trust you like my father did, no matter how wrong everything is around me. I know you hear my prayer. Forgive me if I mix up some of the right with some of the wrong and please, please, please don't forget me." By the end of his first year of slavery, and certain that God had heard his prayer enough and didn't need to be reminded of all the details, Malchus abbreviated even further, so much so that his discourse was less a prayer and more a comment: "Free in you." At first, he would say it with determination, then later as a question, his way of asking, "When?" But as he became more embittered, a sarcastic edge crept in, and he said it disdainfully, almost mockingly, "Free in you!"

Of course, he was going to be free. Time, not God, would take care of that. Eventually, everything he believed was tarnished by cynicism, until all he believed in was his own ingenuity and ability to survive. He would be free—in spite of God.

Hazy shadows became more defined as the sun peeked over the Mount of Olives. The light shone on the workingmen who drove the temple economy.

"Bless you, Holy One."

Caiaphas worked the temple business as if he were a successful farmer. He himself was the tiller. He would plow the fields of Jerusalem deeply by making sure the tradesmen produced the highest-quality merchandise and received the best prices. He would plant seeds by inspiring the people to hold fast to their heritage, especially the traditional pilgrimage to Jerusalem. He was a master at instilling guilt by reminding the Jewish people of their religious obligations. He would water what he planted by sending out speakers on missions throughout all Israel, and wherever else the Semitic people settled after the disbursement, to remind them of their duty to uphold the temple traditions and of their obligation to tithe.

To the leaders throughout the land, Caiaphas would call for unity against those who would attack the Jews and the temple and enlist their financial support for the defense of both. The Jews were always faithful to pull together in times of need, and Caiaphas knew exactly how often he could sound the rallying cry. Finally, at Passover, he would fill the storehouses with a harvest of pilgrims. Pilgrims who gave generously to please both God and Caiaphas.

"Bless you, Holy One."

Malchus would often hear Caiaphas say, "If you don't attack the work, the work will attack you." No one followed this advice more carefully than Caiaphas himself. Rather than sit back and deal with problems as they came, he would seek them out. He had the ability to inspire visiting pilgrims, not only to return the following year, but also to bring others with them. Pilgrims, especially the wealthy ones, were an investment.

People also liked the fact that Caiaphas walked to the temple rather than being carried in a sedan, as if it brought him closer to them. The reality was, he simply did not have the patience to travel by sedan.

Halfway to the temple, the overwhelming and familiar aroma of freshly baked bread momentarily hijacked Caiaphas's attention. His brisk pace almost broke as a baker came out from a shop to intercept him with a cut of fresh, hot bread. Malchus instantly felt hungry and could almost taste the hot bread softening in his mouth. In one motion the high priest reached out, took the bread, nodded a quick thank-you, and continued on his way, never breaking stride. Rude as Caiaphas was, the baker smiled. Malchus remained invisible. And hungry.

Malchus could not help but notice the streets were more crowded than he had ever seen them. He knew Caiaphas took pride in this, and credit for the increase. He had made this happen, and the actual sight of the crowds buying and selling was one of the few things that would put a smile on his face. This was the time to plant for next season. Caiaphas believed with a passion that everything done now, good or bad, directly affected the next harvest. A harvest of people. More people, more money. More for the craftsmen and more for the merchants. They would make as much during Passover as they would during the entire rest of the year. They had all become dependent on that. A time they anticipated with greater expectation every year. The increase in revenues meant more profit to the temple money changers, which meant more for the temple, which would mean more for Caiaphas.

The pilgrims were crowding into the gates of Jerusalem in record numbers. *This will be Caiaphas's best year yet,* Malchus thought.

FOUR

What happened to your eye?" a dove merchant said, staring at Malchus, his head slightly cocked.

"Don't ask," Malchus said. He placed a wood board atop a crate, which was crowded and alive with cooing doves whose little white heads poked in and out of the thin slats. He then placed a handful of pebbles on the board, along with a small bronze plate. Several weatherworn merchants gathered around, pursing their lips and massaging their chins, all focused on the pile of pebbles.

"Now, I'm going to try to explain this as simply as I know how," Malchus said to his class. He took four pebbles and separated them from the pile, placing them in a row an inch apart from one another. "Last year you paid the temple one quarter of your earnings," he said, removing one of the pebbles and dropping it with a clink into the plate.

He looked up to see if his students were following him. They were all frowning in silence, their eyes shifting from the three pebbles that were left to the one in the plate and then back again.

"This year the percentage rate has changed," he said, making a new arrangement of three pebbles. Again, he removed one of the pebbles and dropped it into the plate.

"Last year," he said, pointing to the three pebbles. "And this year," he said, pointing to the two pebbles.

Though they continued to furrow their brows and stare in silence, Malchus knew the merchants were not confused. Of course, they did not like what they had just learned, but, as anticipated, no one would dare argue the temple's portion.

Malchus was simply doing his job, or what used to be Elias's job. He wanted to tell the merchants that their reduced portion was Caiaphas's idea, not his own, but Elias had forbidden him from such conversations.

Now he would have to explain to them that the rate of exchange at the money changer's tables had also changed from last year, again in the temple's favor. For this, he would need more pebbles and would encounter more silent frowns.

Everything bought in the temple had to be bought with Jerusalem currency, which the pilgrims would purchase at the money changer tables with their native money. Of course, there was a fee that would be built into the exchange, and when the merchants cashed in their Jerusalem money for their native money, they would be taxed again.

By the time Malchus finished the temple chores and ran back to the mansion, it was midmorning. *Some day off,* he thought. He felt as if he'd already done a day's work, and the whole time with the memory of Judah mocking him about the way Caiaphas was able to wedge another day into Malchus's workload.

When he got to the kitchen, he found Zara waiting. She was dressed in a white tunic, belted at the waist, revealing the curve of her hips.

"Good morning, Malchus," she said in a cheery voice. Her bright eyes suddenly looked concerned. "What happened?" she said, drawing nearer for a closer look.

"A clumsy slave who works at the temple . . . it was an accident," he said, hoping she would not ask the slave's name. He did not want to lie completely, but he would.

"We need to put something on that, or maybe drain it."

"We'll leave it alone. It will be fine," Malchus said.

"It will be worse tomorrow, you know."

"Tomorrow's tomorrow. I'd rather not think about it anymore today."

Zara just shook her head. "Did you sleep well?"

"Apparently you did," he said.

"Yes, I did, thank you," she said, reaching for a grapefruit. "And I am very excited about our trip. I'm putting together some food for us. Is there anything special you would like me to bring?"

"Whatever you put together is fine with me," he said. He could not take his eyes off her. A flower in the desert. The scar on her cheek meant nothing to him, and apparently meant nothing to her. Admirable. He shook his head and smiled as he considered that she could be part of a plot to keep him there. Why could Caiaphas not have thought of this six years ago?

"Levia left the instructions for you," she said, pointing with her knife to what looked like a note on a small cedar table next to him.

He picked it up and leaned back against the wall to read it to himself, expressionless. Learning to read was something that his father had insisted on. "A man's faith becomes strong from reading the scriptures," he had said. Before putting the letter down, Malchus had to smile slightly.

"What does it say?" asked Zara.

"Oh nothing. Just your usual instructions. We go into Bethany and then to the Garden Stable at the end of town in order to avoid the crowd, then wait there for Seth to arrive. Then there is this little bit at the end that says 'and be nice to Zara.'"

"I like Levia," Zara said as she picked up the note and tucked it into a small pocket.

"What are you doing?"

"Oh . . . nothing," she said with a sly smile. "Just keeping this note in case you need a reminder to be nice to me."

Malchus laughed. "That won't be necessary."

Zara was aglow as she took Malchus's hand and stepped up onto the temple chariot. Compared to Herod's gold-gilded, jewel-laden royal chariots, the temple chariot appeared modest, but was, no less, finely made. The chariot was built to Caiaphas's specifications and sized to hold four standing people, which made it suitable for escorts. It was drawn by two of Caiaphas's horses, muscular, well-kept, matching black Arabians, as impressive as any in Herod's stables. Malchus grabbed the reins and yelled at the animals.

The chest-high wheels of the chariot jerked forward, causing Zara to grab the bronze rim in front of her.

"You're not going to lose me that easily," Zara said, holding on tightly.

"Sorry, I guess I'm a little out of practice," Malchus said as he struggled into the crowded street of the ancient city. Even horses as well trained as these needed a tight rein and knowing hand while going against the steady flow of pilgrims pouring through the city gates.

"How do we get out of the city?" Zara asked.

"Normally, we would exit into the Kidron Valley, but, looking at this crowd, I'm having second thoughts. Most enter that way."

"If you want, I could get out and lead the horses," Zara suggested. Malchus looked at her as if she was crazy. Even if the horses obeyed, the crowd would not. "I—don't think that would be a good idea."

"Why? Because I'm not big and strong like you?" she said sarcastically.

Her feistiness surprised him. Maybe she could part the way, but if anything went wrong, Caiaphas would have him for another seven years. He thought, choosing his words carefully. "Not at all," he said. "I was just considering that we might get through faster if I crack the whip and rear up the horses. The crowd would separate quickly, and we would be on our way. What do you think? And if you like, while I crack the whip you could hold on to the reins."

She looked at him curiously, then glanced down to the reins wrapped around his hands, the leather straps almost cutting into his skin. She looked back up at him again as if studying him, then she shifted her gaze forward. "Do whatever you want," she said, apparently calling his bluff.

Malchus smiled. He was indeed going to enjoy his day with her. "Maybe we'll take the Essenes Gate," he said. "There will be fewer people coming in through the Hinnom Valley."

"How many gates are there?" Zara asked.

"Seven."

She nodded. "I've never seen so many people in one place. The caravans, the colors, the music. There is so much life here. This place is wonderful."

"Sometimes."

"Sometimes?"

"Well, it's not like this all the time. This is a special time. It's the greatest feast of the year. And thank God it comes only once a year. People travel from all over the world to be here just for a week or so and then leave. When they leave, so does most of the excitement, if you want to call it that."

"What do you call it?"

"Work," he grunted, as they squeezed through the gate and into the Hinnom Valley, where the road was wide and well worn and the air dusty. Up the shallow hillside to their left stood the great outer walls of the ancient city. To their right, the hillside was just as shallow, but much rockier and with only sparse foliage. Pilgrims were setting up camps on whatever flat ground they could find.

Malchus sighed in relief as he loosened his grip a little on the reins. He was surprised by how quickly his hands had become sore and sweaty from the friction of the leather bands. temple work had made him soft. Had he gone much longer without loosening his grip, he would have had blistered hands to go with his swollen eye.

Straight ahead was the Kidron Valley and the Mount of Olives. The mount was softly rounded on top, covered with patches of olive trees. It would probably have been called the *"Hill* of Olives" if it were a few feet less in elevation, or would have gone nameless if it were anywhere but just outside the city walls. The eastern slope rising from the Kidron came into view as they drew closer, revealing a thick forest of olive trees and an oil-pressing grove known to the locals as the Garden of Gethsemane.

Zara looked at Malchus, "I envy you and your people. You seem to have so much identity and purpose and belief. Jerusalem is like your home. It's like home for all these people," she said, motioning toward a large group on the hillside who were busy setting up their camp.

"Don't include me in that," Malchus replied sharply. "I don't consider this place my home. I'm just visiting, and not because I want to." Just then it crossed his mind that she might have been instructed to say something like that by Caiaphas.

Zara looked surprised. "Visiting?"

He shrugged. "I have six more months to go, and my debt to Caiaphas will be paid. After that, I'm leaving."

"Leaving? To go where? To do what?" she asked, her disappointment obvious.

Malchus eased the chariot to the right as they entered the Kidron Valley, heading south toward Bethany. Neither Malchus nor Zara mentioned the four crucifixions at the corners of the intersecting roads. These Roman signposts littered the main roads of Palestine and served as a sobering reminder to the Jews as to who was really in charge.

"Well, the first thing I'm going to do—" Suddenly Malchus stopped talking and looked up toward the east to the top of the Mount of Olives.

"What is it?" Zara asked, trying to look around him.

"Listen," he said. "Up there." He motioned with his head toward the summit.

The road coming over the crest was dotted with dozens of animated people that soon swelled into a throng of hundreds yelling something loudly and waving what appeared to be palm branches.

"What's happening up there?" she asked.

"I don't know," replied Malchus. "It's too far to tell. Whatever it is, I'm glad we didn't take that route. Even from here you can see we would never have gotten past that crowd and would have had to turn around and take this road anyway."

The chariot continued slowly but steadily south on its way to Bethany, away from the activity on the Mount of Olives. After straining to see what the commotion was all about, Zara gave up and returned her attention to the road before them.

For a moment she appeared pensive, then bothered. Zara turned to him. "Why don't you want to live here? I don't understand," she said, loud enough to be heard over the noise of the trotting horses and the traffic going the other way.

"There's nothing here for me, Zara."

"At the palace you have so much. Where else could you go and find more comfort and security?"

"A comfortable and secure slave. No, thank you."

"A slave, yes, but you serve the high priest, the holiest man in the world."

Malchus smiled. It would be so easy to tear her high priest perception to shreds with enough detail to terrify her. "I've been a fly on his wall for a long time, Zara. Now you're one too. Flies get to see a lot sometimes."

"But I've heard it said Caiaphas is a great high priest."

"I think maybe we should change the subject."

Zara looked puzzled. "You are jesting?"

Malchus slipped her a glance. "Yes, let's just leave it at that."

"I don't understand."

"Look, we have to be very careful when we talk about these things. I could get into big trouble, and so could you for that matter. Why don't we talk about you for a while. I'd love to hear about you," Malchus said.

Zara smiled. Her smile was heart-melting. "We have all day to talk about me. I want to hear more about my new home and master."

"You should ask Levia."

Zara frowned and stared straight ahead for a while, mostly looking at the oncoming traffic, the many faces. "I think most of these people would like to have the opportunity to have what you want to give up."

"I'm sure you're right. When I first got here, I thought the temple was here to help us all serve and worship God. Maybe it once was, a long time ago. But somewhere along the way it has been transformed. To the visitor it looks like we're serving God, but if God's served at all, it's only after everyone else has been served first."

"Beginning with the high priest?"

Malchus shook his head slowly. "You don't give up, do you?"

"Please tell me."

Malchus shrugged. "I think he believes what he's doing is right. He sees good things happening for the temple. It's getting rich. If it's good for the temple, it's good. If it's bad for the temple, it's bad. Good and evil are translated as more money and less money. Profits have become the measure of blessing. I feel like I'm dying here. I want to reclaim my life."

"If you weren't being freed, would you try to escape?"

"What are you, a spy for Caiaphas?" he said. Maybe this was an innocent way to find out if she was in on something.

She laughed. "Yes, Malchus, I'm a spy."

Either she is good at this, or I have been listening too much to Judah. *He is probably laughing at me right now,* he thought.

"Malchus, I think you sound jealous."

"Of whom?" Malchus said, surprised.

"Caiaphas."

"Really! And why would I be jealous of him?"

"Because he has so much."

Malchus laughed. "In a few months, I will have more than him."

"How?"

"I will be free, but he will remain a slave."

"Caiaphas? A slave?"

"Absolutely. He is his own slave. The more things he owns and controls, the more things own and control him."

"Then I must be very free," Zara said with a laugh.

"You're more free than you might think," he said, then considered how easy it was for him to talk of freedom when his own was so close. Zara, on the other hand, would be a slave the rest of her life. He felt stupidly insensitive and sad for her plight.

"Then where would you go?"

Malchus stared straight ahead for a moment. This was a question he had asked himself a thousand times. "I will tell you, on one condition," he said in a deliberately serious tone.

"Condition?"

"Yes," Malchus said without turning his head. "That you dig into that basket of yours and get me something to drink. You did bring something to drink, didn't you?"

Zara handed him a jug of water. On the bumpy road he could not help but spill some on himself as he drank. Normally he would not have even noticed, but with Zara he found himself self-conscious about his clumsiness. He handed back the jug without a glance.

"Better?"

"Much. Thank you."

Zara giggled.

"What?"

"Nothing," she said. "So tell me, Malchus, where did you come from, and how did you become a slave?"

"Very well," Malchus replied, "but then you have to answer a question of mine."

"Another condition?"

"A request," he said.

"Fine! When you finish answering my question, you can ask me one."

"Fair enough." He took a deep breath and began. "I used to tend sheep with my father, my uncle, and my cousin, Seth. It was a simple life. Easy to understand. Maybe if I had never lived that way, things would be less troubling now. However, when I was out with my father in the fields, he would teach me about the Almighty God of Israel. About incredible things He has done for His people. About Moses and Abraham. But most of all, I loved when we talked about King David. Especially about when he was a shepherd boy—his relationship with God and how he fought the giant Goliath. I loved to listen to my father's stories." Malchus glanced at Zara to make sure she was interested.

She looked back inquisitively. "Would you tell me these stories sometime, Malchus?" she asked sweetly. "I would love to hear them."

Malchus nearly blushed. Was that her way of telling him that she wanted to spend more time with him? Was that possible? Did she actually like him, or was this another part of the plan? He did not want to believe that. He needed to stop suspecting her of this insane scheme Judah put into his head.

He continued. "My father and my uncle Laben had a large flock of sheep in Nabataea. They would be gone for days, sometimes weeks, tending the herd, often traveling great distances to find grazing land. I remember really missing him." Even as Malchus spoke, he felt grief. He still missed his father. He pushed on. "Only my mother missed him more. We would have a feast when he came home. They were wonderful reunions. When Seth and I were old enough, we began to go with them. First for a day or two, because Mother would worry about us, and then for longer and longer. Eventually, she let Seth and me go to the market in Jerusalem with them. I'll never forget it."

"Was it like it is now?" Zara asked.

Malchus saw some pilgrims pulling off the road after spotting a possible campsite. Their belongings banged around noisily as they left the road for the rougher terrain.

"Very much like now," he said. "Jerusalem surpassed all my expectations. I was very young and overwhelmed. Everything my father told me about was there. Just like today. Everything that was being done, all the great preparations and processionals, the prayers and praises that were sung. I thought it was all for one purpose: to thank the 'living God' for all that He had done for us. Like my father, I accepted the whole thing without question. Uncle Laben, on the other hand, did not."

"You're father's brother?"

Malchus smiled and shook his head. "My mother's. He and my father were very . . . different."

"You sound as if you disapprove of him."

"I love my uncle, but if not for him I wouldn't be a slave right now. You see, my uncle Laben liked to celebrate after selling the sheep. He would get together with the merchants after sundown. They would supply the wine and entertainment, and my uncle would take them up on their generosity every time."

"But not your father?"

Malchus shook his head. "My father enjoyed conversation and an occasional wineskin, but after sundown he would be with Seth and me. We'd gather around a fire under the stars. It wasn't uncommon for other shepherds to join us or us them. But if Jerusalem was in sight, Uncle Laben would be missing."

"What would your father have to say about your uncle not being there?"

"He would protect him in our eyes, saying it was business-related."

"Maybe it was."

"We're talking about sheep, Zara. From the shepherds' end, there's not much business that can't be discussed at the temple gates. Besides, most of the people he drank with would regret having met him before very long. He was an angry drunk. His nights almost always ended in a fight. And sometime late the next morning, he would find us and harangue us with a tale of how he had to defend himself or some other poor soul on some matter of principle or other."

"You must be looking forward to seeing your father again."

Malchus was silent.

"Malchus?" she said after a long moment.

"My father died."

"Oh, Malchus, I'm sorry. I didn't mean to—"

"My father died suddenly," Malchus interrupted. "The two of us were walking together when he grabbed his chest and fell to the ground. I screamed to Uncle Laben for help. I had never seen him run before, but he did then. We both grabbed my father and then fell on him and cried. That was the first time I ever saw Uncle Laben cry, and the last. I lost my father and my best friend."

"How old were you?"

"I was sixteen." Malchus did not want to look at Zara because he did not want her to see his watery eyes, but he noticed she was wiping her own.

"At least my father doesn't know I was enslaved. Freedom meant everything to him. And soon I will be free again."

"But how did you become Caiaphas's slave?"

"The very next time we came to the Jerusalem market was six and a half years ago. It was just before Yom Kippur, the Day of Atonement. Now there's justice! It was then that Uncle Laben got into one of his drunken brawls with a Galilean shepherd over who had better sheep. In Jerusalem we got a premium for our sheep because of the pure white fleeces. We were very proud of that. And nobody was prouder than Uncle Laben after he had been drinking for a while. After knocking a Galilean unconscious—"

"Unconscious?" Zara interrupted.

"Oh, yes. My uncle was not very big, but he was very smart . . . fight-wise, that is. He could knock anyone out with one punch."

"Truly?" Zara said. "How?"

Malchus laughed. "I saw him do it so many times, and each time it looked as funny as the time before. He would never punch with his fist."

Zara laughed. "Now you're making this up. How can you punch without your fist?"

"With this," Malchus said, holding up and slapping his right elbow. "Uncle Laben used to tell us that an elbow is bigger and harder than all the knuckles put together. He also counted on surprise. He would grab a man's tunic and pull him close. The man would always be too close to punch back," he said, stopping to laugh. "Then he would swat the man in the head with his elbow as hard as he could . . . putting all his weight into one bone-hard punch." Malchus demonstrated as best he could while holding the reins. "Unbelievably, it would always work, and in the end his hand would never be sore."

Zara laughed, and Malchus was wiping his eyes.

"So then what did he do?"

Malchus stopped laughing and shook his head. "This part of the story is more pathetic than funny. He stole the man's herd and sold the sheep at half their value to make his point. They were all gone, along with my uncle, before the man ever regained consciousness. Apparently the Galilean also had too much to drink and did not know who he was bragging to. I bet he thought twice about bragging about his sheep after that."

"But how did all this get you in trouble?"

"Well, Seth and I were at the usual meeting place the next morning, just outside the city walls under a tree. Uncle Laben finally showed up late, stinking of wine, just as he always did. He didn't say anything about what had occurred. So it came as quite a surprise when we were arrested not even one mile from the gate. It didn't take long for the authorities to figure out who the Galilean was describing. According to the law, we had to pay back four sheep for every one that was stolen. All of a sudden, I was an accomplice. The man's flock was enormous. We couldn't even come close to repaying him. The next thing we knew we were all on the auction stone being sold as slaves. So much for Uncle Laben's protection.

"Caiaphas bought Seth and me but wanted nothing to do with Uncle Laben. In fact, the people there knew my uncle so well that nobody bought him. As a result, he was given to the Galilean shepherd for the usual seven years. I'm not sure who was punished more," Malchus said, laughing. He sensed Zara taking a long look at him as he kept his face fixed straight ahead.

"Now, what was it that you wanted to ask me?" she asked.

Malchus glanced at her, then back to the road. Last night, with Judah's voice in his ear, the idea of asking her if she was part of a Caiaphas plot to secure him forever as his slave didn't seem too illogical. But now the question seemed awkward, even embarrassing. Knowing Caiaphas, she probably was part of a calculated move to keep him enslaved in Jerusalem, but she would likely be kept in the dark while he manipulated the relationship. If he kept his mouth shut, he might find himself on all kinds of strange but pleasant tasks with her.

"Malchus?"

"Oh, I was just wondering if you've . . . ever . . . seen the temple?"

Zara frowned slightly. "Why, no. I haven't."

Malchus nodded. "It's quite big."

"That's what I've heard," she said, still frowning.

FIVE

"Hold on tight," Malchus said as he turned off the busy main road to Jericho and onto the nearly empty road through the middle of the small village of Bethany. "This road will take us right to the Garden Stable. These horses look like they could use a run." Malchus considered himself to be good with the chariot and horses. The road was much narrower than the one they were just on and winding enough to require Malchus's undivided attention.

"The horses need to run?" Zara asked nervously.

"Yes, they've been chomping at the bit since we started."

"Chomping? I thought you were out of practice," she said.

He smiled at her. "Just a little," he said with a wink, then snapped the leather reins. The horses bolted forward.

The powerful legs of Caiaphas's horses effortlessly pulled the chariot. Quickly they were at full gallop. The acceleration caused Malchus and Zara to reflexively bend their knees and tighten their grips. Malchus on the straps and Zara on the rim of the chariot itself. Her knuckles went white. The wind blew off

Zara's head covering, and her long black hair blew freely in the hot arid air.

The stress of the ride along the Jericho road was suddenly gone. Malchus glanced at Zara to see if this new pace was scaring her. When he saw her blowing hair and wide smile, he snapped the reins again.

He glanced back at her. The wind had blown her sleeves up, and tears were streaming backward from the corners of her eyes. What's that? He noticed another scar, this one on her exposed left forearm. It was more pronounced than the one on her face, and it looked as if it had been a deep wound. *More pain,* he thought. *Where had she been? What had she been through?*

"Whoa!" Malchus yelled to the horses, which slowed as the end of the road came quickly upon them.

Malchus and Zara laughed at each other's wind-whipped hair.

"Do you always live so dangerously, or is today just my good fortune?" Zara asked.

"It's not me, Zara, it's the horses." Despite some occasional clumsiness, Malchus considered himself to be quite careful. He found peace in moderation. If he ever appeared to be wild, it was either a mistake or a move he made after careful consideration. He was not a risk-taker by his own estimation. Logic gave him confidence. He added up situations the same as he added up numbers. If a situation added up, he would appear bold. There was no real risk to those who knew the math.

Malchus maneuvered the horses to the end of the dusty road, which widened into a circle so that drawn carts and wagons could easily turn round without backing up. The horses were now shiny with sweat. In the center of the circle was a beautifully manicured flower garden. The stable bordered the far end of the circle. Large shade trees framed either side of the entrance. A flat piece of wood with a star carved into it hung between the trees. For no apparent reason, the entire small area flourished with colorful plants and sweet scents. The leaves on the trees were full and deep green. Unusual shrubs and flowers lined the roadsides and pathways.

"So this is the Garden Stable?" said Zara, as the chariot calmly entered the circle.

"That's not its real name," said Malchus, leading the horses toward the huge trees. "That's just what we call it. It's a pleasant and convenient place to meet someone," he said, stopping the chariot under the second tree, past the entrance.

"Pleasant? It's beautiful!" she said, enjoying the bouquet of colors they were passing.

Malchus looked to his left and shook his head at the trail of dust he left along the length of the road. "I guess I owe the little village an apology." He then stepped off the chariot and extended his hand, offering to help her off. She looked at him and held his eyes with hers for a moment as she took his hand. Her thick, unbound hair fell forward over her shoulders.

"Thank you," she said, holding his hand a little longer than necessary.

"I'll get some water for the horses," Malchus said, pointing to a well fifty feet away. *If she is not part of a plot to keep me here, she should be,* he thought.

"They don't mind if we take water from the well, Malchus?" Zara asked, walking with him.

"'They' is an old man named Japhet. He's . . . different. He runs this place by himself. No one knows exactly how he gets it to look so magnificent. Local rulers, with all their wealth, can't put a garden together to compare with what he's done here."

"He must have the touch—something even gold and silver can't buy," Zara said.

Malchus laughed. "He's been offered plenty to move away and take care of palaces with servants at his beck and call, but that's just not his way. He'd rather stay right here," Malchus indicated the expanse of the garden with a sweep of his outstretched hand. "And a nicer, more generous, man would be hard to find."

"I've never seen a well like this one," Zara ran her hand across the unusually smooth stones atop the waist-high mouth of the well and inspected it closely. Two hewn timber posts stood on opposite sides of the opening, supporting a pointed roof above a curious water drawing device. "How does it work?" she asked, looking upward into the roof's peak.

"Watch this," Malchus said. "You turn this crank that attaches to the roller over the well." Malchus turned the handle and the rope began to ascend with a clicking sound from an attached gear. "The rope is wound up until the bucket appears. That clicking wheel with the wooden teeth prevents the bucket from going back down if you get tired, and it holds it in place after you've wound it all the way up."

"What a great idea!" Zara said. She cranked the handle effortlessly as the gear clicked. "Very clever."

Malchus laughed. "That's Japhet for you. There's another one in the back that's horse run. I'm not sure how it's done, but the horse makes it work, and water goes all over the property—underground!

Zara looked at him in disbelief. "You're making this up."

Malchus shrugged his shoulders and sat on the edge of the well facing her. "Japhet is an inventor. He's full of great ideas. Every time I walk around this farm I see things I've never seen before. Things I never even imagined. He'd probably be famous if he was interested in fame. Most of the things he makes ease his or the animals' workload. If you look at the hooves of the pack animals and horses, you'll see he's fitted the bottoms with metal and he fastened them on with small nails. He claims that, like us, the animals can go farther with sandals on."

"I wonder what gave him that idea?" she said, looking down at her own feet, comfortably inside her sandals. "Is he smart, or are we dull?"

"Do I have to answer that?"

"No," she said with a smile, holding eye contact with Malchus longer than she previously had.

The linger of her gaze prompted Malchus to wonder again if she was knowingly in on a plot. A beautiful slave with an assignment to seduce him. Looking into her eyes, he suddenly found himself hoping it was true.

Malchus cleared his throat. "Uh, ever since we've been meeting at this place, Japhet has been leaving buckets by the well," Malchus said, bending for an empty bucket on the ground.

"The buckets have the same star carved into them as the wood hanging over the entrance," Zara said.

"I know. That star is carved into quite a few things around here. His way of knowing what's his I suppose. When we first thanked him for the water, he laughed and told us it was for the horses. Japhet would say, 'They do all the work.' In truth, I've never seen anyone relate better to animals than old Japhet. He treats them all like they're his children."

They filled the buckets and walked back to the two horses. Malchus placed the water buckets on the ground in front of them.

"Would you like some fruit?" Zara asked.

"Did you bring anything else besides fruit?"

"Like what?"

"Like bread or lamb or chicken," Malchus said. His stomach was making noise.

"No. Just fruit."

"Great, I'd love some." He sighed.

Zara walked to the back of the chariot to get the basket while Malchus sat down under the shade tree and leaned against the trunk. He watched Zara as she walked toward him and allowed himself to imagine they were not slaves, just out enjoying each other's company. The thought was painfully pleasant.

"When do you expect Seth to arrive?" Zara asked as she took a seat next to him.

"You never know. During the rest of the year I could tell you, but at Passover, with all the heavy traffic, you just have to be patient and wait."

While they were waiting, they talked, mostly about Zara's childhood as a slave in Nabataea. She had lived there with her mother, who was also a slave. She did not know who her father was, and her mother had never wanted to talk about it. An hour passed, and the sun was now directly overhead. Malchus had slid down against the tree so that only his head was propped against the trunk. Under the horses he saw legs walking toward them.

Malchus leaned his head to one side, closer to the ground, to see who it was. Shaking off some noontime laziness, he rose to his feet to greet the slow-moving man as he came past the center garden. Walking next to the man was a donkey colt on a rope.

"Hello, Japhet, how have you been?" Malchus asked. Zara stood up as well after pulling on her head covering.

The old man, shrunken with age, looked down and saw Malchus. His wrinkled eyes were red and teary. Malchus thought he looked exhausted, but then realized he had been crying. As the man came closer, his eyes began to focus on Malchus, and his old face lit up.

"Malchus, I thought I recognized your voice. I didn't know you were still doing escorts. It is good to see you," he said, reaching out both his calloused hands and taking hold of Malchus's hands. "What happened to your eye?"

Malchus reflexively touched his swollen eye, determined not to grimace from the increasing tenderness. "A stupid accident this morning. It'll be all right soon enough."

"Try to be more careful, my son. And who is this flower you have with you?"

"Her name is Zara," Malchus said, forcing a smile through his concern for Japhet. "Is there anything wrong?" he asked. "You look like you're upset about something."

"Upset?" he repeated slowly. "No, no, I'm not upset," he said, shaking his head. "No," he repeated slowly and softly. "Malchus," he said, looking into the younger man's eyes, "this is the most joyful day of my entire life. I feel like I'm dreaming." Japhet then turned around and walked a few feet back to the colt. Standing directly in front of it, he took his old, rough hands and put them on either side of the colt's head, bent his head down a little, and kissed the animal between the eyes. Then, pulling his head away but still keeping his hands on either side of the donkey's face, he said, "Malchus, Zara, tell me, what do you see here before me?"

Malchus looked at Zara, who raised her eyebrows and shrugged. Malchus shrugged back at her. "A donkey colt."

"Nothing else?" Japhet asked.

They looked at the colt again and then at each other, both wondering. Malchus said, "Nothing."

"Neither did I," Japhet said, "Neither did I," he repeated. "But I was wrong, and so are you. This little colt is a great treasure. It will be known throughout time, even when you and I are long forgotten. It has taught me that no man knows what great treasure he may have disguised as something simple and ordinary." Japhet let go of the colt's head, turned around and faced Malchus and Zara, and said, "My dear friends, this very donkey colt was spoken of over five hundred years ago by the prophet Zechariah." Japhet closed his eyes, clasped his palms slightly, and quoted the well-known messianic prophecy from memory:

"Rejoice greatly, O daughter of Zion! Shout in triumph, O daughter of Jerusalem! Behold, your king is coming to you; He is just and endowed with salvation, humble, and mounted on a donkey, even on a colt, the foal of a donkey."

Zara moved closer to Malchus and squeezed his arm as the old man recited the scripture. Malchus glanced to his left. Zara's eyes were on the old man standing motionless with his eyes barely opened. He wondered if she was even aware that she was holding him. She looked transfixed, like she had entered some other realm. So, too, did Japhet. Malchus had been there himself, long ago. That is how he recognized it. They were not here right now, he thought. They were somewhere else, the fantasyland of the scriptures. A place some could step into, right in front of you, as if they had walked through a door. Japhet was all the way through, and Zara was on her way.

Malchus had seen it countless times. And on the other side of that door, those lucky enough to pass through received something from God. *Receivers,* in some way, of his holy presence. *All very logical,* he thought. It added up in some mystical way, even from this side of the door. Malchus remembered it with a hint of longing. Many pilgrims were receivers. He liked that about them. But he had spent so much time with Caiaphas, he no longer felt able to enter that place, and, worse, wondered if the place ever really existed or was just the result of wishful thinking and an overactive imagination. *Free in you,* he thought reflexively, cynicism ruining the moment.

"Sir, how is this donkey the one spoken of by your prophet?" Zara asked, caught up in Japhet's amazement and awe.

Japhet nodded knowingly. "Just a few hours ago I saw two men, about your age, Malchus. They ran to that tie post over there by the shade tree and untied this colt," he said, pointing to a waist-high, old, weathered horse rail, just behind the tree trunk that Malchus had been resting against. "I said, 'What are you doing?' They looked at me, excitement beaming in their eyes . . . "

Receivers, Malchus thought.

" . . . and said, 'The Lord has need of your animal. The colt will be returned.' What could I say? I just watched as they took the colt and ran with it back in the direction from which they had come. A peace came over me that told me not to worry. I wondered if the colt would behave, because it had never been ridden before. Then, I had a thought. I wanted to follow them. Be with them. I tried as best I could, but I could not catch them. I lost sight of them as they vanished among hundreds of people atop the Mount of Olives.

"The crowd began to shout, 'Hosanna to the Son of David. Blessed is the King that comes in the name of the Lord!' As the crowd moved over and down the mount, I came to the top. From there I looked down and was able to see. I saw the back of a man, and he was being carried by my donkey colt," he said, again squeezing its head between his hands. "Before Him, people were lying down their garments in the road and waving branches—" Japhet had to stop. His emotions were overwhelming him. He swallowed and took a few slow breaths. "I wanted so much to lay my cloak down with the others, but I couldn't catch up. A sight to behold. This colt," he said, patting it lovingly. "My colt."

The Romans must have gotten a good laugh seeing this, Malchus thought, trying to keep his amusement to himself. They were used to seeing the commanders of their armies roll into cities on polished gold chariots drawn by teams of high-strung horses, each decorated with brilliant armor, followed by rows of marching soldiers. The sight of this man on a donkey colt must have had them in tears.

"Malchus," said Zara, pulling slightly on his tunic, "that must have been what we saw." She then looked again at Japhet, and asked, "Who was the man on your donkey?"

"He was Jesus of Nazareth," Japhet said.

"Who?" Zara asked.

"Jesus of Nazareth," he repeated.

"Who is Jesus of Nazareth?" asked Zara.

"The Messiah!" the old man answered enthusiastically. "I've never met Him myself, but a man named Lazarus who lives here in Bethany is alive because Jesus brought him back from the dead just last week. He was dead. I know both Lazarus and his family, and I was there when he was buried. Four days later, Jesus arrived and brought him back to life. He is who they say. He is the Messiah we have been waiting for. He is the one spoken of by the prophets. He is the One!" Japhet said, his teary eyes further betraying his heart.

Malchus remembered hearing some of the priests talking about something like this, but they had spoken of it as a hoax. Whatever, it was none of Malchus's business, yet it seemed to mean so much to the old man. *Nothing wrong with being quiet,* he thought.

"Did you see Jesus do this?" Zara asked excitedly.

"No, but I saw Lazarus two days later." Japhet paused to laugh. "He came here to tell me. When I first saw, I almost died myself . . . and Jesus had already left."

"What did Lazarus say?" Zara said, very excited. "What was it like to come alive after being dead?"

"He told me death is not to be feared by those who love God. He told me he was in a wonderful place full of light, but he was drawn back to his body from the voice that is the light."

Zara was speechless.

Malchus had to admit, part of him was touched by what he had just heard. Maybe because he heard it from Japhet. Curiously, the story reminded him of something his father had told him long ago of an experience some shepherds had outside Bethlehem one night. His father knew one of the shepherds well. As the story went, the shepherds were in the field one night keeping watch over their flocks when there was an angelic visitation. The shepherds were petrified. The angel told them not to be afraid and went on to tell them of the birth of the Messiah.

Since the time when his father had told him what the shepherd said, Malchus had heard the story repeatedly from many other people. Each time it was different. He was proud he heard such a famous story from his own father, before it was well known and the account of the event had been changed by others. Besides, the original version was amazing enough. As a result of that story, there had been many claims made. Many men demanded their throne. False messiahs insisted the events of that night pointed to them. Each claimed he was the one born that night in Bethlehem—the one of whom the angel spoke—the one the Magi came to see and present with gifts. And, of course, each was the one Herod the Great had miraculously missed when he ordered the slaughter of all the innocent children under the age of two in the attempt to kill the one who was prophesied to be king.

Malchus had seen so many false messiahs, his own father's story lost its impact. His father had left him with the precious memories, stories told to him out in the fields. And he knew this about his father; he definitely had been a receiver. The term sounded so cold when he held it next to the memory of his father's face, but logic was cold and calculating. These days, given the choice between logic or emotion, Malchus chose logic. Logic was sovereign on this side of the door. Logic was the only thing he could hold on to. His father had told him, "Some believe when they see. Others see when they believe." Malchus needed to see first. That is what his service to Caiaphas had wrought. It had to add up.

Malchus had heard of Jesus, although he had not heard much. The little he had heard was from Caiaphas, who was not fond of outsiders to begin with, unless, of course, they were wealthy and coming to pay tithes. Malchus would not dare to mention any hint of doubt to Japhet. If nothing else, the experience was real enough to the old man, and Malchus enjoyed seeing him so fulfilled, even if it was by some strange set of circumstances or curious events.

"Japhet," Malchus said, "the Almighty had the entire world to pick from when He was looking for someone to raise His special colt. If I were Him, I would have made the very same choice. So now we know that this is no ordinary donkey colt, but for a long time we've all known that its owner is no ordinary man."

Japhet smiled. "You're a nice boy, Malchus. Thank you for your kind words." The old man's eyes shifted to Zara. His smile broadened slightly and then he looked back to Malchus and said, "Time is catching up to me. I need to go and rest now." He extended his hands to Malchus and Zara, squeezed their arms gently, then began to make his way around them. "Hope to see you again, Malchus. The God of Israel bless you both. Shalom," he said, walking through the stable entrance. A very ordinary-looking donkey colt followed him.

"Japhet!" Malchus yelled. "One question."

The old man stopped and turned around.

"Will anyone ever ride that donkey again?"

The old man looked at Malchus, smiled, and shook his head. "Malchus, of all the people I have come across today, you are the first to ask me that." The old man turned back around, walked a few steps, and stopped. He turned halfway around and was grinning widely. "No!" he said. He then turned back and continued walking, still shaking his head, still followed by the colt.

"Malchus, I've seen good men and evil men," Zara said. "Japhet is a good man. Is what he said true? Is there really a messiah?"

Malchus looked at Zara, who was standing just two feet away and staring straight into his eyes. Her question seemed more childlike than he would have expected from someone who had been abused. Whatever innocence she had, he certainly did not want to blemish with his own cynicism. Whatever the truth, she would find out soon enough, and he would gently and logically guide her back and be there to ease the blow when it came. He envied her curiosity, but not the inevitable disappointment truth would bring. The truth, as far as Malchus reasoned, was that the Messiah was a Jewish fable—a fable she would see acted out regularly in Jerusalem, the city of acts and actors. He saw a tear of hope in her eye, and that touched him.

"I don't know Zara," Malchus answered, not wanting to raise her expectations any higher than they already were. "I have no answers. But if he's the One, I suspect we will both find out soon. Everyone will."

SIX

Malchus and Zara laid back and watched a parade of puffy white clouds across a blue sky. The still air began to whip up, as it often did by midafternoon. Malchus hardly took notice of the sandy gusts that would otherwise irritate him. He had refused to talk about himself anymore. He wanted to hear all about her, and the more he asked, the more she opened up.

Zara had never known freedom. Sixty-two years earlier, her grandmother had been taken prisoner by the Romans when Herod the Great conquered the territory around Esbus, a Nabataean-owned desert area several days west of the River Jordan. Her grandmother and all the other surviving young women had been taken and sold as slaves, the usual Roman practice. Like many children born into slavery, Zara never knew who her father was. Her mother had raised her until they were separated at the auction block five years before, when she was fourteen.

"Do you know where she is now?" Malchus asked gently as he propped himself up on his left elbow.

Zara closed her eyes and shook her head. When she opened her eyes again, they were moist and glistening. A moment later she wiped her eyes and sat up. "When we were auctioned by our master to cover a debt, I was the first female sold. When my new master took me, I saw my mother for the last time. I was terrified. So was she. She just stood there and cried quietly. She had protected me my whole life, but then she could not do anything. I never saw her again." Her eyes were wet again.

Malchus reached over and took her hand in his. "I want to hear more about you, Zara, but the last thing I want to do is make you miserable."

"Don't worry, Malchus. If I didn't want to talk, I wouldn't."

Malchus decided to continue. "How was your new master?"

"He was an elderly businessman—a Roman. We had . . . an understanding," Zara said, staring straight ahead without emotion.

"Which was?"

"If he wanted to have his way with me, he would have to pay."

Malchus was taken back by her bluntness but tried not to show it. "Pay?"

Zara smiled. "Yes, pay. Occasionally he would have too much to drink. One night he got a little too friendly, and I pulled away. He thought I was playing some sort of game with him, so he came after me. He grabbed me and wouldn't let me go. I slapped him—hard. He was startled, but it did not stop him. He came after me again. This time he was angry. He reminded me that I was the slave and he was the master. I threw something at him, and the next thing I knew he had a knife in his hand," she said, stiffening her chin, a glint of fire coming into her eyes. "I was scared. Very scared. But I wasn't going to just let him have me. Not without his paying for it. Something for him to remember—in case there was a next time."

When Malchus said he wanted to get to know her, this was not what he had had in mind. Zara made him feel as if he had led a sheltered life.

"Did he ever come after you again?"

"I'm sure he thought about it, but he was never willing to pay the price."

"The price?"

"When he attacked me with the knife, I fought back as hard as I could. It was not enough. He was too big and strong. He beat me and cut me, and when I could fight no more, he . . . raped me. But later that night, when he was asleep, I went into his bedroom and broke a vase over his head. I almost killed him. The next day I was privately whipped. He was too embarrassed when he was sober to charge me publicly for my assault and, instead, made up some story to cover his own injuries. Eventually he died, and I was sold to settle his estate, and here I am," she said with a smile.

Malchus did not smile back. He was not going to let her get away with opening her life to him the way she did and end it with a simple smile. He was touched, and he was going to let her know it. She would not have to battle alone as long as he was around.

He slid up the sleeve of her left arm and lightly let his finger glide along her scar. "Is this your battle wound?" he said softly.

She nodded slowly and spoke as softly as he did. "Yes."

He lifted his hand to her cheek wound and slowly moved his finger like a feather along it. "And this too?"

"Yes," she said, and closed her eyes gently as he stroked her.

Malchus was suddenly distracted by the approaching sound of visitors and rolled his eyes. "The escort," he said.

She nodded. She looked a little disappointed at their untimely arrival.

Malchus rose to his feet and helped her up. They then dusted each other off and walked around to the front of the chariot to welcome the party.

The escort came around the center garden. It was Seth. He was on foot, dragging the heels of his sandals as he had done his whole life, the reins of his horse in hand.

Zara leaned toward Malchus's ear. "I can't believe how much Seth looks like you. You look more like brothers than cousins."

"Except I'm better looking," Malchus said, smiling slightly.

"Hmm, maybe," Zara said. "Maybe not."

Sitting on the horse was Evaratus. He was huge, with jowls befitting a man of his size. He had a triple chin, barely hidden beneath a short, sparse, graying patch of beard on his round and sweaty face. He looked like easy prey for any scoundrel, but behind him, on foot, was a hulking muscle-bound slave who would cause anyone to think twice before attacking or robbing the big man. The slave held the reins of a heavily packed ass. Behind the animal stood another slave whose build was the mirror image of the first.

"Greetings, Cousin," Seth said as he approached, then frowned. "What, were you in a fight without me to protect you?"

Malchus was growing weary of explaining his appearance to everyone he came across. "Nothing quite so exciting I'm afraid. An accident."

"Hmm, whatever. I'm surprised to see you here. It's been a while since you've been on an escort. What's the occasion?"

Malchus just shrugged.

"Been waiting long?" Seth continued. Then he looked at Zara standing next to Malchus and said, "Couldn't have been too long. Or maybe not long enough, huh?"

Malchus ignored Seth and addressed Evaratus directly. "Sir, I am Malchus. It is my honor and privilege to escort you to the residence of the high priest, Joseph Caiaphas. He is very much committed to ensuring your safe arrival. If you will now please come with me."

Seth rolled his eyes at Malchus's fawning. He faced away from Evaratus, who could not see him ridiculing his cousin. Seth then turned to steady the horse for the big man to dismount. Evaratus looked as glad to get off the horse as the horse must have been for him to get off. The muscular slave from behind the ass came near to assist if necessary. Evaratus huffed and snorted at the implied need for assistance and waved the slave back. Then, with a grunt, he straightened his legs and hoisted himself over and off the horse. Everyone watched nervously. The spectacle was over the moment the man touched ground, then they all relaxed, hiding their amusement at the odd sight of his unique dismount.

Seth started to excuse himself in order to return to the Jericho road, where the rest of the caravan waited, when Evaratus began giving orders. "My men have walked very far today. I want them to ride with us the rest of the way. The ass can be tied to the rear of the chariot," Evaratus walked past Malchus and stepped onto the chariot.

Evaratus's instructions surprised Malchus. The chariot was made for four average-size passengers. With the size of these three, it would already be a very tight fit. What about Zara? Was he to leave her to find her own way back to Caiaphas's, walking while he and the rest rode? Besides, he was responsible for her.

Malchus watched as the two huge slaves made their way toward the chariot. He looked at Zara and then at Evaratus, and his stomach twisted into a knot. Zara was used to taking orders that belittled and disregarded her. She was a slave for life, and no doubt she had come to expect such indifference.

"I'm sorry, sir," Malchus said. "There is room for only four. Only one of your men can ride at a time. The other must walk."

Evaratus turned to Malchus and eyed him for a moment in apparent disbelief.

Malchus suddenly felt self-conscious about his eye as Evaratus seemed to notice it for the first time. He wondered what kind of message, if any, it was sending to the mountain-like man.

"No!" he finally croaked, his deep voice resonating with authority. "If there is any more walking to do, it will be done by the girl, not my men. Let us go now and stop this foolishness."

Malchus watched the chariot wheels dig into the road as the three men boarded. He had spent most of the last six years passively witnessing giant egos rule over common decencies, often with firsthand experience, but this was different.

Seth left his horse, hurried over to Malchus, and took him aside. "Malchus," Seth said in a stern whisper so not to be overheard, "you never cease to amaze me. First you lay on that thick, flattering garbage for his royal fatness, and then you try to pick a fight with him."

"Don't involve yourself, Seth," Malchus said. "Who does that overstuffed pig think he is?"

"He thinks he is the man entrusted by the entire population of Cos to deliver the tithe, and he thinks you are a slave. And in case you're having a tough time figuring that out, he's right. Besides, Malchus, it's my turn to have the girl for a while," he said, winking. "She can ride with me on the horse."

Malchus shot Seth a look that seemed to surprise him. Then he walked back to the chariot and took a deep breath.

"I am sorry, sir," Malchus said to Evaratus. "The girl is my responsibility, not yours. I had instructions from Caiaphas to take her with me even as I have instructions to take you with me. I am not riding with you, you are riding with me, unless you choose, your grace, to walk, or to steal the high priest's chariot."

Seth looked up to the heavens. Zara could not have looked more surprised. She looked as if she was about to say something, but did not. Evaratus's face, flushed and sweaty, glared at Malchus for what seemed like minutes. Then he looked at Zara, who was watching him for his response. His eyes stayed on her as if he was evaluating her role in what had just transpired. Then he looked at Malchus again. Evaratus's demeanor seemed suddenly to change as the flush left his face, and under his mustache a faint smile was detectable.

"I am used to people around me doing what I tell them to do. I am also used to people around me wanting something from me. Obviously you want something other than what I have, and you are willing to stand up for it. Even to me! I commend you for that, although I would not make it a habit. I have made this trip many times, and each time it is more exhausting than before. We are all hot and tired. I assumed too much. What you propose is acceptable."

Malchus resumed breathing and wiped some sweat off his forehead as Evaratus laughed.

Seth shook his head and walked back to his horse. "I'd like to be around for the rest of the ride. Who knows what will happen next? But I've got people getting restless up the road. Maybe they'll invite me to dinner!" he said to Malchus. Then he leaned toward Malchus so only he could hear. "He practically apologized to you. The girl should be impressed."

"It was my eye," Malchus whispered. "He didn't want his men to get into a fight they weren't prepared for."

"I'm sure that was it, Cousin," Seth said, then waved and rode off, shaking his head.

While Evaratus went through his regular ritual of pushing away the large slaves as they tried to help him onto the chariot, Zara pulled Malchus aside.

"No one has ever done anything like that for me before," she said softly, so only he could hear. She was clearly touched by what had happened. "I could easily have walked, you know. I want you to know I appreciate what you did." Zara stepped back, but then drew up to him again. "You could have gotten yourself into a lot of trouble with Caiaphas. What were you thinking?"

"What's he going to do? Kill me?" Malchus said with a smile, relieved that Evaratus's slaves had not.

All conversation ceased as the chariot crossed the southern ridge of the Mount of Olives. Jerusalem had appeared and filled their view. The walls of the ancient city seemed to be enchanted, rising out of the dusty hillside and reaching into the crimson sky, awash with color from the setting sun. The history that lay buried within the huge stones was as staggering as the walls themselves. Even those who had traveled this road many times before had to gaze at the beauty of the city. The huge perfectly fitted stones that made up the city walls took on dimension as they drew nearer, the shadows giving depth to what looked flat at a distance.

The road was not as busy now that most of the pilgrims had found lodging or rest stops for the night. The lights of their fires dotted the hillside like stars in the sky. The scent of burning locust wood and roasted lamb filled the air. Food quickly became the topic of conversation aboard the chariot. The only topic.

"What is your favorite meal, Evaratus?" Malchus asked.

"Why do you ask?"

"Because I'm getting very hungry and Levia will be serving whatever your favorite meal is. Somehow she will know what you want to eat even before you will. Believe me."

Evaratus laughed. "Well, I'm sure she doesn't know what I don't like to eat."

"What makes you so sure?" asked Malchus.

"Because, young man, I haven't found such a food." They both laughed.

As they approached the Essenes Gate, a thin figure hurried toward them through the twilight, calling Malchus by name.

"Judah!" Malchus yelled back, recognizing the voice. "What are you doing here?"

"I've been waiting for you for hours," Judah yelled, still approaching. "I need to speak to you privately, Malchus. Come out of the chariot," he said, while looking at Zara.

Ordinarily, Malchus would have asked Judah if the conversation could wait a few minutes. After all, he was almost home, and he had tired horses to tend to, with no one else to take care of them. But Judah's urgency was very uncharacteristic.

Malchus looked at the horses and then at Zara, trying to size up her ability to hold them, but her expression told him she knew what he had in mind and that he should not even to think of asking her.

"Evaratus, I'm sorry for this unexpected delay," Malchus said. "Could you please ask one of your slaves to hold the horses? This shouldn't take more than a few minutes."

Evaratus willingly obliged, probably willing to cooperate in any way he could in order to hasten supper.

"Judah, this better be very important," Malchus said, walking him away from the other ears on the chariot.

"I like your eye."

"Never mind that now."

"Just calm down and listen, Malchus," Judah warned. "You'll need your energy. Caiaphas grabbed me as he was storming through the temple and ordered me to tell you not to bring Evaratus to his house. He told me new arrangements would be made at Herod's to receive him there. You are to extend Caiaphas's apologies as best you can and get back to the house as fast as possible."

"Why? What happened?"

"Don't ask. There's too much to tell, and we don't have time right now. I can tell you this—You're lucky you weren't at the temple today. And don't expect a quiet evening. I'll try to find you later, hopefully before you see Caiaphas. Once he gets hold of you, I might not see you till morning."

"I'll see you outside Caiaphas's in two hours," Malchus said as he turned to leave.

"Malchus, one more thing."

"What?" he said, turning back to Judah.

"Is that the girl you were telling us about?"

"Yes."

"Did you ask her?"

"Of course not."

"She denied it, didn't she?"

"You're insane."

"She punched you in the eye, didn't she?"

"Leave."

Judah walked away, grinning.

On his way back to the chariot, Malchus tried to think of an easy way to not only tell Evaratus his dinner would have to wait, but that Caiaphas was not going to receive him. Looking at the size of him, he thought his first run-in with him may have been the easier task. What could possibly have occurred at the temple today that would keep Evaratus from staying at Caiaphas's?

"I'm afraid I'm going to have to apologize again, sir," Malchus said, taking back the reins from Evaratus's slave. "I've been instructed to take you to Herod's for reasons I do not yet know."

"Herod's?" Evaratus said, disappointment tingeing his words. "What do you suppose the problem is? Is it just for tonight?" he asked, somewhat irritated, as they went through the gateway.

"I'm sorry, sir," Malchus answered, "but I cannot answer any questions right now. This is all very unusual. But whatever the immediate problem, it appears to be well under control. Please don't let this change of plans trouble you. Caiaphas is looking forward to spending time with you, and I know he'll get word to you as soon as possible."

Herod's palace was located near the palatial homes of both Caiaphas and Annas. Malchus did not take long to drop off his charge and start back toward home. Alone with Zara again, Malchus let the horses trot through the narrow streets.

"What's happening?" Zara asked.

"I'm not sure, but we'll both find out soon. I'll drop you off at the house and then bring the horses back to the stable. Hopefully, I'll speak to Judah again before I see Caiaphas and find out. I was lying to Evaratus. Whatever the problem is, it's massive. It has to be. I've never known Caiaphas to miss an opportunity to influence the likes of Evaratus. That's what Caiaphas lives for. I can't imagine what could have happened today that would make him pass Evaratus off to Herod. I'll tell you this—Whatever it was, it took him by surprise. And Caiaphas hates surprises."

SEVEN

Malchus And Judah stood in the street outside Caiaphas's home. Above them, shouts were blaring from the high priest's balcony. Malchus pictured Caiaphas ranting and screaming into the aching ears of the captain of the guard and hoped that by the time he got there, his master would be exhausted.

"Malchus, that Nabataean slave girl is beautiful!"

"I told you."

"I didn't know you knew what beautiful was."

"Do you think you can get your mind off the girl long enough to tell me what happened today at the temple?" Malchus said, looking up at shadows moving on the balcony wall.

"You're going to hate to hear this, but you picked the wrong day not to be at the temple." Judah bent down and picked up a stone and held it out in front of Malchus. "He had the entire city the way I have this rock. Right in the palm of his hand." He tossed the stone back to the ground.

"He who?" Malchus said, too tired for riddles. He had not had much sleep the night before, and even though it had not been a strenuous day physically, he still felt drained from it. All he wanted to do now was lie down on his bed. The only thoughts tugging at his mind were good ones, thoughts he could relax with. Just because Caiaphas was in a rage did not mean he had to be. "Can you please just tell me what happened without the analogies?"

"Jesus happened. Jesus of Nazareth. You must have heard of him."

Malchus furrowed his brow. "Japhet was talking to Zara and me about him earlier today. Other than that, I've heard only some passing comments from Caiaphas."

"Well, you better prepare for his comments to be a bit more pointed," Judah said.

"Just tell me why, Judah."

Judah, who could get very demonstrative when excited, positioned himself squarely in front of Malchus. "Now, try to envision this—"

Malchus rolled his eyes.

"He comes through the Golden Gate on a donkey, with the whole world singing and shouting, 'Hosanna to the Son of David.' People were laying their garments on the ground for the animal to walk on. He gets off the donkey and marches straight to the temple. He circles around Solomon's Porch to the Royal Portico, all the while looking up at the temple walls. I walked over to the sheep merchants next to some of the temple guard. I can tell you, they weren't prepared for—"

"Forget them," Malchus interrupted. "What did Jesus do?"

"He stared at the walls for a little while. Then he started saying something. At first I thought he was talking to himself or maybe praying, but then—" Judah's eyes widened for effect "—I realize he's talking to the walls. To the walls!"

"He was praying, Judah."

"Not like I've ever seen."

"Just continue."

"All right, he closes his eyes and bows his head. A hush comes over the entire place. Scary. This was the first time I ever saw a messiah who scared me. All the people had been singing and dancing and shouting. The next thing, you can hear the wind blow. The entire temple was that quiet."

"And then?"

"Then he raised his head and looked toward us. He gave us a look I'll never forget. Eerie. Like he saw right through us."

"I can see right through you too."

"Just listen, the best is coming. He points his finger our way and yells. I remember every word. His voice echoed through the whole temple. 'It is written, *My house shall be called a house of prayer, but you have made it a den of thieves.*' My legs felt like stone. I looked at the temple guard. Every man was still. No one could even speak. If I wasn't so scared myself, I would have laughed at how sorry they all looked."

Malchus was no longer thinking about how tired he was. *A den of thieves,* he thought. He had never heard a more appropriate description.

"Then he just storms to the money changers' tables. You know, the new ones. The heavy ones."

"I remember."

"Remember how well constructed they were? How fine they looked? Not anymore. He turns them over. By himself. It was not that he was big or strong-looking either, but he just runs right through those things. One after another. A one-man army!"

"Wasn't anyone helping him?" Malchus asked. "His followers?"

"No," Judah said, shaking his head. "The people who were singing and shouting for him just a few minutes before were all watching with their hands at their sides without saying a word. Nobody could have predicted this. Even those who appeared to be his disciples looked as surprised as the rest of us. If this was planned, they definitely were not informed."

"Did the temple guard go after him then?"

"Wait, he wasn't finished yet. He was just getting started. He busts open the sealed money bins that had been under the tables and empties them into the crowd. The temple was raining shekels. That was enough to wake everyone out of their trances. People came from all over, grabbing up coins that were now everywhere, and stuffing them wherever they could. Another few seconds, and I think I would have joined them myself, but then he flashes his gaze down the line of merchants' tables, stopping us all where we stood, and grabs a staff."

"A staff?" asked Malchus. As good a time as he had had with Zara, he was envious of what Judah had witnessed. Hearing from Judah was good, but he wished his own eyes had seen the event. Malchus was convinced the Messiah was a Jewish invention or, at best, another empty hope. Yet there was something about what he was hearing that rang true. Unless, of course, the man was simply insane.

"Yes, that was the most frightening part. Malchus, as a shepherd, you would have been impressed at how he handled the thing. You would think he had been born with it in his hands. He swung it like a warrior, like he had been trained, hitting the perfect spot on the table legs of the dove merchants. The table collapsed in a heap. You know how well those things are put together. Three swings. One. Two. Three. Next table—One, two, three. Next. Then, next. It was like they bowed before him. Doves were everywhere, squawking and flying and scurrying for cover. He threw the staff at the oxen pen, riling the beasts into a frenzy. Then, he grabbed a whip."

"A whip? A messiah with a whip? Now that's new." Malchus had trouble envisioning this scene happening at the temple, but he grinned as he now hung on Judah's every word. In the years Malchus had been enslaved, there had been many "what ifs" that wandered in and out of his imagination. But never in his wildest daydreams had he ever envisioned a scenario playing out like this.

"Well, he made it a whip. He scoops up these tie ropes, wound them up, and made his whip whistle through the air faster than you could tell the temple guard to find real work!" They both laughed, then Malchus quickly shushed Judah, cautioning him with his hands to be quiet. He looked up the stairway at the guards. "Don't worry, they didn't hear," Judah said, waving at the guards as if they were personal friends. The guards waved back.

Malchus laughed. "I guess they can't recognize me from there. They'll be mad if they find out they waved at me."

"Malchus, listen, there's more," Judah said, getting back to the story. "He goes over to the sheep pen, kicks open the gate, and cracks the whip over their fuzzy little heads. In their hurry to get out, they trample the pen down. Then he does the same thing to the oxen. It's amazing no animal was hurt. In fact, come to think of it, no one was hurt, animal or person.

"After that, while we all keep a safe distance, he drops the whip and slowly walks over to the crowd, extends his hands toward them, and says, 'Come, you who are sick and in need, and I will make you well.'

"Malchus," Judah said with dead seriousness in his voice as he looked the other man in the eyes, "Everything I've told you has been the truth. I saw it. I'm not exaggerating a bit. As incredible as all that was, what happened next was beyond belief. He healed the sick of everything, of whatever that was wrong with them."

Malchus stepped back and frowned.

"He healed them," Judah repeated, nodding.

"You mean he made them feel better, right?"

Judah shook his head no.

Malchus stared at Judah for a moment, then smirked. "I hope you've been drinking, because if you haven't, I'm very disappointed that you, of all people, would try this one on me," he said, shaking his head. "You had me fooled, you really did, but you went too far, as usual."

Judah got closer, closing the gap between them. "There were people leaving him who were laughing and crying for joy, and running and leaping—people who just moments before were carried over to him on stretchers, moaning, sick, or crippled. Helpless. I swear. Before my own eyes, I saw sores disappear and walking sticks left behind by people who could only cry with relief. Even I cried."

"You cried?"

"Well, I wasn't going to tell you that part, but yes, I did."

"Wasted tears, my friend. You were had by actors."

"You wouldn't say that if you had been there, Malchus."

"This place attracts fake healers like flies to honey. Always has, always will. And no one is ever really healed. Never have been, never will be."

"You think I don't know that? I've been here longer than you! I wouldn't waste my breath if what I saw today was the usual. But what I saw was anything but the usual. It was different. Completely different. I know what I saw today was impossible. Impossible for anyone. Except him.

"Then he started wading through the crowd like it was a body of water until he disappeared in it. Chasing after him were some of the chief priests. I heard later they actually cornered him. I don't know what they were thinking. They were like sheep cornering a lion. And about as effective."

"How's that?" Malchus asked. He wanted to hear this part more than anything he had been told. Any time a messiah made it as far as the temple, the priests would verbally cut him to shreds, especially if Caiaphas was there.

"He tore them to pieces," Judah said.

"Why?" He immediately thought of several reasons. "I mean, how?"

"You should have seen the old priests," Judah said, grabbing Malchus by the shoulder. "You could almost see the hair on their backs bristling like a jackal's. They began challenging his authority to tear up the temple. Like he's got a right! Imagine that. Jesus comes in like a Roman legion destroying the place, and instead of the temple guard trying to tie him up and cart him away, the priests come after him shaking their fingers, yelling, 'By who's authority . . . blah, blah, blah?' He shut their mouths faster than he shut down the money changers."

"What did he say?"

"I know I sound like I'm repeating myself, but I have never seen anyone speak to the priests this way. Caesar himself couldn't have spoken with more authority. Every word was chillingly accurate as he ran through a list of indictments. He left them speechless and naked. It was awesome."

"I'm sorry to hear that," Malchus said somberly.

"Sorry? Why, I thought you'd be delighted."

"He caught them by surprise, Judah. If I know Caiaphas, the next time they'll all be ready for him."

†

Malchus ascended the steps to Caiaphas's home with trepidation. So much had happened, first with Zara, and now with Jesus. As Malchus walked under the entry arch, he could imagine Caiaphas, the master planner, executing a painstakingly calculated counterattack on the unsuspecting Jesus. He would never let an incident like today's go unanswered.

Passing the temple guards, Malchus resisted goading them for their comrade's pitiful response to the day's events. He would have settled for his usual *Shalom* and door slam, but instead he entered quietly. He slipped into the kitchen that was across from Caiaphas's meeting room. Zara and Levia were preparing a tray of food for the high priest and whomever he was yelling at.

Malchus walked in front of them with his right index finger over his lip to keep his name from being mentioned, then he motioned toward the meeting room. The women nodded, and Levia sent Zara away with the tray. Malchus stationed himself in a shadow by the outside wall so he could see what was happening across the hall. He wanted to test the waters before going in.

"Sir, would you—"

"No! He doesn't want any fruit, and he isn't going to want any fruit unless I say so," Caiaphas yelled. He was screaming at Zara, who was holding a tray of fruit, carrying out Levia's orders. His intensity caused her to stop in midstep. As she did, an orange dropped from her tray to the floor. It rolled toward Caiaphas. He looked angry enough to kill.

"Leave it there and get out," he ordered, slowly overenunciating every word. Zara turned, quickly left the room, and returned to the kitchen.

Malchus motioned her over. She came to him, clearly shaken and cowering. "Don't take anything personally when he's like this. You're doing your job, and that's what he'll remember."

"Thanks. I'll be fine. But I better leave before he sees you," she said. Just then, Levia called for Zara to follow her out of the room.

Levia was just doing her usual good job of seeing to the needs of any and all guests. And this guest was certainly not one to be overlooked. This was Jonathan, son of Annas, brother-in-law of Caiaphas and captain of the temple guard. His office was second only to the high priest. If anything untoward were to happen to Caiaphas, the captain of the temple guard would take his place.

Jonathan was a big man, and strong, with a reputation for being ill-tempered, arrogant, and nasty to his subordinates. His size suited him well in his position, and he used it to intimidate. But here with Caiaphas, size meant nothing. If anything, Caiaphas routinely intimidated Jonathan—and more so tonight than usual. He would not dare to say so, but he probably wanted a piece of fruit, especially from the pretty new slave girl who had, undoubtedly, caught his eye the moment she entered the room. He had to be disappointed she left so quickly. Women were one of Jonathan's better-known weaknesses. He was even more ill-tempered and nasty to them than to the men under his command. Almost no one spoke of his social depravity, and most women around the temple simply avoided him. He was, after all, the son of Annas and captain of the temple guard.

"A den of thieves!" Caiaphas said through clenched teeth. He stood at the open balcony, facing the cool night air. "A den of thieves!" he repeated, slightly louder this time. He grasped his forehead with his right hand and squeezed his hand closed until he held only the bridge of his nose between his fingers. Then he turned and started to walk toward Jonathan, who was sitting at the meeting room table looking at his folded hands before him. Caiaphas looked up at the ceiling, raised both hands, palms up, and yelled, "A den of thieves! Who does he think he is talking to? Who does he think he is?"

"The Messiah," said Jonathan.

Caiaphas shot him a look, and Jonathan immediately looked back at his own folded hands.

The high priest walked over to his captain and whispered sternly into his ear. "Would you like to try to explain to me again, before we go and explain it to Annas, why the temple guard did absolutely nothing to stop him? After all, Jonathan, you were in charge," he said, then stood up. "Well?" he screamed.

Jonathan lifted his hand to his ear and cringed. He sat there like a child, shaking his head and folding and unfolding his hands. A moment later, he shrugged slightly, and said, "In all honesty, the men were a little confused. When he entered the city, there was quite a fanfare. He received more attention than even Caesar would have gotten. We wondered ourselves if he was the Messiah. Just for a moment," he quickly added, seeing the vein in Caiaphas's forehead ready to burst at the suggestion. "An enormous crowd followed him. It seemed like the whole city had gathered, and they were all with him. And for him. They were chanting like children, 'Hosanna to the Son of David.' I think the whole thing just caught the men by surprise. They were simply unprepared for this."

"You, Jonathan. You. You. You," Caiaphas yelled, emphasizing every word by pointing his finger at Jonathan's face. "Don't say, 'they.' They're your men. You're responsible. You were unprepared! You were caught by surprise! You were confused, and not 'a little.' Now, continue," he said, turning abruptly and pacing away.

"The vandalism took them, uhh . . . took us . . . took me by surprise, and before I knew what was happening, it was over. The damage was done, and he had moved off into the crowd that surrounded him. I won't even tell you what I saw then. I think my eyes were playing tricks on me. If we were to advance then, we would have had a riot on our hands. But I assure you, Caiaphas, it won't happen again. The next time he gets anywhere near the merchants, we'll be on him like—"

"You had better be!" Caiaphas yelled. "You need to assemble the temple guard. You need to remind them," he said, "that they are here to protect us." He was screaming again by the time he finished the sentence. "I will not permit this! Do you understand? I've worked too hard for what we have, to let this—this maniac ruin it.

"As high priest I have tolerated more than my share of messiahs. They strut in with their poisonous tongues, prophesying and promising deliverance from foreign oppression, preying on the disaffected and weak-minded. Occasionally, one even has the nerve to hurl an insult my way, to make himself look brave. So let them be brave to the indolent. No one cares. Why, they even do us a service, drawing together bands of the lazy and disgruntled and leaving with them.

"But not him. This one is different. His goals are higher. His following bigger. And does he attack Rome? No, he attacks me and the temple. And at Passover, of all times. I will not tolerate him like the others. He must be dealt with and dealt with quickly. Very quickly. Who knows how much damage he caused today, or how far the impact will be felt? Merchants actually ran away from him. We haven't seen them since. We may never see them again—not to mention the shocked pilgrims."

He looked down at the floor and saw the orange Zara had dropped. He thought to pick it up, but instead kicked it without looking where it would go. The orange went flying. Cracked, it flew toward the balcony and went clean through the railing and into the open air. Shreds of rind hung off its flesh like broken wings.

The man is too enraged to tire, Malchus thought, still crouched in a shadow on the kitchen floor. *I can't stay here all night. In the mood he's in, if Caiaphas finds me hiding here, he'll have me flogged. Jonathan would love that. Maybe I should just report in and get it over with. How much better could his mood be in the morning?* He looked at Caiaphas again through the archway. He had never seen him so mad. *Maybe while his back is turned I should try to get by and go to bed. Tough choice. I'll go to bed,* he thought.

He almost made it past the meeting room doorway.

"Malchus!" Caiaphas yelled.

Malchus stopped obediently and backed up a step. He started to enter the room when he heard someone clear her throat. From the end of the hall, Zara smiled at him. He forgot himself for a moment.

"Malchus!" Caiaphas shouted again. "If it's not too much trouble."

Malchus quickly entered and walked halfway across the meeting room. "Yes?" He looked at Jonathan, who sat back, half-turned in his seat to face him. Malchus figured Jonathan must be glad Caiaphas's attention would no longer be focused just on him.

"I've been waiting for you," snapped Caiaphas. "Haven't you heard?"

"About what happened in the temple?"

"No, about—" Caiaphas cut short his sarcasm, squinting at Malchus in the dim lighting. "Your eye . . . "

"An accident, sir. I'll be fine, thank you." Malchus was surprised and touched that Caiaphas had taken notice in this moment of insanity.

Caiaphas nodded. Then, apparently restraining himself in a forced calm, he repeated himself, "The temple. Judah told you?"

In the midst of this whirlwind, Malchus could see everyone was moving much too slowly for Caiaphas. A long time had passed since the high priest had allowed his temper to rule the day, but his steely discipline appeared ready to crack. He looked worn. His right hand, palm down on the table, supported his weight as he stood there. The hint of compassion Caiaphas had toward him at this moment surprised Malchus. He knew how hard Caiaphas worked for everything to be perfect. And Malchus knew what kind of stress this Jesus was causing him. As for Jonathan, he sat there quietly, trying to keep a low profile and avoid Caiaphas's acerbic barbs.

"Yes, Judah told me how—uh, what happened," Malchus replied respectfully. "If there is anything you want me to do, tell me what it is, and I'll take care of it."

"I want you in the temple at dawn. I want you talking to the merchants, helping to calm them down. Just help them in any way you can. Tomorrow we will see how many return." Caiaphas straightened. "And how many don't."

Suddenly Malchus realized the real reason for Caiaphas's concern over his eye—the sake of appearance in the temple. Simple math.

Caiaphas turned to Jonathan. "They must be assured that next time the temple guard will protect them. And that there won't be a next time! They *must* be made to feel safe. I want you personally to apologize to each and every one of them for the inconvenience and distraction that heretic caused, and for the losses resulting from your inaction."

"There won't be a next time," Jonathan said, trying to sound confident. "If he comes again, we'll be right there with him."

"Oh, he'll be back. I have no doubt about that. The madman is on a mission," Caiaphas said, shaking his finger. "And yes, you will be right there with him. And you will stop him. Passover begins in less than two days. We can't afford another episode like today's. Who knows how many people he's scared away from next year's feast. Also, I want an emergency meeting of the Sanhedrin, tomorrow, here in my personal court," he rubbed his chin in thought. "Not the whole Sanhedrin. Not yet. I will send you a list of exactly which members later this evening."

Jonathan pushed his seat back and stood to attention. "Shalom, Caiaphas, I will see you in the morning," he said. Still deep in thought, the high priest just waved him off. Jonathan shrugged at being ignored, then headed for the door. Malchus thought the opportunity to leave was as good as it was going to get.

"Shalom," Malchus said. He began to accompany Jonathan to the door. The captain said nothing, as if Malchus were not there.

Free in you, Malchus thought. With his freedom in sight, he felt less like a slave with each passing day. Consequently, shallow, pompous attitudes like Jonathan's, which Malchus had surrendered to for years, were appearing as rude as when he had first arrived.

"One more thing," Caiaphas said, just as they were exiting into the hallway. They both stopped and turned. "Jonathan, I want a list of the people who give him an audience. Those who listened to his rantings. I want to know who's being poisoned with his lies—who we need to keep an eye on."

EIGHT

Be there at dawn, Malchus tripped on the strap of his untied sandals and fell by the kitchen doorway as he hurried down the hall. He stared at the doorpost he had crashed into the previous morning. It loomed inches away.

Zara gasped as Malchus tumbled by. "Malchus . . . are you—"

"I'm fine," Malchus said, sitting on the hallway floor trying to tie his sandal. "But I won't be for long. I'm late. And when Caiaphas gives you an order to be somewhere, the one thing you can't be is late."

Zara looked a little puzzled. "How late can you be? It's so early?"

"If there's light in my room when I open my eyes, then I'm late. That's true today at least. How long has it been light out?"

Zara shrugged. "Since I've been up. An hour, maybe."

"I'm very late."

"Your eye looks worse than it did yesterday, you know. I knew it would."

"You're so smart," he said, admitting to himself that his vision had been impaired by the swelling. "That's because I slept on it all night. It will be back to normal soon."

Zara laughed. "Soon it will be very colorful. And it won't be normal for another week or two."

"We'll see," Malchus said pridefully.

"You should be glad you can see at all."

"As long as I can see you, I am content," he said.

She smiled and seemed to blush. "Malchus, before you go, can you help me with something?"

"My time is very expensive, you know."

"Name your price. Money is no object," she said.

"No object that you possess, that is." They laughed. "How can I help you?"

"Levia asked me to find some fresh flowers for the meeting room table. When I asked her where to get them, she told me to walk outside the west temple walls. She gave me directions, and said I would have no trouble finding my way, but I'm afraid I'll get lost."

Malchus knew of a better place and wished he could take her there and back, but Caiaphas would be mad enough to punish the both of them. "Follow me," he said. "I'm going to the temple and can easily point you in the right direction once we're there."

Zara was beaming. "I've never seen the temple."

Although just a couple of hours after dawn, the streets were already buzzing with activity. News traveled fast in the ancient city, and Passover did nothing but increase the speed. Malchus and Zara were at the southern end of the city, not far from Caiaphas's home, when they heard. Malchus saw the word being passed about from person to person like water moving through a bucket brigade, but he didn't recognize what was happening until his turn came to hear and pass on the message. Apparently, joyous splashing of water in the Pool of Bethesda had caused waves of news that rippled from the northern most walls of the city, southward through the Sheep Gate, through the temple, and into the streets. "Jesus is at the Pool of Bethesda!" At the repeating of the words, a charge electrified the air. The message was coming from everywhere.

Zara grabbed Malchus's right arm with both her hands. "Malchus, please take me to see this man." She tugged at him like a little girl pulling on her grandfather's arm.

Malchus looked into her eyes. They sparkled with life and anticipation and all but made him forget his duty. How could he say no to her? But what about Caiaphas?

Zara had been sent out by Levia. She could explain she had simply been lost and caught up in the flow of the crowd. But if she got too close to this man Jesus, who was now an enemy of the high priest, her explanation might not be worth much. She could get punished.

"I don't know, Zara. This might not be a good idea," Malchus said.

"But I must, Malchus. I *must*. Tell me the way to this pool, and I will find it myself if you can't take me."

"Come, I'll take you," he said, knowing he had no choice. If he did not take her, she was determined to go anyway. And she would. Malchus had seen this fever before. Japhet had it yesterday, and Zara had apparently caught it from him. He knew there was no talking to someone who thought she was hearing from God. And the Messiah, according to the scriptures, was to be God in the flesh. Enough to grab anyone's soul. Anyone who had not already seen over a dozen of them, that is.

"How far is this pool?" Zara asked, pulling him to move faster as they entered into the flow toward the temple. "Why is he there? Will he still be there when we get there?"

Malchus laughed at her excitement but thought it might be a good idea to temper some of her energy with some reality. "The Pool of Bethesda is just beyond the temple, through the Sheep Gate. People who are sick or lame will be there, looking and hoping for a touch from God. If someone is healthy, they are not likely to be there."

"Why?" asked Zara as they flowed with the crowd.

"There's a Jewish belief that an angel occasionally comes by and stirs up the waters at the pool. When that happens, the first person to step into the water will be healed."

"Have you ever seen that happen?"

"No," Malchus said. "But I don't make a habit of going there."

"Why?"

"It's not clean, especially during Passover. It's right next to the Sheep Gate, where the animals are brought into the temple to be sold and sacrificed. The sheep make the immediate area smell of animal droppings and wet wool. On a hot, still day, the stench outside the Sheep Gate can get bad if you're with a flock waiting to get in."

Zara's bouncing enthusiasm seemed momentarily slowed.

"People who are at the pool are there for a reason. From any direction, you would have to pass several far more hospitable and less offensive gates. The Sheep Gate itself is mainly used as a convenient way to get livestock into the temple without burdening the rest of the city."

"Sounds like I'd have a hard time finding it if you weren't with me," Zara said.

"You might have to ask a few people, but once you were outside the Sheep Gate you'd see it. The pool is open and obvious. In fact, anything going on there is in full view of the Roman fortress known as the Castle of Antonia, which has a tower higher than any other building in Jerusalem. And with any unusual activity, like now, the Romans will be keeping a watchful eye on it from the tower."

Malchus could see Zara had one destination in mind. She was going to see Jesus, and she was not going to let animal stench or thoughts about being spotted by the Romans get in her way.

The closer they came to the temple, the more crowded the streets became. Zara looked at Malchus anxiously, as if there was something he could do to speed the flow of traffic. She jumped up into the air, looking to see if there was a path through which they could move faster. There wasn't. Malchus was not about to start pushing and squeezing his way through with Zara in tow. He would probably get into a fight and somehow have to explain that to Caiaphas too.

And what if he lost the fight—with Zara watching? No. Zara would just have to be patient. Jesus would still be there.

Zara took control. An opening appeared before her, and she quickly moved ahead, pulling Malchus, who was still holding her hand. Malchus resisted weakly with his weight. She turned and met his eyes with a slight frown.

"Come!" she demanded.

"I'm coming," he said as they continued to press through.

"Humph. Excuse me!" someone complained sarcastically.

"Slow down!"

"We're all going to get there."

"Sorry," Malchus apologized as he went. He called to Zara, "He's not going to leave any time soon. He's here to be seen and heard." *Like all of them,* he thought.

"I can't explain," she said over her shoulder. "I just need to be there."

The crowd was getting even thicker. Finally it pressed in all around them and became impassable. Zara attempted to peer around shoulders and heads to find a way through. There was none. Malchus felt pressure from behind. They were stuck where they stood.

After standing there for a few moments, staring only at backs, Zara turned to Malchus. Her face was inches from his and looked disturbed. "Malchus, I just had a thought."

"What?" he asked. Those in the crowd pressing around them would have been uncomfortable and tired, but Malchus enjoyed how close he was to Zara. He was almost touching her. He wanted to be touching her. *I could stay right here all day,* he thought.

"You will be easy to recognize at the temple, will you not?"

"I practically live there."

Then you must not come with me to see Jesus. Caiaphas was so angry with him. If you are seen listening to him, word might get back to Caiaphas, and you could get punished . . . because of me."

Malchus was touched. "We'll see what happens when we get there."

"Are you going to move or just stand there?" came a voice from behind Malchus. Malchus looked up to see that there was room to continue forward. Before Malchus could say more, the slow movement brought them past a corner house.

"Malchus, look!" Zara said, peering over the heads of all the people down the new street they had turned onto.

Malchus instantly remembered when he'd seen it for the first time. The sheer size of its walls. It was a marvel that had not lost its splendor like the system it housed.

"Is that . . . ?"

"Yes, Zara. The Holy Temple. People travel across the world to see what your eyes are beholding right now."

Malchus was glad he was able to be there and share this time with her. Zara looked at him with all the excitement that had sent them on this small trek. The bounce was back in her step. *Her heart must be racing,* he thought. The anxiety about being discovered was apparently gone—forgotten.

In front of them, the crowd slowed almost to a standstill, again. Each person waited for his or her turn to reach and ascend the stairs, which led to the great open gates of the outer courts. A human flood, spilling into a narrow funnel. They were staring up at the temple, Malchus realizing Zara must be unaware that she was looking at only a small corner of its outer wall. He marveled with her at the sheer size and beauty of the gates to the temple.

There were nine gates visible from their approach. A massive one in the middle, flanked on either side by four slightly smaller ones. All the gates were stone arches, and each contained two doors. Gold and silver plating trimmed the eight side gates, and they shone so brightly in the sunlight, you could not look directly at them for longer than a second or two. Though each of the eight gates was bigger than any gate in the city itself, by far the most magnificent was the center gate, the main entrance to the temple. It was cast out of dazzling Corinthian brass and was richly engraved and trimmed. The huge double doors required the collective strength of twenty men to open and close them. This gate was known as the "Beautiful Gate," and the polished white marble steps that led up to it reflected the sun nearly as brightly as the gate itself. Malchus loved the sight before him. With every turn, Zara appeared awestruck.

After a long while, they had finally made their way to the first step leading up to the far left gate, to begin their final assent into the temple.

"Give to the blind. Help an old blind man, please," came a sorrowful wail over the din of the crowd. The people in front of them shifted slowly around a man sitting about ten steps up. He protected his face with his arms as people pushed their way past him, tripping and bumping into him as they made their way up the steps. "Please," he repeated, grabbing at unseen arms and legs that quickly pulled free from his grip. He grabbed Zara by the hem of her tunic. "Give to the blind. Please. Help an old blind man," he said again. A pitiful sight, his clothes dirty, his face weathered by the sun, he leaned on his right elbow and held a cup in his left hand. His eyes moved, unseeing, behind a milky blue film. Zara stared at him as the pulsating crowd moved her around him, his hand still tightly clutching her tunic.

Many times before, Malchus had seen the blind man. He was a fixture on these steps, crowd or no. Malcus considered yanking Zara's garment free, but then hesitated, not wanting to appear cruel. Zara was not in danger, and she seemed interested in the man. She probably felt sorry for him, but had nothing to drop into his cup. Malchus had some money. Maybe Zara would like it if he gave a coin to the blind man.

"Move on, keep going," came a voice farther down the stairs. Others chimed in.

"It's not me, it's her," another voice said.

"What's going on? Is she going to move?"

"I don't know. Are you going to move?" Everyone seemed to be shouting at Zara.

"No!" she said, suddenly indignant at their rudeness.

Oh no, Malchus thought. *Here comes the fire.* But to his surprise, instead of continuing her fight with the crowd, she ignored them. She kept her ground and bent over to the blind man.

"Go around her," someone shouted as the people began to pass, pushing her so close to the blind man, she almost fell on top of him. The shouts and the sudden crowding of his space seemed to make the blind man very nervous.

Malchus suddenly felt a swell of anger. He positioned himself to take on the next person who dared to push either Zara or him.

"Can you walk?" Zara asked.

"What?" Malchus said. Now what's she going to do?

"Walk where? Leave me alone. Who are you?"

"I want to help you," Zara said in a soothing voice.

"Help me? You cannot help me, unless you have something to give me. How can you help me? No one can help me. Can't you see I'm blind? Are you blind too?"

"He wants money, Zara. I've got some he can have," Malchus offered. He was confused. He could not read her thoughts, but he was intuitively against it.

"Malchus, I know he wants money. Do you think I'm stupid?" Zara said.

"No. Of course not. But—"

"All we've heard since we left home was about Jesus healing people." She looked at the old man. "If Jesus is the one Japhet spoke of, then this man can be healed."

"Zara," Malchus said, trying to remain calm. "This man has been blind since birth. Everyone knows that to be true. No one can heal his blindness." *Or anything else,* he thought.

"Not even the Messiah?" she asked, point blank.

Malchus was tongue-tied. He wanted to tell her there was really no such thing as a real messiah. But how could he do that now? And here?

She turned back to the blind man. "Please, let me help you," she persisted tenderly.

"You want to help me? Then help me," he said, thrusting out his cup in her direction and staring blankly ahead. He released her tunic.

"I have no money, but if you will let me, I will bring you to someone who can give you sight," Zara said.

The blind man was silent for a second. Then he reached out his hand in the direction of her voice. His hardness seemed to leave him as hope, inspired by Zara's promise, welled up within him. She took hold of his hand and helped him as he struggled to his feet.

Malchus could not believe what was happening. He felt incredibly awkward. *There is no logic in this,* he thought. Then, against everything he thought he should do, he took the blind man's other arm. The bony feel of it under the ripped and dirty rag in which he was clothed repulsed him. And the man smelled. Malchus tried not to breathe deeply. *He needs to be washed in the Pool of Bethesda,* Malchus thought. *No, he was probably sent away even from there.*

"Get away," the blind man yelled, yanking his arm away from Malchus. "Would you steal coins from a blind man? Only she can touch me."

Malchus saw the arm he had been holding was the one with the money cup. *This is insane,* he thought. *We can't do this. What if Caiaphas sees this? This is no way to be inconspicuous.*

They made their way up the stairs, moving at half the pace of the crowd. Then, they were inside the gate. The grandeur inside the temple seemed to strike Zara, who was now clearly lost in another world. The pillars and gateways, chambers and courts must have seemed like a dream come to life.

"Where do we go from here, Malchus?" she asked. The crowd, which had been like an appendage to their flesh, dispersed after entering the temple, people going in every direction. Presently they were standing in the Court of the Gentiles.

Malchus looked around nervously. In the distant left corner of the court a large gathering of people crowded around someone who seemed to be talking to them. *That must be Jesus,* he thought.

"Over there, Zara." Malchus pointed. "He must have left the pool to come inside the temple. The healing must be over. He's teaching now." Malchus was guessing, but he hoped Zara would believe him. Maybe she would forget this insane venture. The blind man could beg from where he was. *Leave him right there,* he thought.

"Malchus," called a familiar voice from behind.

Just what Malchus feared—being recognized by someone who knew he should be working. At least it was not Caiaphas or Jonathan. Only Elias. Malchus could handle the old man, but still he had to be careful. Elias was a chief priest and long-trusted assistant of Caiaphas.

"Zara," Malchus said. She was staring in the direction of the gathering. "Zara," he said again. She turned. "Elias is calling me and probably heading this way. He doesn't know you yet. When I turn around to talk to him, you turn the other way. I don't want him to somehow recognize you when he sees you back at Caiaphas's." She nodded and turned.

"Malchus," came the voice again, much closer.

Malchus let out a deep breath and turned around. "Elias."

"Malchus, where have you been?"

"I—"

"You must get over to the east end immediately. The merchants are causing us much trouble." The old man took Malchus by the arm and led him away. As he walked, Malchus looked over his shoulder for Zara. She was gone.

NINE

Don't worry. There's no need to be concerned. Everything is under control," the man shouted, mimicking Malchus. "That's easy for you to say. Your sheep weren't running loose through the temple. Your doves weren't flying away, never to be seen again. And you—you weren't even here yesterday, so how would you know how I feel?"

All Malchus knew was Zara was on the other side of the temple leading a blind man by his bony hand to a man who was probably under surveillance from every direction. He hoped Caiaphas had left the job up to Jonathan and the temple guard. Jonathan never seemed to do anything right, and the guard did not know her . . . yet.

"Look, what happened yesterday is not going to happen again," Malchus said, trying to reason with and reassure the merchant. He could not remember when he had addressed more complaints—complaints he actually thought were valid. But he had his orders.

"And why not?"

"Because the temple guard will stop him."

"Like it did yesterday? Oh, now I feel so much better."

"Today is different. The guard is ready today—"

"Forget it! I would have to be a bigger fool than you to believe that! You should have seen the temple guard yesterday. As long as that man is in town, I set up nothing. I sell nothing. I can't afford the losses."

Just then they heard loud shouts coming from the other side of the temple in the Court of the Gentiles.

"You see what I'm saying? It's happening again," the merchant said, slapping his forehead with his right hand.

Malchus turned to see the entire area around him draining of pilgrims and merchants. Tables were being left unmanned.

Malchus took off in a run to the other side of the temple. *Yesterday everyone must have seen quite an event, and they probably don't want to be late for the next one,* Malchus thought. He only hoped Zara was a spectator and not the center of attention.

When Malchus stood within view of the disturbance, he stepped up onto the base of a pillar to search for Zara. People were swarming after a man who was running with his arms stretched straight out, like wings flailing wildly in giant circles, shouting deliriously, "I can see! I can see!" He repeated it over and over. "I can see you! I can see you!" He yelled, running from one person to another. "I can see all of you," he shouted. He began twirling again, like a dancer. "I can see everything. My eyes! They work!"

As Malchus watched this odd dance, his gaze fell upon Jonathan standing next to a scribe who was writing at a table. Jonathan seemed to be alternately searching the crowd and dictating to him.

Malchus jumped off his perch and cut across the flow of the crowd toward Jonathan, although at this point the flow seemed to be governed by the traveling yells of the supposedly healed blind man. He did not know what excuse he would use for not being with the merchants, but maybe from that vantage point he would be able to locate Zara. On his way to Jonathan, Malchus leapt into the air several times, hoping to catch a glimpse of Zara, but the size of the crowd made the task impossible.

"Malchus," Jonathan said loudly. He was smiling.

Malchus sensed trouble. Jonathan almost never spoke to him. It was beneath him. The only thing that would make him smile was someone else's misfortune. Malchus approached Jonathan around the back of the scribe, hoping to see what was being written. He paused and looked over the scribe's shoulder, but the writing was small and illegible. He could tell, though, that it was a list. His chest tightened at the thought of what names were on the list and what their fate would be.

"Malchus," Jonathan said. "You should get that new slave girl out of here before she gets into any more trouble. She not only made my list of possible rebels, but she gets a mark next to her name for bringing others with her."

"Who could she bring? She doesn't know anyone. She's been here only a day."

Jonathan motioned toward the blind man.

"Him?" Malchus said.

"That's right, the blind man," Jonathan said, looking over Malchus's head as he talked. "She seems quite zealous."

"Oh, I'm sure she's just overwhelmed with being in the temple for the first time. This is her first time, you know.

Besides, the blind man practically lives here. She can't be accused of bringing him."

"Look, I have work to do. Don't bother me."

"Jonathan, you can't put her name on the list. If Caiaphas sees her name there, he'll be incensed. He'll have her flogged."

"That's not my decision to make."

"But you know that's what he'll do," Malchus said, pleading with him.

"Talk to him about it," Jonathan said.

Malchus stepped in front of the scribe and, in frustration, almost made the mistake of grabbing Jonathan's list. When, spotting Caiaphas coming from a distance, accompanied by a few other chief priests and scribes, Malchus quickly stepped back and returned his attention to Jonathan. "Where is she, Jonathan? Where is Zara?"

"Is that her name? Thank you. She's over there," he said, pointing with his finger. "I've been keeping an eye on her. A pity. She's very attractive."

At that instant, Malchus realized he actually hated Jonathan. He spun around to the area where all of the commotion had started. Malchus left Jonathan without another word, his heart pounding. He pressed and fought past the throng of people until he could see the one who had started all the commotion. Malchus paused, somewhat surprised at what he saw. The Nazarene did not look like any of the half dozen or more previous messiahs Malchus had seen since his enslavement. They all had the same look, priestlike, sitting in the shadows, with a pale, drawn face from fasting. Jesus looked anything but sick. In fact, he had all the appearance of one of the bystanders, thoroughly enjoying a festive event. His garment gave no hint of pretense, and he was busy with the crowd, not aloof. He seemed to have something to say to each individual, as well as addressing the entire group as he walked about a large column under the Royal Porch at the west end of the Court of the Gentiles. He was smiling broadly and even laughed as the once-blind man yelled out.

Malchus was interested and wanted to stay, but he could not be part of this. There was no time. He had to turn his attention back to Zara. She had to be found. Now. He searched the faces in the crowd and tried to peer in between the people to find her. Caiaphas was coming, and Malchus had to find Zara before he did.

"Whoa there! What's your hurry?" a man said as Malchus bumped into him.

"Sorry," Malchus said, then realized it was Evaratus. He had been so focused on Jesus and now in his search for Zara, he did not recognize the big man as he was passing by him. His giant slaves were with him.

"What do you make of this?" Evaratus said, motioning toward Jesus.

"I . . . I haven't really heard him, sir. I'm looking for—"

"Well, his claims are extraordinary," Evaratus interrupted, frowning heavily. "What does Caiaphas have to say about him?"

"I'm sure you'll find out soon enough."

Suddenly, the man whose sight had been restored hurried clumsily into a space between Jesus and the listeners, and fell at the Nazarene's feet. Evaratus's attention followed. With his forehead bowed to the marble floor, the man thanked the Nazarene over and over again. Then he began to cry convulsively, wailing for joy. The crowd that had followed the man also began to close in. As they pressed together toward Jesus, Malchus saw Caiaphas and his band getting dangerously close, slowed only by the wall of bodies surrounding their destination. Desperately he searched the crowd. She must be right here, he thought. Why can't I find her?

"Dear God, where is she?" he muttered in desperation.

"Malchus," came a voice from behind, as if in response.

He turned abruptly and grabbed her by the shoulders. "Zara!" he shouted. "Are you trying to get yourself killed? Are you oblivious to the danger you're in?" he said, only now seeing her face. Her eyes were filled with joyful tears, and her nose was red and sniffling. He felt terrible that he had screamed at her, but there was no time for explanations and apologies. Malchus looked up and saw Caiaphas wedging into the crowd.

"I'm sorry, Malchus. I had to," Zara said. She blinked, spilling out tears that rolled down her cheeks.

"Make way for the high priest," shouted a temple guard, trying to keep in front of Caiaphas as Caiaphas impatiently tried to pass him to get to Jesus. The determination to confront the Nazarene was all over his face.

The immediate crowd gave Caiaphas room as he and several other chief priests stood before Jesus. With Caiaphas's focus fixed, Malchus motioned to Zara to keep quiet and listen.

"Rabbi . . . " Caiaphas said calmly.

Malchus knew how difficult it must have been for Caiaphas to call Jesus a rabbi and how inside the high priest must be seething.

". . . By what authority are you doing these things, and who gave you this authority?"

Jesus turned to Caiaphas, the old man still at his feet, and said, "I will ask you one thing, too, which if you tell me, I will also tell you by what authority I do these things. The baptism of John was from what source, from Heaven or from men?"

Caiaphas stood there as the chief priests at his side whispered into his ear. Malchus could not hear them, but he could just imagine what the problem was and almost smiled. The John whom Jesus referred to was a local wild man, who had lived in the desert and had baptized people in the Jordan River near Jericho before Herod beheaded him. Most of the people in the crowd had passed him on previous journeys to get here, and many held him to be a prophet, an opinion Caiaphas would never encourage. But he did not want to alienate himself from the crowd either.

"We don't know," Caiaphas finally said, choosing diplomacy over honesty.

"Then neither will I tell you by what authority I do what I do," Jesus said, then knelt down to help the old man stand up.

Caiaphas's face reddened, but he could say nothing with the crowd there.

Malchus could have fallen over. This was the first time he had ever seen Caiaphas stumped. He listened as Jesus continued to speak in parable stories that were obviously about the priesthood and not very complimentary.

Evaratus now stood next to the priests, still frowning as Jesus continued. Malchus wondered if he would send his giant slaves to the high priest's aid before the confrontation was over. *That would be interesting,* Malchus thought. But with Caiaphas flabbergasted, Malchus took the opportunity to sneak Zara behind a nearby column. He hated the situation he was in and the fear he felt. He wanted to move freely alongside Zara without the curse of bondage. "Free in you," he mouthed as he leaned against the cold stone.

His eyes were on the priests. His ears were in the heavens. His heart was with the people. Yet, with all of their yearnings combined, they could not muffle for Jesus the silent cry of the slave hiding behind the pillar.

Caiaphas turned to leave but had only taken a few steps when Jesus pointed in the direction of the priests and began to speak. "These have seated themselves in the chair of Moses. Therefore, do all they tell you, but do not do according to their deeds, for they say things and do not do them. They tie up heavy loads and lay them on men's shoulders, but they themselves are unwilling to move them with so much as a finger. The deeds they do are for themselves and to be noticed by men. They love the place of honor at banquets and the chief seats at synagogues and the respectful greetings in the marketplaces and being called rabbi. The greatest among you shall be the servant."

Caiaphas turned and again faced Jesus, as did the other priests. Malchus, who had come out momentarily for a better look, cautiously eased Zara and himself back behind a large pillar, though, at the moment, there didn't seem much chance of Caiaphas seeing anything but Jesus' unprecedented assault.

Jesus leveled his gaze directly at Caiaphas and continued. "Whoever exalts himself shall be humbled, and whoever humbles himself shall be exalted."

Malchus wanted to take this excellent opportunity to sneak out of the temple with Zara, but he just could not. If no one else understood what Jesus was saying, Malchus did.

Caiaphas smiled thinly and, with a peaceful hand gesture, offered to speak. But before his words could be heard, Jesus raised his voice and continued with even more intensity.

"Woe to you, hypocrites, because you shut off the kingdom of heaven from men, for you do not enter in yourselves, nor do you allow those who are entering to go in.

"Woe to you, hypocrites, because you devour widows' houses, even while, for a pretense, you make long prayers. Therefore, you shall receive greater condemnation.

"Woe to you, hypocrites, because you travel on sea and land to gain followers, and when you gain even one, you make him twice as much a son of hell as yourselves.

"Woe to you, blind guides, who say, 'Whoever swears by the temple, that is nothing, but whoever swears by the gold of the temple, he is obligated.' You fools and blind men! Which is more important, the gold or the temple that sanctified the gold?"

Malchus winced for Caiaphas. Insulting him was enough, but now he was hitting him where it hurt most. But how did this man know these things? He had never been at any Sanhedrin meetings. He had never worked at the temple, at least not as long as Caiaphas had been there. He had not seen the records. With the exception of Caiaphas, Elias, Annas, and himself, no one really knew enough to say the things he was saying. And why wasn't he afraid of anyone, even those two towering bodyguards with Evaratus, who still stood next to the priests?

"Woe to you, hypocrites! For you clean the outside of the cup, but inside you are full of robbery and self-indulgence.

"Woe to you, hypocrites! For you are like whitewashed tombs, which on the outside appear beautiful, but inside are full of dead men's bones and filth. Even so, you, too, appear righteous to men, but inwardly you are full of lawlessness.

"You serpents, you brood of vipers, how shall you escape the sentence of hell?"

Malchus was nearly as immobilized as Caiaphas appeared to be, but looking past the high priest, he could see Jonathan marching toward them with a dozen guards.

"Now, Zara. We have to go. Now!" Malchus said, pulling Zara by the arm.

She resisted, transfixed by Jesus, who continued to scold the high priest.

In desperation, Malchus grabbed her chin in his hand and, stepping aside, held her face so she could clearly see Caiaphas. "Look at his face, Zara. Remember how mad he was last night? That was nothing compared to how he will be after this. I can't let him see you here. Jonathan already has your name on a list that places you in the temple today, listening to Jesus. If Caiaphas gives the order, you'll be whipped."

Zara's gaze finally met Malchus's.

"Zara, if you anger Caiaphas, the consequences are severe. He can be ruthless." He stepped back in front of her, shielding her again from Caiaphas's view.

Zara looked back toward Jesus. Whatever the attraction was, it was as strong as Malchus had ever seen. Finally, she looked back at Malchus, and, as if in pain, she said, "Let's go."

"Good. Don't turn your head around until we're outside the gate," Malchus said. "We'll talk when we're outside and away from the temple." He grabbed her hand and pulled her through the crowd and away from Jesus. Zara had responded quickly when Malchus mentioned the whip. He remembered her story of being privately whipped at the orders of her previous master—an experience she obviously did not want to repeat.

TEN

Malchus was scared. If only he had not taken Zara to the temple. If only she had not been so determined to go. And he definitely should not have let her get involved with that blind man. But again, she had made up her mind. *And what about that blind man?* Malchus wondered. *Was he really healed? Can that happen?* Malchus shook his head in disbelief as he and Zara hurried to distance themselves from the temple. He had to remember he was in Jerusalem, where nothing is as it appears.

But Jonathan's list was real enough. If not for that wretched list with Zara's name on it, he would have remembered this day fondly as the day Caiaphas and the temple business were exposed. He needed to organize his thoughts. What was Caiaphas going to do about the Nazarene? The high priest was not the type to take such abuse without a response. A strong response. And what was Caiaphas going to do with Jonathan's list? Zara was not supposed to have been in the temple in the first place.

Malchus tried to calm himself with some logic. With the consuming demands of the Passover obligations, coupled with the task of getting rid of the Nazarene, how could Caiaphas spend time reading through what had to be a huge list of names?

Or was the list only part of another calculated business move to find the important people he would have to win back? And when would he have time for that? Maybe if the Nazarene left soon, he would throw the list out without even a glance. Not likely.

They were now several blocks away from the temple. Malchus looked over his shoulder to see if they were being followed, but observed only usual activities. A marketplace disguised as a holy city, or was it the other way around? Merchants and craftsmen were at the roadsides with their merchandise displayed across tables or dangling from overhead beams. Layers of pilgrims were busy haggling with sellers while an endless stream of traffic flowed down the center of the street. And the ever-present aroma of carob tea was occasionally interrupted by a crosscurrent of lamb smoke or fresh bread.

"Malchus, you should have seen it," Zara said, snatching Malchus from his thoughts.

"Seen what?"

"The miracle!" she said.

"Whatever you do, don't use that word back home . . . especially tonight."

"But it was a miracle."

"Uh-huh."

"You don't sound very impressed," she said, looking at him with concern.

"I'm too worried to be impressed."

"Don't be worried. Caiaphas has more important things on his mind. He has his hands full with Jesus. And Jesus is a problem that won't go away."

"Why do you say that?" he asked.

"Because what happens will be determined by Jesus, not Caiaphas. Caiaphas is going to have to get use to that."

Malchus laughed. "I'm sorry, Zara, but it's hard for me to imagine Caiaphas getting use to anything if he doesn't want to. He has a way of making problems disappear.

Zara smiled. "Did Caiaphas ever heal a blind man?"

"I love your smile, Zara, but it will lead to trouble in Caiaphas's house. Like I said, Caiaphas has a way of making his problems disappear."

"Malchus, Malchus," Zara said, looking into his eyes. "How can I not smile? If you'd seen the expression on the blind man's face when light first entered his eyes. The eyes that just a moment before were pale and crusted over were suddenly as clear as yours or mine. As soon as I saw him start to blink, I burst into tears," Zara said, her own eyes welling up again as she spoke.

How could he tell her that she must be somehow mistaken? He was having a hard time telling himself. He remembered seeing the confidence Jesus had as he spoke. *Such dominance,* he thought. But to align with Jesus would be more dangerous right now than she could imagine. What would Caiaphas do if he thought Zara felt anything toward the Nazarene? Just imagining the possibilities made it difficult to think clearly.

Malchus needed to calm himself. Maybe some carob tea would help. He was confused, but one thing did seem to make sense to him—being with Zara. If only he could run away with her, far enough to be safely out of reach.

They stopped at a small wooden sidewalk table where tea was being steeped, and he ordered two cups.

"Do you know what *Jerusalem* means, Zara?" Malchus asked, hoping that a change of subject would help calm him.

"No, what does it mean?"

"City of Peace."

"That's beautiful."

"Yes, but it's anything but a city of peace! I don't know how it got the name. It's said that there's been more blood shed here than anywhere else in the world. It probably should have been named *City of Blood.* Throughout history it's been a very dangerous place to be."

"Especially if you're a sheep."

Malchus laughed. *"Especially* if you're a sheep."

"Why do they do that, Malchus? Why do they kill so many sheep?"

"They don't kill them. They sacrifice them. It's different. It's an old tradition, or maybe I should say belief," Malchus explained. "The sheep suffers the penalty of sin on behalf of the sinner, which, of course, is death. As the lifeblood flows from the sheep, the sin is paid for."

"That seems unfair to the sheep, don't you think?" Zara said with a pout. "They don't do anything wrong."

Malchus smiled at her. "I think that's what makes them eligible." Malchus found it hard to believe. Just a short time of normal conversation with Zara had brought peace to his weary mind. If anything was a miracle, it was she. He looked at her warmly, put his hand on hers, and moved closer. "Please understand me, Zara. I know Jesus is very special, but right now he's also very dangerous."

"Zara looked at Malchus's hand, then smiled, putting her other hand on his, and said, "Is love dangerous, Malchus?"

"Love?" Malchus repeated. He hoped he was not blushing, but when Zara took his hand and spoke of love, a surprising warmth rushed through him.

"Jesus said the greatest commandment was love and that all of the other commandments are fulfilled by loving God and one another."

Malchus wanted to roll his eyes, but he resisted, staring into hers. "He didn't seem very loving toward Caiaphas."

Zara furrowed her brow.

"But I have to admit, he spoke accurately about the priesthood. Curiously accurate," he said, as if thinking aloud.

"Do you have any money, Malchus?" Zara asked as an old man poured the tea with his back to them.

"Yes. A little. Occasionally merchants tip me during the feast for helping them do this and that. But next week I will make much more. Judah and I skin sheep during Passover and sell the fleeces to the Romans. It's the one time of the year that I actually feel like a free man."

"Be careful, it's very hot," said the old man, carefully placing two cups of tea on the wooden table.

"Thank you," Malchus said, breathing in the steamy rich carob aroma.

The man smiled and nodded. "You don't want your tongue to look like that eye. That must have hurt," the old man said, staring awkwardly at Malchus's eye.

"You know," Zara chimed in. "It is getting quite colorful."

"Wonderful," Malchus said sarcastically.

Suddenly the man's pleasant expression changed as he looked past them, up the street. They turned around to see what had affected him so.

Four Roman soldiers were marching down the street, double file. They looked intimidating, but that was deliberate, and typical. Small contingents of them would occasionally strut about in military formation, particularly during feast times, to remind the rebellious and the pilgrims that Rome was in complete control.

"Heathen dogs!" the old man hissed so only Malchus and Zara could hear. "I only hope I live to see the day scorpions make their homes in the dusty bones of those murderous animals. May God curse them and their children to Sheol for eternity!" There was spit clinging to the old man's lip, and the veins in his neck were stretched to breaking.

As the soldiers approached, Malchus worried he would end up in the middle of something ugly, but the old man apparently knew better than to let his curses fall on their Roman ears. When they passed, Malchus and Zara both turned back to him.

"What have these soldiers done to you?" Zara asked tenderly, placing her hand on the old man's.

"They cut my heart out and made me bury it. They killed my son. My only son." He pulled out a cloth and wiped his eyes.

"Why?" Malchus asked.

"One evening, ten years ago, near the Pool of Siloam, my son happened upon two of those venomous creatures having their way with a young slave girl. About your age," he said, nodding to Zara. "They started smacking her and tearing her clothes off, laughing the whole while. My son ran over and yelled at them to stop, to leave her alone. They ignored him. Then he grabbed one of them by the wrist and pleaded with him to stop hitting her. The coward was much bigger than my son, and he threw him to the side. They laughed at him, finding it amusing at first that he would try to stop them. But this distraction gave the girl an opportunity to get away. For that, they beat him and arrested him. That night they whipped him mercilessly until he died. The next day, when their superiors heard what had happened, the two soldiers were warned to be more discreet when they entertained themselves. I hate them! Murderous vipers without souls. That's all they are."

Malchus knew of Roman cruelty, but thankfully not from his own experience. His relationship with them had been mostly positive, based largely on the business dealings he and Judah had with them. Being a slave of Caiaphas also helped. The Romans did not want to have to explain to their supervisors why the leader of the Jewish people was unhappy with the way his slave was being treated. Malchus knew his situation was unique. He also knew the old man's feelings toward the Romans were shared by most of the Jews. Some of Malchus's own acquaintances had been whipped by Roman soldiers. They ruled by intimidation. As in many parts of the Roman Empire, in Jerusalem the numbers and fervor of rebels were on the rise. For this reason, whenever the Romans had an opportunity to make an example of someone, they took it and were exceedingly cruel and heartless in order to instill fear as a means of control. Their approach worked. However, they also instilled hatred for Rome.

Malchus and Zara finished their tea and said good-bye to the old man, who once again smiled and seemed completely relaxed. Zara, on the other hand, neither smiled nor relaxed. The story seemed to have unsettled her. Malchus was not sure if it was the story itself or if a deeper memory had been disturbed.

Zara took Malchus's hand as they walked. He looked at her. She seemed afraid.

"Do you really think Caiaphas will have me whipped if he sees my name on that list?" Zara asked.

"I don't know. Much will depend on what else is happening. If he's enraged like he is now, I think he'll try. But I won't let him."

Zara frowned at him curiously. "What do you mean by that?"

"Don't worry, just don't give him any more reason to do it," Malchus said, trying to reassure her. He wondered how he could ever save her from the whip if the orders were given.

She looked at him blankly. "I'll die before going through that again."

He looked at the scar on her cheek. "Some scars go deeper than others," he said.

"This!" Zara scoffed, touching the scar on her cheek. This is nothing."

"Your back?" Malchus said.

Zara shifted her gaze from Malchus to the street before her, chin straight and expression steeled. "It's not pretty, if that's what you're asking," she said coolly.

"That's not what I was asking," Malchus said.

"I'm sorry. You didn't deserve that. All you've done is watch out for me."

Malchus turned to her and took both her hands in his. "I won't allow him to touch you."

Zara stopped in her tracks and stared at him. "You would protect me?" she said, the meaning of what he said not lost on her. "You can't do that. A few more months, and you'll be free."

"Free? Knowing you've been beaten to death? No thank you."

Zara's eyes welled up with tears. "You barely know me."

She was right. They had known each other only a short time. But he also knew something had kindled in his heart. "If the situation arises, I promise I'll be there for you, but you have to promise me something."

"What?" Zara said as she wiped her eyes with the back of the hand he was still holding.

"You have to stay away from Jesus," he whispered.

†

They were back in plenty of time for the meeting, but Levia had many questions, not the least of which was why she had returned without any flowers.

ELEVEN

Malchus was in the hallway on his way to the kitchen when the heavy, olive-wood entry doors swung open violently, hitting the wall, then slammed shut just as abruptly. As Caiaphas stormed forward, his robe pulled back, and Malchus heard a tear. Caiaphas looked down. The doors had caught his robe, ripping it unceremoniously.

Caiaphas screamed and yanked at the robe in frustration until it was torn free. The lower portion of the garment was in tatters, the damage reaching upward to the high priest's thigh. He showed no signs of caring.

Malchus did not have to wonder how the rest of Caiaphas's encounter with the Nazarene went. Again, Malchus wished he had witnessed it all. He could probably get the details dramatized from Judah later tonight at the fire. He could just imagine the high priest's march back from the temple. He would have had to keep up his appearance regardless of how he really felt. He wondered if the baker had had the poor timing to offer Caiaphas some fresh baked bread.

"Blind! How dare he accuse me of being a 'blind guide,'" Caiaphas yelled. "How dare he!" he said loudly, through clenched teeth.

Malchus was about to head back the way he came when Caiaphas saw him.

"Malchus. What are you doing here?" Caiaphas demanded.

"I, uh . . ."

"Whatever," he said, shushing him with a wave. "I'm glad you're here. It saves me the trouble of sending for you."

You're glad I'm here? Malchus thought.

Caiaphas furrowed his brow. "Your eye looks worse," he said, then changed the subject again before Malchus could respond. "People will be arriving very shortly for a meeting, and I want you to be here."

"Yes, sir," Malchus said. *Me?*

Caiaphas stormed past him and turned into the meeting room, waving for Malchus to follow. "There's an important job I want done tonight. You should be perfect for it," he said, pacing.

"Yes, sir," Malchus said. *What job?* He did not like the sound of this at all.

Caiaphas turned and faced Malchus. "I can't explain the details to you now, but it will be an honor for you to do it. So as for tonight, be here!" Caiaphas's robe spun as he turned to walk away, revealing the long tear suffered in the door.

"Your robe is torn, sir," Malchus said, somehow feeling obligated to report the obvious. He regretted he had spoken as soon as the words left his mouth.

"I know it's—" Caiaphas said, raising his voice, then stopped himself. "I know it's torn. Thank you." He turned and left.

"I'm in trouble," Malchus mouthed to himself. He was feeling anything but honored. *An honor,* Caiaphas had called it. That alone scared him. And Caiaphas had never told him to do anything at night before. I'm going to hate this, and Caiaphas knows it. Why else didn't he scream at me for not being at the temple? Why else would he try to be polite?"

A knock rattled the doors. Before Malchus could make a move, Levia entered from the kitchen to answer it. The meeting was not supposed to start for another half hour, but Malchus would be shocked if everyone was not here and seated at least fifteen minutes beforehand. One of Caiaphas's unspoken rules was punctuality, and everyone knew it. Caiaphas sanctimoniously declared his meetings to be God-ordained, and any latecomer, with the exception of Annas, would be accused of having his priorities out of order and of exalting himself above the Almighty. They all hated this about Caiaphas, but nevertheless, they made a point of arriving on time to avoid such confrontations. No one ever arrived late twice.

To be sure, this afternoon's meeting was to be very exclusive. He would not be able to meet with the entire Sanhedrin in a meeting room this size. There were forty-five members of the Sanhedrin, and they fell into three groups: "chief priests," who, in the person of the high priest, held the presidency and defacto leadership; "scribes," who were mostly rabbis, were immersed deeply in the study of theologies; and "elders," men of ancient ruling families, were mostly from the tribe of Judah. The chief priests were divided into two sects: "Sadducees," who were the majority, and "Pharisees," upper-class Jews who lived in closed communities, separated from the rest of Israel, and were dedicated to holy living and purity. Caiaphas had to have calculated exactly who he wanted and who he didn't.

TWELVE

Malchus had never been to a meeting like this. He was not sure if there had ever been one. He felt awkward and out of place, a lowly slave among the elite of the Jewish world. He would not dare come near the large olive wood table where everyone else was finding their seats. Instead, he found a corner by the doorway and attempted to blend into the wall. He wished he were invisible. Occasionally a curious glance fell on him, but no one would openly question Caiaphas's decision to have him here. The criticism would no doubt come later, when the meeting was over and the members could talk among themselves. For now, the slave was here. Those who knew Caiaphas knew the slave was here for a reason. No one yet knew why, but, even so, no one wanted to be in Malchus's sandals.

Though a wide beam of sunlight came through the balcony opening and generously splashed the meeting room, both the oil lamps on the huge table and the ones set into wall niches were lit and turned high.

Malchus's attention shifted to the large man entering the room. It was Bebai, chief priest and temple jailer. To Malchus's delight, his slave, Judah, directly followed him. Bebai saw Malchus and motioned for Judah to join him in the corner. Judah looked as relieved to see Malchus as Malchus was to see him.

"Why are *you* here?" Malchus whispered discreetly.

"I was hoping you knew. Bebai just told me to follow him. Your eye looks worse."

"Do you think so?" Malchus deadpanned.

"What's this about?" Judah nodded his head almost imperceptibly toward the assembly of priests.

"Jesus. What else could it possibly be about?" Malchus said, keeping an eye on the table. "And I don't like the fact that I was ordered to be here."

Judah nodded very slowly.

"You were there for all of it?" Malchus asked, his curiosity hardly concealed by his whisper.

Again, Judah nodded slowly.

"Later," Malchus whispered nervously as several officials turned from the table and stared. Everyone was finding his seat at the exceptionally long table, which was wide enough to seat everyone in the room, with space for a few more. Before each man sat a beautifully engraved silver wine goblet. Zara came in with a decanter and kept the glasses full, topping them off after every sip. Malchus watched as several of the priests took more than a little notice of her. A few of them could not take their eyes off her as she moved around the table. When the decanter was empty, she left. She gave Malchus a warm smile as she exited. Malchus returned a smile that remained even after she was gone.

"I'm jealous," Judah said. "And stop smiling already. You're making me sick."

Malchus looked back at the table. Caiaphas and Jonathan were missing. He assumed the two would walk in together. Caiaphas would always walk into a meeting at the exact moment it was scheduled, and heaven help anyone not prepared to proceed. He never needed to warm up.

Caiaphas would sit at the head of the table closest to the balcony and face the door so he could see anyone coming in or leaving. The seat itself, however, would be empty for most of the meeting. Caiaphas would move about the room when he spoke, as well as when he listened. Malchus figured he did it out of both force of habit and animal instinct—his way of stalking his prey and sizing up friends and enemies alike. The pacing intimidated the others, and Caiaphas knew it.

Malchus recognized all who were there as those who had been at the temple when the Nazarene was there. To the left of Caiaphas's place was Elias, the ubiquitous bookkeeper and chief inspector. His job had not existed until Caiaphas created it. Elias had been with Caiaphas before he was high priest and had been unquestionably loyal. He was the liaison between Caiaphas and the treasurers and collectors. Caiaphas trusted him completely. This way, no matter what Caiaphas was doing, he had one eye on the money. However sharp he was with the money, Elias's age was catching up with him. He would not be able to offer much in wisdom or insight regarding Jesus, even if he were asked. His hearing was going, his eyes were going, but, loyal to a fault, he would agree with anything Caiaphas said.

In the two seats next to Elias were Jesse and Shet, two of the three temple treasurers. By law, there could be no less than three treasurers to collect temple monies. Caiaphas went with the minimum to better keep track of what they collected. Caiaphas did not pick them. They had already been the treasurers when he became high priest, and they were experts in their specialty. They were collectors of the pledges. They collected objects dedicated to the temple, demised property, offerings, the first tithe, and the second tithe. In short, everything of value that came into the temple, and did not have to do with exchanges or purchases, went through their hands.

Next to Shet sat Johanan, the chief gatekeeper. Johanan loved his work more than anyone Malchus had ever seen at the temple. His job was simple and routine, at least in description. He opened and closed the temple gates and doors, allowed the priests and people in, then let them out. But Johanan transformed this simple task into a daily event, one he infused with passion and artistry. With twenty-five common priests at his command, Johanan was like a director with a huge cast of performers at his disposal. At the same time every morning he would first open the priests' door on the east side of the temple, allowing the clerics to enter and ready themselves in whatever ways were necessary. Then, he would open the Beautiful Gate with the help of twenty other priests, directing their every move. When all the priests were at their stations, they would simultaneously open the double doors of each of the eight smaller gates. Johanan's vote was always respected, and he had more influence than most of the priests.

Sitting to the right of Jonathan's empty seat at the end of the table was Mattiah, the chief priest in charge of the casting of lots. Many priests did not have one specific job or title. For them the casting of lots provided a frequent method of delegating responsibility and resolving conflict. Mattiah was also responsible for the direction and supervision of the ceremonial sacrifices that were offered every morning and evening.

Judah had mentioned the fact that Mattiah and a few other priests had chased after Jesus after he ransacked the temple businesses and had heard him say that he would never forget the tongue-lashing he had received from the Nazarene.

Directly across from Mattiah was Bebai. Bebai would probably be the least informed of anyone about Jesus. As temple jailer, he kept mostly to himself and had few friends. He did not mind the solitude. A big burly man with a hard appearance that suited his position, he had a heart for Judah and treated him like a son. In his time, his punishments were unforgettable, but Bebai did not swing the whip anymore. That was now Judah's job. Some thought his swing was excessively hard, but whenever any priests had a complaint about how Judah was doing his job, Bebai would typically threaten to administer punishment himself. That usually ended all complaints. Besides Bebai's being at the temple during the assault, Caiaphas may also have wanted Bebai here because no one would feel comfortable arguing with him for fear of his having a long memory.

Moving up the table, next came Petahiah, who was in charge of the bird offerings. A perfectionist, he took great pride in the way the dove tables were set up and in the way the birds were presented before sacrifice. He was there when Jesus smashed the tables, cracked open the cages, and sent the birds flying. Petahiah would take the offense very personally.

Ahijah, the temple physician, sat in the next seat. He was responsible for the care and treatment of the priests, most of whom had one ailment in common—bowel sickness. The condition seemed epidemic during the feasts, when so many offerings were made. Because of the priests' unusually meat-rich diet, bowel sickness was so common, full-time care was necessary. To make matters worse, wine, which seemed to help their digestion, was forbidden during feasts. Ahijah would treat the priests with remedies passed from one temple physician to another, all of which stank and tended to make them even sicker. Real relief for these patients came at the end of the feasts with a change of diet. Ahijah had been at Caiaphas's side when the Nazarene tore into them.

Eleazar and Pinhas occupied the two remaining seats. During most of the year Eleazar was superintendent of curtains, and Pinhas, of priestly vestments. At Passover, however, they ran the money-changing tables. The curtains and vestments had, by then, been made ready for the feasts, and they needed little or no attention. This freed them up to change foreign currency into Jerusalem currency. More money was made for the temple exchanging currencies than anywhere else in the market. Caiaphas handpicked them for the job for the same reason he made Elias bookkeeper. Loyalty.

"Do you think, what's her name—Zara—could save the leftover wine for us to drink after the meeting?" Judah asked.

Malchus turned back to Judah. "You're disgusting." Looking past Judah through the doorway, he could see Caiaphas marching down the hallway. He was alone.

THIRTEEN

Jonathan rushed around the temple, giving last-minute orders to his subordinates. He, better than anyone, knew not to arrive late for one of Caiaphas's meetings. Especially this one. "I don't care what happens, you keep those doors guarded!" He shouted, trying to do all that Caiaphas had assigned him. Taking care of these matters while trying to get to the meeting on time gave Jonathan indigestion. He was frantic. He looked around to see that his men were in position. Not paying attention to where he was walking, he bumped into someone. He turned to excuse himself, knowing he had not been watching where he had been going.

"I'm sorry, I—"

"You did nothing. I stepped in front of you," said a young man with curly black hair. He made eye contact with Jonathan only briefly, then quickly scanned around to see who might be looking at them. "I have something you want badly," the man said, still looking around nervously, sweat dripping off his forehead and onto his short, thick black beard. "Can we go some place a little more private?"

"Look, I don't have time to take a stroll. Tell me here and now what this is all about. I have a very important meeting to get to," Jonathan started to walk back in the direction of the main doors. The man moved in front of him again, blocking his path.

"Do you want Jesus alone?" the man asked quietly, his eyes darting about. "I can give him to you."

For the first time Jonathan focused on the man. "Who are you?"

"Who I am is not important, but who I can deliver to you is . . . and you know it."

Jonathan still wanted to be on time for the meeting, but Caiaphas would never forgive him if he let this opportunity slip away. "Come with me to Caiaphas's palace."

"No, I can't go far or I might be missed," said the man, standing in such a way as to use Jonathan as a cover in case anyone was looking.

This was a big decision for Jonathan, and he had bad memories of big decisions. Too many times in the past when he had decided to take charge, he found himself desperately trying to justify what he had done and explain how things ended up the way they did. "Your problem is threefold," his father would say. "You're gullible, shortsighted, and ill-informed."

Jonathan drummed his sides nervously with his fingers. "Very well then, come with me to the council chamber. We can be alone there. But you'd better not be wasting my time." He desperately hoped he had made the right decision.

The man agreed, and Jonathan motioned for a couple of guards to follow them. Once inside, they shut the door tight. Jonathan offered the man a seat at the council table, but he refused.

Apparently too nervous to sit, the man paced back and forth, repeatedly wiping sweat off his brow with the back of his hand.

"Now tell me who you are?" Jonathan demanded.

"I am someone who knows a good opportunity when he sees it. I can see the frustration on your faces. And I know where it comes from. You have a big problem. You'd like to get rid of Jesus, but you can't get near him without risking a riot—something you can't afford at Passover."

"All you're doing is stating the obvious. Tell me something that I don't already know!"

"I can tell you where Jesus is going to be tonight with only a dozen unarmed men accompanying him."

Jonathan narrowed his eyes. "And how would you know that?"

"Jesus has a core group of twelve disciples. I am one of them." The man retraced his steps toward the one window opening, which was the only source of light in the dreary room. He stopped a few feet from it and turned back toward Jonathan. "The type of disorder he has caused you is nothing compared to what he has planned for the coming days."

Jonathan was confused and frowned. "What does he expect to gain from this?"

The man looked at Jonathan for a moment, then laughed in his face. "Gain? Jesus doesn't care about gain. Who knows why he does what he does. He makes less and less sense to me every day. He's not bothered in the least by the oppressive Roman rule over Judea, but he whips you all out of the temple for trying to make a little profit. One day he's flowing with miracles at every turn, and then, just when you think he can rule the world, he claims he can't do anything because of someone's lack of faith. He's constantly speaking of peace, then he tells some of us to get swords. One day he flees to avoid arrest and now this."

Jonathan's eyes widened at the mention of sword procuration.

"He's continually making the most unbelievable claims about himself and then tells us to be quiet about most of the miracles."

"You are not talking to a peasant, fool. Do you think that I don't know the healings are staged," Jonathan said.

The man paused, staring straight into Jonathan's eyes, then spoke with a quiet confidence. "They're real. I know. I've seen him walk on water as if it were solid ground, and command a raging storm to fall instantly still, just as you would your temple guard."

The man held Jonathan's gaze for a long moment, but then Jonathan broke it off with a shiver. "If you are one of them, why are you telling me all this?"

"He's headed for trouble and we with him if he's not made to listen to reason. For the right price, I can tell you where he is going to be this very evening, and you can avoid enormous problems if you act. We both know the value of this information," the man said.

Jonathan nodded knowingly. "I knew the issue of money would appear sooner or later."

"You're no one to judge me. I'm in charge of all the money that is given to us, and I could have left with quite a sum whenever I wanted."

"But then you wouldn't be able to help yourself upon occasion, would you?" Jonathan said with a smile. "And this way you won't be a thief on the run."

The man looked away. "The truth is I've also grown tired of roaming the countryside, rarely knowing where I'm going to be the next day or where I'm going to sleep. That's no life for me," he said, the conviction in his voice disappearing. "I need a change. And the way he has been acting lately has been less predictable than ever. I'm not sure he's seeing things the way they are anymore, and I don't want to be left with nothing. Not after all I've been through."

"Enough about you. How much did you have in mind?"

The man straightened and spoke bluntly. "Thirty pieces of silver and nothing less."

"Thirty pieces of silver?" Jonathan laughed. "Are you insane?"

"Maybe, but that's the price."

"I could have you arrested right now," Jonathan warned.

"What good would that do you? I wouldn't cooperate with you. And while Jesus is destroying your feast, the people would be demanding my release."

"If you are one of the twelve, I'm sure I'll be speaking to more of you with similar offers for their so-called leader," Jonathan said.

The man laughed. "What, do you think you can get a better price? Forget it! I am a Judean like you. All the rest of them are Galileans. He is their life. You would be wasting your time—something you have very little of."

Jonathan raised a brow at the fact that the man was Judean. Certainly more educated than the troublesome Galileans. But how could he be certain anything the man was telling him was true. He massaged his chin. "What do you think Jesus would say if we told him you were here telling us this?" Jonathan asked, taking another tack in the negotiations.

"He wouldn't believe you. He trusts me so much, I am the only one he allows to handle the money—and a good thing too. If it was up to him, I would starve. He gives away everything that's given to us."

"Very well then. You will have your thirty pieces of silver. But you will have to do more than just tell us where he is going to be. You are going to have to take us to him. Or aren't you man enough for that?"

The man stared blankly for a moment. He obviously had not considered open betrayal. His face turned slightly pale.

"Yes or no?" Jonathan yelled. "As it is I'm late because of you."

"Agreed, agreed," the man said with a hint of anger. We will be having our Passover meal soon. Afterward he will be bringing us to a private location where you can have him. I will meet you at the Beautiful Gate at nine. There you will give me the thirty pieces of silver, and I will bring you to him." He walked to the door, opened it, and left, never once looking back.

After the door to the chamber closed, Jonathan shouted, "Yes!" and shook his fist triumphantly in the air. He had made the right decision and could arrive at the meeting late, without fear. In fact, he would be the very guest of honor.

FOURTEEN

The high priest was in full stride as he entered the room. All discussions stopped abruptly. Without as much as a "Shalom," and before those who were seated could even rise to greet him, he let everyone know this was no ordinary business meeting.

"No more wine," he demanded loudly. "We have work to do and a long night ahead, and I want everyone's attention."

One by one the priests pushed their goblets toward the center of the table, some more hesitant than others.

"We have a crisis at hand that must be dealt with swiftly. This Jesus from Nazareth is no longer a curiosity. He—this vagrant—has prophesied his own kingship openly and is being heralded as King of the Jews by the misfits, peasants, and women who have followed him from who knows where. From our observations, he has put together a core band of conspirators from Galilee, a town notorious for rebel activity. This so-called king then proceeds to lead his followers by creating disorder in the temple, trying to destroy our traditions and even the law itself. Unless he is stopped, and stopped quickly, he will succeed." Caiaphas banged his fist down on the table.

Most of the priests nodded in agreement, occasionally glancing to one another to confirm their mutual support.

"You have all witnessed the divisive accusations against the temple and the priesthood. You stood and watched, as did all the people, and saw that there was no reasoning with the man as he attacked us publicly. I have labored and toiled and analyzed this—this most dangerous situation—first as a man. But it was not until I, as high priest, prayed and sought the Lord that I received an answer. As a holy man, I always desire peace first. But there is a counsel from one holier than us all that must be observed and reckoned with. The only answer given to me, I believe, was from the Almighty." Caiaphas let his words sink in, waited a long moment, then pulled back his seat and sat down.

"The drastic measures of this false messiah, gathering the pilgrims to himself with his blasphemous silver tongue and so-called miraculous healings, which, as anyone can see, are no more than prearranged theatrics, must be met with measures equally as drastic. After much prayer, I can see that further reasoning would only be giving the enemy of the Lord an opportunity to do more irreparable damage.

Caiaphas surveyed everyone at the table, making eye contact with each one of them. Malchus and Judah, who were still wedged in the corner of the room, maintained their low profile.

"The Lord has revealed it would be expedient that one man die, so the whole nation does not perish. So sayeth the Lord," Caiaphas said without even a blink.

There was a stunned silence. There was no misunderstanding what the high priest had just said, and even if there was the slightest doubt, no one asked him to please repeat himself. The Nazarene was somehow to die, and the only thing that would shock Malchus more would be if Caiaphas did not already know how.

Caiaphas operated with a boldness Malchus had never witnessed before. He was not talking about just any false messiah who found his way into Jerusalem. He was talking about a man who seemed to have the whole world on his side. *Has he lost his mind?* Malchus wondered.

The ones who were against Jesus were, no doubt, being stirred in their hearts by what they saw as true courage coming from their leader, the high priest. Some of the priests began to fidget nervously with their hands, but none seemed willing to look to one another anymore. All knew the high priest would be highly observant of any questioning eyes that could cast a descenting vote.

Malchus still had no idea why he was there, and the thought frightened him. This was a meeting he should have been shut out from, not brought into.

Caiaphas spread his hands out on the table. "In years gone by, when our fathers led our nation without the intrusive Roman ways, there would be no question as to what must be done. But I tell you the truth, though our times have changed, the Almighty has not. We will be held accountable for our response regardless of Rome's influence. And, in fact, the Lord has shown me how even Rome will bow to the will of our Lord. Before we get into how this might be accomplished so as to satisfy the legal and procedural covenants of the law," Caiaphas continued, "I want to know your suggestions."

He couldn't care less, Malchus thought. But Caiaphas did need for everything to at least appear legal. As high priest, he was head of the Sanhedrin, but he still could not take the law into his own hands. He needed the majority to agree on this course of action. To minimize the risk of the entire Sanhedrin thwarting his plan, he would first work on these members. Using this meeting to stir them, he would have the necessary key support and momentum to swing an official meeting his way. He could then turn the meeting into the trial itself. The time to work on the select jurors he had personally sequestered had arrived.

Surprisingly, Elias was the first to speak. "How is it again that our nation would be destroyed, Joseph?"

Malchus and Judah looked at each other by moving only their eyes, then looked back at the table. Caiaphas could not disguise that he did not believe his ears. He could not publicly tell the old man to be silent and let someone else speak after opening the meeting to all. Elias was supposed to be here only to nod his head, agreeing with everything he said. Not to think. And certainly not to question the very justification at the heart of Caiaphas's plan. For the sake of appearance, Caiaphas refrained from orally bashing Elias. Besides, the question was arguably valid, and someone else might ask it eventually.

"He is an infection, Elias. A deadly infection that is spreading by the minute."

"Blasphemer is what he is!" shouted Ahijah, the temple physician, leaning forward in his chair. "I've heard his blasphemy, telling people that their sins were forgiven. Only the Almighty can forgive sins. The next thing you know he'll be telling them that they don't have to come to Jerusalem."

Caiaphas nodded.

"I, too, have heard the man speak, and have watched him perform what I consider to be miraculous acts of mercy," said Johanan, the doorkeeper. "The words I have heard him—"

"Miraculous acts of mercy? To whom?" interrupted Jesse, the treasurer. "Have you seen the company he keeps? Prostitutes, adulterers, tax collectors . . . sinners. And he treats women as if they're men, and I wouldn't be surprised if he disciples them as well."

The other treasurer, Shet, nodded vigorously and chimed in. "If it were up to him, he'd march the women and *the Gentiles* right into the Priest's Court, defiling the temple. He seems to take pleasure in that sort of thing."

"The Holy of Holies," Jesse added, stirring up a moment of murmuring around the table.

Johanan shook his head and tried to finish what he had been saying. "The words I have heard him speak were precious, even inspiring. Could we be so arrogant to believe that if the Messiah were to come, he would have no correction for us? If, as scripture declares, he is to be our light, are we to believe that we have no darkness for him to enlighten? We should consider the rebukes that the Nazarene brings us may well be from God, and if they are from God, we need to heed them in holy fear of the Lord."

Malchus's respect for the gatekeeper had just elevated.

"But what of his violence in the temple?" asked Shet.

"Remarkably, maybe even supernaturally by the hand of God Himself, nobody was hurt," Johanan answered. "What he did, he did to make a point. And make it he did. I personally don't feel threatened in the least."

"That's because you're not a dove, Johanan," shot Petahiah from directly across the table. "The man is insane. Anyone can see that. He is wrapped looser than Herod's loincloth. One minute he is laughing and playing with children, the next he is trying to kill us. Then he tells the people to love their enemies and bless those who curse them. And if all that is not insane enough, he tells us if we destroy the temple he will raise it up in three days. He's mad and ought to be locked up and punished, and if that means death, I'm with Caiaphas. At least we'll be rid of him before anyone else gets hurt," he said, rising up out of his seat. "He's no light for me, and he's not my messiah!"

"Locked up where?" Elias said. The Roman's have taken over the temple fortress as their own."

"That is not a problem," Caiaphas said.

Malchus's eyes widened. He knew what Caiaphas was thinking even if no one else did. There was a sort of dungeon in the cellar with shackles on the wall that had been there before Caiaphas's tenure began. But as far as Malchus knew, it had not been used as long as he had been there. Tonight, however, Caiaphas was full of surprises, and Malchus was wondering, not about what he knew, but what he did not know about Caiaphas. The thought of the man he had witnessed in the temple today being chained in the dungeon below him, in this very building, made him cringe.

Bebai, Judah's master, sitting to Petahiah's right, reached his big left hand up to Petahiah's shoulder. "Settle down, Petahiah," he said, pulling him back into his chair. Petahiah jerked his shoulder away, then fussed with his robe, straightening it back into place. He looked briefly at Bebai, then sat back down indignantly.

"Let's not lose control of ourselves," said Mattiah, the one in charge of casting lots. "I agree the man has done us some serious harm and is well capable of doing much more. I am also not fond of being publicly humiliated or referred to as a 'whitewashed tomb full of dead men's bones.' But even if we all agreed that he should die—" he paused, looking at Johanan, "—and we don't. There is nothing to charge him with that even approaches a capital offense. Even if such accusations were to be made, I cannot see how we could catch him, try him, and sentence him, all before Passover. The sun will be setting before this meeting ends. Passover is upon us, and so, too, is the Sabbath. Why, we don't even know where he is. Our hands are tied, and he's out there, free to plan more rebellion and dissent."

"But the Romans' hands are not so tied," said Caiaphas.

Silence.

Malchus grimaced, as did some of the priests, at the mention of Rome. He remembered back to when he had first become a slave. There was a certain mentally ill peasant who would cry out, "Woe to Jerusalem!" during Passover and other popular feasts, disturbing and annoying the crowds. Malchus and most of the other slaves were amused, but not Caiaphas. The Sanhedrin had the temple guard punish the peasant, but he persisted. Finally, in an unprecedented move, they turned him over to the Romans, who promptly whipped the man to the bone. The peasant was never heard from again.

But the Nazarene in Roman hands? The thought made Malchus shudder. He felt all the more fearful of why he was present at this meeting.

"Yes, of course, the Romans!" Petahiah said as his words were echoed about with nodding approval. "Any reason is good enough for them. All they need to know is that he calls himself 'King of the Jews.' They'll take that personally. That's treason in their book."

"The Romans?" Johanan yelled in disbelief. "The Romans?" He repeated. "We, the Sanhedrin, legislators of the Law of Moses for the entire Jewish world would yoke ourselves to—no, employ—the Romans to have a holy man killed?"

"Holy man?" Ahijah blurted excitedly. "Have you paid attention to how he heals? No man from God would touch the sick and not go through a day of purification. He shows absolutely no regard for the laws of defilement, touching one after another after another—and in the temple, as if to do it in the Almighty's face. I tell you, only the devil would behave in such a way. I'm convinced. The healings are of the devil." He sat back in his seat, folded his arms defiantly, and began nodding his head in confirmation of what he had just spoken, muttering, "holy man," while laughing to himself.

Caiaphas cleared his throat, gaining the table's attention. "Every year since I have been high priest, the pilgrims have increased, and, along with their numbers the revenues have also risen. In just moments, this man has singlehandedly set us back years. I fear that should he be allowed to remain through Passover, he will crush our spirits and perhaps even physically destroy all that the years of labor have built in the way of trade, goodwill, and religious commitments, the very things upon which we all depend to sustain us. In addition, he has accused us directly, and publicly, vilifying us as corrupt hypocrites. He is bent on destroying us if we do not destroy him first. We are the people of Israel. We are its leaders. If he destroys us, he destroys Israel. We cannot coexist with this Nazarene in harmony. He's a usurper!"

Johanan stood up in his place. "So *that's* it! This meeting has nothing to do with whether he is right or wrong; it has to do with our survival. Our financial survival. The Lord will not be pleased, and I will have no part of it!" Johanan pushed his seat away and stormed away from the table.

"The Lord will not be pleased?" Shet chided, his hands spread out extended to the others. "The Lord will not be pleased?" he repeated. "Can't you see, Johanan? The work we do is the Lord's. The man has set out to abolish the law itself. He is the one doing the work of the devil, and that, I agree, is how he is able to perform these so-called marvelous deeds—these miracles. He is doing them in the name of Beelzebub. He is no more than a sorcerer; only he also wants to destroy us."

Johanan stopped at the archway and turned around. "I stand by what I've said." He looked at Malchus and Judah in the corner. "And what are they doing here? What dirty work will they be doing that we cannot do ourselves?"

"That's enough," Caiaphas warned. "I have let you continue because I wanted to give everyone his say, but I will not tolerate any more accusations, nor will I tolerate dissension in our ranks. That's just what the Nazarene would want."

Johanan bowed his head out of habit and left.

Bebai then got up without a word and also left the table. On the way to the exit, he turned and said, "The Nazarene has not escaped the eye of Rome. If they had considered the man a threat, he would already be dead." Bebai then bowed slightly, turned to Judah, motioned him to follow, and continued out.

Judah looked at Malchus but could not say anything with all the attention in his direction. He turned and followed his master.

Malchus's heart sank. He wanted to leave so badly, he almost followed them out the door. Judah had been propping him up emotionally. Now he was alone and more frightened than before.

With the vocal opposition gone, Caiaphas seized the moment. "Obviously there are some strong feelings here," Caiaphas said, apparently trying to regroup, "but let us be deterred no longer from the emergency at hand. We have two problems: first, to find out where the Nazarene is going to be this evening, so that he can be arrested away from the crowds. I've given Jonathan instructions to have two of the guard follow him out of the—"

"It's done. Your first problem has been taken care of," interrupted a voice from the entranceway. All heads turned. There stood Jonathan, a crooked smile on his face.

FIFTEEN

Cheers came from around the table as Jonathan told how he had discovered where the Nazarene was going to be that evening, and the priests were allowed to finish whatever was left of their wine.

"So basically it comes down to this," Jonathan said proudly, obviously enjoying the accolades and attention he received. "Sometime after sundown the Nazarene will take his Passover meal in a secret place. Afterward, his traitor will meet us at the Beautiful Gate and lead us to the place where he will be with only his core group, minus, of course, the one who now works for me—us."

"How much will we have to pay him?" Caiaphas asked, smiling broadly for the first time since Jesus showed up.

"Uh, thirty pieces of silver," Jonathan said.

"A tidy sum, but well worth it," Caiaphas said, the amount not even causing him to flinch, his face still beaming.

Well worth it? Malchus could not believe his ears. Thirty pieces of silver was more than a tidy sum. It was enough to buy a house in Jerusalem. Unbelievably, Caiaphas was still smiling.

Caiaphas stood up, absolutely aglow. He did not say anything at first, just stared straight off into space as if he were viewing another dimension. Then he began. "Fellow priests . . . " He stopped long enough to make eye contact with all who were still there. "Do you all realize what we have here? More than a fortuitous turn of events. More than luck. Even more than the fruit of careful planning. It is, rather, an answer to prayer from God Himself. A confirmation, if you will. It is deliverance! If you shared any of the doubt some of the others expressed concerning our Lord and exactly whom He supports, doubt no more! Clearly, he has spoken. In this He has told us He is on our side. The incredible irony of it all, that the information we so desperately needed would be delivered into our very hands from a key member of the man's own band. The timing is too perfect. This cannot be a mere coincidence. No, it is the Lord's providence. God is with us. He has greatly provided for us in our hour of need, and as we go forth to do His work, He will lead us and guide us. And He will not forsake us."

Malchus could not determine what Caiaphas was doing. Was this real or more melodrama? Did Caiaphas actually believe what he was saying, or was he just seizing the opportunity and using it to his own advantage? And this was some opportunity. He had a lot with which to work. Whether he believed what he was saying or not, he had these priests convinced that God had just acted, and they were energized, ready, it seemed, to commit murder in God's name. It was quite an accomplishment for Caiaphas, achieving exactly the purpose of this meeting.

They were all now giving thanks to God for His gracious provision, and momentum was building. It was palpable. And scary. Malchus could not remember when he had seen them so genuinely enthusiastic about anything, let alone something as odious as this. There they are, he thought, totally unified in purpose, purpose of which he wanted no part. But why else was he there? Why could not this have happened next year when he was miles away. *Free in you,* he thought.

"It is good that we give thanks to God for allowing His face to shine on us. I know in my heart He is with us and He will continue to be with us, no matter what comes against us," Caiaphas said. "But we have much left to do before this evening is over." The high priest stepped away from his seat and looked at Malchus. Malchus looked back, seeing malevolence and cunning in Caiaphas's eyes. Then, with the voice of an angel, he spoke. "Come, Malchus, we need your help. I will tell you how you can be of great service to us and to your people."

Malchus hesitated, not wanting nor able to move. The words went through him like a knife. *This is it,* he thought. Could he tell them he wouldn't participate without being the first person in who knows how long to be shackled and flogged for rebellion in Caiaphas's private dungeon? If Bebai was here, he at least would go easy on him. But with Jonathan, he would get no such mercy.

"Come on, Malchus. We have no time to waste."

Jonathan stood up and walked over to Malchus and whispered in his ear. "Before you speak I think we should step outside the room for a moment and have a little talk." Jonathan then looked at the others and politely bowed. "Would you all excuse us; this should only take a moment," Jonathan gave a reassuring smile to Caiaphas, then proceeded to escort Malchus, by the elbow, into the hallway. "Someone of your position should feel privileged to be a part of anything the high priest should require, but you don't seem very enthused."

Malchus wanted to tell the captain the Nazarene was a threat to his and Caiaphas's world, and not to the people or any of their slaves. He wanted to tell Jonathan he enjoyed what Jesus had to say and that no truer words had ever been spoken about Caiaphas and the way the temple was run. He would love to tell Jonathan all that and more, but those words would fall on a seared heart and result in a sound lashing. "You plan to kill the man. I don't like killing," Malchus said.

"You know what this is, don't you?" Jonathan said, pulling out the list that Malchus immediately recognized. "Caiaphas is going to honor you by directing you to be our eyes and ears in escorting the Romans to arrest Jesus. If you refuse, your punishment will be nothing compared to the punishment to certain people on this list," he said as he ran his finger up and down the piece of parchment as if looking for a specific name. "There's someone in particular. A woman. I don't have to mention her by name. But I perceive her as an unusually dangerous threat to peace and order. I'm sure Caiaphas would agree, don't you?"

"How do I know that if I cooperate, Zara's name will come off the list?"

"You don't!" Jonathan said, smiling strangely. "But if you don't comply, don't do your job well, I can guarantee she will receive a most exquisite punishment. In fact, I'll see to it personally. I'll see to it privately," he said, the same smile returning. "And I'll look forward to it."

Malchus felt truly, completely helpless and powerless. Cornered like an animal. Trapped, bound, and gagged.

Jonathan bowed his head toward Malchus's face, their eyes just inches apart. "Do we understand each other?"

Hate burned in Malchus's heart as he stared into Jonathan's face. He looked down to the ground and nodded.

"Good, a wise choice," Jonathan said. "Let's go back inside now. We don't want to keep the others waiting."

When they entered the room, Caiaphas looked inquiringly at Jonathan. Jonathan responded with a simple nod of reassurance. "Malchus, I hope whatever words of encouragement Jonathan shared with you had their desired effect," Caiaphas said gravely.

Malchus nodded in submission. "How can I serve you?"

"Good, very good. Let's move on then," Caiaphas said, appearing relieved that this unexpected detour was quickly resolved. He apparently had not anticipated Malchus to be anything less than the faithful slave he had always been. "I want you to understand why we need you, Malchus. If the Sanhedrin was officially involved and made the arrest, we would not be able to punish this . . . this menace properly. We need someone not constrained by our laws to do it. That's where the Romans come in. When it comes to efficiently, effectively, and officially arresting, trying, and punishing, I'm sure you agree, no one is more expert than the Romans."

Except for you, Malchus thought.

"You, Malchus, have a unique relationship with the Romans because of your trade with them, and you also have a unique relationship with us. You are my slave, beholden to me by law and yet not bound as a priest when it comes to the law or even the Sabbath, which could also prove to be a problem for us. We don't trust the Romans to carry out the arrest properly and lawfully without being supervised, or at least being accompanied to ensure they carry out their duty. And Malchus, that's where you come in."

The oily words and gross hypocrisy of Caiaphas made Malchus's skin crawl. Yet, he could do nothing.

"We must all go to the Castle of Antonia now, while there is still daylight, and meet with the Romans," Caiaphas said, signaling for the others to rise.

SIXTEEN

Malchus paced back and forth as he waited for Caiaphas to return. At one point he walked by the doorway and noticed Zara in the kitchen, motioning for him to come over to her. She was alone. Malchus was excited to see her, but his feelings dampened by the queasiness that had overtaken him since being "honored" by Caiaphas and the leadership. He walked over to her, trying to conceal his anxiety, at least for the moment. She took his hand.

"Malchus, it looks like it's going to be a beautiful evening tonight. Let's go for a walk after supper. There will be a moon out. We'll go wherever you want."

Malchus wanted to cry. Zara would have no idea what was going to take place this evening. As per Caiaphas's usual policy, she had been ordered by Levia not to return to the council chamber after the meeting had begun. Zara probably considered that a blessing since she would not have to clean up when the men finished their business. Now she was looking forward to making the most of this free time, and Malchus was deeply moved that she had chosen to spend it with him. After the experience she had at the temple with the blind man, what Malchus had to tell her was going to be his worst nightmare, and hers too.

The thought of fleeing surfaced. What if he took her with him and fled the country? Where would he go? How far would he get? If they were caught, which was very likely, would their punishment be any worse than what Jonathan was looking forward to giving her sometime in the future. *Of course it would,* he thought. *There would be more for which to punish her. Much more. And knowing Jonathan's reputation with women . . .*

"Zara, I don't know how to tell you this," Malchus said sadly. "It isn't going to be a beautiful evening tonight, Zara, it's going to be a horrible night."

"Why, Malchus? What's wrong?" Zara said, her hand on his arm.

"They plan to arrest Jesus tonight with the help of Roman soldiers, and they want me to go with them."

"The Romans?" Zara said, apparently more startled by that than by the news of the arrest.

Malchus could only nod. He did not have to tell her Caiaphas was planning to kill the Nazarene if the Romans were involved. The Romans had a very small list of punishments, regardless of the crime and, depending on the administrator, any of them could result in death.

"Malchus, no! They cannot! They must not! Do they not know what they are doing? He is the One. The Messiah. Oh, Malchus, tell them they can't!" She looked intensely at Malchus through watery eyes.

"There's nothing I can say."

"Tell them he's the Messiah."

"Then they'll kill me too. And I'm not certain he is."

"No one could know what he knows and speak what he speaks."

"Another reason they want him gone. The man sees right through them, and it scares them to death."

"But he heals the sick."

Malchus shook his head. "They just claim that's the devil. Another reason to have him executed."

"What are they, blind?" Zara said, loudly enough to cause Malchus to look quickly behind him.

"Shhhh. Remember, that's one of the accusations that infuriated Caiaphas the most."

Zara's eyes were ablaze. "I don't care," she whispered through clenched teeth. "It's the truth . . . and Jesus said the truth would set you free."

"Yes, at the end of a sword."

"And you're going to take part in this?"

"Yes," he said, looking to the ground. "And I can't refuse them."

"Why not?" she asked as she pulled her hand away from his. "Why not?" she repeated, raising her voice again.

"Look, Zara. Jonathan warned me that if I did not cooperate, he would report you to Caiaphas and personally see to your punishment. I can't let that happen."

"Malchus, he's going to hang that over your head forever. So Jonathan has a stupid list. Tomorrow he will have witnesses to say what he wants. And then some other list to threaten you with. If it's not one thing, it'll be another. The next thing you know, he'll demand something in exchange for your freedom."

"Zara, I don't think you understand. If I go in there and tell them no, Jonathan will likely bring both of us into the cellar and have us shackled to the wall. Not after a trial, but after a moment. At his whim. I can't let that happen, Zara. I care about you." He blurted out. The words that left his mouth had barely formed in his mind. "I've never seen them more serious about anything as long as I've been here. They believe arresting Jesus is the will of God."

"Whatever they do to us, or to me, is better than being part of their plot against Jesus," Zara said.

Malchus could hardly believe how adamant she was, especially after she had already told him she would rather die than get whipped again. Maybe he could soften her martyrlike mentality.

"Try to forget about the Messiah thing. I don't even know if there is such a person. For all I know, the Messiah is just an old Jewish fable. Most of the time you only hear about him when a rabbi is looking to stir up an assembly, and I'm certainly not going to gamble with *your* life over a priest's ploy to conjure up zeal. I can't believe we're even arguing about it. You know I can't refuse them. It would be suicide."

"And going with them could be murder—what does your law say about that?" Zara said coldly, turning away from him and walking to the window.

Malchus walked up behind her and gently placed his hand on her shoulder. "It's not even certain that the Romans will go along with this. They'll probably laugh in our faces," he said, trying to reassure her.

Zara pulled her shoulder away from his hand. "How could I have been so wrong about you?"

"Malchus!" came a commanding voice from the hallway. "Let's go. We're waiting for you." It was Jonathan.

Malchus turned toward the hallway, then back to Zara. "I have no choice."

Zara glared at him. "Apparently you've just made a choice," she said sharply, then walked away.

SEVENTEEN

As the sun began to set, a crimson glow fell across the western walls of the homes in the ancient city. Zara was right. It was going to be a beautiful night. But the beginning of the spectacular sunset went unappreciated by the lone slave and the band of priests hurrying to the Roman fortress known as the Castle of Antonia. For them, time was running out, and they were determined to carry out their business before the Sabbath was upon them. The busy noises of the day had quieted, except for the occasional shouting of a Roman soldier trying to control his horses. Prayers could be heard through the windows of some homes where celebrants were getting an early start before the Passover meal. As the band passed through the street, Malchus and the priests drew curious stares from the locals. Judging from the direction they were traveling, the onlookers assumed they were heading to the temple on some priestly mission. No one could have thought, even for an instant, that their destination was the Castle of Antonia, command post of the hated Roman conquerors.

The castle, its famous tower punctuating the skyline, was situated at the northwest corner of the temple. Malchus had become very familiar with the tower's rich history. Beneath the tower ran a subterranean passage into the temple itself. It also had stairways, which descended into the northern and western porches of the Court of the Gentiles. Some of the most cherished traditions and historical milestones of Jewish history were tied to the Castle of Antonia. It had been the ancient armory of King David, the palace of Hezekiah and Nehemiah, and the fortress of the Maccabees. But to Malchus, the history was history. Now it served as a police station—Jerusalem's headquarters for the pagan Roman army that kept watch over Israel, even in its sanctuary. It was the perfect lookout. The Tower of Antonia, built upon a seven-story-high rock, rose over ten stories from its base and offered a commanding panoramic view of the temple and the surrounding area. From this vantage point the Romans could respond to virtually any situation, immediately deploying a detachment of soldiers to quell any uprising or disturbance of the peace.

Although Malchus rushed alongside the priests to the castle with its Roman tenants, his mind still remained back in the kitchen with Zara. He could not get their conversation out of his thoughts. Why did she have to get so intense? And why did she have to give him that it's-either-them-or-me attitude?

She is right, too, he thought, reflecting on what she had said about Jonathan. He would continue to use the information about Zara and Jesus to blackmail Malchus into doing whatever he wanted. He hated that Jonathan was in control. If only there was a way to reverse the roles, he thought. The idea of grabbing Zara and running for it was looking better and better. With all that was happening tonight, they would not be missed until they were long gone. *Long gone with no provision,* he thought. Away from the city, from his home, from food and water. Alone and helpless. No, running was not a plan. Just a fantasy. He needed to wait until after Passover so he would have money from the lambskins he would sell. With enough money, anything might be possible. *Free in you,* he thought sarcastically. And then his mind came back to the business at hand as he realized they were fast approaching their destination.

The idea of going into the Castle of Antonia had to intimidate every man who followed the high priest. None of them, except for Caiaphas, had ever been inside, although each one of them saw it daily, since it was physically a part of the outer walls of the city and the temple courts. Seeing it in the background was one thing, but going inside on business was another.

The men pressed on. Onlookers appeared confused. Some looked alarmed at the sight of the high priest and the captain of the guard, followed by half a dozen black-robed chief priests and a slave, all hurrying through the streets at dusk as Passover was about to begin.

Once outside the Damascus Gate, Malchus followed like a mule on a rope as the band immediately turned right onto a small but well-kept road that hugged the city wall until it entered a large, gated archway into the Roman fortress. Without the city walls as a shield, the setting sun struck Malchus's eyes directly. He shaded them with his left hand, bringing Antonia into focus. No one looked down as they walked. All eyes were fixed upon the giant fortress before them, their breathing becoming ever more labored.

The pace had not slowed since Caiaphas started out for the garrison. His flushed but determined face was now set straight toward the entrance a few hundred feet away. In his wake, several steps behind him, the rest panted and tried to keep up.

Before them were Roman guards on either side of the archway, and another guard paced the turret above the arch. The guard in the turret abruptly stopped pacing when he saw the priests approaching and yelled something down inside the fortress. Moments later the gates opened outward and another soldier appeared. Unlike the temple guard, the Roman soldiers were seasoned warriors, armed with sharpened weapons they held at the ready, seemingly prepared to use them.

"State your business," the soldier said sharply to the priests as they arrived at the threshold of the castle.

"Tell the procurator that Joseph Caiaphas, the high priest, is here, and it is urgent I speak to him now," Caiaphas said with authority, though he was breathing heavily. His tone was deadly serious, and his delivery was classic Caiaphas, commanding the attention of both the Romans and his own priests.

"Wait here," the soldier told them less confidently, then disappeared behind the arch, the gate closing behind him.

Caiaphas paced until the gate reopened and the soldier stepped back out. The Roman looked over the band of priests as he walked around them suspiciously, eyeing each one of them, pausing to take special notice of Malchus, who was obviously not a priest. Then he walked back to the front of the group, directly in their path. "Three of you can enter. The rest must remain outside," he ordered, staring back at the one who was their leader.

Caiaphas looked about to argue, but did not. He turned and faced them. "Jonathan, Malchus, come with me," he said. "The rest of you wait here in case you're needed to testify as witnesses." Then he turned and the three of them followed the soldier inside. The priests left behind grumbled indignantly at having to remain out on the dusty road, but Malchus knew they must have been relieved they did not have to go inside.

Caiaphas, Jonathan, and Malchus entered into a large rectangular central courtyard surrounded by long walls with turrets and towers rising up from each of the four corners. The tower facing the temple was much taller than the other three. The turrets all had soldiers stationed upon them.

Malchus was wide-eyed as they walked through the courtyard. The crack of a whip followed by an agonizing, blood-curdling scream froze Malchus in his steps as he turned toward the sickening cry. Caiaphas and Jonathan showed little reaction. Two men were strapped to a locust wood whipping post in the very center of the courtyard. A muscular soldier snapped the whip with obvious expertise and indifference as the blood-soaked cord tore away the flesh of the two prisoners.

The difference between a Jewish whipping and a Roman whipping could be likened to the difference between discipline and torment. By law, the most the Jews were allowed to flog someone was thirty-nine lashes, and that on the rarest of occasions. The Romans had no upward limit, and they used different whips—more sadistic and cruel whips. Roman whips had sharp pieces of stone and metal embedded into them in order to rip the skin on the return stroke. They were instruments of torture and death.

As they passed within a few yards of the whipping post, Malchus felt queasy at the sight of the flesh and bone the Roman whip had exposed. The two bloodied men were delirious with pain and barely cognizant of the visitors as they passed by. Caiaphas and Jonathan barely took notice. If anything, Caiaphas seemed irritated at the slow pace of the soldier they were following.

The soldier looked back and seemed to take notice that Malchus looked sickened. He grinned but said nothing.

They followed the Roman to the tall and famous Tower of Antonia at the northeast corner of the castle. At its base there was a large arched door with a heavy bronze knocker ring. The soldier grabbed the ring and knocked on the door. A moment later it opened. Another soldier let them in and led them up four long, dimly lit flights of stone steps to a large open room. The first soldier followed behind them.

The room was richly adorned with Roman statues and red draperies, and it had windows on every side. In the light of the western window was the silhouette of a short stout man looking out at the sunset. Caiaphas moved to the center of the room; Jonathan and Malchus followed. The two soldiers stood off to the sides, but positioned between the silhouetted man and the visitors.

Although Malchus had never seen Pontius Pilate at Caiaphas's home, he had heard Caiaphas speak of him. From what Malchus could gather, Caiaphas's relationship with the procurator was strictly business. And outside his home, Caiaphas's contact with him had been intermittent at best. The few times their paths had crossed, however, Caiaphas refused to call him by anything but his official title, *procurator,* a Roman designation for the governing administrator of a specific geographic area. Caiaphas decided that would be the way he would address him after the first time they met.

Malchus was trying to piece together memory fragments of conversations from way back when Caiaphas still traveled with Annas. When Caiaphas became high priest fifteen years ago, the procurator was Valerius Gratus. At that time, Gratus had been there only one year, and Caiaphas got along well with him. They were both new at their jobs and were getting settled in their respective positions at the same time. Gratus was mostly a career politician interested in maintaining good relationships with those whom the people respected. The high priest was at the top of the list. The last thing he wanted was a report of unrest going home to Rome. Malchus remembered Caiaphas mentioning that Gratus was a consummate politician, and had done whatever he could to keep his job and prevent anyone from disturbing his peace. If that meant treating Caiaphas with a measure of respect for his position, so be it. Theirs was, at least, a cordial relationship, even if it was premised on the subjugation of Jerusalem. Eight years later, Gratus became ill. In a short time, his condition deteriorated to the point that he could no longer govern.

Pontius Pilate was then appointed procurator through the recommendation and sponsorship of a man named Sejanus. Pilate was his protégé. Sejanus rose to near supreme power as the ruthless commander of the praetorian guard under the Roman emperor Tiberius. When Pilate replaced the ailing Gratus, he brought in his own people with the ruthlessness and thoroughness his mentor had inspired. All members of the old guard were replaced with Pilate's own men, who were brought from Rome, where they had served under him previously and had proven their loyalty.

When Caiaphas first greeted the new procurator, he welcomed him to Jerusalem. Pilate coldly informed him that he would tolerate no problems from the Sanhedrin or second-guessing of his decisions, and, if the Sanhedrin did not abide by his rule, he would hold Caiaphas personally responsible. This approach worked for a time. Recently, however, Pilate's position had become less secure. The anti-Jewish Sejanus had been accused of treason against Rome, and although the charges were dropped, he was under intense investigation and fell from power. All those associated with Sejanus were now under suspicion, including Pilate. As a result, Pilate was never certain of who his friends were, and he was often looking over his shoulder, fearful of every shadow. Caiaphas kept his distance, recognizing how dangerously paranoid Pilate actually was. He made a rule to deal with him only when absolutely necessary. This was such a time.

"A beautiful sunset this evening," said the man at the window. "I suppose that means you're in a great hurry, aren't you, Caiaphas?"

So this is Pontius Pilate, Malchus thought. Judging by the comfortable surroundings, he probably spent much of his time here.

"We came here on a matter of great urgency," Caiaphas said. "And yes, time is of the essence."

"Well, I suppose it must be, since the high priest of God's 'chosen people' comes to see me, in my unholy abode, with the renowned Jonathan, his captain of the amazing temple guard," he said sarcastically. "You must feel terribly soiled just being here, don't you?"

Jonathan gaped with apparent surprise when he realized Pilate knew him. Caiaphas seemed less surprised. And if he were not addressing Pilate from a place of such extreme need and urgency, he probably would challenge Pilate for his contemptible sarcasm. Malchus figured Pilate was also aware of that, and he was enjoying the additional advantage he had, toying with the high priest.

"The view up here is exceptional, even on the temple side, and I stay better informed than you might think. I must confess, though,

I don't know this young man," Pilate said, motioning toward Malchus. "That's quite an eye. Is he your bodyguard, Caiaphas?"

The high priest impatiently closed his eyes for a moment, refusing to answer.

"His name is Malchus, sir," came a voice from behind. The three visitors turned around to find that two other soldiers had come in unnoticed, and were standing behind them. One of them was Alexander, a friend of Malchus.

"Alexander," Malchus said, a bit surprised to see him.

Alexander acknowledged him with a nod. "He is the slave of the high priest, sir."

"Your slave, Caiaphas?" Pilate asked. "Oh, this must really be important." He laughed mockingly. "Tell me, then, what is so urgent?"

Caiaphas was undistracted by Pilate's obnoxious comments. Instead he spoke with authority and urgency. "There is an extremely dangerous and destructive revolutionary on the loose at this very moment. People all over Jerusalem are allying with him, and we firmly believe that if he is allowed to continue to move freely among us for even one more day, the result will be disastrous for both your country and mine. We report him to you so you can arrest him this very night for treason against Rome. Moreover, now is the opportunity, since he is accompanied by only a few men and is away from the crowds that would follow his orders."

"Since when is treason against Rome one of your concerns?" asked Pilate.

"Since he also preaches treason against our temple and law."

"And I suppose you have some kind of evidence to substantiate these very serious accusations. Against Rome, that is. I could care less about your law and the temple. That's your business."

"We have many witnesses who are prepared to testify against the man."

"Who is this treacherous instigator whom you speak of, *Your Chosenship,* this man who has somehow evaded our eyes and ears?" Pilate asked dramatically.

Caiaphas must hate every moment of this, Malchus thought. He knew Pilate did not like him. In fact, he knew Pilate resented him, if for no other reason than the fact that he was Jewish. That he was high priest and able to petition him also annoyed the procurator. "His name is Jesus. He is from Nazareth. He claims to be the king of the Jews."

"Jesus? Please, Caiaphas. Jesus? We know of him," he said with a belittling chuckle. "He may be a revolutionary by your holy standards, but he is no threat to Rome."

"I assure you, Procurator, he is a severe threat to Rome," Caiaphas said with intensity in his voice. "The way the people are flocking to him, all Jerusalem—nay, the whole world—will be his before long, and then it will be too late. If that were to happen, you will remember this conversation as the opportunity lost, and all Rome will know your name for the havoc you allowed to be reeked under your very watch."

Pilate laughed, though not as heartily as before. "Bah!" Pilate said, waving his hand. "You people are afraid of your own shadows. Our reports on him have done little more than amuse us. He is a religious fanatic preaching some of the most absurd teachings we have ever heard. Absurd, Caiaphas," he said, poking his index finger at the high priest, "not dangerous."

"You are wrong, Procurator. He is very dangerous. He stirs people into a frenzy. They would jump at his command. All he need do is point to Rome, declare it their enemy, and you will have an insurrection on your hands that will be hard to contain. And harder still to explain, since all of Rome will hear of such an uprising. Why, some of your own soldiers may secretly be with him already," Caiaphas said.

Malchus mused that however badly Jesus had bested Caiaphas, Caiaphas certainly showed no lack of his usual craftiness and confidence. Even Malchus could see Caiaphas had sufficiently played into Pilate's fears to ensure some action would be taken.

"Enemy of Rome, Caiaphas? Hardly. What he tells the crowds to do to their enemies would make you want to be his enemy. We hear he says, 'Love your enemy.'" Pilate laughed. "If someone strikes you on one cheek, give him the other," he said, laughing louder. "If someone takes your tunic, give him your cloak as well. Bless those who curse you. Is that what you want, Caiaphas? A blessing? That must be why you're trying to curse him!" Pilate continued, laughing as he spoke and shaking his head back and forth in disbelief.

Malchus did not believe Pilate could last much longer. He had seen Caiaphas crack people before, and Pilate was giving off some of the same telltale signs he had seen in the past. The man no longer had the same authority in his voice. He had lost some of his volume and projection, and he spent less time looking directly at Caiaphas, who was steadily looking straight at him. Pilate probably was wondering if any of his men had secretly joined forces with the Nazarene, or had brought back false reports of his activities.

The soldiers, still standing at attention, were being careful not to smile. Pilate's mocking laughter suddenly stopped. He walked up to Caiaphas, stood directly in front of him, and spoke in a harsh whisper. "Now, do you think me a fool, Caiaphas, to believe that you, the high priest, would come out here with Passover knocking at your door, with the captain of the temple guard and your slave, to convince me that a man who preaches love and peace, a nobody from Nazareth of all places, is a threat to the great Roman Empire? What has he done to you? What has he really done to you, Caiaphas? What has he done to you that you want him arrested for treason? What has he done that you should come to me to give him the death penalty? Did he embarrass you? How did he provoke you to this, I wonder?" As he spoke, Pilate's face almost touched the priest's face.

"I am not the issue here, Procurator," Caiaphas said sternly, not moving an inch. Then louder: "The man is a deceiver. He may preach love with his mouth, but he has no respect for authority. Yesterday, as I'm sure by now you must be aware, he violently assaulted merchants within the temple and vandalized the marketing area," Caiaphas said, with his own touch of sarcasm. "If this 'king of the Jews' turns on his own subjects, how hard do you think it will be for him to turn against you? Can you take that chance from someone claiming to be a king? Today he's king of the Jews. Tomorrow he'll claim to be king of Sparta." Pilate looked toward the window as he heard the sound of the whip, followed by an agonizing cry of pain. "Come see what it is that you request," he said to the three, escorting them to the window facing the courtyard below. They looked down. "The two men whom you see down there are thieves. They were caught trying to rob a Roman pilgrim on the road from Caesarea. Right now we are just beginning. Tomorrow at this time they will be dead. They are scheduled to be crucified. Once on the cross, they will look back at this treatment longingly."

He turned and looked Caiaphas in the eyes again. "What you are accusing this Nazarene of is a worse offense. If you can imagine it, treason is punished even more severely."

"The man may be from Nazareth, but his disciples are from Galilee, a place that harbors many rebels."

Pilate's eyebrows rose at this comment. He apparently had not known that. There had been recent problems with rebels from Galilee.

"And, I repeat, the people are flocking to him by the hundreds. His following grows by the day, if not the hour. Is this the first you heard of the disorder he created in the temple? Have you not also heard that he threatened to actually destroy the temple? Do you think that, as time goes by, he will not create a disturbance of which even Rome will be alarmed? Will you have answers, Procurator? How will you explain it and deflect the blame? What will you tell them? 'Oh, it's nothing to worry about; he just thinks he's the king.' How do you think that will sit with Caesar?"

Pilate was silent. Caiaphas had him, and Malchus knew it. He had shut him up, and Rome would soon do his bidding.

"Do you work long and hard at this, Caiaphas, or does it just come naturally for you? You seem to have it all figured out, the questions and the answers. Unfortunately, you may be correct. The situation could well develop into something that would be difficult to explain—especially now." Pilate sighed.

"We will arrest this man, Caiaphas. But I do it for me, not for you. You have made a very serious accusation, and as you point out, it is in Rome's interest to investigate the man. Then I will make my own judgment. He will be arrested for suspicion of treason and may well be released if there is no evidence against him. If so, I might come after you for bringing false accusations.

"And," Pilate continued, "there are a few conditions that must be met, or there will be no arrest tonight."

"What might *they* be?" Caiaphas asked, half mocking, knowing any conditions would be incidental. Pilate was too convinced not to act.

"I want the Sanhedrin officially to find him guilty before he comes before me. My soldiers will deliver him to you first. I do not need an uprising among your people, with accusations that this arrest is Rome's idea. If anyone is going to be blamed for this arrest and its aftermath, it is going to be you, not me. Is that understood?"

"I'll do even better, Procurator," Caiaphas said confidently. "We'll first bring him to the house of Annas. He will personally give the initial approval. Then we will bring him before the Sanhedrin and authorize his arrest. What else?"

"We'll arrest him, Caiaphas, but I want your people there as well. Again, I don't want it even to appear that it's our idea."

"Procurator," Caiaphas said assuringly, "that is why I brought my slave, in anticipation of this very request."

"One slave, Caiaphas? Don't make me laugh," Pilate said, raising his voice. "One slave is hardly a representative of your people. In fact, what I want are the leaders themselves. I want to see chief priests, scribes, elders, and anyone else to whom you've given some religious title."

"But Procurator, it is the Sabbath. By law, they cannot work." Caiaphas was now annoyed.

"They don't have to work. We will do the work. They can just be out for an evening stroll. I don't know; you work it out. You're adept at taking hypocrisy and compromise and making it look good. Your people believe whatever you say. Tell them these conditions are accomplishments. Wonderful! God's chosen people, breaking their law on the high holy day. Hypocrites on parade. Perfect!"

Caiaphas let the insults roll off without return. "Is there anything else, Procurator?"

"There may be, depending on where and when this is going to take place."

"For that information I defer to the captain of the guard," Caiaphas said, an open hand waving toward Jonathan, who was standing behind him and to the side.

"At the present, his whereabouts are unknown to us," said Jonathan in his best military demeanor, plainly trying to impress Pilate. "Except to say that he is in Jerusalem at a secret location having his Passover meal with his band of followers." Jonathan went on to tell Pilate about the scheduled rendezvous with the one who was willing to betray Jesus for money, and that he personally would be leading them to him. Pilate was glad to hear as much. The more Jews who were pointing fingers at Jesus, the better.

When Jonathan finished briefing Pilate about the planning, execution, timing, and meeting locations, the procurator turned to Caiaphas to take him to task one final time, this time on a philosophical note.

"Just one more thing, Caiaphas. You Jews, you claim there is only one God, and that your precious laws come from Him, isn't that right?" Pilate asked.

"That is correct, Procurator," responded Caiaphas.

"And your only God has left you a conquered, defeated people?"

"Conquered, yes, Procurator."

"Well, since your God has obviously forgotten you, maybe he is with this king of the Jews whom you want arrested," he suggested, goading Caiaphas. "And maybe his proclamations are the new laws for your people," he said, grinning mischievously.

"There is only one God, Procurator. He has given us the law. His law. He has delivered us in the past. He has given us the law to guide the people of Abraham. And he has given us patience. God is not, Procurator, with this deranged madman from Nazareth, nor is God giving us new laws that make even the Romans laugh. Yes, Procurator, there is only one God, and he is still with us."

"We shall see, Caiaphas, we shall see," said Pilate as he turned and left the room.

EIGHTEEN

So much had happened in the last few days, Malchus lost track of what came first or where it had started. All the events seemed to bunch together and lose definition. The only thing he knew for sure was that he was exhausted, both mentally and physically. His face felt thick and heavy from stress. And now he was on another one of Caiaphas's "most important" errands, getting word to the chief priests, scribes, and elders of what Pilate had demanded for the arrest. Someone had to relay the instructions, and Malchus again seemed Caiaphas's logical choice. By the time he finished his job and rejoined Jonathan at the Beautiful Gate, a crowd of dark-robed priests had assembled. Malchus sat on the cool, hard steps several yards to the side of the Beautiful Gate, tired and hungry, his head in his hands. His eye picked up a gray vein in the white marble, crooked, erratic, confusingly trailing its way through the stone, and he found an instant of comfort that he was not alone.

He swore to himself that this time next week he would run away from Jerusalem, never to return. Somehow he would convince Zara to go with him. Caiaphas had turned from ambitious to ruthless. How could he allow Zara to live in a house where such a madman lived? *She has to forgive me,* he thought.

The hour had finally come. The sun had completely set over the west walls of the city, and the fading silhouette of the Tower of Antonia was blending into the darkening sky. People with torches and lanterns were converging near the gate, gathering into small groups according to their type, priests with priests, elders with elders, scribes with scribes. Malchus was desperately trying to find a way out as momentum continued to grow. Why was it still so necessary for him to be there? Maybe they would forget about him, lose him in the activity of the moment, and he could go back and tell Zara he had escaped. Then she would forgive him.

There was a man standing alone under the arch of the gate, nearly concealed in the shadows of the torchlight. He looked as if he was hiding. Malchus had never seen him before, and he figured the man must be the traitor. Malchus wondered what he knew about Jesus that would make him do such a thing. Then he wondered if he even knew what he had gotten the Nazarene into. Whether he knew or not, he had apparently done it for the money. Why not? Everyone else around here had a price.

Two more groups with torches approached from opposite directions. The first to arrive were the temple police, with Jonathan at their lead. Jonathan made his way straight to the man who was hiding in the shadows. The man moved into the light as Jonathan approached him. His face was pale and drawn; his only color came from the yellow glow of the torches. Malchus felt no pity for him as Jonathan pulled out a weighted coin sack and began to count out pieces of silver. *You couldn't pay me enough to be in his place,* Malchus thought, watching the man stare at the silver in his hand, then put it back into the sack and clumsily tie it around his waist.

The other group marched in next. The Roman soldiers. The traitor looked surprised at the arrival of the Romans. Again, Malchus wondered if the man knew what he had gotten himself into. There would be no turning back now if he valued his life.

The temple guard looked frail, almost pathetic, in comparison to the Romans. These were battle-worn soldiers, trained in actual combat. They were armed with small circular shields fastened to their forearms and with gladiuses, the standard Roman battle sword, about two feet in length, worn on their sides. In addition to the standard breastplate, the highly polished armor worn on their necks, shoulders, and thighs glistened in the torchlight.

Malchus watched as the Roman leader, a centurion, made his way quickly to Jonathan, who smiled and waved to him. Malchus smirked and almost shook his head. He knew the Romans were not there to socialize or wait for anyone else to arrive. They had been ordered to come and wanted to complete their assignment as quickly as possible and get back to Antonia. They seemed irritated even to be on such an errand and probably annoyed that these Jews were somehow involved in the mission. Malchus knew the official orders about being here to arrest a dangerous rebel were believed by no one in a Roman uniform. In fact, the whole thing had to be embarrassing to them.

"Let's go," shouted Jonathan, motioning with his torch in the chilly night air. His people now looked more like an angry mob than the teachers, leaders, and peacekeepers of Israel. The traitor reluctantly allowed himself to be led by Jonathan to the front of the gathering. The rumble of voices in the mob grew louder.

Malchus brought up the rear, coughing from their dust. Was he anything more than a scapegoat, a shield, someone to point fingers at should anything go awry? There were more than enough witnesses present to ensure that the Romans arrest Jesus. He slowed his pace, dropping back until a scary thought came to mind. If Jonathan were to find him missing, he might use it as an excuse to abuse Zara, something he actually sounded eager to do.

There seemed no safe option but to follow along. Logically, he had no other choice. He would keep a low profile, insulated by the crowd that had gathered. Somehow he would make Zara understand when it was all over.

The traitor led the mob southeast, down a narrow street toward the Pool of Siloam. Before reaching the pool, the traitor took a sharp right, then continued uphill a few hundred feet along an even narrower road. The houses on either side were so tightly packed together, they were touching each other.

As they noisily marched up the street, every window seemed to have a face staring out of it. Jonathan was in his glory, strutting his torch in the front of the pack, the center of all the local attention. Malchus, however, felt embarrassed to be attached to the angry crowd and was glad to be in the rear with the darkness that followed behind them.

Arriving at a two-story home with an external stairway leading up to the second-floor door, the traitor slowed to a stop and pointed up to the door. The traitor's fingers looked eerily bony against the sleeve of his tunic and the torch-lit night. "You first," Jonathan said to the ex-disciple, taking him by the arm and pushing him toward the old timber stairs. The traitor braced himself as he fell against the stairs and quickly turned to

Jonathan, his liquid glare revealing the broken trust of a man he thought he knew.

"I don't want to miss their faces when they see yours," Jonathan said, almost giddy with excitement, sweat beading up on his oily face. The man reluctantly walked up the stairs, the mob pushing up right behind him, testing the integrity of the stairs. When he reached the door, the man again glanced behind him. He appeared frightened, and Malchus wondered if it was because the traitor was thinking about the one he was about to ambush or about the hungry-for-blood look of those behind him. There was murder in everyone's eyes.

"Come on, what are you waiting for?" shouted a voice from the stairway. Suddenly Jonathan pushed the man to the side and violently kicked the door open. It slammed against the inside wall, snapping the top hinge, and, still attached to the hinge at the threshold, fell into the room with a crash. The mob surged into the room over the broken door, pushing the traitor in as well, the silver coins jingling loudly as he vanished from Malchus's sight.

Malchus, content to stay at the bottom of the stairs, was not too far away to hear what happened next.

"What kind of treachery is this?" he heard Jonathan scream. "Where are they?"

Malchus had heard that pitch before. It meant Jonathan probably had the traitor by the neck, his face close enough to kill with his foul breath alone. Jonathan was used to being at a loss for words, but this scenario could push him over the edge. He could just picture Jonathan explaining this one to Caiaphas.

Malchus was relieved to hear that the Nazarene was not there. Finally he had something positive he could report to Zara. Jesus had somehow outsmarted them all.

"They've already left, but I know where they've gone," he heard the traitor plead. Malchus hoped this was simply a desperate appeal for a few more minutes of life.

"This is all a hoax to get money for you and them, isn't it?" Jonathan accused wildly. "This man has tried to take advantage of us all," he cried out to the crowd.

"No, it's not true, I swear, they left earlier than I thought, that's all," the man begged.

"Look, Captain," the centurion said. "He could be telling us the truth. The table looks like it was recently used, and there are a dozen seats set up. There was a pause. "And the wine goblet—there's still a little wine in this goblet, and the ants haven't yet found the bread crumbs on the table. "I would think we just missed them, but not by much."

"May I have that goblet?" Jonathan said. Malchus then heard what sounded like the goblet hitting someone, followed instantly by a painful cry, he imagined, resulting from getting hit in the face. "Now, last chance. Where is he?" Jonathan yelled.

"At the oil press on the Mount of Olives," the man screamed through sobs of fear. "At the Garden of Gethsemane."

Jonathan then pushed the man out the door where Malchus could see him. The man had a dark swell on his forehead.

"He's at the Garden of Gethsemane," Jonathan yelled out, waving his torch in the air like some mighty warrior on the hunt. Echoes of Jonathan's words sounded throughout the crowd as its members got their bearings for the next leg of the pursuit.

Jonathan reeled on the traitor and screamed in his sunken face as he grabbed him by his hair. "You, too," Jonathan ordered, roughly grabbing the traitor by the arm and shoving him indifferently down the stairs. Humiliated, he tumbled to the dirt street in front of Malchus. Breathing heavily, the man rose slowly and brushed off his bruised and soiled arms and legs. *He is at the mercy of the same men to whom he had betrayed his master,* Malchus thought. He was completely helpless and powerless, and all he could see were the angry faces in the crowd descending upon him. The only interest they had in him now was to make sure he had told them the truth, and, of course, to see him scorned by the ones he had betrayed. If they did not find Jesus at the Garden of Gethsemane, the Romans would surely kill him.

The man looked up, his sweat-soaked face taking in all the angry eyes, which stared at him with such hatred, he seemed paralyzed. The crowd swept him up as it surged back down the road again, toward the Pool of Siloam where they would leave the city by way of the Water Gate. Malchus watched the traitor walk down the road in stiff, wooden movements, as if he did not feel his legs. The fascination with the bag of silver, still tied to his waist, had to be long gone. He looked ready for death.

NINETEEN

The torch light spread like liquid into the Kidron Valley. The clear sky had given way to billowy, fragmented clouds, which reflected silver and gray with great black shadows as they blotted out the moonlight. Darkening the night further and casting a pall over the evening sky was the oil-stenched torch smoke drifting back up the hill from the easterly breeze coming off the Mount of Olives, where the Garden of Gethsemane lay. Malchus coughed spasmodically as the thick black smoke filled his nostrils. He covered his mouth and nose with the sleeve of his tunic and quickened his pace to the valley.

Malchus thought of the Garden of Gethsemane. When he had first become a slave, Levia had sent him there to purchase the very purest of oil from the man who owned and ran the press. A small operation. In fact, the garden itself was small. Malchus remembered how serene and peaceful it was there. It was a place he would like to visit with Zara. Now, as he saw the mob approach the path that would lead them up to the garden, he only hoped it would not be the site of a bloodbath. What if Jesus and his followers resisted? From what he heard of Jesus at the temple, how he stood up to the priests and wrecked the market, the mob coming for him could run into trouble. *Then again,* he thought, *at the temple Jesus does not have armed Roman soldiers to contend with.*

†

Unknown to anyone, up on the hillside in the garden itself, a bowed head, drenched in sweat, saw, through closed eyes, the approach of the torch-lit crowd.

†

Climbing the footpath to the garden, Malchus found himself passing the older chief priests and elders, some of whom were winded and bent over at the waist. Others struggled uphill, breathing heavily through wide-open mouths. Looking up ahead, he could see the traitor being savagely pushed forward by Jonathan, the Romans following right behind him. As for the temple guard, its members had dropped back and were now surrounding Malchus as they continued to climb.

"I hope this doesn't take long," a struggling guard said. "Let's just grab this peasant messiah and get out of here. This place is starting to give me a strange feeling."

Lit by the mosaic of torches, the entrance gate to the garden looked eerily inviting. Shadows fell in every direction, and as Malchus watched them dance, he became aware of a different feeling. The air seemed thick, almost heavy. Not warm, not humid. Just dense. He could think of no other way to describe it, and he had never experienced anything quite like it. It caused a heaviness about his chest, not quite painful, and not unlike water pressure, but dry. For no apparent reason, walking was becoming more difficult, and became harder still with every step, until he felt as if he were walking up the Jordan River. From the indiscernible mumblings of men talking to themselves, Malchus guessed others around him were noting the same phenomenon. Closing his eyes for a moment, Malchus realized what the thickness really reminded him of. It seemed as if the approach to the garden was crowded, really crowded, like being packed into a small space with barely enough air to breath, a crush of bodies on every side, leaving no room to bend or stretch or even turn one's head. He wanted to say something about it, but even his jaw felt heavy. Then he looked up and saw something that made him want to turn and run, yet, he froze where he stood. The clouds that had been passing straight overhead were now curving around the garden, as if they were brushing up against a similar invisible resistance just as he was, an invisible wall surrounding just the garden. The night sky above the garden was amazingly clear, as if a window to the universe had been opened, and he could not remember ever before seeing so many stars. In the clear air above he sensed, but did not actually see, movement.

What was that? he wondered. He had the distinct impression he saw someone, only he was looking up. The very idea sent a chill down his spine.

Once inside the garden, the traitor and Jonathan stopped. So did the Romans and everyone following. Three men, who apparently had been sleeping on the ground just inside the entrance to the garden, bolted upright in surprise as the sounds of the crowd awoke them.

"Seize them," Jonathan shouted, pointing to the three. Before anyone could respond to his order, a strangely authoritative voice was heard from a little farther up in the garden, just out of torchlight.

"For whom do you seek?"

The words sent a shock wave through the already heavily laden air. *There is no mistaking it,* Malchus thought. Instantaneously, as the words were spoken, he sensed a presence in the air. For a moment he wondered if he were going crazy, but he felt the presence again, only this time it was as if he were in the middle of the temple courts with thousands of people around him.

"Jesus of Nazareth," said the centurion in response to the question. His words sounded strangely muffled, and Malchus wondered what was wrong with the man, or his own hearing.

Up the hill Malchus could see the reflection of fire and moonlight off a white tunic moving toward them.

"Go ahead," Jonathan said, shoving the traitor forward. "Greet the one we want. Right now I don't care about the rest."

The traitor looked back to Jonathan who was now flanked by Roman soldiers, then he continued into the garden. He walked, head low, toward the approaching man, whom Malchus presumed to be the one who had just asked the question. The man paused in the shadows as the traitor took his hand, then kissed him on the cheek. The man spoke softly to the traitor, who then backed away with his head bowed shamefully in his hands.

"I am he," the man said as he continued his approach through shards of moonlight cutting through olive tree brances.

Suddenly, Malchus felt another surge—like a wave—and it moved right through him. He felt vulnerably exposed to that invisible, crowded presence about him. His feet seemed stuck to the ground. His body felt so heavy, he struggled to hold himself up. His legs trembled in betrayal. Before he knew it, he was on the ground. Looking from side to side, he could see he was not alone. In fact, nobody was standing. The members of the mob all lay scattered on the ground. Some were flat out on their backs. Some seemed to have their faces buried in the dirt. Some were crumpled up, like dirty laundry that had been tossed to the floor. Lanterns had broken and gone out. The oil-soaked torches were also strewn about on the dirt, still burning, their flickering casting shadows into the surrounding olive trees. Slowly, the sensation of heaviness began to dissipate, and everyone struggled to get off the ground. Some still could not rise, and gave up, accepting their predicament, at least for the moment.

Malchus had gotten to one knee when he saw the man they had come for standing a few yards away. He rubbed his eyes a few times, uncertain he was seeing clearly. The Nazarene was absolutely soaking wet, as if he had just climbed out of water. Both the long dark hair on his head and the beard on his face were dripping. His tunic, which clung to his soaked body, had a pink hue that could be seen, even in the torchlight.

"For whom do you seek?" Jesus said again.

"Jesus of Nazareth," the centurion repeated, his response barely audible, as he collapsed to the ground in midsentence.

"I am he," Jesus also repeated, with the same result as before. Waves of energy ripped through the air as if to punctuate his every word. The same words, the same effect. Malchus wondered if the chief priests were thinking the same thing he was. The words, *I am he,* were pregnant with meaning,. Every learned Jew knew this was the way the Almighty identified Himself to Moses. These words spoken by Jesus were blasphemy to the priests, but they were unable to protest as they lay prostrate on the ground.

"What is happening?" Jonathan demanded of the ex-disciple, trying to pull the man toward him by grabbing a handful of his tunic. Both were on the ground, as was everyone else in the arresting party. The ex-disciple did not answer. Instead he kept his face to the ground and hands over his ears, surrounding his senses like a tomb.

"What kind of wizardry is this?" One of the soldiers asked, the fear in his voice obvious.

"What he does, he does from the powers of Beelzebub," whispered one of the chief priests, fear and loathing dripping from his words.

"You have come for me, and I am here," Jesus said to them while they were again struggling to their feet against the garden's heavy air. "Let these others go, and I will go with you," Jesus said, motioning toward his disciples with a barely perceptible hitch of his bearded chin. Just as discreetly, Jesus looked at the one who betrayed him, saying nothing, speaking volumes. The traitor looked back with a watery gaze, then quickly away.

"We have no orders other than to take the Nazarene. As far as we're concerned, the others can go," said a Roman soldier who had managed to get to his feet and was now leaning on Malchus.

"Well, what are you waiting for?" Jonathan said to the Romans from behind the traitor. "Go ahead and get him."

The Romans looked at one another, no one wanting to be the first to advance. Each was waiting for the other to make the first move toward Jesus. None of their extensive training had ever prepared them for what had just occurred. Everyone in the arresting party appeared afraid, Romans and Jews alike. How could they seize a man who could knock them down simply by speaking? And what would Jesus do if he got mad?

Malchus struggled back to his feet as the Roman soldiers, renowned for their bravery, quarreled amongst themselves regarding who would step forward first. If not for their agitated expressions, it would appear from a distance that they were being overly polite with one another. Finally, one of them, probably the one of least rank, grumbled as he took the first step. He then, with no warning, shoved Malchus ahead with all his strength, sending him stumbling and falling at Jesus's feet. The sudden surge forward did not go unanswered. Unexpectedly, one of Jesus' disciples lunged in front of his master and drew his sword.

Malchus managed to keep himself from landing, face first, in the dirt, but as he regained his footing, he turned his head to the left to yell at whoever had pushed him. Before he uttered a word, he saw the soldier, wide-eyed, looking past Malchus and reaching for his sword. For an instant Malchus stared blankly at the soldier. Suddenly, he heard a loud *whack*. The right side of his head was slapped by something icy cold. In reflex action, he put his hands to the sides of his head. Warm fluid rushed between the fingers of his right hand. His legs involuntarily collapsed out from under him, and he hit the ground again. The frozen sensation he had felt just a second earlier turned into a blazing fire. He screamed in agony, barely aware of the sound of his own cry. He writhed about on the ground, blood flowing between his fingers. His ear had been completely severed from his head.

"No more of this," Jesus said loudly. As he spoke the words, the arms of both the disciple and the Roman soldier went limp involuntarily, each no longer able to hold the weight of his sword. Again, ripples of energy sent them all backward and to the ground.

Jesus looked down at Malchus, who was in a fetal position kicking his feet uncontrollably in the dirt, holding his bleeding head, and screaming in searing pain. Jesus began to bend toward Malchus, whose terror multiplied as he saw the man they had come to arrest reach out to him.

Jesus touched Malchus's blood-drenched hands, which were pressed against the huge open gash on the right side of his head.

Malchus continued to scream, wondering what terrible and mysterious fate would befall him. Then it happened. Malchus would later remember it as a cool breeze, which started in the center of his head and slowly worked its way to the gashed opening, where his ear had been. His hands, still pressing tightly on the wound, went numb—unable to feel what was transpiring beneath them. He did not consciously realize he had stopped screaming until, in astonishment, he lay motionless. The pain had completely ceased. Everyone in the arresting party who saw Jesus touch Malchus gasped, probably thinking Jesus had killed him simply by touching his head. They certainly all would have run away if their legs had let them.

"Put your sword into its sheath," Jesus said to the disciple. "He who lives by the sword will die by the sword. Will I not drink from the cup which the Father has given me?" Then he turned his gaze to the arresting party. Its members were frozen with fear. He raised his arms and began to speak. "Have you come out against a robber with swords and clubs? When I was with you in the temple, you could not lay hands on me. Do you think I cannot appeal to my Father, and he will at once have more than twelve legions of angels appear before your very eyes in my behalf? But this hour has been given to you and the power of darkness so that the scriptures of the prophets might be fulfilled." Having said this, he stepped forward into their midst, dropped his arms to his sides, closed his eyes, and slowly bowed his head in surrender. At that moment the heaviness in the air seemed to disappear.

"Seize him," Jonathan said, still behind the ex-disciple. Two of the Roman soldiers took hold of Jesus' arms and then paused and looked at each other, each still hesitant, perhaps wondering whether any further supernatural phenomena would occur, or whether Jesus would also kill them by his touch.

When nothing occurred and they saw his surrender was genuine, they tightened their grip. The other Roman soldiers became emboldened and drew leather cords and bound Jesus' hands behind his back. He offered no resistance at all. Neither did he speak another word. They had their man. Their courage returning, they pushed through the mob and led him down the way they had come. The rest of the mob followed, angrily jeering as they went. The disciples, one by one, followed behind at a distance, until only Malchus was left in the Garden of Gethsemane.

TWENTY

Time seemed to stand still. Malchus had not moved since Jesus had touched him, and that had to have been over an hour ago, maybe two. No one had stopped or come back to assess his condition. Maybe they had not noticed he was missing. That would be typical. Or maybe they really did think he was dead. Caiaphas would love to be able to stick Jesus with a solid crime like that, even if it was at the expense of his own slave.

Whatever, he did not care what any of them thought about him now. He was enjoying a foreign crispness of thought. Oh, his doubting, analytical mind did stage a meager attack in trying to explain what had actually happened after the Roman soldier had pushed him toward Jesus. But every explanation was a reach. Like maybe he had just been hit on his head with the sword . . . hard enough to cause his mind to play tricks on him. There was no doubt he had been hit very hard—hard enough to send him straight to the ground. And the rest could then have been a dream, like those all-so-real ones he had been having of the high priest lately.

He smiled at the lack of evidence and illogic of his defense. Beneath his right hand, he felt his ear. Not only was the wound healed, but he had an entirely new ear, as if the dismemberment had never happened. Dreams do not produce real blood, he thought for the tenth time, then stared incredulously at his still bloodied hands—sticky and drying proof that he had not imagined the whole thing. And pain of that magnitude does not simply vanish. With just the gentle touch of his hand. Effortlessly. No, there was nothing staged about *this* healing, and he would now be shocked if he were to find the others were anything but genuine.

What about my severed ear? It must be on the ground somewhere. He lifted his head in a halfhearted attempt to look. Too dark. Too peaceful. *Who needs it anyway,* he thought.

He rolled over onto his back. Looking up at the stars, he noticed the clouds were once again moving straight over the garden, no longer detouring around some unseen resistance. He moved his arms back and forth to see if the thickness in the air was still present. It was not. All the weight—the anxiety, the fear, and the tension that had been building all day was gone. Vanished. As if it had never been. In its place, peace. As he lay there, he actually felt as if he were floating. He did not want this experience ever to end.

Although still marveling, his mind had moved beyond the physical healing. Half the questions he had in life had been answered in a moment. He also felt as if he had answers to questions he had never asked. His mind was illuminated with a living ah-ha! Jesus was the long-awaited Messiah! Not at all a fable as Malchus had come to believe.

Something had definitely changed inside him. At that moment he could not remember ever having felt so content. He felt as if he were a new man. Fulfilled. So at peace with the world. So at peace with his Maker. That was what was different. He was, for the first time in his life, at peace with God. And it had happened because of Jesus, the true Messiah, whom Malchus had been there to help arrest. *God help them,* he thought, and then smiled. *Why not, he helped me.*

His mind drifted back to when he had been a boy out in the fields with his father. He remembered his father telling of the satisfaction to be found in knowing God—satisfaction beyond description or understanding, a fulfillment in being in the plan of the One who made the plan. So this is what his father had meant. And it must have been what he meant when he spoke of either choosing God's way or man's way. Malchus enjoyed the clarity of the moment and wondered—hoped—it would last forever.

Malchus considered some of the miracle's other implications. He knew now whom he was to follow, whose side he was on. He certainly was not, and never had been, a supporter of the religious order. He thought he had always been his own man. Even as a slave he considered himself a free spirit. But now he knew. His spirit had never been free. In retrospect, he had not known true freedom. Jesus, however, appeared completely free, even when arrested. He had allowed them to arrest him. That much was obvious. A totally free captive—free to the point that the bewildered mob was more his than he theirs.

Malchus suddenly did not care he was a slave. The realization amazed him. All he had thought about since he was enslaved was the day he would once again be free. Now, that did not seem to matter. He could serve God as a slave or as a free man. What was important now was that he serve the Messiah. Even if Jesus was a wild man at times. Malchus's eyes had been opened, and there was nothing he wanted to do more. He felt as if he was home, but home was a person, not a place.

His eyes closed, and then opened, and then closed again. He touched his ear and smiled and fell into a most restful sleep.

TWENTY-ONE

Malchus slowly opened his eyes to the soft glow of presunrise light that outlined the horizon of the Mount of Olives. He took a moment to remember where he was. He reached for his ear, then closed his eyes and sighed in confidence that the previous night had not been a dream. He remembered in awe the wave of energy that sent everyone to the ground whenever Jesus spoke. He tried to imagine what the angels would have looked like and how many of them he would have seen. He wondered what mission Jesus was saving them for. Probably in Jerusalem. Probably today. Again he opened his eyes but was surprised to discover that enough time had passed for the dawning sunlight to splash quietly into the Garden of Gethsemane. He watched peacefully as sparrows flew in and about the olive trees that surrounded him, speaking to one another, probably about the stranger on the ground.

"Malchus," a voice called from just below the garden, down a way on the footpath.

Malchus stirred at the call of his name, then lifted his head enough to see someone hurrying up the footpath toward him.

"Malchus, are you here?"

Malchus smiled. He recognized the voice. What better way could there possibly be to waken from this perfect sleep? "Yes, Zara, I'm over here," Malchus said sleepily, propping himself on one elbow.

"Malchus. Malchus, I got here as quickly as I could. I heard something happened to you," she cried. She ran up to him and dropped to her knees. He must have looked mortally wounded, there on the ground, with dried blood on his face, hands, and garments. "Where are you hurt?"

Malchus laid his head back to the ground. "My ear. One of them attacked me with a sword."

"Oh, dear God," she said, her eyes welling up, gently touching the skin and hair by his ear, cautiously examining the wounded area.

"The other side," Malchus said.

"I knew something terrible was going to happen," she whimpered as she leaned over him to examine the other side of his head. Her tears dripped on his cheeks, and her long black hair fell over his face like a veil. His hair was hard with dried blood. After carefully searching with the softest touch, she began to bend his ear over. "Am I hurting you?" she asked, deeply concerned.

Malchus wanted to grab her and not let go, but he resisted. "No," he said.

"Let me know."

"I will."

"I—I don't see the cut. It must be under your hair."

"No, it was my ear."

"Well, that might be where it hurts, but the ear isn't cut."

"Zara?"

"Yes, Malchus?"

"Did you bring anything to eat?"

"Eat? Well, no, I uh—" She drew back and stared at him. "Did you say eat?"

Malchus laughed. "I'm not hurt, Zara," he said. "I've just been resting here." He hated to admit it because he was so touched by her concern. And he did not want her to stop fussing over him, but he also could not wait to tell her what had happened.

"What do you mean you're not hurt?" She pushed him away from her for a better look at him. Seeing all the blood, she looked confused. "What do you mean you're not hurt?" she repeated, no longer crying.

"I'm not hurt, Zara, I'm just not hurt." He shrugged his shoulders. Then he stood up slowly. "I was hurt. I was very hurt. More hurt than I've ever been. I should still be very hurt." He laughed louder, seeing Zara's confused expression. His laughter echoed down the hillside. He was giddy now, and his laughter was infectious. Zara began to smile, even laugh a little, but with a slight, uncomprehending frown.

"Then where have you been all night? What is all this blood from? Whose blood is it?"

"It's mine," Malchus said with a smile. "And I've been right here."

"You're not making any sense, Malchus," Zara said shaking her head, then her eyes widened. "Your eye!"

"What about my eye?" he said, reaching for it.

"It's—It's better."

Malchus touched his eye, then, feeling no pain or swelling, he pressed it harder and massaged it. He paused, then let out a loud laugh.

"Malchus, tell me what's happening here," Zara demanded, still staring in disbelief at his eye.

"Jesus healed me. Completely. Just like he did to the blind man, I guess. Me, of all people. I was his enemy, coming to help arrest him, but that didn't matter." He told Zara what had happened, trying not to leave anything out.

Zara listened intently. Her large feline eyes took in everything he said as if she were seeing the events unfold before her. Malchus watched her as he spoke, her beauty almost caused him to forget what he was saying. When he finished, she told Malchus what she had heard at Caiaphas's. "One of the chief priests came to the house to tell Caiaphas that Jesus had been taken to Annas's house. Then I heard him say that you had been seriously hurt, maybe killed, and that someone should be sent here to get you. I asked if I could go. I'm not even sure if he really heard me when I asked. He just nodded and waved his hand on his way out the door with the other man. Levia wouldn't give me directions at first. She said it was too dangerous for me to come at night by myself. I started to leave and told her I would ask someone else. When she saw I was actually planning on going, she changed her mind and told me how to get here." Zara spoke so quickly, she was breathless.

"I'm glad you came," Malchus said, squeezing both her hands.

Zara began to laugh again. Tears welled up in her eyes.

"You were right, Zara," Malchus said, bending down to her. She was still on her knees, laughing. He cupped her face in his hands and looked at her longingly. "You were one hundred percent right. He is the Messiah. He's got to be. He can't be anyone but the Messiah. He can do anything he wants. Look what he did to me. I guess I just needed to be shown a little more directly." He sighed.

Zara reached out, grabbed him around the neck, and pulled him toward her. "What are you doing?" Malchus protested as he allowed himself to be pulled to the ground next to her. He playfully pulled her over him to his other side. He looked at her face as her girlish smile faded and her eyes focused on his, drawing him closer. He kissed her lightly on the lips, drew back slightly as if to see if this was really Zara, then he kissed her again.

After a moment Zara eased her head away. "Malchus, I'm sorry about the way I spoke to you in the kitchen. I realize now the risk you took," she said, still looking deep into his eyes. "You risked your life for me," she said softly. She brushed her hand against his face, lightly tracing the curve of his new ear with the soft underside of her finger. "What will they do to Jesus?" she asked.

Malchus laughed. "What will *they* do to *him?*" he asked, smiling back at her, his face reassuring as he answered. "What will the mice do to the lion? They will do anything he *allows* them to do and nothing more. That's what will happen. Jesus said that at any time he could call thousands of angels to his side, and I believe it. I thought I was going crazy last night when it felt as if the whole garden was crowded, like at the temple. But now I know better. The angels were right here, just waiting for the word. I know it. Jesus can handle himself, believe me."

"So what do we do, Malchus?" Zara asked. "Caiaphas hates Jesus. If he finds out what happened to your ear, he'll hate you, too. And if he hears what we believe, won't he punish us?"

Malchus looked at her for a moment. "Punish us? Caiaphas would definitely punish us. He'd probably try to kill us along with Jesus. You should have seen him and Jonathan last night. They were bloodthirsty. Don't say anything to anyone, Zara. Not yet. Let's just go back to the house and let everyone know that I'm all right, not that anyone else cares. Jesus definitely has a plan. I'm sure of it. He was completely in control last night, and very decisive. I've never seen such power and authority. He just has it. I don't know if anyone knows what he's going to do, but he definitely has a plan. You could see by the way he gave himself over to them that he had other options. He could have done something else, but he didn't. His surrender was calculated and intentional. Whatever he does, I want to be part of it."

"Then we should find him," Zara said.

TWENTY-TWO

Malchus and Zara entered the old city through the Water Gate by the Pool of Siloam. Malchus was so euphoric, he was oblivious to his crusted hair and soiled clothes. Zara was not. She had told him—ordered him—to take a bath, and they were heading to the pool.

Malchus, in a state of bliss, saw nothing, heard nothing, and was thinking about nothing but Jesus and Zara. He walked down the smooth marble steps to the water and failed to notice the obvious. And Zara, not being a native, would not have understood what she was looking at. Malchus still did not notice as he bent down and looked at his reflection in the clear, motionless water.

"Wash up, Malchus, or do I have to push you in?" Zara said, waiting behind him with her hands on her hips, her smile a stage for her beautiful dimples.

"All right," he said dreamily, hardly listening to what she said, still looking at his reflection. He studied his ear in the still water. It looked as if nothing had happened but for his hard, matted hair. Then it dawned on him that something was missing. There were no ripples in the water. *Where is everyone?*

Malchus had half-turned around when Zara gave him just enough of a push to send him spilling into the water. He emerged and threw back his head and hair from his eyes. Zara smiled and gave him a wave. He smiled and waved back, allowing himself to fall straight back into the cold water.

"That should wake you up," Zara said as he came up for air. "And stay in there until I say you're clean." She wagged her finger at him like his mother.

Malchus looked at her from the pool. No one had ever been so loving with him. The sun had been up barely two hours, and he was already having the best day of his life. If this wasn't love he was feeling, than what was it? He felt protected. Invincible. As if he was in God's perfect will, and that this peace, this bliss, would somehow last for the rest of his life, that he would never be alone again.

Alone! His mind shot back to what he was thinking just before Zara pushed him into the pool. *There's no one here but us!*

"Something strange is going on, Zara." Malchus said, disturbed. He looked past her and searched the area surrounding them.

"Strange?"

"Yes. This is the Pool of Siloam. Jerusalem. Passover. Why are we the only ones here?"

Zara looked puzzled and shrugged her shoulders. "I guess we're just lucky today."

"This place should be mobbed. We should have had to wait hours to approach the water. Where is everyone?"

Zara turned around and saw only a few people, but heard voices in the distance. Lots of voices. "I think most of Jerusalem is that way. Listen," she said, pointing.

"The temple? Antonia?" Malchus said, climbing out of the pool. "What's happening?"

Zara ran her fingers through his hair and over his ear. "Hmm. better," she said, inspecting. "I'd forgotten how handsome you were without a black eye, but you need another dip," she said, wiping a smear of blood from her fingers.

"Jesus!" Malchus said, looking in the direction of the noise. "Come on, Zara. Maybe that's why everyone is there," he said, smiling broadly.

Malchus and Zara had barely started in the direction of the temple before they could hear Jesus' name being spoken by those on the fringe of the crowd. Just hearing the Messiah's name sent a rush of excitement and anticipation through Malchus. What words of wisdom is he confounding the Romans with now? What miraculous deeds are the people of Jerusalem witnessing at this very moment? What display of his awesome power is being unleashed as a testimony to his authenticity? Malchus pulled Zara by the hand, quickening his pace as the traffic closed in around him. People emptied out of houses and inns, all heading in the same direction. The noise of the crowd grew louder with every step.

Within a block of the temple, Malchus knew whatever was happening was coming from the direction of the Roman fortress. Malchus thought the clamor they were heading toward had a strange feel to it. Instead of the choruslike praises that welcomed Jesus into the gates just a few days ago, or the isolated proclamations of joy and thanksgiving from those who were healed of all kinds of infirmities, there was yelling. It sounded angry. Ugly.

Just ahead, on a road that led diagonally away from Antonia to the Damascus Gate, there was a thick wall of people, pushing, shoving, and vying for position to see. It appeared impenetrable. Malchus stopped.

"What's the matter, Malchus?" Zara asked.

Malchus's chest felt tight. He was overcome with a wave of anxiety. Over the years he had seen many people sentenced to death by the Romans. Through the city and out the Damascus Gate to a hillside called Golgotha, known to all as the Place of the Skull, the condemned had been forced to carry the very cross on which they were to be crucified. The death walk usually attracted an angry crowd comprised of curious onlookers, noisy radicals, and those against whom the crime had been committed. The crush of humanity before him reminded him of such a crowd, but this was different. Larger. Louder. More intense. Scary.

"I'm not sure, but I think it's a Roman execution."

"A what?"

"A Roman execution."

"Do you think it's—"

"How could it be? Jesus would never allow such a thing to happen to him," he said. It was more a question than reassurance. He could see his own concern in Zara's face, and realized his face was betraying him. "I have to get to the front and see," he said.

"How? Everyone is trying to do the same thing. Look at all these people."

Malchus looked but could not give her an answer. He glanced back at Zara and felt his frustration change to near panic as he heard mocking laughter over the shouts of the mob. To the front of the crowd he could see people becoming more animated. At first it looked as if they were waving their arms, but as he watched, he realized they were shaking their fists. Some even looked as if they were throwing things. Beyond the crowd he saw people filling the flat rooftops on the other side of the street. They were jeering and pointing.

"Stay here," Malchus said. "I'll take the rooftops past the crowd. From there, I'll be able to see everything, and then I'll come back and let you know." He looked at the tops of the buildings that lined the road.

Zara grabbed his wrist tightly. "You're not going anywhere without me."

Malchus saw the determination in her face. There was nothing to discuss. He grabbed her hand and led her into the backyard of the house immediately to their left. Malchus expected to find a ladder to the roof, and he did. But he also found others who were making their way up on other ladders.

He and Zara hurried up, and, once on the roof, Malchus saw there were six other roofs to cross before they had a view of the road. The distances between the houses were no more than a few feet. He wondered if Zara could do it. Before he could even ask her, Zara sprinted past him. To his shock, she jumped and easily cleared the gap to the next roof and was continuing toward the next. She was like a deer in flight. Malchus could hardly keep up with her.

Zara jumped to the last roof and was on her way to the edge by the cross-street to join a dozen other people who were pointing and shouting angrily. Malchus could not believe Zara's leap across the rooftops, but his attention immediately refocused on the dread that gripped his chest. All he could think about was the street below. He rushed to her side, sweating, breathing heavily, and petrified to look at what she was already seeing.

"Who are they?" Zara asked, grimacing.

Two bloody, half-naked men were coming up the street one story below them, single file, each carrying a large splintery beam across savagely whipped shoulders.

"The thieves." Malchus sighed. *Of course,* he thought. The thieves he had seen yesterday in the courtyard.

"How do you know?" she asked.

"They were tied to the whipping post when I was at Antonia," Malchus said, feeling the tightness in his chest dissipate. As disgusted as he was by the sight, he was relieved.

Four Roman soldiers led the way, now just below, clearing a path with only their presence. The thieves struggled behind them, followed by two more soldiers, each of whom cracked a whip randomly as a painful reminder that they were to press on toward their death.

This gruesome parade was nothing new to Malchus, but the size of the crowd was. Still, there was something else, something different about it. He looked at Zara, who was staring at the events below, then at the crowd of people who were roaring and shaking their fists. *Something is definitely not right,* he thought, trying to figure out what was going on. He looked again at the crowd and almost forgot entirely the impending executions.

Malchus looked down the street in the direction from which the thieves had come. The crowd wasn't closing in behind. They were not following. There was always a mob that thrived on the misfortune of the sentenced. And always they followed so they could be within earshot when the hammer drove the nails through the flesh of the doomed. Why were they lingering on the roadside? What were they waiting for?

"I don't understand why this crowd is so big and crazy. These men are nobodies. These people do not know them or even what their crimes were. I wouldn't know myself if I hadn't seen them inside Antonia just yesterday. And even if they were known, their crimes wouldn't stir such a huge re—"

Malchus suddenly felt the bottom drop out of his stomach. He felt as if he were falling. His chest constricted again.

Zara turned to him when he stopped speaking. His face was pained, and he was holding back tears as his eyes became transfixed. She spun around to see what had so gripped his attention. A gasp escaped her lips. She quickly turned away and buried her face in his chest. Malchus wanted to turn away, too, but he could not. He was in shock. Overwhelmed. Unable to move or look away. He could not possibly be seeing right. His tears fell onto Zara's thick black hair.

"Oh, God, no!" Malchus whispered, looking down from the roof as Jesus slowly approached. Hearing him, Zara turned to look again. Upon seeing Jesus closer now, her knees buckled, and she fainted. Malchus grabbed hold of her as she fell into him. He held her dead weight, mesmerized by the scene below.

A triangle of three soldiers slowly marched ahead of Jesus. He had been beaten far more severely than the two thieves. Malchus could not imagine how he was even still alive, much less carrying the heavy wooden beam, its splinters digging deeply into ripped and bleeding shoulders. The back of his outer garment was soaked red with blood. There was also a stream of blood running down his face and into his eyes and mouth. It came from under his hair, which was pinned down by what looked like a woven hyssop vine, its long, pointy thorns puncturing and tearing at his already bruised and swollen head. Malchus was paralyzed. It hurt him to look. He could not imagine how intense the pain must be for Jesus, under the heavy load of the tree, being prodded forward just like the two thieves.

Behind Jesus there were also two soldiers with whips, and after them, about a dozen women following. Malchus could see their faces. They were crying hysterically and helping one another to stand as they moved along with the beaten pulp of a man.

"Save yourself, Messiah," the people mocked. Many fell to their knees as he approached, shouting sarcastically, "Hail, King of the Jews."

"Let's hear a prophecy now, Jesus—or do you want us to tell you *your* future?" a man near Malchus yelled, laughing. Malchus wanted to kill the man, but the taunts were coming from all around him, getting louder and louder.

"A fitting crown for a king." "Teach us more rabbi." "Who needs to be healed now, O Great Healer?" Everyone seemed to be yelling at him.

Malchus clenched his fist and stamped his foot on the roof. *Shut their mouths, Jesus!* his thoughts screamed. "Why don't you save yourself?" he whispered. "Please, Jesus, please. Don't allow this to go any further," he said, more loudly. "Show them your power. Call your angels." He was shouting now. Everyone around him stopped yelling and suddenly turned and glared at him. *They all look crazy,* he thought. Malchus was about to tell them that Jesus truly was the Messiah, but fell silent and looked down instead. Still holding Zara by his side, he dropped to his knees.

Zara's eyes opened. She saw she was sitting on the roof and leaning into Malchus's embrace. She looked at Malchus. All the color had drained from her face. She looked as if she was about to vomit.

"Zara?"

"I'm all right," she said, wiping sweat from her face. Then she looked to the street in time to see Jesus directly below. Spit hit him from every direction.

Jesus tripped and fell face first into the hard-packed dirt, the weight of the beam driving the thorns deeper as his head slammed forward. One of the soldiers leading the way came back to him and pulled the cross beam off his shoulders, revealing skin so raw and dirty that it looked as if it had been burned with a torch.

Zara threw up, then wiped her mouth with the sleeve of her garment.

The soldier yelled something in Roman to the other soldiers. Two of them lurched into the crowd, seized a man, and hurried him to the beam. The man struggled to get it on his shoulders as a whip cracked on Jesus' back, causing Malchus's own back to stiffen. The women behind Jesus flinched. Insults were hurled at them, too. Many walked bent over as if their stomachs ached. Others covered their faces in both hands.

"I know where they're going," Malchus said. "If we go back to the temple and out the Sheep Gate, we won't have to fight the crowd through the Damascus Gate to Golgotha. Can you make it?"

"Golgotha?" Zara said weakly.

Malchus nodded, unable to elaborate. To describe what the Romans would do at Golgotha would be to admit it to himself.

Malchus helped Zara to her feet. She felt weak in his arms, and she moved with uncertainty, no longer the gazellelike athlete racing across rooftops. They managed to negotiate the aerial maze and descend the same ladder that had given them access to this ramshackle mezzanine. Once on the street, they worked their way against the flow of the crowd and headed to the temple.

Zara looked a little better as they pressed on. Some color was back in her face now. They climbed up the outer temple steps and hurried through the far-left gate. Malchus could not remember ever seeing less activity going on in the temple area during Passover. Jesus was still disrupting temple business, and he was not even there.

"Malchus!" Someone was calling him. Malchus turned. It was Judah. He was waving him over.

"Not now, Judah," Malchus yelled back.

"But I heard you were—"

"I'll find you later," Malchus yelled, then hurriedly turned back to his mission.

The warm morning sun that had bathed them since they were united in the garden was eclipsed by the cool shade of the high west walls of Jerusalem. For a moment he felt a chill as they rushed along in the shadow of the ancient walls. The normally busy avenue to the Pool of Bethesda was as eerily quiet as the Pool of Siloam. They did not see the sun again until they made their way around the Roman fortress, and then the bright hot light was directly in their eyes.

Leading Zara by the hand, Malchus stepped off the pathway and across a short span of untraveled hillside to the road to Damascus. Beyond that, at the end of a narrow footpath worn from the dragging feet of hundreds of others who had been executed under Roman law, loomed Golgotha.

Zara followed Malchus in silence. Malchus did not notice. He was lost in his own thoughts, sorting through the events rapidly unfolding before him, succeeding in finding questions but not answers. Were the executioners so blind that they could not see this was no ordinary man? Wasn't anyone going to stop this crime—this atrocity—from being committed? And if Jesus were crucified, *murdered,* what would be the penalty? How would God respond to such savagery? To the rejection and murder of the Messiah? Malchus shuddered.

He imagined what he would do if he sent the long-awaited Messiah to his chosen people and they thanked him by torturing and murdering his emissary. Anger gripped him as vivid images of what his own wrathful judgment might be. Merciless infliction of painful and fatal diseases, pestilence, catastrophes, the likes of which man could not imagine. And special vengeance for the instigators and perpetrators of this offense. Caiaphas would be first. Then the priests at the meeting room table. Then Pilate, Jonathan, the traitor, the soldiers, the arresting mob, the hecklers, and finally the ones who let it all happen. He saw himself in that latter group, frozen like a rodent before a flock of descending ravens, hoping desperately not to be seen and devoured. Even in his own vision of revenge, he himself was guilty.

Malchus shut out his own thoughts. Every scenario seemed horrible. All he could hold onto was the remote hope that, at the last minute, Jesus would somehow turn everything around as part of God's plan. He found some hope there. Certainly no man had ever come away the victor from a crucifixion.

He picked up his pace again. This once-perfect day, this new life of love and fulfillment, had turned wretched and black, leaving him lost and alone. Overhead, recently freed doves flew and swooped off the city wall, dancing in the clear morning sunlight. Oblivious. They caught his attention for a second. Then he saw it.

The human flood of the death march poured out of the Damascus Gate and surrounded the edge of the shallow pit know as Golgotha. Somehow still breathing, the three broken men emerged from the throng to a battery of ready soldiers.

TWENTY-THREE

Malchus leaned against the shaded wall, its huge cold rocks still damp from the morning dew. Zara, drained, leaned against him, blending in like a human stone. Her face was drawn and expressionless. She dropped to her knees, her right hand resting lifelessly on his calf. Malchus expected her to faint again.

Four soldiers attached the three cross beams that had been delivered by their intended victims. Malchus thought the soldiers looked more like carpenters than executioners, tying and nailing and running out lengths of rope.

The three exhausted prisoners were made to kneel a few feet from two soldiers with long spears. Meanwhile, several other soldiers formed a large half circle around their busy comrades, keeping the crowd safely away while they tied and hammered.

Jonathan was there with a proud contingent of the temple guard. He was too far away to see clearly, but Malchus knew he was smiling. Unfortunately, Jonathan knew better than to get too close to the Romans while they were working.

Malchus was worn out. His search for answers had only exhausted him further. He slid down against the wall next to Zara, who continued to stare without expression. "Did last night really happen?" he asked.

Zara looked him in the eye. "Yes," she said, her face smeared dirty from swiping at tears. "We can't deny what has happened." She looked back toward the pit.

Malchus moved his hand slowly through the air before him, wanting to detect the thickness he had experienced the night before. "Why aren't they here? Don't they see?" He then touched his ear and eye, wondering if he had gone completely insane.

"Who?" Zara said.

"Them. The unseen ones I told you about."

Zara nodded, but not very convincingly.

With the work on the crosses complete, the two thieves were seized and thrown down on them. Before they had a chance to struggle, their arms were positioned over the cross beams and, with large rusted spikes hammered through each wrist, they were quickly nailed secure. A brief eerie moment later, when their minds caught up to their shocked bodies, the thieves screamed and writhed in agony. The echoing cries sent a chilling hush through the swelling crowd. Unfazed, the soldiers moved down to their feet and attached them in the same efficient manner, as if they were still putting the cross together.

The bottoms of the long posts were positioned by the openings of two narrow holes, each about a cubit deep. Without as much as a nod of instruction, a pair of soldiers securely grabbed the ends of the ropes that were fastened to the top of the cross and pulled as another pair of soldiers lifted at the head. When the cross was almost vertical, it dropped a few feet into the hole and hit bottom, causing the convulsing thief to shriek. He cried pitifully as he tried to support himself on the nail through his heels to keep his own weight from tearing at his wrists and eventually collapsing his lungs.

Malchus winced as he heard the thud of the second cross hit the bottom of its hole. Zara tightened her grip on his knee as the soldiers methodically moved toward Jesus. They grabbed him, stood him straight up, and tore off his outer garment, leaving him naked except for his loincloth. Malchus cringed when he saw his back. It was so ravaged from Roman whips, all that was left was a meaty pulp, flayed to the bone.

"This is it," Malchus said. "If he's ever going to turn this thing around, it's now or never." Malchus rose to his feet. He was barely able to stop himself from screaming out as he watched them position Jesus on the cross without the least bit of resistance.

Zara rose slowly, leaning into Malchus the whole way up. Then, she embraced his waist and leaned her head on his chest, tears dripping from her bloodshot eyes. Jesus was staring straight up as the spikes were driven through his wrists, causing his eyes to shut tight and his body to straighten. He grimaced but did not cry out. Many of the women who had followed him dropped to the ground at the sight.

Near the top of the cross, the soldiers nailed a wooden sign. Malchus had never seen a sign on a cross before. He could not see what it said until the cross was raised. Some of the people in the crowd reacted to it. A murmur could be heard, and several chief priests began to argue with one of the soldiers, demanding that it be removed, saying, "He's not our king." The Romans ignored them, becoming impatient and surly as the nagging priests pressed the issue further.

"What does it say?" Zara said.

"Jesus of Nazareth, King of the Jews."

"I don't understand," she said.

Malchus was not sure if the sign was simple sarcasm from a centurion or a direct affront to the priests from Pilate. The message could not be to Jesus, who was in no position to read it. Whatever the reason, Malchus found it to be more sad than insulting, and he could not concentrate on it long enough to care. The man who had miraculously healed Malchus, the man he had just come to know as the Messiah, was now a public spectacle, nailed to a cross, having not uttered a word of protest or explanation.

Malchus's thoughts screamed out to Jesus, silent shouts of frustrated anger. *Why are you letting this happen? I know you can stop it. Why don't you? Why? Please! Show them! Show them all!*

Nothing. Nothing happened. Then, in a moment of utter frustration and defeat, he slipped into his prayer of habit. To himself, and as a question, he thought it bitterly: *Free in you? Free yourself! Can't you? How are you supposed to free me if you cannot free yourself?* Tears rolled down his face as the prayer echoed in his head.

Jesus slowly lifted his head and opened his eyes. He stared straight at Malchus, who was still at the rear of the crowd against the city wall. Suddenly, Malchus felt pierced by Jesus' gaze. Just as in the Garden of Gethsemane, Malchus's mind became crisply illuminated.

"Do not forget in the darkness what you have heard in the light."

Instantly, Malchus glanced at Zara. She did not appear to have heard anything. He looked back to Jesus, who was still gazing *at him.* Impossible. Malchus blinked hard to squeeze the tears of disbelief from his eyes.

He had to be simply remembering something Jesus had said. He thought for an instant but could not remember Jesus ever saying these words. Was Jesus communicating to him? Now? From the cross? Malchus was confused. The thought did not even have Jesus' voice attached to it, yet the statement rang out so clear, the words so specific. Still held by Jesus' gaze, Malchus focused on the thought as if it were a message. *What light? What darkness?*

As soon as his mind asked the questions, he remembered the garden had been physically dark when his ear, and everything else, had been healed. But it was also there that his mind had become enlightened and, though now the sun was shining brightly, this was the darkest moment he had ever experienced.

He had barely digested that thought when another message came. This time he could hear Jesus' voice clearly in his mind, and the words were so personal that his weakened knees almost gave out.

"Free in Me."

This *was* impossible. *Jesus had heard his thoughts?* Hope suddenly gripped him, but he was still terribly afraid of doing anything about it. The Romans were standing ready to brutalize anyone who would dare interfere, and the priests would surely remember any protest or claim and report it back to Caiaphas. He felt like a coward before the Messiah who could read and speak into his mind, and Malchus looked downward for a second in shame. But then he wondered why Jesus didn't speak into the soldiers' minds, reveal his powers to them?

The only answer that made any sense to Malchus was that he was going insane and, under the stress of the moment, was cracking. He looked back to Jesus in the hope of another response, but Jesus now appeared to be speaking to one of the thieves.

Malchus continued to cry out in his mind to the dying man on the cross, but to no avail. Jesus never so much as glanced in his direction again, only confirming the notion of Malchus's own mental instability. How could he have been so wrong?

Malchus and Zara stayed for hours. A small group, probably family, was finally allowed to approach the cross. Jesus did little more than raise his battered face and speak a few words before the group fell to their knees in sobbing grief. Malchus could bear no more. He had come to see supernatural life, not pitiful death. Maybe it would have been better if he had never gone to Gethsemane in the first place. At least then he would not have had such high hopes, and he would not now be in the depths of such crushing despair.

Malchus's gaze strayed from what now looked like an everyday crucifixion and was suddenly startled. Jonathan was still there. He and a few of the temple guard had drifted toward the Damascus Gate and, despite the arrow shot of distance between them, appeared to be staring at him. Malchus looked away and instinctively drew Zara closer to him, presuming Jonathan might still be refining his list.

He pulled Zara by the hand and slowly walked away in the direction of Caiaphas's, looking back once to assure himself that nothing had changed with Jesus. Meanwhile, the doves continued to swoop off the city wall in the pleasant sunlight. *Good for them,* he thought.

TWENTY-FOUR

Malchus wandered aimlessly about the city with Zara. He was as bewildered as he was depressed. Wherever they went, people were talking about Jesus and, with most of the grieving population praying in the shadows or behind closed doors, the consensus on the street was that he had gotten what he deserved. *Amazing,* Malchus thought. He rides into town on a donkey, with the world praising him and proclaiming him to be the chosen one of God, their ears burning to hear him speak. Now, they claim crucifixion was his just reward.

Malchus's affinity toward numbers and logic was being tested beyond computation. Equations always added up and were either correct or incorrect. And he *always* knew the right answer. But not this time. Nothing added up. The equation did not make sense. He kept going over the facts about Jesus in his mind—the scene at the temple, the healings, the miracles, his own experience, and he could not understand how the outcome resulted in an execution. Every time he reviewed it, his mind screamed out, *wrong!* The more he searched for the error, the more hopeless he became. And the more hopeless he became, the more he despaired at what would come next.

With nowhere else to go, they arrived at the steps to Caiaphas's home by late afternoon. They had taken one step toward the entrance when a rogue gust of wind blew Zara's hair into her face.

"Look, Malchus," Zara said emotionlessly, staring at the sky, pulling her hair back so she could see.

Malchus looked up as sand whipped into his eyes. He rubbed them with the backs of his hands, then looked again. The weather was changing rapidly. Dense black clouds were chasing away the clear blue sky above. Malchus turned in the direction of the storm. A chill ran down his spine when he saw that the clouds were not blowing in from anywhere. They were forming right over the city and spreading outward. The peculiarity of it made Malchus think of the evening before, at Gethsemane. *Now what?*

"I've never seen anything like this before," Zara said, her chin jutting upward, head back, as she followed the outer perimeter of the cloud cover passing overhead.

Malchus squinted as the clouds covered the sun, then eclipsed it completely. "I don't think anyone has," he said, the clouds continuing to form and billow until they touched the horizon in every direction for as far as Malchus could see. The sky turned almost as dark as night.

Malchus felt a large drop hit his forehead, then another. "Come on, Zara. Let's get inside."

"Tears from God," she said, still looking up as a drop landed on her cheek.

Malchus took her hand and led her up the stairs. A moment later, the rain fell with such fury that they were drenched by the time they reached the door.

"Aren't you coming in?" Malchus asked the two guards standing in the rain as he hurried through the door, knowing they would ignore him and stay at attention. "Well, you know best," he said after holding the door open a moment longer. He pushed the door tight and turned just in time to see Zara disappear into the kitchen. He heard Levia greet her. He was about to join them when Caiaphas caught his eye from the meeting room across the hall. The look summoned him. Malchus tried to make himself presentable, pulling his waterlogged clothes away from his body and pressing his wet hair back with both hands.

Caiaphas stood sideways at the balcony, looking at the sky. He backed away as a gust of wind caused the draperies to lick at him as they whipped in the air. "Unusual weather we're having," he said matter-of-factly.

"Yes, sir," Malchus answered, repulsed by the casual tone of the high priest's voice. He had just orchestrated the murder of an innocent man, and he was discussing the weather. The thought of remaining his slave for another six months was unbearable. He hated Caiaphas. All he wanted to do was frustrate his plans. He could think of nothing more meaningful. Nothing that would give him more purpose. Nothing but vengeance.

"Sit down, Malchus," Caiaphas said, motioning toward chairs around the table. "I'm glad to see that you're all right. I was, um, very distressed by the accounts of the attack upon you by one of the rebels. I, um, was about to dispatch some men to aid you, but Zara insisted that she should be the one to go to you. She was adamant. You know how women can be." He grinned awkwardly. "She wouldn't wait for anyone to accompany her," he said, sitting himself down at the head of the table. He arranged himself in the chair and looked up with a slight smile. "Apparently she thinks very highly of you. We all do." He had on his best "concerned, loving father" look.

Malchus thought Caiaphas's concern was both amusing and offensive, but he tried to look unaffected.

Caiaphas then directed his gaze to Malchus's ear. "Obviously the reports of your condition were exaggerated. You look fine. That's good. I was *very* concerned. In fact—" he frowned slightly "—your eye looks much better, also."

Malchus was amazed at Caiaphas's ability to look so loving when he knew he couldn't care less. He was so good at it that, for a second, Malchus thought he was really interested in him. The very last thing Malchus wanted from Caiaphas was anything that resembled genuine concern.

"This day has much good news," he said, changing the subject.

Malchus immediately returned to reality. *That's the man I know,* he thought. *Back to business.*

The high priest spoke louder to be heard above the driving rain. "As I'm sure you know by now, the heretic, Jesus, has been executed by the Romans for his crimes. And his band of rebels has dispersed in fear, as I knew they would. At least they have some sense."

The words hit Malchus like a club. Now the man was gloating over Jesus' murder. Malchus could not contain himself. "Actually, sir, I was attacked."

"Excuse me?" Caiaphas said, apparently not expecting any reply.

"The reports of my condition, sir. They could not have been very exaggerated. I *was* violently attacked with a sword by one of the disciples."

"You were? Oh, I'm sorry to hear that. It's too bad you didn't report it sooner. We could probably have had him crucified as well. At least you weren't injured," he said as a curtain ripped loose and blew across the floor.

Normally Malchus would have hurried to gather the curtain, but he stayed firm in the conversation. "I was terribly injured, sir. Mutilated. The disciple cut off my ear with his sword."

Caiaphas's eyes narrowed as he leaned forward. "He what?"

"He cut off my ear," Malchus said evenly.

"Your ear?" Caiaphas looked confused.

"Yes, sir, this one right here," Malchus said, pulling on his right ear. His boldness began to wane as he realized the weakness in his claim.

Caiaphas's expression did not change. He folded his hands. "Do you think I'm in the mood for this? If this is your idea of a joke, let me warn you—"

"No, sir," Malchus said, surprised at himself for interrupting. "It's no joke." He began to defend himself. The facts about what had happened began to charge his response. "I was on the ground, screaming in agony. My ear was completely off. *Severed from my head!* The Nazarene just touched me as he was being taken by the soldiers. The next thing I knew, the pain was gone, and my ear had been completely restored. Everyone had to have seen it happen. Even Jonathan!"

Caiaphas's face turned red. The veins in his neck were bulging to the point of bursting. "Don't tell me about your hallucinations,"

Caiaphas screamed. "You were undoubtedly knocked unconscious and dreamed this preposterous—"

"And my eye," Malchus said, suddenly remembering. "My eye was healed too. Yesterday at this time I could barely see out of it, and now . . . "

Caiaphas stopped yelling and just stared at Malchus, or more specifically, at his completely cleared eye. The high priest's expression was blank, which now spelled concern.

There was a sudden flash of lightning, followed instantly by deafening booms of thunder and more lightning. The entire house shook. It kept shaking even after the thunder had rolled by. Caiaphas grabbed the table by its edge. His eyes darted around the room. Pieces of the ceiling crashed onto the table as stone and plaster broke loose and shattered all about the room. Wall hangings crashed to the floor, and plates, urns, and vases could be heard shattering throughout the house.

Malchus suddenly feared he was in the wrong place, at the wrong time, and that God's wrath was about to smite the high priest and everyone associated with him. Caiaphas had to be the first one on God's list for retribution. Screams came from the kitchen. Then, as abruptly as the earthquake had started, it stopped.

Malchus ran to the kitchen doorway. Zara and Levia were safe in each other's arms. Zara looked at him in the dim light, as if expecting Malchus to tell her what to expect next. Maybe she had had some of the same dreadful thoughts as he.

The front entry door was flung open. Two chief priests squeezed through the door together, holding up a third priest by the arms. The priest who was being carried by the two was

Eleazar, the superintendent of the curtains. His face was drained of color, and he looked barely conscious.

"Now what?" Caiaphas shouted, seeing the three priests.

"He saw the hand of God!" shrieked one of the priests, his eyes wild and unblinking.

"What are you saying?" Caiaphas said. "Bring him into the meeting room!" he directed sharply as he turned. "Or what's left of it. And you three, come in as well," he said to Malchus, Zara, and Levia, all of whom had heard what the priest had said.

The priests helped Eleazar into a chair. He was trembling.

Caiaphas swept broken plaster off his seat with his hand. "Now," he said, sitting down and holding his palm out. "Speak."

"He was at the altar when—"

"Not you!" Caiaphas yelled at the man who had helped Eleazar into Caiaphas's home. Caiaphas took a moment before he spoke again, apparently trying to regain his composure. "Him," he said, just above a whisper as he pointed at Eleazar.

The priest's teeth were chattering. The words came slowly at first. "Well, I was just making my rounds in the Priest's Court as I—I usually do, and when I passed by the altar," the priest looked up and stared blankly at the ceiling for a moment, "I thought I heard something behind me at the holy place. I quickly turned around to see what it was, and—and—I saw the veil that covers the entrance to the Holy of Holies divide. No, tear. It ri-ripped down its entire length. It was loud. Very loud. And the wind. The wind was coming from inside. Loud. Make it stop." He was screaming, covering his head with both arms, and rocking back and forth. He looked and sounded completely crazy.

"Stop that now!" Caiaphas ordered with his most official and threatening tone. "Stop it!" he shouted above the man's yells. "Just tell me what happened. What do you mean the veil ripped?"

"Yes, yes, it was being stretched. No, pulled. I just don't know. Then—" he held his fists straight out, knuckles touching "—it burst apart from top to bottom!" he said, throwing his arms wide apart, staring at the imaginary tear. "Torn by the very hands of God!" he screamed. His lips trembled, and he gazed into space. "I'm doomed. We're all doomed!"

"Silence!" the high priest bellowed.

Eleazar looked startled. He stopped groaning, looked at Caiaphas, and then buried his head in his hands on the table. It sounded as if he was sobbing.

Caiaphas just sat there staring at Eleazar. Everyone else was silent. They were all staring at Caiaphas and Eleazar.

"Listen to me, all of you," the high priest enunciated with great exaggeration. "All of these things have logical explanations, as you all know, but weaker minds won't look for answers. They will just see these things as part of their delusion and connect them to that madman. I will not do that. And I will not allow you to do it either! I charge you all before God not to speak of any of this until we find out what happened. We will not give these people food for their overactive minds." He turned to Malchus. "Go to the temple and find Jonathan. Tell him to seal off the Priest's Court until we take care of the veil." He turned sharply to Eleazar. "You go with Malchus and stitch that thing back together immediately until we can replace it. That will have to do for—"

"No!" Eleazar shouted back desperately, waving his hands back and forth frantically. "I will not. Absolutely not!"

Malchus could not believe the way the old man was talking to Caiaphas. He had never seen anyone yell at the high priest before.

"What God has torn apart I will not put back together!" Eleazar was shouting. At that moment, a piece of loose plaster fell from the ceiling and crashed and shattered on the far end of the table.

"Ah!" Eleazar screamed. He passed out and fell to the floor like a sack of flour. All everyone in the room could do was stare.

Caiaphas rolled his eyes and looked back at Malchus. "All right. Eleazar cannot go. Tell Jonathan to find Petahiah and have him do it. He used to be in charge of the veil before Eleazar took it over. And if he won't do it, then you take care of it."

"Me?" Malchus said incredulously, his eyebrows rising as he pointed a finger at his own chest.

"No, no, of course not you. It has to be a priest, but I don't care which one. Just make sure it gets done. Now," Caiaphas said, raising his voice again. There will be no rumors associating this coincidence with the death of that maniac. "I will not allow Jerusalem to become a haven for the insane," he shouted to no one in particular while pounding the plaster-covered table.

Caiaphas himself looked insane, pontificating over the prostrate body of Eleazar. He was losing his famous steely composure, and he was becoming outwardly bothered by the onslaught of disturbances and distractions that had stolen his moment of triumph over the Nazarene.

"And Malchus," he called, his finger in the air. "Remember. Not a word about what you've heard from Eleazar. He has obviously lost his mind," he said, looking down at the motionless body lying on the floor. "Say the curtain ripped because of its age—or vandals. And please. Nothing about that ear of yours. People will think you're crazy too!" he yelled.

As Malchus went through the front door, he heard Caiaphas yell for all in the house to hear, "Somebody clean up this mess!"

Levia and Zara scrambled to comply.

TWENTY-FIVE

Malchus entered the temple through the Priest's Gate. All the others were locked for the evening. "Where's Jonathan?" Malchus asked a guard stationed by the door. The guard motioned with his head in the direction of the Priest's Court. Malchus turned. There were about two dozen priests and guards gathered near the entrance to the sanctuary. Jonathan was among them. So, too, was Petahiah.

"Well, well," Jonathan said as Malchus approached. "I thought it was you I saw at Golgotha. I told you there was nothing wrong with him," he said, looking back at the others.

No thanks to you, Malchus thought. "Jonathan, Caiaphas wants you to seal off the priest's court, and Petahiah, he told me to tell you to begin repairs immediately on the veil." Everyone seemed to be staring at him as he spoke. He wondered what kind of rumors had spread about the sword attack.

"Not me!" Petahiah said stepping forward defiantly. "It's Eleazar's job."

"Eleazar won't do it," Malchus said, enjoying the predicament the priests seemed to feel they were in.

"And why's that?" Petahiah asked, folding his arms and cocking his head slightly, as if he knew the answer.

"He, uh, seemed somewhat . . . troubled," Malchus said flatly, keeping his usual straight face.

"Somewhat troubled?" Petahiah answered. "Somewhat troubled, you say? Petrified is more like it! Or did he forget to tell you about his little accident and the puddle of urine he left by the altar?"

Malchus expected snickering, but there was none. With the exception of Jonathan who, as usual, looked as if he had somewhere else to be, they all appeared afraid. That was why they were outside the Priest's Court. Nobody wanted to be in the chamber near the ripped veil that would expose to his eyes the holiest place on earth—the very place where the presence of God supposedly dwelt. Men had been known to die instantly from simply stepping into the room known as the Holy of Holies, or by inadvertently touching the Ark of the Covenant, the sacred vault containing the stone tablets that Moses had brought down from Mount Sinai. Only the high priest was allowed in there, and only on one day a year.

"And you can tell Caiaphas that from what little I saw, the veil is completely destroyed. Beyond repair!" Petahiah said, his hands moving dramatically with every word. "Not only is the cloth shredded too deeply to mend, but its colors have almost disappeared—and I have no plan to vanish with them! You can tell Caiaphas that he can deal with me however he wants, but I may never go into the Priest's Court again. And I most certainly will not touch that veil. Ever!"

Jonathan rolled his eyes.

Malchus could not believe what he was seeing. All the priests were vigorously nodding in agreement, encouraging and affirming Petahiah with shouts of "Yes! Yes!" and "Amen." This was the first time he had ever seen the priests openly defy Caiaphas as a body, and he did not want to be the one to deliver their message of protest. Especially now with Caiaphas so agitated.

"I am here only to relay Caiaphas's orders. What you do in response is up to you," Malchus said, turning quickly, hoping he could get away before Jonathan called him. The priests continued to rant about the temple. What Caiaphas wanted done was "not right." The more they debated, the surer of themselves they sounded. Malchus wondered how bold they would be if Caiaphas had ordered them to their faces.

"Malchus," came a voice from behind.

Uh-oh, he thought. He turned around. It was Judah. He breathed a sigh of relief. Looking past Judah, Malchus saw the priests in an animated discussion with Jonathan. Malchus shook his head, wondering whether the priests actually believed they could convince Jonathan of anything. As if Jonathan cared. As if Caiaphas would care what Jonathan thought.

Malchus let Judah catch up to him, then took him by the arm. "Come with me," he said, continuing away from the priests and guards. "We'll talk outside."

"Malchus!" someone shouted from a distance as they were halfway out the temple gate. He recognized the voice. Judah started to turn around, but Malchus squeezed his arm and kept them going in the opposite direction.

"We have to get out of here. I'll tell Jonathan I didn't hear him. He'll think I'm lying, but I don't care. He can take it up with Caiaphas if he wants."

"Well, aren't you the rebellious one?" Judah said. "Where are we going?"

"Away from here. Anywhere. My head feels like it's going to burst, and I feel like I'm about to cry, or kill someone, or both. You would not believe what I have been through in the last three days. I don't even know if I believe it. My mind keeps running in every direction. I need to get out of this city, Judah," Malchus said, exasperated and weary.

"My friend, I think I know just what you need," Judah said, putting his arm around Malchus's shoulder and giving him a quick squeeze.

"Well, that makes one of us."

"Find some firewood and meet me outside the Essenes Gate. And Malchus!"

"What?"

"Your eye. It looks—better."

"Later."

Malchus and Judah sat comfortably against the ancient city wall outside the Essenes Gate. They had found a spot a few hundred feet off the road and were drinking wine and warming themselves by a fire in the night-chilled air. Down the slope from their perch was Hinnom Valley. Campfires dotted the opposite slope and rolling hills beyond.

"Feeling any better yet?" Judah asked with a gleam in his eye as he watched Malchus finish off the first wineskin.

"A little," Malchus answered, wiping wine from his mouth with the back of his hand. "It feels good to not think," Malchus said. "Am I that thirsty or does Bebai stock better wine than Caiaphas?"

"Bebai enjoys wine far more than Caiaphas, and won't share it with a soul—except, of course, with us," Judah said, winking. He pulled a wood peg from the mouth of the second wineskin with his teeth, and drank heartily.

"So tell me. What happened to that ugly eye you had yesterday?"

"I think I need a little more to drink first."

Judah shrugged. "So drink."

Malchus drank. He felt his face getting warm from the fire. Or was it from the wine? Whatever it was, he was starting to feel a little better. Confusion and pain were slowly fading into the background. For tonight, that is all he wanted. And Judah was good to be with right now. Their relationship came naturally. Effortlessly. He could talk to Judah about anything, and, as the wine lowered his guard, he decided he would do just that. He needed a fresh opinion. Someone more removed, more objective. Judah's perspective might be valuable. Maybe he could make sense of the things Malchus was too close to—much too close to.

Judah leaned forward and stirred the fire with a stick. "What do you think of Petahiah refusing Caiaphas's order to mend the veil?" he asked.

"Wouldn't you?"

"Wouldn't I what?"

"Refuse."

Judah stared blankly for a long moment, as if he had never asked himself the question. He took a quick draw from the wineskin and turned his attention back to Malchus. "I don't know. Would you?" Judah asked, lowering the skin.

Malchus took the drink from him, drew a large mouthful, swallowed deep, and then belched. "I'll tell you what I know for certain," Malchus said, finding confidence in the wine.

"And what's that?" Judah asked, leaning back on his right elbow and looking a little sleepy.

"Veils don't just rip—they have to *be* ripped. Especially one that size," Malchus declared, proud that he finally had a coherent thought.

"It's no wonder they have you doing the book work. Who do you think ripped it?"

"Who?" Malchus asked incredulously. "Well, let's see. Let's eliminate who couldn't have torn it. The veil is how many stories high? Three? Four? And how wide is it? A seamless fabric that has hung for how long? And, oh yes, there's that troubling matter of its fading when it was torn. And—"

"Enough!" Judah interrupted, raising a hand. "I get your point. But I don't understand how you can be the one telling this to me. You're the first one to ridicule anyone who makes a claim that has anything to do with God doing anything. You're the most cynical Jew I know."

"Not anymore I'm not," Malchus said. "I've traded in my cynicism for confusion and depression," Malchus said, lifting a wineskin up over his head.

"Never do that," Judah said, shaking his finger at him.

"But this I do know, Judah. Jesus was not just a man. He did things that only God could do." He squeezed the skin at the last word and drank.

Judah leaned toward Malchus. "What are we talking about, Malchus? I must be missing something. Only the day before yesterday I was the one telling you about inexplicable healings. You didn't believe me. What's changed your mind?"

Malchus put down the wineskin and rolled to his knees. "We're going to need more wood on the fire," he said as he stretched for another branch.

Malchus sat back down and tried to recount the last couple of days to his friend. The wine impared his ability to get started, but once he began to talk about climbing up to the Garden of Gethsemane, the words and events came easier. In fact, he was surprised at how the images crystallized in his mind and came to life. His words gave fresh vitality to what had occurred. He was not just telling a story but reliving it, observing what had occurred without the constraint of time and space. Looking at the garden like a spectator, not a participant. Malchus could almost feel the air thicken around him when he told of the angelic presence that had been in that place. He could hear Jonathan yelling orders. Judah was speechless and fixated on every detail. Malchus winced and felt the pain of the disciple's sword attack. "And my eye got healed too."

"What?" Judah yelled, eyes bulging when Malchus told of his ear being severed. He reached out and pushed Malchus's chin so the fire would light the wounded side of his head.

After a second, Malchus moved his head away from Judah's hand. He continued the story. Judah sat up and rearranged his legs. At that point, Malchus would have continued even if he knew

Judah didn't believe a word he said. Voicing the events as they had occurred gave Malchus a sense of confidence. In hearing his own words, he felt strengthened. He was no longer simply telling a story; he was hearing it. Malchus ended the saga with Zara finding him the next morning with blood all over his hair and clothes.

"And?" Judah said.

"The rest is personal." Malchus smiled.

"Just when it was getting interesting," Judah said, and then quickly added, "Sorry, I couldn't resist."

Judah stood up and stretched. Malchus followed, rubbing numbness from his buttocks. He suddenly felt dizzy, but he steadied himself against the wall. He'd definitely had too much to drink.

"Looks like you're more than just confused," Judah said.

Malchus nodded. He was having difficulty focusing on Judah.

"You believe Jesus was the Messiah?"

"That's right."

"And the Messiah could have conquered Rome with just a nod to his angels?"

"That's right."

"So why is he dead?"

"I don't know."

"You think God tore the veil because he was upset."

"Judah, I'm upset. I can't imagine how God views this."

"That's what those priests were discussing just before you got there."

"Really?" Malchus raised an eyebrow. "What did they say?"

"They're divided as usual, but some of them think like you—they think that they might have actually killed the real Messiah. And with the veil ripping after the earthquake, which happened after that weird thing the clouds were doing just before it rained harder than anyone around here has ever seen, and all of that just after Jesus died. They were too afraid to argue much about it."

"Caiaphas won't be when he gets hold of them," Malchus said.

"Well, I guess we'll find out soon enough," Judah said, then drained the last of the fourth wineskin.

"Find out what?" Malchus said.

"If he really *is* the Messiah."

"You mean *was,* and what are you talking about?"

"I mean is. The priests were talking about some prophecy—something Jesus said to them about resurrection. Didn't you hear?"

"Resurrection?" Malchus said, his eyes fixed on Judah's. He felt hope stirring within him, but he was ready for more disappointment. He did not want to be lifted up to a great height just to be dropped again. If he was going to be disappointed, he wanted his feet on the ground, not in the clouds.

"He said something about destroying the temple and then rebuilding it in three days. I'm not sure who started it, but there's a rumor that he's coming back from the dead on the third day," Judah said, poking Malchus in the side.

Suddenly, Malchus wished he wasn't drunk. And with the poke, he noticed how queasy his stomach felt. He tried to focus on Judah, but everything seemed to be moving. He was starting to feel nauseous. Slimy saliva was beginning to fill his mouth.

"Judah, I think we better get back. I'm not feeling very well."

TWENTY-SIX

"Malchus! Maaaaalchus!"

The shout came from a distance, but it was loud enough to shatter his rest. His head felt huge, and every syllable out of Caiaphas's mouth pounded his eardrums like a mallet. He started to open his eyes, but the burst of light that invaded his slightly parted lids slammed him with pain at the back of his skull. He rolled over and buried his head into the cloth of his mattress, protecting his eyes and covering his ears with a blanket clutched tightly with both hands and pulled down around his head. "Ugh," was all he could utter, and even that hurt his ears. He had felt ill before he fell asleep last night. This was worse.

"Malchus!" Caiaphas snapped from the doorway. "Get up. I am meeting with Pilate. Hurry up," he ordered, and then abruptly stormed away.

Malchus could barely think. He waited for the throbbing to stop from Caiaphas's verbal assault, and then he sorted through what he had just heard. Pilate? Now? *This cannot be happening,* he thought. Since it was Passover, if there was any work that needed to be done, Caiaphas would not do it. *So what is it this time?* he wondered, trying again to open his eyes as the mattress pressed against his face.

"Good morning," sang a quiet voice.

Malchus peeked out through one bloodshot eye. He tried to smile at Zara, but even that effort sent pain to his temples.

"If my head didn't hurt so much, I would be embarrassed to be seen in this condition," Malchus whispered, his voice muffled in the mattress.

Zara stuck her head into the room to hear better, then pulled it quickly back out. "You smell awful," she said. "How are you feeling today?"

"Some days are worse than others," he said hoarsely, attempting to lift his head. "This is the worst."

"You *looked* worse yesterday morning," she said, "but you *smell* worse today. You had better wake up. Caiaphas has been busy all morning." She disappeared before he could think of anything endearing to say.

Malchus sat up ever so slowly. His face felt like swollen leather. His arms and legs were shaky. If his breath smelled anything like the dry putrid taste in his mouth, it was no wonder Zara had not stayed. He leaned forward and placed his head in his hands and rubbed his eyes. *And Caiaphas wants to see Pilate?* he thought, wondering what Pilate would say if he could see him now.

"Try this."

Malchus looked up. He shielded his eyes with his right hand. Zara was back with a large goblet in her hands. She walked in and handed it to him. He took it, trying to steady his hands as he reached out to her. He took a sip. It was fresh grapefruit juice that ripped through the stale taste in his mouth like a knife. It felt good.

"Keep drinking. It will wake you up."

The way she spoke made Malchus think again of his mother. He managed a smile and finished what she had given him, but he was still incredibly thirsty. He held the goblet, draining every drop of juice from it, then looked at Zara like a little boy.

"Would you like another?" she asked, not waiting for an answer.

"If you could. That was just what I needed," he said as she left. The dry mouth was going, and his voice sounded almost clear. By the time she returned he had composed his thoughts and his appearance somewhat, and he could feel at least some of his energy returning.

Malchus peered past the second goblet as he drank. Zara was watching him. She was still beautiful, but the smile was gone and so, too, was the exuberance she had had when she pushed him into the Siloam Pool. She looked melancholy now. In mourning. And still she was there for him. He reached for her hand. She took it and helped him up from the bed.

"Thank you," he said in Nabataean.

She forced a smile. "My pleasure," she replied, also in Nabataean.

Nabataean had never sounded so sweet, so comforting. "Are you all right?" he asked. His voice still sounded very coarse. She looked grateful that he asked, like she had been waiting until he was ready to talk.

"Last night was very difficult. I—"

"Malchus!" Caiaphas yelled from down the hall.

Zara bit her lower lip and shrugged. "You have to go," she said, her disappointment obvious.

"I'm sorry." He looked into her eyes. Her sadness made him feel desperate to do something to lighten her burden. "I don't know what Caiaphas is doing now, but I'll return as soon as I can." He kissed her softly on the lips. Their eyes spoke, but neither had a chance to say a word.

"Now Malchus! We have to go." Caiaphas sounded as if he was coming to get him, so Malchus quickly leaned forward, kissed Zara again, and hurried to meet him in the hall.

†

Malchus usually did not have a problem keeping up with Caiaphas, but at this moment he didn't know if he would even make it to Antonia. He was already sweating profusely and they had just started out. His head hurt with every step, and he was afraid if they went any faster, he would vomit.

"You look ill, Malchus," Caiaphas said after a backward glance. "Could it be that you celebrated the demise of our enemy with a little too much fruit of the vine?"

Celebrated? He was outraged by the question. "Are you—"

"I suppose I can't blame you," Caiaphas interrupted, not noticing how angry Malchus looked. "I was tempted to toast our success as well, but I dare not celebrate yet. This one can be more dangerous to us dead."

"Sir?" Malchus asked, wanting to hear what Caiaphas had to say about the prophecy Judah had described.

"If that deranged madman thought he was a prophet and one who could take advantage of the faith of our people, he has grossly underestimated us. And he has overestimated his own omnipotence. He is dead. We are still here."

Malchus restrained himself so he could hear more about what Jesus had said. "A prophet?" he asked, baiting Caiaphas.

"Are you the only one in Jerusalem who is unaware of the plot by his disciples to steal his body from the grave?"

"Steal his body? For what?"

"So they can say he rose from the dead according to his own prophecy. Well, the dead prophet will get no help from the living. I will not permit their chicanery. They will not mislead the Jews with lies and tricks. I will stop them."

"You will?" Malchus asked, almost to himself. He did not like the sound of this. Caiaphas seemed worse today. More paranoid. Malchus thought for a minute, then smiled. He could not believe the effect Jesus was having on Caiaphas. And then it dawned on him. Why would anyone prophesy his own death and resurrection, then go to the cross without protest *unless he knew* it would come to pass? Otherwise, it would be—suicide.

"Yes, Malchus. I'll demand Pilate guard the tomb with however many soldiers it will take to thwart such an attempt. The conspirators will see the soldiers and scatter. And if I even hear so much as a sneeze from them again, I'll hunt them down to meet the same fate as their precious rebel leader," Caiaphas said, looking back and forth at people on the road as he strode toward Antonia.

Malchus wondered if he thought some of Jesus' followers were listening. The very thought that Jesus still had followers seemed to be enraging him to the point of distraction. As they approached Antonia, he began to wonder how Pilate was dealing with all this.

TWENTY-SEVEN

"Wait here," the Roman guard ordered, then returned to his station at the doorway. Caiaphas, Malchus, and Jonathan—whom Caiaphas had also summoned to attend—were left standing a good thirty feet from Pilate, who was busy at his desk reading and sealing documents in hot wax with a massive ring on his left hand. The morning sunlight coming through the window conveniently fell upon him and his immediate workspace. He went about his business as if no one else were in the room, much less waiting. Caiaphas, who was now noisily clearing his throat, had no patience for this type of impertinent treatment and would play this game only so long. Pilate, however, seemed to be sending the message that the high priest was not his priority.

Jonathan, who stood taller than either Caiaphas or Malchus, looked around the room curiously, probably basking in the presence of so much power. *Idiot,* Malchus thought.

Pilate finally put down his quill, organized the tabletop, arranged himself in his seat, and looked up. His expression dripped annoyance. After a moment of silent observance, he motioned them forward with a single slow wave of his hand, then halted them when they were half the distance to him. "You should do something for that cough, Caiaphas," he mocked. "To what do I owe the delight of seeing you here again? This is the second time in less than three days, Caiaphas. Do you think I have no other concerns except the Jews?"

Caiaphas ignored the last question. "We have an urgent matter that requires your help," Caiaphas said quickly, as if he were giving an order.

"Which is?" Pilate said, closing his eyes in botheration as he spoke.

"The Nazarene."

"Great Jupiter! The man has been executed. He is dead. Is that not enough for you? What more can he do? What more can I do?" Pilate yelled.

"We have strong reason to believe that some of the Nazarene's followers plan on stealing his body and—"

"So?" Pilate interrupted.

"So they can perpetrate a myth that he rose on the third day after his death," Caiaphas said, maintaining an even volume.

Pilate massaged his chin and shook his head slowly. "So?" he repeated again.

"Anyone rising from the dead—"

"No," he interrupted, "not you," Pilate said, wagging his finger to stop him. "Him. The big one. The one enamored with the statue of our goddess, Venus. I'm curious if he shares your concerns. Do you find her attractive, Jonathan?"

Jonathan snapped his attention to Pilate. He had been staring at the nude figure. "I, uh—"

"As I was saying," Caiaphas said, with measured annoyance, "anyone who appears to have risen from the dead, especially after prophesying that he would . . . "

Upon hearing that Jesus prophesied he would rise from the dead, Pilate's eyebrows rose.

" . . . He would be recognized as having divine authority. He would be seen as a god. If that were to happen, the many false stories that surround him would take on new dimensions. Wild rumors would be treated as miraculous truths. The man would become a legend," he said, counting his fingers for emphasis as he spoke. "The heresy that he preached would become law, overruling the Law of Moses." He touched another finger. "The sacrificing on the feast days would become obsolete since he has claimed himself to be the forgiver of sins. There would be division between the Jewish people, the likes of which you've never seen. There would be a civil unrest of such proportion that word would quickly reach the ears of Rome."

Pilate laughed loudly. "All of which means you would be out of a job." He glared at Caiaphas through narrowed eyes. "Dogs stick their noses where they don't belong, Caiaphas, and only for their own purposes. Let me worry about civil unrest. You mind your own business."

Good start, Pilate. Sounds like the beginning of a fight I would like to see, Malchus thought. *But from a distance.*

Caiaphas squeezed his fingers into a fist. "How dare you address me in that way, Procurator," he said, emotion finally detectable in his voice. "I have done nothing more than report useful information to you to help you head off a disaster before it happens."

The procurator drummed his chin, sunlight flashing off the signet ring on his finger. "As far as I can see, your people could only be helped if they believed the Nazarene was a god. The only one who would lose is you."

"Helped? You cannot be serious. How?" he said angrily.

Malchus thought he saw Pilate smile.

"Simple. Rebels are constantly trying to turn the people against the ruling powers. In our case, that is me. As I recall, the Nazarene taught that the Jews should turn the other cheek and pay taxes to Rome. As far as I'm concerned, his followers would be model citizens."

Does Pilate actually believe that? Malchus wondered. *Or is he just trying to aggravate Caiaphas?*

"You couldn't be more wrong, Procurator," Caiaphas said. He unclenched his fist and now pointed directly at Pilate. "His followers would quickly destroy the entire city's economy by crippling the temple business, making it impossible for people to afford the tax burden you have imposed on them. What you will reap is more rebellion, not less."

Pilate pushed himself away from the table and stood up. "Enough of this conversation. You're interested only in your own personal kingdom, and we both know it. Tell me what it is that you propose so I can deny it and be rid of you. The mere sight of you is irritating," Pilate said, making his way around the table.

"Simple. Station guards—at least a dozen—at the Nazarene's tomb until the third day has passed. If any of his followers show up, have them arrested for disturbing the peace and punish them so severely they will find another, less disruptive lunatic to follow. Then, so we can be done with this for the last time, set your seal to a proclamation forbidding public recognition of the Nazarene. That way you will have officially identified him as an enemy of Israel *and* Rome. He could not be anything but that now, could he, Procurator, since he was convicted under Roman law? By your authority."

Pilate leaned back against the table, shaking his head and looking at the floor. He looked up. "Simple, you say?" He walked over to Jonathan, his hands behind his back, and looked up into his face. "Simple? Arresting a single man—an unarmed man, a man who did not believe in fighting—that sounded like it should have been *simple.* Wouldn't you agree, Captain?"

Jonathan looked straight ahead and said nothing.

"From what I've heard, it wasn't as simple as one would have thought. There were . . . things, inexplicable things. Things that nobody expected." Pilate said. "I don't like to hear about unexplainable things, particularly where my men are concerned. You know what I'm talking about, don't you, Jonathan?" He looked at Caiaphas. "Did you know everyone at the Garden of Gethsemane fell to the ground whenever the Nazarene spoke?"

Caiaphas frowned. Apparently he had been left uninformed. Apparently no one had had the nerve to tell him.

"Why, you fell down, didn't you, Jonathan?" Pilate said.

"The traitor leaned back against me, and I must have slipped. I also wanted to make sure it was not a trap. We were in their camp and we—"

"Please," Pilate said holding up a hand. "Spare me."

"It was dark and crowded," Caiaphas interjected. "He was seized and arrested. What is there to explain? He is dead, Procurator. There is nothing unusual about that."

Pilate shook his head, then moved away from Jonathan, back to Caiaphas. "I don't know. According to him, he allowed you to arrest him."

"Allowed us?" Caiaphas said. "I suppose he *allowed* your soldiers to nail him to the cross?"

"To tell you the truth, I asked myself that exact question."

Pilate's admission perked Malchus's attention. Apparently Pilate witnessed some of that same authority Jesus had demonstrated in the Garden of Gethsemane.

"Please, Procurator. He was an ordinary man. Nothing more."

"I'm not saying he was not a man. But ordinary?" he said, shaking his head and index finger as he walked. "I've put to death countless enemies of Rome without losing a wink of sleep. Last night I could not sleep. And I am sure I was not alone. Did you sleep, Priest? After the strange display of clouds in the sky and the earthquake, many of my men were saying that Jesus was the Son of God, a term not likely ever to be found on a Roman's lips."

Caiaphas shrugged his shoulders. "Natural events. A coincidence."

Pilate shook his head. "Unexplainable things. Unnatural things. Even *supernatural* things. And at this time?" He turned and moved on to Malchus and frowned. "You look different. What unexplainable thing happened to you?"

Malchus's eyes widened. Had he heard about his ear, or did he remember the ugly eye? Should he tell Pilate here? Now? Dare he speak in front of these men? He turned to Caiaphas. The high priest's eyes commanded him to remain silent. *I will tell Pilate,* he thought. *But not now. Later. When the time was right. When Caiaphas wasn't here.*

Pilate looked to Caiaphas and smiled at him, causing the priest to divert his gaze from Malchus. Then he looked back at Malchus, and again to Caiaphas. "This was no ordinary man," Pilate continued. "And the absurdity of your request to outlaw and punish his followers makes my answer too easy. No."

Caiaphas closed his eyes. Malchus knew this was not yet over. *If he had to, Caiaphas would send a slave to guard the tomb. Me,* Malchus thought. *And if not me, Jonathan. Or maybe Caiaphas would guard it himself.*

No. Passover was more than a small problem, since it was not lawful to be doing even the simplest of chores. Caiaphas, of course, would break the law if he had to, but only as a last resort.

"So what you're telling me is that you are afraid," Caiaphas said.

"Afraid?"

"Yes. Afraid of bad weather. The dark. Dead men seem to haunt you. Not something you would expect from a Roman."

"You would be wise not to forget to whom you are talking, and wiser still to open your ears. Did you hear what happened to the man who betrayed that Nazarene?"

Caiaphas frowned but said nothing.

"He hung himself. He was found hanging from a tree."

"Sounds like he was murdered by one of the other followers," Caiaphas said.

"He died of shame, and you know it. Do you think I don't know he threw the money you gave him back at you?"

Malchus glanced at Caiaphas, who did not deny it.

"I will tell you something else, Priest," Pilate said, waving his finger and pacing and raising his voice with every word. "My wife had a dream the night before you brought me your so-called criminal. When she saw him, she knew he was the one in her dream. She warned me. 'Do nothing against this righteous man,' she said. Whatever he says will be the truth. He is a man who cannot lie . . . " His words trailed off into silence. Pilate appeared distant, lost in thought.

Malchus could not believe his ears. Pilate's wife had a dream about Jesus before the arrest? More unseen forces at work in the night? Was this something else that angels could do? He wanted to hear more.

"Procurator?" Caiaphas finally said.

"What is it?" Pilate snapped, as if returning from a dream. Or a nightmare.

"You were saying."

"Yes, yes, yes. I know this probably will not mean much to you, Priest, but when you are gone, it will make me feel better knowing you've heard it. Jesus spoke to me before he was taken away."

"Begging for his life, no doubt," Caiaphas said.

"Hardly. He told me things. Troubling things. Things that continue to arrest my thoughts. He told me that he was indeed a king, but that his kingdom was not of this world."

Not of this world, Malchus repeated to himself. He was not sure what it meant, but he liked the sound of it. He could hardly wait to tell Zara.

"And when I told him I had the authority to crucify him, he had a presence about him I will never forget. He said I would have no authority over him unless it had been given to me from above. I don't understand what he meant, but the thought of it haunts me."

"He was playing games with your mind, Procurator, just like he tried to do with all of Jerusalem."

"He was bloody, beaten, thorns were puncturing his skull. He was in no condition to play games . . . and remember what my wife warned. The man cannot lie."

Caiaphas rolled his eyes, but Pilate did not see it.

"Then he told me something you should appreciate, Priest. He said that because the authority was given to me from above, the one who delivered him to me had the greater sin. And that, Your High Priestness, is you," Pilate said, jabbing his finger into Caiaphas's chest.

"You don't say," Caiaphas said, unmoved.

Pilate stared at Caiaphas, eye-to-eye. They were only inches from each other. "You speak of fear, Priest. You are more afraid of him than he was of the cross. That says a lot to me about you. And him."

"He was an insane zealot, and if you don't grant my request, you will find yourself crucifying his followers for crimes even you will recognize."

Pilate laughed loudly. "Should I start with my wife? She believes what the Nazarene says. Does that make her one of the followers? She has been right many times, she and her dreams. I believe what she says to be true. Does that make me a follower? Should I have myself flogged?"

Suddenly Pilate's laughing stopped, and he moved up close to Caiaphas again. "I'll tell you what. I will put soldiers at the

Nazarene's tomb. You may call them guards, or anything else your sordid little mind comes up with, but they will be there to be my eyes. I don't believe there will be any attempt to steal a body tomorrow. But if the body does somehow disappear, then you may find Rome itself spreading the news you so dread. Hah! I can just imagine it. Rome embracing the very Messiah whom you have rejected. A wonderful irony, wouldn't you agree, High Priest?"

†

Outside the Roman fortress, Malchus asked if he could be excused. He felt terrible and wanted to return home to be cared for and babied by Zara. Caiaphas, who was now headed toward the temple at a relaxed pace, granted his request with a brief wave of his hand. He looked unsettled. Caiaphas, as usual, had gotten what he wanted, but this time it was not the *way* he wanted it. Malchus wondered if Caiaphas was relieved to know the tomb would be guarded, or worried that Pilate himself might cause trouble.

The thought made Malchus shudder. If Caiaphas dwelled on what Pilate might do at the tomb, Malchus would be the likely candidate to spend the night in the graveyard. Then again, if Jesus did rise up from the tomb, he would be there to see it happen. But had Jesus really said he would resurrect, or was the whole idea conjured up from speculative paranoia and hype? No wonder Caiaphas looked distraught.

This was all getting very complicated—even for the high priest. Too many events. Too much fatigue. Too many thoughts. *God will do what God will do,* Malchus thought, *with or without men like Pilate and Caiaphas, or me for that matter.*

In the meantime, Zara. Grapefruit juice. Sleep.

TWENTY-EIGHT

The following morning, Levia joined Malchus and Zara for breakfast in the kitchen.

Malchus looked up from his bowl of grain to find Levia staring at him—again. He widened his eyes and stared back. "What am I, a freak?" he said.

"Relax," Zara said, coming to Levia's defense. "Leave her alone. You'd stare, too, if she told you she'd just grown a new ear and her ugly eye had been completely healed a few hours later." Zara seemed to be in much better spirits since Malchus told her about the meeting with Caiaphas and Pilate. All she kept asking was, "Can it happen?" And all Malchus could say was, "I hope so." That was enough for her.

"I didn't grow a new ear. It appeared. It was cut off. Completely. It wasn't there. Then it was," he said. "And my ugly eye didn't heal in a few hours, it healed instantly."

Zara and Levia laughed at him.

Malchus took the bowl in his lap and turned away from them.

"Oh, don't be so sensitive," Zara said. She leaned over and pecked him on the cheek.

Malchus smiled. "Fine, but at least say it right."

"All right. It didn't grow. It was gone, and then it appeared. Do we have it right?" Zara asked. The two women laughed again.

"I wonder if the guards Pilate stationed at the tomb caught anyone trying to steal the body," Levia said.

Malchus shook his head. "Only if it was a staged arrest, and I don't have to tell you who would be behind that. And for all I know, Jesus never even said he would rise from the dead. Whatever happens, he was the Messiah. We just weren't ready for God's kingdom to arrive." He moved his head closer and spoke lower. "Because some of us are too interested in our own kingdom to care about God's."

"Quiet, Malchus," Levia whispered sharply. "Be careful."

"Don't worry, I will be," Malchus said.

Levia and Zara looked at each other, and then back at Malchus. "What do you mean, 'I will be'? I don't like the way you said that," Levia said.

"Look, after seeing them crucify him and listening to what Caiaphas told Pilate, I know how dangerous it is to be one of Jesus' followers. But Caiaphas openly makes plans in front of me and even includes me in on them. He thinks that I'm with him. If I could warn others of what—"

Suddenly, there was a loud crash in the foyer. Malchus jumped from the table in midsentence and darted into the hallway. Zara and Levia ran after him to see what had happened. Malchus stopped right outside the door, the women right behind him. A ceramic vase was shattered across the floor. Caiaphas was standing over it. Behind him, the entrance guards watched through the open doorway. When he turned and saw them staring at him blankly, he grabbed the door edge with both hands and slammed it closed in their startled faces, then he picked up a piece of broken ceramic and threw it at the closed wood door. "Incompetents! Idiots, idiots, idiots," he yelled.

Before Caiaphas turned back around, Malchus had quietly ushered Zara and Levia back into the kitchen. He could not help but smile when he heard Caiaphas bellow out a primal roar of frustration.

"What is it?" Levia asked. She seemed completely confused.

"I would guess that Jesus' body is missing and no one was arrested."

"But how?" Levia said.

Malchus was about to shrug his shoulders, but then, glancing at Zara, he felt a tingle run up his back. Her eyes begged the question.

Caiaphas stormed past the kitchen but stopped when he saw Malchus. "I told him this would happen. I told him. But no. He couldn't take me seriously."

"Sir?" Malchus said. He knew what Caiaphas was referring to, but he wanted to hear the specifics from the high priest's own mouth.

"The body of that heretic. It's been stolen."

"How? Didn't Pilate have the tomb guarded?"

Caiaphas shook his head. "Obviously not. He claims he had two soldiers there and that they must have fallen asleep, but he is lying. The boulder in front of the tomb would have taken several men to move, and that would have awakened anyone guarding it. Now it starts."

"Sir?" Malchus said, with his best confused look.

"The stories, the rumors, the fires we have to stomp out. Listen, Malchus. We have to pull together and stop this thing before it gets going. I want you to tell your cousin Seth, and Judah, and anyone else you come across that you know for a fact the body was stolen by his disciples."

"Was it?" Malchus said.

"Of course it was. What else could have happened? I have already spoken to Jonathan. Now get to it. Immediately," Caiaphas yelled, and then left.

†

Malchus and Zara ran out the Essenes Gate, across Hinnom Valley, up the opposite hillside, over the top, and out of view. They praised God and danced about like children at play.

Malchus looked at himself and had to laugh. He was as dirty as he had ever been as a boy tending sheep. He reached down and ripped up a handful of dried grass and threw it into the air as some kind of spontaneous joy offering. He watched as the wind swept it up the hillside and away. The wind effortlessly blew away the straw and made him recall the moment in the garden when he realized his own anxieties and intense confusions had been lifted, like a great weight, off his shoulders. In a moment, relieved and dismissed—simply blown away with a puff of God's breath.

Suddenly Zara stopped and fell to her knees in the shade of a large boulder.

Malchus ran to her. "What's wrong?" he asked, winded and panting.

Zara closed her eyes, frowned slightly, and motioned with her hand for Malchus to give her a moment.

Malchus slowly knelt next to her and waited, wondering what in the world was happening. She did not appear to be in pain. Finally, he gently placed his right hand on her shoulder. "Zara?" he whispered.

She slowly turned to him and opened her eyes, her pupils rapidly adjusting to the light. She smiled just enough for her dimple to swallow the scar on her cheek.

"Are you all right?"

She nodded and stood up, Malchus helping her, but she did not seem to need it. "That never happened to me before."

"What?"

"It was as if I was dreaming. My mind was filled with a voice," Zara said.

Malchus paused. A week ago he would have received this news with skepticism at best, and would then apologize for his unrestrained sarcasm. Now, however, he wanted to hear what the voice had said. At least he could comfort himself knowing he was not the only one hearing voices.

"You don't believe me," Zara said.

"That's not at all true. Tell me what you heard. I want to know."

Zara smiled. "I can't tell you."

"Why not?"

"Because it makes no sense. Just words without a beginning or end. But I did hear them."

"Then what harm can they do? Tell me, I promise I won't laugh."

"If you do, I'll give you another ugly eye."

"Yes, yes, yes, you can give me two ugly eyes, just tell me already."

"Free in me," she shouted, throwing her hands in the air and twirling around. "I keep hearing *Free in me.*"

"What did you say?"

"Free in me," she repeated.

Malchus stopped breathing. He stared at her, feeling as blindsided as when the sword had first severed his ear. He had not told her about his experience hearing Jesus' voice at Golgotha because he still questioned his own sanity, and he had never spoken those words to her—to anyone. Except God.

Though looking at Zara, he could not see past the image of Jesus speaking to him from the cross. The question of Jesus' ability to do such a thing was now far overshadowed by the fact that he would even bother. First, while suffering on a cross, and now, from some unseen world or kingdom. He was completely known by someone who was more interested in him than he was in himself. He was numb with peace showering him from head to toe. He did not want to move or even think. Just receive.

Malchus blinked, and he was back on the hillside with Zara. He dropped to his knees and wept, his face in the sand, astonished and overwhelmed at God's mercy. The Almighty had heard his prayer through all his sarcastic accusations.

Zara knelt down beside him. When he explained to her through his tears what her words meant to him, she cradled his shoulders and wept with him.

TWENTY-NINE

Another dove flew off the windowsill into the early-morning sky as the high priest approached. Caiaphas looked up at the rustle of its wings and watched as it flew out of sight. He ignored Jonathan as he walked by.

"Another sacrifice that the Almighty has been robbed of. Another one of his little mementos," Caiaphas said angrily, cursing under his breath. He looked out the window into the Court of the Gentiles just below.

"How could the Roman Empire be so successful yet so totally incompetent? How could they bungle guarding a sealed tomb—a hole in the wall with a huge rock in front of it? What's wrong with them?" he seethed. "And then there's always the possibility that Pilate himself arranged the theft. Would he dare?"

Jonathan wondered if he should answer. He was not sure if Caiaphas was talking to him or to himself.

"Through their ineptness or stupidity, whatever the case may be, the Nazarene will continue to irritate us through his followers. Now they will claim proof, and the pilgrims will carry that news back with them. The success I've built will be ravaged with twisted stories. We will be made to look like the criminals—unless we strike first," Caiaphas said.

"His followers are mice," Jonathan ridiculed, trying to reassure Caiaphas. "They hide from us in holes, afraid to admit they ever even knew him. They will vanish, just as he did."

"Are you an idiot?" Caiaphas snapped. "If his body isn't found, they'll be jubilant. Just watch. They will claim he actually rose from the dead. Those who were afraid to admit they were with him will crawl out of their holes. They will be like locusts, a plague upon our people, a threat to our very existence. The only chance we have is to stomp them out before they find their courage and spread the lie. Before they organize. Stomp them out and do it emphatically!" Caiaphas shouted.

"That will be easy," Jonathan said, trying to sound confident and capable.

"Nothing about this is easy," Caiaphas screamed. "Do you hear me? Nothing! What is wrong with you? You completely underestimate everything. If there is anyone alive more dangerous than Jesus, it's you! Just shut up and let me sort this out!"

Jonathan opened his mouth, about to say something, but Caiaphas glared furiously at him. He froze in midthought, closed his mouth, and waited expectantly for the next verbal barrage. He watched Caiaphas as the high priest paced back and forth. He would suddenly stop in his tracks, and then begin pacing again. Finally, Caiaphas turned his attention back to Jonathan.

"Do you still have that list of names of the deceived who were sitting at his feet?" Caiaphas asked.

"Yes," said Jonathan, in reflex reaching to his sash to make sure he had it.

"Start with them. Find the people on the list," Caiaphas said, then he continued to pace. "We need to separate the curious onlookers from the—the—believers. Those rebels somehow need to be made an example of to satisfy the onlookers' curiosity. The more those who are unsure about what they have heard see us taking control of the situation, the more comfortable they will be dismissing the rumors as the rantings of dangerous rebels. And yes, everyone, and I mean *everyone* on the list must be told the missing body was the result of a plot. That it was his people—conspirators all—who stole the body and will be punished by both the temple authorities and the Romans. You must instruct your men to spread this word! And anyone outwardly defiant must go on a separate list."

Jonathan nodded his head in affirmation and turned to leave.

"And I want you to act as if I'm standing right next to you. Do you understand what I'm saying?" was the last thing Jonathan heard before the door closed.

Jonathan was glad to leave. Going down the stairs from the chamber, he pulled out the list and opened it. He surveyed the names, wondering how he would divide them among his men. His eyes stopped at one name. His lips curled in a lascivious smile. "Zara," he read aloud. He immediately decided his men could wait while he had one practice interrogation. He felt a twinge of excitement in his gut. "She is first." He began to fantasize about the way he would investigate her. The more he thought about it, the more excited he became. And the faster he walked.

THIRTY

Malchus held open a small cloth satchel while he and Judah watched Alexander drop coins into it. The soldier counted, with a pronounced Roman accent, to the clink of each coin.

Malchus thanked God—something he had not done since he was a boy with his father. He remembered thanking God when they found water for the flock, or when a lamb was born, or when being paid for the sheep they had raised. Now, after years of religious apathy, he was thanking God again.

"That's it. We're even," Alexander said. "You bring me more, I'll pay you more, as always."

"There won't be much more to come for a while," Judah said.

Alexander nodded. "Just make sure that when the time comes, you bring the goods to me first. I'll take care of you," he said. They shook hands and went their separate ways.

This was payment to Malchus and Judah for the sheepskins and fleeces they had secured. With all that had occurred in the past week, the take was not nearly as much as it had been in past years. The other merchants were also experiencing the previous week's impact on their finances, and most were cursing Jesus for it. The chief priests supported that view at every opportunity, as per Caiaphas's orders. They did not get much opposition.

Malchus knew he would need another way to supplement the difference. His mother depended on their funds for the coming year and needed money by now. For once, though, Malchus was not worried.

His faith in God's provision, that somehow God would provide for him personally, was strong—stronger, even, than when he had been a boy with his father. He knew now everything would work out. God was in control. Really in control. Really God. Malchus was amazed at how much his thinking had changed. Before last week, he had difficulty believing God was interested in the world, let alone in any one person. If the Messiah was interested in his well-being in the garden, at the cross, and with Zara in the field, he would be interested now. Now that he was alive again.

"So, what are you going to do now, Malchus?" Judah asked. They had just split their earnings and were walking together along the outside of the city wall.

"I'm going to bring this money back to the house and put it in a safe place before I lose it," Malchus said, patting the small bag of coins that hung from his waistband. As they continued to walk, Malchus picked up a stone, examined it, and rolled it in his fingers, seemingly lost in thought.

"Malchus, that wasn't what I was asking, and you know it. You aren't thinking of slipping away with that new slave girl now that you have some money, are you?"

"Yes, as a matter of fact, I'm on my way right now to get her. We'll leave with the pilgrim flow. No one will know we're gone until we're in Jericho, and by then we'll be out of reach."

Judah stared blankly at him. "I hope you're not serious."

"Of course I am. And now that you know our plans, we either have to take you with us or kill you."

"That's not much of a choice. If you take me with you, Caiaphas will find us and have us killed anyway. So really, you're staying, right?"

Malchus smiled, then nodded. "What else can I do? I still don't know if Caiaphas bought Zara to keep me here, but he may as well have. In six months I'll be free and, if Caiaphas hasn't had me arrested for believing Jesus was—and is—the Messiah, well, I might have to get used to seeing your face a little longer."

Judah shook his head. "I really can't believe you're telling me this. You'd start all over again in a place you've been dying to leave since I met you six years ago?"

"Maybe. I'm not making any decisions just now. We'll see what God's plans are. I know God has a path planned for my life, and I'm already on it. When I was a boy, my father told me that when God created everything, all he needed to say was 'Begin,' and everything began. I think last week God said 'Begin' to me. I can't speak for anyone else, but I know I'm not alone." Malchus threw his rock down the gentle hillside that fell away from the road. They both watched it disappear from sight.

"If Caiaphas hears you talk like this, you'll be a *missing* piece of God's plan."

They both laughed. "I know, Judah. But you know what? I don't care who hears me say these things. It's all so new. I feel so alive. I want to talk about it more and more."

"I'm telling you, if Caiaphas hears you, you'll feel dead, not alive. Be very careful, my friend."

"Seriously, Judah, Caiaphas's consuming hatred of the believers makes me want to stay more than leave. He speaks so freely around me. I wonder sometimes if he even knows I'm there. With my hearing all that is spoken in his home, I could probably help other followers of Jesus keep a step ahead of Caiaphas. Information like that might even save their lives and give them time to spread the news that he's alive. He's alive!" Malchus shouted.

"Now I know why you sound different, Malchus. You've gone crazy!" Judah said, pushing him on the shoulder. "What do you want to do, get us both killed? Quiet! Caiaphas is too smart. He would be on to you before you knew what was happening. I will admit, though, it would be fun while it lasted. Watching his carefully planned schemes foiled at every turn. Talk about justice! But, forget it. After a couple of botched plans, the joke would be on you. He'd figure it out and have you torn in half and fed to the crows. Forget about it, Malchus. It's suicide."

"Well, Judah, whatever I do, I have time to think about it. I don't have to make my decision today. God will make it clear to me."

"Let's hope so," said Judah. "If he leaves the planning to you, you're as good as dead." They both laughed again.

Entering the city through the Damascus Gate, the two friends embraced, slapped each other on the back affectionately, then went their separate ways to put their money in a safe place.

THIRTY-ONE

Jonathan knew what the guards were thinking as he approached Caiaphas's entrance. They admired him and hoped somehow to emulate him, even in some small way. He was their mentor. They recognized his authority. His stature. And after he entered the home they guarded, they would no doubt talk about him with envy and approval, looking forward to the day when he would be high priest.

"Shalom," Jonathan said in his deepest voice.

They nodded without expression as he passed.

Jonathan quietly closed the door behind him and stood in the grand foyer gathering his thoughts. He was here to fulfill the responsibility with which Caiaphas had entrusted him. She just happened to be at the top of the list, or near enough, and certainly one of the more dangerous since she lived in the same home as the high priest. No matter. No one would question why she was first. Who would dare?

Jonathan let out a deep breath. The familiar image of Zara appeared in his mind. Again. Strangely, he felt anxious. Caiaphas might want to know why he had not been told in advance that his own slave was on the list. And then there was the warning to behave as if Caiaphas were supervising the interrogation in person.

If his motivations were questioned at all, he could always tell Caiaphas that the news of his own slave being a follower could be too disturbing at the wrong time. As difficult as it was, he had kept the problem to himself to save the high priest unnecessary stress, all the while keeping a watchful eye on the situation to make sure everything was under control. After all, he was captain of the temple guard; keeping things under control was his job. Of course, it was his job to hide this information. The more he repeated this explanation, the better he felt.

Jonathan looked down the hall, hearing voices in the kitchen. He reached behind, opened the door again, and closed it loud enough to be heard.

"Malc—" Zara said, stepping into the hallway from the kitchen. Once in the hall, her eyes met his, she stopped abruptly, then turned back toward the kitchen.

"Wait," Jonathan called. He tugged his robes straight, pulled himself up to his full height, and walked toward her.

Zara had stopped but had not turned around.

"What's wrong? Were you expecting someone else?"

She turned hesitantly. "I thought Malchus might—"

"Malchus? Malchus is working at the temple. Or should be."

Zara slowly looked to the floor.

"Sorry to disappoint you, but I'm here on official duty, and I need to speak to you."

Zara suddenly looked up and then into the kitchen.

Jonathan followed her gaze into the kitchen to find Levia looking at Zara but remaining silent.

Jonathan pulled out the list, keeping his eye on the Gentile slave. He could sense her fear and found it exciting. Apparently she had been told about the list. Excellent. Levia, however, was frowning. She probably should be enlightened.

"Last week the high priest alertly ordered a list be made of possible followers of our most recent false messiah—people who appeared eager to accept his lies. Some seemed more enthused than others. Some even brought people to him to be healed, encouraging even more criminal behavior and blasphemy."

The slave's fear caused her to look repeatedly to Levia.

"Look at me when I speak to you," Jonathan said evenly, emphasizing every word.

The slave looked at him, standing perfectly still.

Her eyes. He was suddenly taken by her eyes. He had seen her in passing for over a week now, but he had never held eye contact with her, especially up close. Splendid. Stirring. Almost enough to make him nervous. Almost.

"This is the list," he said, pretending to be reading it. "This morning I was ordered to see if anyone on this list actually believed that blaspheming Nazarene was the Messiah. He especially wanted to know the names of anyone who embraced the preposterous rumor that he rose from the dead. I told him no one could actually believe such nonsense, but you know Caiaphas, he thinks some of these people might have fallen for the lies. That couldn't possibly be, now could it?" he said.

The girl just stood there before him. She did not turn away. *Very obedient,* he thought. *Excellent. She is indeed special.*

"We know his body was stolen to perpetuate the lie of his resurrection. The plotters will be found and punished, and information leading to their arrest will be rewarded."

"I cannot help you," she said, breaking her silence.

"Cannot or will not?"

She did not answer.

"Are you a follower of the Nazarene?"

"Jonathan, does Caiaphas know you are here interrogating Zara?" Levia finally asked.

"You dare question my authority?" Jonathan said angrily. He wished Levia was not there. He would dispose of her if he had to. "Caiaphas gave specific orders, and anyone interfering with them will be subject to punishment." He turned back to Zara. "I'll ask you once more. Are you or are you not a believer in the Nazarene you seemed to be so attracted to in the temple?"

"Don't answer him, Zara," Levia said sternly. "Don't give him an excuse. Caiaphas deals with his own people. He wouldn't have sent this bully after you."

"Silence, woman," Jonathan screamed. He shoved Levia to the side, sending her reeling into the wall where she banged her head. She slumped to the floor, moaning. He then grabbed Zara by the arm. "My orders were to get answers, and I intend on getting them." He dragged her toward the cellar door and then turned to Levia. "I'm not done with you, either." Then he grabbed Zara firmly by the back of her arm and directed her down the stone stairs, closing the door behind him.

At the bottom of the stairs, Jonathan pushed Zara away. She remained silent in the darkness. He felt along the cold stone wall until he touched the oil lamp hanging from a spike. He found the flints in a small dugout shelf in the wall next to the lamp and struck them together at the lamp's wick. The sparks lit the room for a brief moment, revealing Zara standing motionless. He wanted to see her eyes again. Her eyes would reveal her heart. A small yellow flame appeared and quickly grew. He left the wick unadjusted, causing the lamp to burn inefficiently and cast a dull light with black smoke rising and mushrooming at the ceiling.

Zara stood before him in the middle of the room. He was puzzled. Her eyes were closed. "Are you . . . praying?" he asked.

She made no attempt to respond. She simply stood there, hands at her side, chin up slightly, motionless.

"To whom might you be praying? Your messiah?" Jonathan said calmly, softly.

Still no response.

"He's dead," he yelled in her face.

Nothing but the movement of breathing and even that was not as rapid as he wanted. And he could not even enjoy her eyes with this incessant praying. Maybe another approach.

"Any disciple should be willing to walk the path of her master," Jonathan said as he slowly walked around her, his eyes taking in the details of her body. "Was the Nazarene your master?"

She had no response except for her continued silence.

"I'll take that as a *yes,* but feel free to correct me at any time. Do you see those shackles on the wall over there?" He pointed to the two rusted iron chains dangling from the adjacent stone wall. She still did not look.

Jonathan pushed her chin in the direction of the chains. Her eyes opened but revealed no expression. When he took his hand away from her chin, she turned her head back and stared him in the face blankly.

This was not happening the way he had envisioned. If she was going to resist, then she should resist. He wanted her to respond, to fight, claw, scream, not just stand there and . . . pray.

Enough! he thought. He pushed back her head covering, grabbed her hair with his right hand, tightened his fist, and spun her head around to the wall again. She gasped as he tightened his grip. "Those shackles. Now do you see them? Now do you?" he yelled into her left ear. "Your messiah was right there, in those very chains. And now it's your turn to follow him."

He shoved her head toward the wall. She hit the wall hard with her hands and face, unable to stop herself. A trickle of blood ran out from her nose. She groaned from the impact, and her breathing was now heavy and rapid. She still said nothing. Her unwillingness to fight with him was disappointing, but her labored breathing excited him.

Finally, he thought. He grabbed each of her hands in turn, and secured the shackles to her wrists. Her arms were spread wide. He checked the iron clasps to make sure they were secure.

"You should consider this to be quite a privilege, slave girl. If you had not been out looking for your friend, you might appreciate your position a little better. I'm sure that one day you'll look back on this and thank me." He leaned to speak into her ear, then paused to smell the scent of her skin. "His hands were against the same metal yours are, and his wet back was against the same stone as your face. We had just brought him here from my father's house. This is where we began the serious questioning," he said, his mouth almost touching her ear.

She moved her head away from him.

"Ah, now I can see we're getting somewhere." He laughed low. "We had the Romans leave. This was not for them. Most of the chief priests you saw, before you left to find your little friend, came down here to witness your messiah's blasphemy. All members of the Sanhedrin, to make it perfectly legal. You know how important that is to us. What happened down here was strictly confidential, but since you're being so . . . cooperative, I'll draw you a picture you'll be sure to appreciate."

Finally he was seeing a response. She no longer seemed to be praying. Her face was now pained with every word he spoke. He had found a tender spot, a bruise he could press.

"He didn't say much, but the little he said was enough to earn him this," Jonathan said, displaying to her face his closed fist. "See how the knuckles are still red. With all as a witness, Caiaphas asked him about his teachings. He said nothing. Then he was asked about his threat to destroy the temple and rebuild it in three days. He stood right here on the same dirt on which you're standing. Right here, Slave. Can you feel him? He said nothing. He just stood there, guilty, wearing that 'innocent me' face. I wanted to hit him . . . just punch his . . ."

Jonathan's hands had become tight fists as he remembered. If there was an hour of his life he could repeat, he would choose the one he was now describing. He would never allow himself to forget it.

"Then it happened, Slave. The Nazarene actually said what everyone had come to hear. He couldn't have given us a better gift, and he was too stupid to realize he should have remained silent. Caiaphas asked him if he was the Messiah, the son of God. His next words were so condemningly perfect, I'll never forget them. He said Caiaphas had spoken correctly, and that we would see him sitting at the right hand of the power of God, coming on the clouds of Heaven. Whatever that meant."

Jonathan grabbed her chin and turned her face toward his, pinching her cheeks until she winced. "Your loyalty is for nothing. He was a fake. Right then and right here I put him to the test, and he failed miserably. After I saw Caiaphas tear his robes, I knew I had to take control of that lying mouth. I hit him hard so he wouldn't be able to mock us anymore. And as soon as I hit him a few times, other priests joined in. *That* was justice," he said, and then threw her face back into the wall.

Jonathan took a moment and let out a long sigh. "But it doesn't have to be that way with you, Zara," he said, whispering close again. "There are other ways to handle this that aren't so—extreme." He slowly slid his hand down the inside of her sleeve and leaned against her buttocks. Touching her skin aroused him. "This doesn't have to be painful, Zara. Just tell me you believe Jesus was a fake. I don't want to have to do to you what I did to him. I can be very forgiving to someone like you," he said, his lips touching her right ear as he spoke.

She closed her eyes tightly. Tears began to run down her cheeks. She pressed her head into the wall as Jonathan again slid his hands up her arms then down over the front of her tunic, squeezing her with both hands, then reaching lower until he touched her bare legs. Then he ran his hand slowly up her smooth skin, lifting her tunic as he went.

"Now this doesn't hurt, does it?" Jonathan asked, moaning in her ear, his body pressing against her from behind.

"Noooo!" Zara screamed. She twisted herself to face him and stared defiantly into his eyes. Then she screamed into his face: "I believe in Jesus. He *is* the Messiah. I also believe that he is alive again, as he told you he would be. And I believe you will pay for this at his hand, you coward!" Tears streamed down her face. She began to scream for help, but as soon as the first sounds escaped her mouth, Jonathan's hand exploded across her face.

Jonathan stepped back, startled by her outburst. But his desires were already controlling him. "Good, very good. I knew you would come to life sooner or later." He then grabbed the back of her tunic at the neck with his right hand, and ripped it open, baring her back. Then he grabbed hold of the garment at the lower back and tore at it again, until it was completely ripped off, revealing her naked body. He had never seen such beauty, and now she was his. He grabbed her hips. His mind was completely lost in the moment. Nothing else existed but her.

He sighed and slid his hands up her back. He felt a peculiar wrinkle in her skin. He moved his hand curiously and felt another. He stepped back to allow the light to shine upon her. "Well, well. Not a bad idea. And I thought I was going to be the first," he said, examining the whip scars, then running his fingers along their length. "Very good work. This should warm you up nicely."

"Don't—please, don't," she pleaded. "Not that."

"What a pity," he said. He saw a whip hanging on the wall a few feet away and grabbed it. "I'm sorry it has to be this way," he said, but I have a job to do, and nobody is better at this than me. He then stepped back and cracked the whip in the stale musty air. Zara's scream sent a rush through his veins.

THIRTY-TWO

"Shalom," Malchus said, smiling broadly at the stone-faced guards. He was not the least bit sarcastic. He even closed the door gently behind him and wondered whether the guards might want something to drink or some fruit.

He needed to hide his money and get back to the temple, but not yet. He could spare a moment. He walked expectantly to the kitchen where he knew he would find Zara and Levia. He was half right.

Malchus rushed to Levia, who was on her hands and knees, trying to get to her feet. No sooner did he ask her what happened, when he heard a muffled scream. He spun around, his eyes boring through the cellar door. His feet barely touched the floor as he raced to the door, flung it open, and flew down the stone stairs into the dark dungeon.

His eyes did not adjust quickly to the poor light, but he was able to hurl himself in the direction of the dark form he knew to be Jonathan. Malchus was in midair, only an arm's length away, when he made out the sweaty face of his enemy glaring back at him from the darkness. A sadistic, twisted grin revealing the yellow glow of teeth moved quickly to the side. Malchus reached for the shadowy figure but missed. Instead, his outstretched arm was grabbed and pushed, causing Malchus to lose his balance and smash his forehead into the hard clay floor. He sprang back to his feet before he felt any pain. His eyesight adjusted to the dark just in time to see Jonathan send a crushing kick to his midsection. The blow forced the air out of him. He gasped for air and struggled to remain standing, when another blow to his left cheekbone sent him to the dirt at Zara's feet.

"What more could I ask for?" Jonathan shouted. "Would you like to try that again?" he said, laughing.

Malchus was lying on his side, bent at the waist, still trying to fill his lungs. He could not even spit out the bloody, mildewed dirt from his mouth. As he lay there, he felt cloth under his right hand. He looked toward it. It was white. It was Zara's robe. He could see her naked calf against the wall. With whatever consciousness he had left, all he wanted to do was kill Jonathan. But he could not move or breathe.

"Your friend here has just confessed to me her faith in the dead Nazarene. What about you, Slave? Shall I assume you both share the same beliefs?"

"Malchus!" Zara cried.

Malchus coughed violently through purple lips as air finally entered his lungs. He spit and struggled painfully to his hands and knees. He looked toward Zara and saw that she was completely naked. She was looking back at him from over her shoulder. Even in the dim light he could see the blood and dirt on her face and the tears in her eyes. *Kill him!* his primal thoughts screamed. He glared in Jonathan's direction just in time to duck away as the whip lashed the back of his neck, just missing his face.

"The penalty for attacking the captain of the temple is, of course, determined by me. But then, this isn't an attack, is it? You're trying to kill me, aren't you?" he yelled at the near prostrate body of Malchus on the floor.

"Defending myself against an insanely jealous slave trying to kill me. If I kill you in self-defense, I will only have to worry about one side of the story. Mine."

Malchus had never been flogged. The searing sting of the whip was worse than he could have imagined. Jonathan snapped it again, catching him in the upper arm. It felt as if he was being cut with fire. He turned quickly and looked at Zara. She had said she would rather die than get whipped again. Now he knew why. His heart pounded in his chest. He clutched her torn tunic and stood up slowly, pain stabbing his side and his face. He draped what was left of her clothes over her shoulders and saw glistening red stripes on her back. The beast.

Malchus turned back toward Jonathan, who seemed to enjoy his view of them. "You miserable coward. Yes. Yes, I believe in Jesus! And I'm astounded that you don't. You were there at the Garden of Gethsemane. You witnessed the power of his words, his presence. You felt the thickness in the air. You saw what happened to my ear. And now you do this?" Malchus yelled.

"You're insane. I saw nothing, and neither did you. You don't know what you're talking about," Jonathan said in a raised voice, stepping back a bit in anticipation of the confrontation for which they were readying. "But I do know that you're both traitors," he said, raising the whip. And my orders are to make an example of you. Caiaphas will be relieved you were found out and dealt with swiftly."

"You've either been blinded by God or by your own perversity," Malchus said, instinctively bending at the knees, readying for combat.

Jonathan made his move, snapping the lash across Malchus's chest. It struck him with pinpoint accuracy, tearing a hole in Malchus's robe and ripping into his flesh. Again Jonathan cracked the whip. Malchus tried to grab it with his hand but missed. Instead, it landed across his midsection, its lash licking his belly, leaving a trail of blood soaking into the front of his robe.

Malchus glanced back to make sure he was shielding Zara. As he looked, another lash caught him in the neck, and then another across the shoulders. He grunted, biting back sounds of pain, as his body stiffened.

"Malchus, run, get away!" Zara screamed.

"Not without you," he said as another lash came whipping across and past him, its end hitting Zara's bared back. She instantly jerked against the chains and shrieked in pain. Her cry went right through him.

"Oh, did that one get Zara?" Jonathan asked sarcastically. "You better start doing a better job, Malchus, or your woman's going to get hurt." He laughed.

"Agghh," Malchus yelled, spinning and lunging upward at Jonathan. The captain swung the whip, but Malchus was too close. Just as he had seen his uncle Laben do more times than he could believe, he swung his right arm around, driving all of his weight through his elbow. Still too short to hit the big man's face, he rammed Jonathan hard in the middle of his throat with the point of his elbow. The hit was solid.

Jonathan gasped for air. Eyes bulging, he dropped the whip and grabbed his neck with both hands. He staggered backward until he hit the stone wall where the lantern was hanging. He was coughing, gurgling, gasping for air. After a moment he slid down the wall until he was sitting upright on the floor, just staring wide-eyed at Malchus. He shook his head convulsively a couple of times, and then his hands fell away from his neck. His eyes closed, and then his whole body slid sideways down the rest of the wall until his head banged onto the stone floor. He did not move again.

"What is it, Malchus? What's happening?" Zara screamed.

"Shhh," Malchus said gently. "It's over."

Malchus quickly released the shackles that held Zara, revealing wrists that were cut and bruised. As her arms fell, she turned and embraced him. He hugged her tightly and closed his eyes for a moment, absorbing the fact that they were suddenly both safe. He clumsily did his best to adjust her torn tunic, taking off his belt and wrapping it around her to hold the torn garment together. Then he brought his hands up and cupped her face. "When I heard your scream, I stopped thinking."

"Malchus, no one in my life has ever cared so much for me," she said.

"Come on, Zara, we have to get out of here," he whispered in her ear.

"Is he dead?" Zara asked, looking toward Jonathan.

Malchus went over to him and put his ear near Jonathan's face. He was still breathing. "Unfortunately, no. Now let's go. When he comes to, he's not going to be very happy." He started for the door, then suddenly stopped. "Wait," he said. "Zara, give me a hand."

Malchus and Zara grabbed hold of Jonathan's hands, spun him around, and dragged him to the chains hanging down the wall. Struggling with the dead weight of his large frame, they managed to lift him just high enough to hook his left arm up to one of the shackles. They struggled to secure his right arm also, but he was too heavy and they were running out of time. Instead Malchus secured Jonathan's right hand to a foot clasp. As long as one hand could not reach the other, he would have to rely on outside help to get free.

Malchus wanted to wake Jonathan up and whip him to death, but he needed to try to think rationally again. They had to leave as quickly as possible. The longer Jonathan was unconscious and shackled, the better.

"He's not going to like this when he wakes up," Malchus said. "Oh, what I wouldn't give to see him explain to whoever finds him how he wound up in the shackles."

"Come on, Malchus," Zara said, pulling him by the hand toward the stairs. She was still shaking.

They ran up the steps and into the hall, then past Levia who was on her feet but leaning against the wall. She gasped, seeing the torn open back of Zara's tunic. Zara did not stop to talk. Instead, she ran down the hall to her room to change her clothes.

Malchus took Levia gently by the arm. They went into the kitchen, and Malchus quickly told Levia what had taken place in the dungeon.

"Where's Jonathan?" Levia said.

"For the moment, he's unconscious."

"Unconscious?"

"Yes, but I don't know for how long."

"How did—"

"Levia, we have to leave. Fast. We both admitted to believing in Jesus. If we stay here and we're lucky, we'll be flogged severely and end up in prison for the rest of our lives. Make sure you tell Seth what really happened here. Say good-bye to him and Judah for me. Someday, I'll get in touch with them, if we get out of here alive. Thanks for your help all these years, Levia. You've been like an older sister to me," he said, smiling.

"I've felt like your mother, the way I've had to clean up after you," Levia said.

He grabbed her hand and squeezed it. "Thanks," he repeated. Levia wiped a tear from her eye.

"One more thing," Malchus said. "If you hear any noise coming out of the cellar, don't do anything yourself, but make sure Caiaphas or one of the guards goes down to see what it is." Malchus gave her a farewell hug as Zara ran back into the room. Zara smiled at Levia for a moment, and then both embraced, hugging each other tightly.

"Shalom," Malchus said as he and Zara calmly walked out between the temple guards as if nothing was wrong. Neither guard responded. Halfway down the stone steps and out of view of the guards, they broke into a run and quickly disappeared into the rush of the busy street below.

"Malchus, where are we going?" Zara asked, staying directly behind Malchus as he opened a trail through the crowd of people as quickly as possible.

"Japhet's, to buy a horse, or mule, or whatever he's got that can get us out of here. Where after that? I don't know yet," Malchus said, talking over his right shoulder and holding Zara's hand tightly. "Where would you like to go?"

"Wherever we're going is fine with me, as long as we're together."

Malchus suddenly stopped short, and Zara bumped into him. He turned around to her and then looked past her.

"What?" Zara asked nervously, turning toward Caiaphas's home also, trying to see what Malchus was looking at.

"We have to go back."

"What?" Zara said. "Why?"

"The list," Malchus answered. Did he dare go back for it? Every moment was precious. Time meant distance, and they needed to put as much distance between themselves and Jerusalem as possible. Even if they continued, their chances of escape were slim, but to go back would make escape next to impossible. The math definitely did not add up to going back. But how could he not? Who would be the next victim?

In the second it took Malchus to decide, so, too, had Zara. She turned and began running back toward Caiaphas's. Malchus ran after her. He had not seen her move like this since the rooftop, and he actually had some trouble keeping up with her, his bruised ribs aching as he ran.

The guards are still at the entrance, so Jonathan should still be unconscious, Malchus thought. One of the guards glared at Malchus as they came to the door. He was immediately paranoid that the guard was looking at his face, which was now bruised and swelling from the fight in the dungeon. He did not look that way when he had entered a short time before. In fact, he had been physically perfect since the healing. And when he and Zara had left moments ago, the guards would have seen only the backs of their heads, no doubt mistaking Malchus's escape for his usual rudeness.

Malchus slammed the door when they entered, trying not to arouse any more suspicion. "The guards know something is wrong," he said quietly to Zara when they were in the foyer.

"What are you doing here?" Levia whispered, obviously shocked to see them again.

"We have to get the list of names from Jonathan," Zara said.

"The list?" Levia rolled her eyes. "This is madness," she said.

Malchus glided stealthily down the steps into the dimly lit dungeon. Jonathan looked just as he had when Malchus left, sitting against the wall, his left arm stretched out in a shackle as if he were reaching up to catch a tossed orange.

He grabbed the lamp from the wall and quickly moved around the room, searching its dark confines for the list. Where is it? Come on, Jonathan, what did you do with it?

He heard people walking about upstairs and froze in midstep. He waited a moment, listened for more movement, then continued the search when he heard none. After looking again in the same corners, he was about to give up when he realized there was one place he had not searched. Jonathan. Was it stuffed somewhere in his robe?

Malchus bent over Jonathan and slowly pulled open the top of his robe, keeping careful watch of the big man's right arm, which was well in reach of Malchus's neck.

No list.

He looked into Jonathan's sleeves. They had slid down from his shackled wrists almost to his shoulders, revealing the captain's large hairy arms.

No list.

He reached behind Jonathan's slumped back and felt along the wall and ground. The nervous sweat dripping down Malchus's face was stinging his eyes, and his clothes were sticking to his skin. Suddenly, Jonathan's head rolled to the side, and the man groaned. Malchus's breathing stopped. He waited a second that seemed like an eternity. No movement. He exhaled, then began to feel around behind the captain. *Where is it, Jonathan? You're not that clever,* he thought. *Wait. What's this?*

He felt something half buried under Jonathan's behind. Malchus could hardly get at it, his fingertips barely pinching it. He tugged, but Jonathan's weight was on all but the corner he had in his fingers. He pulled again, tearing the corner off. He held the ripped piece up to the lamp. Finally! He must have somehow dragged it with Jonathan to the shackles.

"Oh God, now what do I do?" Malchus whispered in prayer. The very last thing he wanted to do was awaken this viper. But he was going to get that list. He leaned into Jonathan's side and pushed. Jonathan's head flopped from his left shoulder to his right, but he was still sitting on the list. Malchus pushed again, this time upward, certain Jonathan would be shaken into consciousness. He lifted him imperceptibly as he stretched his fingers and grabbed at the paper beneath him.

Got it.

Malchus eased Jonathan back until he was no longer touching him. He took the list with all its names and touched its corner to the flickering flame. He put the lamp down on the ground and dropped the burning parchment as well. He watched as the names disappeared into ashes. Malchus did not wait for the list to turn to embers. As the last name blackened and crumpled by fire, he quickly and quietly ran back up the steps.

"Done," Malchus said.

"I was ready to come down there," Zara said tensely. "I thought I heard you struggling and . . ."

"I'm fine," he said. "Let's go."

Zara nodded and exhaled, then started with Levia toward the front doorway.

"No," Malchus said. "We can't go that way. I didn't like the way the guards looked at me on the way in. We'll go this way," he said, leading Zara by the hand.

Malchus climbed out the kitchen window, hung, and dropped twice the height of a man to the hard ground, crumbling on his side when he hit. He grunted and grabbed his tender, bruised ribs, then quickly looked in the direction of the guards. All they would need now was to be seen leaving through the window. He did not have the slightest idea what he would tell them.

Zara followed him and dropped in the same way, and Malchus caught her to soften her fall. They looked up and waved to Levia, then sneaked around to the front, well below the grand entrance steps.

From the street Malchus could see the guards. They were facing each other and appeared to be talking. They never did that. Malchus did not like the math. Their chances of getting away were small enough. Their only hope was that whoever came after them would first go in the wrong direction, allowing them to buy some distance before their trail was picked up.

They emerged from the crowd out through the Essenes Gate and into Hinnom Valley. Once out of the confines of the city walls, they were free to run.

†

On the hillside, just outside the Water Gate below the Pool of Siloam, Seth was enjoying a hot cup of tea with some friends. He had just returned from an escort. He was taking his time getting back to Caiaphas's because he knew the moment he stepped past the guards, Levia would have orders for another escort. Seth did not like the escorts, but preferred the job to working with the priests. At least he could pretend he was free. He sat back, watching the stream of people merging through the two valleys.

"More tea?" a man said, extending a bronze tray with several small clay cups on it. Both Seth and a man next to him nodded appreciatively, exchanged their empty cups for the two new steaming ones, and then resettled themselves.

Seth blew softly across the steam and was about to take a sip but then lowered his cup. He saw Malchus hurrying in exodus. The new slave girl was right behind him. Seth furrowed his brow and stood up. At first he thought they were trying to steal some time together before Levia missed her new assistant, and he smiled. That is what he would be doing, but not Malchus. Malchus was most definitely on an errand, maybe to show the girl fresh figs or hidden locust trees still full with carob pods. He probably had to keep the girl from getting lost, and then race back to the temple before Caiaphas found him missing.

Suddenly, Seth wondered if he could show the girl the valley's secrets and free Malchus to serve the temple, where he belonged. They were almost at a run and nearly out of earshot. He cupped his mouth with his right hand and yelled to his cousin.

There was no acknowledgement. He thought they should have heard him.

"Malchus," he yelled louder.

Malchus turned his head, but did not stop.

Seth flagged his arm but Malchus turned back around, still weaving through traffic. Too far now for Malchus to see who was calling. "Ahh," he said as he waved them off.

Already standing, Seth finished his tea and bid his friends safe travels. He was envious. If only he was with his cousin instead of heading back to Caiaphas's. He longed for the day when he and Malchus would be free again. *Soon,* he thought.

"Malchus," someone yelled.

Malchus heart skipped a beat. "Keep going. Don't turn around," he said, pulling Zara along.

"Malchus!" someone yelled again, louder this time.

Malchus looked over his shoulder toward the hillside near the Water Gate by the Pool of Siloam. Someone was waving. He tried to focus while running but could not quite make out the person. Who was that? he wondered. He looked familiar. Well, at least it was not Jonathan, he thought. "Come on, Zara," he said, turning back toward her. "We're still alive."

THIRTY-THREE

Like rainfall, a hissing sound filled Jonathan's ears. Louder, softer, then louder again. The flickering flame of the lantern and its reflection dancing across the room were barely in focus. He had no idea where he was or what time it was. Was it evening or morning? As his eyes adjusted, the shadowy stone walls reminded him of where he was, but he couldn't understand how it could be. Then, suddenly, a sharp piercing pain shot through his head and throat.

"Aghhh," he screamed, then bit his lip to stop. Screaming made the unbelievable pain in his throat even more intense. He instinctively reached for the pain. He could not. He was—chained? "How could this have happened?" he whispered, discovering he had no voice and that talking was almost as painful as screaming. He swallowed and grimaced. More pain. *What am I doing here?* he wondered.

His thoughts were all very hazy, and his head was swimming. At first Jonathan did not remember a thing. Then, he vaguely recalled bringing Zara down here, and after a few confusing minutes, he remembered Malchus arriving. Finally, Jonathan remembered being struck in the throat.

Also baffling was how one of his arms had been chained to a foot clasp. He pulled hard on the chains, but they were securely fastened to his wrists. He struggled, and even tried to free himself with his teeth.

Head pounding, throat cramped and burning, he suddenly came to one dreadfully clear reality. He was going to need help.

"Is there somebody down there?" Levia asked innocently from the top of the stairs.

"Levia," Jonathan called hoarsely. "Levia, come here. Help me." The pain from yelling was unbearable. He was trying to fight back tears but could not.

"Who's down there?" Levia yelled.

"Get me out of these," he said in a loud, grave whisper, shaking his wrists.

"You . . . do you want me to help you?" Levia said, placing her hands on her hips. "Sorry, those things are much too complicated for me. I'll go and get some help. I'll go and get a Roman soldier. He'll know how to open those clasps."

"No!" he shrieked in a higher pitch, straining his unrecognizable voice to the breaking point. "No," he said softer. "Get the guards." His pain caused sweat to stream down his face and neck.

"The guards? Oh, of course. I'll go get them," Levia said. Then she halted midway up the stairs and asked, "Wasn't Zara down here with you?"

Jonathan said nothing. He rolled his eyes, knowing hers was not the last word he was going to hear about this. If he had been free, he would have strangled Levia, he was so frustrated.

Levia left. Moments later, she returned with the guards who had been posted outside at the house entrance. The guards looked at Jonathan, then at each other, and then back to Jonathan.

"Don't just stand there gaping, get me out if these things," Jonathan ordered in his new tenor voice. The pain made him wince like a man possessed.

Both guards rushed to his assistance.

"Who did this to you?" one of them asked as he unshackled his wrists.

"Zara," Levia quickly volunteered. "Zara must have done it. She was the only one down here with him. It must have been Zara," she repeated.

"The slave girl?" they both asked at the same time.

"It was Malchus also," Jonathan snapped.

"The slave?" they said incredulously, this time looking at Jonathan but still speaking in unison.

"Silence! Don't say another word if you know what's good for you," Jonathan warned in a barely audible whisper. He looked menacing, and both guards knew better than to say anything further.

The guards helped Jonathan up the stairs. He wished he had an explanation of some kind for them, but he could not think of anything. He was not really sure himself what had happened. The only thing he knew for sure was that he was going to catch and kill Malchus and Zara. Never before had he been so thoroughly humiliated and embarrassed, no small feat for a man who spent most of his time being publicly rebuked and corrected by Caiaphas for just about everything he did. This, however, was different. Much different.

"We must find them and bring them to justice," Jonathan fumed. "We must find out where they went. When I get my hands on them, they'll wish they had received their punishments and been done with it. When I'm done with them, they'll wish they were dead. Levia? You must know where they were headed. Where did they go? You're their friend," he said, glaring at her.

Levia shrugged her shoulders. "I didn't know Malchus was here. I only saw you and Zara and—"

"Enough! You old fool! He screamed, forgetting for a moment the pain that yelling caused. He grabbed his throat with both hands to stop the throbbing.

"They were headed toward Bethany," came a voice matter-of-factly from the hallway. It was Seth. He took one look at Levia and immediately knew he had said the wrong thing.

Without another word, Jonathan and the two guards hurried past Levia and Seth and out the door.

THIRTY-FOUR

Winded and gasping for air, Malchus looked over his shoulder as he and Zara came within view of the garden stables. The softer temple life had not done Malchus any favors. His thighs were cramped and his sandals, which had been ready for mending before they started, were falling apart and in need of emergency repair. Zara said her legs were fine, but that the wounds on her back were stinging from the salt of her sweat.

A young boy, one Malchus hadn't seen on previous ventures, was using one of Japhet's star-engraved buckets to water the many assorted flowers in the middle of the dirt circle near the stable entrance. The flowers were lush and plentiful and turned what would have been a dreary, ordinary-looking stable entrance into a collage of colors that people throughout the area would make a point to visit, especially in early spring. Japhet had to have taught the boy how to take care of the flowers, for no one would dare to add their touch to anything Japhet had designed. Gardening, especially collecting rare flower seed, was one of

Japhet's numerous passions. The boy looked up as Malchus and Zara hurried by, heading up the driveway to the barn.

"Just a moment," Malchus said as they ran behind the old barn door to hide. "I need to catch my breath. When I used to chase sheep with my cousin, I could run all day long. What's happened to me?" He peered out from behind the door at the empty road and hoped to God it would stay that way. It was the first time since they left Caiaphas's palace that they were hidden from public view.

"We're free, Malchus. Soon you'll be running after sheep again."

"We're alive, but far from free. We're escaped slaves. The moment we acknowledged to Jonathan that Jesus was the Messiah, we kissed away our freedom."

Zara did not respond. Malchus knew she had probably just wanted to instill a sense of hope, but they could not afford to look to the future, only the present.

There were half a dozen roads leading away from Jerusalem. Their chances of survival depended on which direction Jonathan chose to follow first. In any case, once Jonathan decided to search the road to Jericho, Japhet's would be a logical stop.

"We have to get out of here," Malchus said, then turned to Zara. "They could be here any minute. If Jonathan has any common sense, he'll know to come here." Her face was beaded with sweat, and the back of her tunic was so drenched, he could see her skin where the cloth stuck to her.

Malchus was acrawl with fear as he considered capture and punishment. Zara would be far better off if he had never rescued her from Jonathan in the dungeon. The penalty for being a runaway slave was harsh, especially for a Gentile. And punishment could be inflicted not only by the Jewish slave owner, but by the Romans as well for breaking the civil laws. Also, the punishment for a runaway slave would be in addition to what was in store for those who believed Jesus was the Messiah. Malchus wondered what the punishment for the believers would be. Whatever, they were guilty of both offenses, and Malchus knew if they were caught, they would be longing for death before their punishment was over.

Malchus took another look at the road. Still empty. He took Zara by the hand and went deeper into the barn. He had to find Japhet and obtain some kind of transportation for the long journey out of Palestine. To where, he still did not know. He needed to speak to Japhet now, get a beast, and get on the road.

"Japhet," Malchus yelled, walking through the stable. "Japhet!" He knew Japhet's hearing wasn't the best. If he didn't find him in another second or two, he would have to help himself to a horse or mule and work it out somehow in the future. "Japh—" The old man suddenly emerged from a stall, pitchfork in hand, scaring Malchus half to death.

"Enough, enough, stop shouting. What do you think, I'm hard of hearing?" The old man had a smile on his face as he spoke even before he realized it was Malchus. Seeing Malchus and Zara, his eyes lit up, but his expression quickly changed upon closer focus.

"What's wrong, Malchus?" he asked.

"Japhet, we desperately need your help." Malchus quickly explained their situation to him. He told him how he had been part of the mob that had arrested Jesus, and of the miracle Jesus had performed. He showed Japhet his new ear.

Japhet nodded affirmingly as he closely inspected and touched Malchus's ear. "You must not be silent about this, my son. Your words are stirring and have the breath of God on them. You will be a witness to a people."

"Not if Caiaphas gets hold of me," he said. But there was something more than casual about Japhet's words. They came with an unexpected weight and impact. The urgency of the moment was sharply cut with a surprising sense of promise and purpose.

"Of course," Japhet said, leaning the pitchfork against the stall door. The pitchfork handle had been tapered and split open at the end and connected horizontally for the grip. Another one-of-a-kind Japhet tool.

"I'll need a beast. I'll pay you whatever it cost," Malchus said, showing him his money while he spoke.

"Put that away. You'll need it," he said, pushing away Malchus's hand. He motioned for them to follow.

The old man's slow pace heightened Malchus's anxiety to where he considered scooping Japhet up in his arms and carrying him to speed things along.

Stepping out through the rear of the barn, Japhet pointed to a large, muscular black horse eating grass in a large corral. There were four other horses in the corral, along with three mules, three donkeys, and his beloved donkey colt. "That's my selection for you, Malchus. He's very strong. Not the fastest of the bunch, but he has no quit in him. He'll pull my wagon with you and Zara as far as you want to go.

"A wagon?" Malchus asked. "You have a wagon we can use?"

"Not *a* wagon," Japhet said with a proud smile. "My wagon. The wagon I made especially for my trips down to Jericho. As you know from your escorts, that road is treacherous in many ways. So I built a wagon that is worthy of the challenge. You know, I'm not so young anymore, so I needed some, shall we say, assistance. But first, let's get the horse."

"How can I help?" Malchus said, constantly looking over his shoulder, waiting for the front doors to smash open any second.

Japhet waved him off. "Thank you, but we don't have time for help." The old man brought his fingers to his mouth, whistled, and every animal in the corral stopped whatever it was doing, lifted its head, and looked toward the old man.

Malchus and Zara looked at each other, then back at Japhet.

Japhet called the large black horse by its name. "Julius." The animal obediently trotted over to Japhet and lowered its head. Then Japhet kissed it between the eyes.

"Julius?" Malchus asked. "Caesar must be flattered. You couldn't name him something a little less risky, like Herod or Pilate?"

"He likes the name *Julius,*" Japhet said nonchalantly.

Malchus wondered if he was serious.

Japhet proceeded to harness Julius effortlessly with the proper tack and lead him into the barn. If Malchus did not know better, he would have sworn that the horse practically dressed itself. Japhet then checked the hooves and picked clean anything stuck in the bottoms. He inspected the horseshoes he had fashioned, explaining what they were, how they worked, and their benefit to the horse. Julius then gently lowered his foot, and Japhet slapped him affectionately on the rump. Julius raised his head in such a way that Malchus half expected the horse to speak. Japhet and Julius had quite a relationship, but Malchus was getting impatient. What if the road to Jericho was Jonathan's first choice?

Japhet then walked over to something that was covered with a large cloth. "Take it off, will you, please?" Japhet directed.

Malchus and Zara each grabbed an end and quickly pulled. There was nothing outwardly special about the wagon, and Malchus wondered why the old man had bothered to cover it. It was almost as wide as Malchus could stretch his arms and one and a half times that in length, with deep sides that had the usual Japhet star carved into them and two large, solid wooden wheels to roll on. Except for the star, it was standard.

"It's beautiful," Zara said. "Thank you."

Japhet nodded humbly, then called for Julius.

Again, Malchus could only watch as the horse positioned itself without further prompting in front of the wagon, waiting to be hooked up.

"Look under it, Malchus," Japhet said, making adjustments to the tack.

Malchus took a quick look at the front doors, then got down on his knees and ducked his head under the wagon. The wagon itself was supported not by timber, as Malchus had expected, but by what looked to be bows, like the ones used to fire arrows. He ran his hand over them. "What do these do?"

"I made them from local locust trees. The wood is very hard, but shaped in layers, it bends without breaking. Fastened to the wagon it absorbs the roughness out of the ride on a road even as bumpy and pitted as the one to Jericho. Believe me, it saves your back and your—" He looked to Zara, then slapped his own backside to finish the sentence. "You'll see. But that's not all. Let me show you something else that just might come in handy." Japhet reached into the cargo area of the wagon and pulled out a stick that was about two feet in length. He then inserted it into a hole in the floor from underneath the wagon and pushed the stick upward. A section of planking in the floor of the wagon flipped over.

Malchus and Zara leaned over the wagon and looked into a compartment that was revealed. The wagon had a false bottom. Neither had noticed it before Japhet showed them.

Malchus shook his head. "And what is this for?"

"On the rode to Jericho you never know if you're going to be robbed. I take anything of value and put it in there," Japhet said, pointing to the previously hidden area a little more than a foot deep. "Then I drop it down like so," he said, letting the planks fall snugly back into place. "And nobody is the wiser."

"Here, Japhet. Take this, please," Malchus said, with coins in his hand. He felt indebted to the man.

Japhet again pushed the money away. "I do this unto the Lord. If you want to give me something, there is only one thing I will ask."

Without time to argue further, Malchus put the coins back in his pouch. "Name it," he said, and then helped Zara up to the bench seat in the front of the wagon.

"The children of Bethany will miss Julius's dance."

"Dance?" Zara said.

"Yes, I've trained him for their enjoyment. I would greatly appreciate it if you would allow him to dance for the children you come to know."

"Of course," she said. "But how—"

"Take this," Japhet said, removing a small, thin, hollowed-out wooden tube on a leather lace from around his neck. He handed it up to Zara.

"What's this," Zara said, examining the wooden tube.

"Blow into it."

Malchus looked to the door anxiously. He didn't want to be rude, but he had no time for this.

Zara took a deep breath and blew. A sharp high-pitched whistle echoed through the barn.

Upon hearing the sound, Julius instantly reared up on his hind legs and whinnied, then after a moment settled softly back to earth.

Zara's eyes were wide and both arms were latched to her seat.

"Children love when he does that. He'll do it every time," Japhet said, obviously very proud of Julius.

Before anything else could happen, Malchus hopped aboard and grabbed the reins. The seat moved up and down ever so slightly, initially causing Malchus to brace himself. He looked at Japhet quizzically.

"A similar concept to the springs on the bottom, my boy," Japhet volunteered.

"Japhet, we can't thank you enough," Zara said.

"You're very welcome. The Lamb of God is with you both."

"The Lamb of God?" Malchus asked.

"Jesus! He is the Lamb of God. Everyone brought a lamb to be sacrificed for his or her sins. This Passover, so did God. God brought a Lamb, and now there is no need for another. The event was prophesied hundreds of years ago. Now the prophecy is fulfilled. The world will never be the same. He will be with you

always, and you will spread the seeds of this good news to others," Japhet then pulled a knob on the side of the wagon and a step hinged down for him.

"What are you doing?" Malchus said, wondering if there was anything else about the wagon Japhet had not told them.

"I'll ride with you until you get to the Jericho road."

"If you're caught with us, you could get in severe trouble."

"I'll be off soon enough," Japhet said, then whistled a signal. The barn doors swung open with the gentle nudge of Julius's nose, and they were off.

Malchus had knots in his stomach. He had half expected soldiers to be standing there in front of them. He wished there was another road than the one he had to double back on to get to the road to Jericho. Jonathan could be turning the corner right now, and they would not know until they were upon them.

Julius's beastly strength became immediately apparent as he effortlessly pulled the wagon in tow. Riding around the circle, Japhet waved to the boy who was still busy watering the flowers. "That's Martha's boy," Japhet said.

"Who's Martha?" Malchus asked.

THIRTY-FIVE

At the top of the Bethany road where the road to Jericho intersects, Japhet got off the wagon, finally accepting Malchus's help. As Japhet climbed down, Malchus heard a loud, deep voice call him from behind. He turned cautiously, his knees feeling suddenly weak. Then, seeing the man behind the voice, he was relieved, but only somewhat.

"Evaratus!" Another delay. He tried to sound glad to see him, but the last thing Malchus wanted was to be seen by someone whom he and Jonathan both knew. Then he remembered the last time he saw Evaratus he was standing next to Caiaphas when Jesus was verbally undressing to the skin him and the other priests. For all Malchus knew, Evaratus could have suggested the whole Roman execution idea to Caiaphas in the first place. Wonderful timing. *Free in you,* he thought, then quickly apologized, knowing he had just been heard.

"Yes, yes. It's good to see your eye has cleared up. You're a fast healer," Evaratus said, but then he frowned slightly, looking closer at Malchus's face. "But you seem to have a few new scuffs."

"Well, you know how it is. Some horses are harder to bring out of the pasture than others," he said, patting Julius on the rump.

"Are you headed back to Cos?" Malchus said, asking the obvious while keeping an eye toward Jerusalem.

"Yes, indeed," the big man answered as his horse stepped out of the busy road and alongside the wagon. As usual, his two huge, muscular slaves accompanied him, each dressed only in loincloth and sandals. One was leading a mule, packed so heavily the animal was barely seen. Evaratus bowed his head to Zara. "And good day to you, Zara. It's a pleasure to see you again. I trust Malchus is still fighting for you?" Evaratus said pleasantly.

"More than ever," Zara said, glancing at Malchus.

Malchus looked back at her as if she were crazy.

"Good, good," Evaratus said with a deep chuckle.

Evaratus seemed in a good mood for someone starting out on such a long journey. Maybe with all that had happened in Jerusalem, he was just glad to leave.

"See you next year?" Malchus asked, again glancing toward the old city. He wanted desperately to leave, but if he cracked the reins and took off toward Jericho, he would likely have not only the temple guard chasing him but the pilgrims' exodus as well, led by Evaratus and the two hulks.

Evaratus furrowed his thick brow and considered the simple question longer than Malchus had expected, or was it that everything seemed to be taking too long? "I don't know. Much can happen in a year," he finally said.

That was not what Evaratus would have said on the way *into* Jerusalem, and Malchus knew it. Something had happened to this annually faithful delegate of Cos's tithe. Last week's experience had either soured him or scared him away from future trips. This was exactly what Caiaphas had feared. Jerusalem had become too dangerous for the pilgrims—a viable rationalization to forego an already inconvenient journey, a notion Caiaphas had labored so hard to conquer over the years.

"Don't you think you should get going, Malchus?" Japhet said.

Malchus would have preferred for Evaratus to leave first, but Japhet was right. "Well, I suppose I should," Malchus said as calmly as he could, despite the sweat dripping off his brow. He climbed back into his seat. "May your trip be a safe one," he said.

Zara waved with a weak smile. They both nodded another brief farewell to Japhet, then started off.

"Wait!" Evaratus commanded.

Malchus was about to snap the reins and take off, but did not, fearing the world was closing in around him. He turned to Evaratus and nervously watched the two giant slaves walk in front of the wagon. Japhet closed his eyes, presumably in prayer. So did Zara. He knew what the question would be, and he did not have anything to say. Except the truth.

Evaratus stepped up to the wagon. "Where are you two going?" His eyes narrowed. "Jerusalem is in the other direction."

"But we're not going to Jerusalem," Malchus answered quickly, knowing hesitation would surely give him away.

"Then where?"

Malchus had never been very good at lying, especially when he did not have a good one thought out. "Jericho. Oranges," he said, which was partially true. Jericho did grow the world's best oranges, but it was a day's ride just to get there by wagon, even under the best of conditions.

"Oranges?" Evaratus said with a strong air of skepticism. "Are there not enough oranges in Jerusalem's marketplace that you have to travel to Jericho?"

Malchus had no quick answer, and Evaratus was no idiot.

"And the high priest appears to be showing unusual trust, is he not?"

"Trust?" Malchus said, but his mock confusion felt painfully transparent.

"Why, yes. After all, you're bringing his Gentile slave girl halfway to her homeland . . . and this can't be one of Caiaphas's wagons," he said, stepping back to see it better. "If I'm not mistaken, that star is the same as the one I saw carved into a piece of wood at the garden stable." Evaratus stepped closer and looked Malchus in the eye. "You weren't planning on bringing those oranges back to Jerusalem, were you?"

"No," Malchus said boldly, ending what had become a charade and a waste of precious time.

Evaratus appeared surprised at the sudden admission of guilt. "But why? Were you not to be freed soon?" he said with an unexpected tenderness in his deep voice.

Malchus looked back toward Jerusalem again. "We're running for our lives, Evaratus. Try to stop us if you must, but if we don't leave now we'll surely be dead before sunset."

"Why?" Evaratus demanded.

"Because they believe Jesus is the Messiah. And so do I," Japhet said loudly and boldly enough to raise a few passing eyebrows.

Evaratus quickly looked about to see what trouble the sudden proclamation might have stirred. He then looked at Japhet, who was standing proudly, then back to Malchus and Zara. In a hushed voice he rasped, "So do I."

THIRTY-SIX

Jonathan could feel his left hand crushing Malchus's neck as he and five other horsemen galloped through the Kidron Valley on the temple's finest horses. He had left the stable master with a hand-size welt on the side of his face for taking so long to ready the horses, and he would have hit him again if he had had the time. He repeatedly pumped his fist, envisioning himself hammering Malchus's face until there was only dripping red pulp.

Jonathan had not felt this alive and full of purpose since he dragged the Nazarene's betrayer to the Garden of Gethsemane. Like then, he was free to do whatever was necessary to accomplish the mission. His way.

Stallion hooves pounded the dirt roadway. Behind them, a wake of dust left pilgrims coughing and choking. The Levitical robes of the temple guards and their captain blew freely in the wind, revealing razor-sharp swords flashing sunlight as they bounced with each stride. Malchus and Zara, possibly in disguise, were hiding among one of the many caravans leaving Jerusalem, and they *would* be found.

Near Bethany, Jonathan signaled for the guards to come to him. He did not want to yell above the noise of the crowd. They pulled the reins of their high-strung horses, slowing them to a trot, and maneuvered them next to Jonathan. "They can't be very far ahead," Jonathan said hoarsely. "If they're on foot, we'll probably see them within the next five miles. More than likely, though, they went to Japhet's to get an animal. You three go ahead. If you find them, take them captive. If they give you the least resistance, kill them both where they stand. Then bring them back. And you two," he said, pointing, "come with me to Japhet's. We'll find out if they were there."

All the guards looked at one another. Jonathan knew what they were thinking. These were slaves of the high priest they were being ordered to kill.

"Now!" he yelled through gritted teeth. "Or you'll answer to me personally."

Jonathan watched for a moment as the three guards rode ahead. They went right to work. They checked everyone, stopping to peer into covered carts, lifting tarps from covered wagons, and ordering hoods removed from anyone who couldn't be seen clearly from atop their mounts. Satisfied, Jonathan and the other two rode through Bethany, heading for Japhet's.

Japhet was thanking God for the opportunity to help these new disciples while walking back to his stable. He saw the young boy about two hundred feet ahead, still tending the garden. The boy abruptly stopped watering and looked up the road. Japhet, his hearing not what it used to be, stopped and turned around to see what had caught the boy's attention. Something was happening around the bend. Although Japhet could not yet see what it was, he did see a cloud of dust rising above the road and moving quickly toward him. He thanked God for the boy's keen hearing and his own sharp vision and quickly got off the road and hid behind a nearby boulder.

He finally heard the unwelcome approach and felt the ground tremble. His palms were against the rock as he crouched behind its cover. The horses were at full gallop. Japhet leaned closer into the boulder to make sure he wasn't seen, squatting as the captain of the temple and two of his guards thundered by. They rode past the boy and into the stable grounds dangerously fast.

Jonathan dismounted even before his horse came to a stop. He drew his sword and went into the barn with one of the guards. The other guard remained on his horse and kept watch from outside. He was eyeing the boy, the barn, and the road they had just traveled. Japhet was surprised at Jonathan's intensity. He had never seen him like this before. No wonder Malchus and Zara were in such a hurry to leave. Japhet closed his eyes and prayed that none of the animals would be hurt. There was no telling what Jonathan would do when he discovered that the objects of his hunt were nowhere to be found.

Jonathan kicked open the barn door, sending it crashing against the wall. He and one of the guards entered the barn, then emerged a few minutes later. Jonathan then kicked the dirt and began yelling something at his men before mounting his horse. Japhet hoped the tantrum was over and that his animals were safe. The guard who was with him simply followed his lead without any display of emotion.

Japhet winced as Jonathan jammed his heels into the horse's ribs. The poor animal took off with a burst and a whinny loud enough for Japhet to hear. Jonathan stormed out of the entrance and past the flower garden, the guards behind him trying to keep up. Japhet tried to focus on Jonathan's sword to see if there was any blood on it. It appeared clean. Then Japhet bent down as low as he could, praying he would not be seen. He was grateful they were leaving. He sighed heavily after the hooves stomped past him, but before he could take his next breath, the horses whinnied again and came to a sudden halt in midgallop.

Japhet's heart sank. *How stupid of me to allow myself to be seen,* he thought. He braced himself for the inevitable, but decided that, no matter what, he would tell Jonathan nothing. He would not say anything that would jeopardize Malchus and Zara. He would die first. Japhet figured Jonathan would try to beat it out of him and then run him through with his sword. *So be it,* he thought, as he looked skyward. *Before that time comes, I still might be able to slow Jonathan down. God, give me strength,* he prayed. *Every minute I keep him here increases their chance of escape,* he thought, prepared to make the ultimate sacrifice.

Japhet pushed away from the boulder and stood up. He turned around to look Jonathan straight in the face, but to his surprise, Jonathan was not there. Jonathan had turned around and gone back to the stables again, the guards following slowly behind. Japhet had been so deep in thought, he had not realized they left. For a moment he was confused but relieved they had not seen him. He would not have to deal with Jonathan after all.

Then, just as quickly, he was overcome with dread. His heart sank as he realized why Jonathan had returned to the stable.

†

Jonathan yanked back on the reins, and his horse reared its head and whinnied, skidding in a cloud of dust that the wind quickly carried away.

Japhet winced for the tortured horse but was more concerned for the safety of his young worker.

"Boy!" Jonathan shouted angrily, then cringed and reached for his throat. "Did you see a man and woman come or leave within the last hour?" he snarled in a quieter voice.

The boy looked up at him and then at the other approaching horsemen but said nothing.

"Look at me when I speak to you!" Jonathan screamed hoarsely. "I said, look at me," he repeated, grabbing his sword.

The boy's desperate gaze dashed about. Japhet knew the frightened youngster was looking for him.

Jonathan drew his sword, startling the other horsemen who also began to look about, presumably for witnesses.

"The question is a simple one," Jonathan said with eery calm, pointing his polished sword between the boy's watering eyes. "Now tell me. You saw a man and woman leave here?"

The frightened boy nodded his head in obedience and quickly said, "Yes."

"Good. Now, when they came here, were they on foot?"

"Yes," he said, wiping one eye with his sleeve.

"And when they left, were they on foot?"

"No," was all he said.

"Well, what were they on?" Jonathan said louder, apparently tiring of the exchange.

"The wagon," the boy said.

"They were given a wagon?" Jonathan raged.

Suddenly a voice demanded Jonathan's attention from behind.

"They had my horse and wagon, and as you already know, my name is Japhet, you snake," Japhet said, angry and unashamed. "How dare you threaten a defenseless boy. You call yourself a priest?"

"Bah! I am in the pursuit of criminals as commissioned by the high priest, not that I need explain to you," Jonathan said, with the point of his sword now in Japhet's direction.

"The only criminal I've seen today is still here," Japhet said boldly as he faced the glistening, cold metal.

Jonathan raised his brow, then looked at the other horsemen, each of whom wore blank expressions. "Tell me they stole the horse and wagon from you, and I won't have you arrested and brought to Jerusalem in chains. Then we will see who the criminal is."

"I gave them my best horse and sturdiest wagon."

"Gave them?"

"*Gave* them!" Japhet said, holding his chin high, daring Jonathan to run him through with his shiny weapon. Japhet was now thanking God for the courage empowering his old limbs to stand up to this enemy. The more rage he could stir up in this, this priest, the longer he could keep him here.

"Yes," Japhet answered. "I gladly gave them my best after hearing the good news they had to share."

"What good news?" he said, dripping with disdain.

"That Jesus is the Messiah."

"I thought as much. Good. Then you're a traitor and a blasphemer as well, and you'll receive no sympathy when the high priest hears of your punishment."

Japhet ignored Jonathan and made his way over to the boy to help him up. His tearstained face was filthy from wiping his eyes with mud-covered hands. Japhet brushed some dirt from the boy's face and put his right arm around his shoulder. Then Japhet looked back to Jonathan. "Come off your horse and arrest me then. Take me to Caiaphas so I may tell him myself who the Holy One of Israel is."

"Ha! You would like that, Japhet, wouldn't you? But I have no time to waste with you while they're escaping. Just answer me this, old man. Where is your Messiah now . . . when you need him?"

"He is here, with me," Japhet declared.

"We shall see. And you, boy," Jonathan said. "Do you also believe this?"

"Yes," the boy said, nodding innocently.

"Jonathan, he's only a boy. Must you bully him? Deal with me. He believes what he's been told." Japhet held the boy closely. "I'm the one who explained it to him."

Jonathan turned his horse around to face the two guards and unstrapped the whip tied to his saddle. "Flog the old man the usual thirty-nine. If he dies before you're done, give the rest to the boy." He tossed the whip to one of the horsemen who caught it and looked down at them.

"Tie him to that tree," Jonathan ordered. "The one with that ridiculous sign attached to it."

Japhet followed Jonathan's gaze, which remained on the sign for a moment, then dropped lower to the similarly engraved buckets left near the road. He hoped he was wrong and needed to break Jonathan's focus. "You may stop Malchus and Zara, coward, but you will not stop the spread of God's Word. The Living Word."

"I'm only sorry I can't stay and whip you myself," Jonathan said, then he flicked the reins and rode off, his horse kicking dust and sand back on him and the boy.

Japhet closed his eyes and prayed for the Lord to give him the strength to make it through the full thirty-nine lashes for the boy's sake. His arm still around his young friend, he bent his head and whispered into the boy's ear. "This is the privilege I have prayed for my whole life. The Lord has counted me worthy to suffer for His name. God is good."

The two guards descended on him like raptors, dragged him away from the island of flowers, and tied him to the shade tree, under the wood plank with the star engraving like the one on the wagon.

THIRTY-SEVEN

With all the tension, Evaratus somehow found time to be amused with the suspension springs under the seat. Though almost bottomed out under his lone mass, they provided a profoundly smooth ride for such a challenging road. As Japhet had suggested, one of the slaves was on Evaratus's horse in front of the wagon and the other was on the mule behind it. The wagon was full of the mule's former cargo of traveling supplies, gifts, and two large white stow bags, and all was covered by a single burlap tarp tied to the sides of the wagon with rope. In all appearance a very ordinary sight, inconspicuous among the pilgrims. Except, of course, for Evaratus and his slaves, an extraordinary sight under any circumstance.

Malchus sneezed, lying flat on his stomach in the secret compartment with his head toward the front of the wagon. He was grateful for whatever cushion the lower springs could provide on this painful ride. There was not enough room for him to turn onto his side, and the splintery, rough boards were much more uncomfortable than when they had started out a couple of hours ago. Any decent jolt would slam the floorboard into his chin or the false floor to the back of his head. At least the worst of the lash stripes from Jonathan's whip were on his back and not his front. Though the sting of the whip was not as intense as earlier, any lateral movement became an immediate reminder. Meanwhile, Evaratus apparently thought it unnecessary to warn him of deteriorated road conditions in advance.

Zara was right next to him. She had the benefit of a turban Evaratus had been kind enough to render, since he had a spare for himself. The turban could have been thicker, but it afforded her enough cushion for her head that she could relax her neck.

The horizontal seams in the old wood gave them visibility, albeit restricted, on all sides. Though twisting and stretching his neck was painful and looking past his feet was frustrating while the wagon was moving, Malchus could also see through cracks and knot holes in the rear of the compartment. While they were appreciative of whatever visibility the seams afforded, there was little to be thankful for in the way of ventilation or light. They kept their faces near a grapefruit-size hole Malchus had carved out of the bottom to allow for precious air. As clever as the hidden compartment was, it was stiflingly hot, and without the air hole it would have been maddening if not fatal. The hole also allowed a bit more light to enter, enough so that the couple could see each other's face. Malchus would have made the hole wider, and indeed was doing so, when dust that had kicked up from Julius's hooves billowed into the opening, causing them to cough uncontrollably. Unfortunately, this was not to be a one-time occurrence.

"I'm glad we have some light," Malchus said to Zara, their faces almost touching.

"Why?"

"I can see your beautiful face," he answered as another cloud of dust burst through the hole, causing them both to choke and cough.

"Shhhhh," Evaratus cautioned.

"You mean dirty face," Zara said between coughs. Tightly crammed into the compartment, she labored to bring her hand to her face to wipe the dust from her eyes. A tear slipped onto her finger and mixed with the dirt as she tried to rub away the irritation.

Malchus worked his hand forward and gently pulled Zara's hand away from her eyes. Movement was painful to his sore back, but he was determined not to reveal that while helping her. He pulled the cork from their water sack with his teeth and carefully squeezed a little on the side of her face and then a few drops in her open mouth. He wanted to give her more, but they would need every drop for the desert.

"Ahh," she said peacefully. "I've never known warm water to feel so good."

"Soon we'll find a place for you to bathe."

She stared at him, blinking. He slid his sleeve over his hand and slowly wiped the streaking mud from her face. He never lost eye contact with her. "I've dreamed of running away with you," he said, letting go of his sleeve and stroking her face with his fingers.

Zara smiled. "How long have you been dreaming this?"

"Ever since Judah told me that you were Caiaphas's plot to permanently keep me a slave."

"What?"

"I knew that you knew nothing about it when you chose Jesus' safety over me the night of the arrest. But if Caiaphas could get me to fall in love with and marry a Gentile slave, he could keep me for the rest of my life. It's been done. I told you, if it's good for the temple . . . "

Zara was silent for a long moment. "But why didn't you tell me?"

"At first, I thought it might embarrass you, but later I didn't want you to like me because you thought you had to," Malchus said, then chuckled slightly. "His plan actually worked, but now he doesn't have either of us. How ironic."

Zara wasn't laughing. "What do you mean his plan worked. You would have stayed?"

Malchus just stared at her. He didn't want this moment to pass too quickly. "Yes . . ."

Zara took his hand in hers and kissed it. Apparently the moment meant as much to her as it did to him. "When you dream about our escape, do we get away safely?" she said.

"Sometimes," he said, taking a sip of the water before plugging it up again.

"But not always?"

"Not always."

Zara was silent for a moment. "I've had dreams about you too."

Malchus was surprised. "Escape dreams?"

"No . . . but they're always good."

Malchus smiled, then stretched his neck over and pressed his lips to her forehead. She kissed him softly on his bruised cheekbone. An exchange of physical pain for emotional tenderness. Another cloud of dust blew into their faces. "I'm beginning to hate this hole," Malchus said an instant before a bump in the road banged the floor into his sore cheekbone. He cringed and did not know if he could take another hit like that without crying.

Evaratus laughed.

"Why don't you—" Malchus yelled until a hand came over his mouth.

"Shhh," Zara interrupted with a smile. "You'll just encourage him."

Malchus sighed. "I'm glad this is so entertaining for everyone."

Trying to move faster than the traffic on the road proved futile, even though Evaratus kept attempting it. Most of the road was still too narrow for the wagon to pass the other pilgrims.

"Uh-oh! Trouble," Evaratus said in a more serious tone, his head half turned so that Malchus and Zara could hear him. The wagon slowed down, then eventually stopped.

"What's happening?" Zara whispered. "Why are we stopped?

"Don't worry," Malchus said, wondering the same thing and trying to listen to the sounds outside. "We're safe in here."

"A wagon just up ahead slid half off the road," Evaratus said. "It's a narrow turn. They have to be helped back onto the road before anyone can continue. There's no way anyone can pass, except on foot."

"Can it be moved?"

"Don't speak so loud, it's getting a little crowded out here," Evaratus said in a hushed voice. "Moving the wagon won't be easy. The embankment is treacherous. There's a steep hill on the inside of the road too. No place to maneuver."

Malchus could hear the complaints of the stopped pilgrims behind them, the voices getting louder with each passing moment. He whispered to Zara, "Maybe we should get out and hide over the hill until we get moving again. If the wagons are stopped when the soldiers get here, the advantage is theirs. And I wouldn't mind getting some fresh air."

"And what if we're seen?" Zara said.

"With a little help from Evaratus and his slaves, I might be able to sneak out unnoticed. And maybe with my help, that ditched wagon could get back on the road and we could be on our way."

"Your help? What about me?"

"You'll be safer in here. If I'm spotted, they won't search the wagons."

"Forget it. I'm not staying in here alone. If you're going, I'm going."

Malchus nodded, then knocked on the wood for Evaratus. "Should we come out and help?"

"No! Absolutely not."

Malchus turned back to Zara and managed an awkward shrug. "That settles that."

"Good," Zara said. "This isn't comfortable, but at the moment it's safe. Right now, I will take safe. We just need to be patient."

"Well, it might be hot and sweaty and tight, but at least we can relax our muscles without getting beat up for it," he said, then leaned forward and kissed her. She responded immediately, but the moment was interrupted by the sound of Evaratus's heel rapping against the wooden wall by their heads.

"Company," Evaratus said. "Keep still."

Malchus immediately slid his right arm to his side and stretched his neck to peer past his right shoulder. The position pained him, and it was difficult to hold with the movement of the wagon. But through the seam and knot hole in the rear planks he saw hints and glimpses of three temple guards rudely maneuvering through the traffic, causing pilgrims to jump and dart aside or risk injury. Malchus strained to see and cursed the unpredictable motion of the wagon and the Romans for their negligence in maintaining roads that did not lead to Rome.

"They seem to be examining everyone they pass," said Zara, who was also straining to see.

"You can see that?" Malchus said.

"I think so," she said.

Malchus wondered how much of what they were seeing was actually visualizing what they did not want to see. Though he continued to hold his awkward position, he didn't have to see them to know they would be searching anything sheltered. One guard would search while the other two would continue on to the next. However difficult it was to see their every movement, one thing was for certain . . . they were gaining ground quickly.

Zara took Malchus's hand as the shiny black horse hair of a stallion and a guard's leg became visible through a side seam, almost touching the wooden planks.

Evaratus reacted without delay.

"Oh good! Thank God you're here," he shouted to the guards enthusiastically. "You've come to help us." He stood up on the wagon as he spoke, causing everyone, including the guards, to take notice, his huge frame commanding their attention. "Over there," he said, waving them on and gesturing toward the accident just ahead.

The guards slowed their horses to a walk as they neared the wagon. They eyed it and stared at Evaratus.

"If you hadn't come, these travelers would have backed up all the way to Jerusalem," he bellowed, even though they were very close. "Look at this mess," he said, pointing up and down the road to distract their attention from his own wagon. "Why, the journey of these faithful pilgrims would have been a nightmare if you hadn't come."

"What has happened?" said one of the guards.

Evaratus did not answer but began to applaud, shouting, "Thank you, thank you," as he clapped vigorously. All around him, other pilgrims began to clap and cheer. Then still others joined in.

Malchus could not believe his eyes, or at least his left eye, which was pressed up against the seam. Evaratus was a master of mass mania. The crowd on the road was roaring and clapping wildly, treating the guards as if they were heroes. He and Zara remained silently amused.

The guards appeared a little confused. And embarrassed. They looked around. Behind them the traffic was at a halt as far as they could see. Ahead, a few pilgrims were trying unsuccessfully to move the fallen wagon. And all the while the cheers and encouragement of the crowd grew louder and louder. Finally, one of the guards waved to the others to follow him, and the three of them led their horses ahead, to what had become their new mission. As they rode away from his wagon, Malchus raised his eyes to the heavens and shook his head.

"Relax down there," Evaratus said to his stowaways. "You wouldn't believe this even if you could see it."

"We can," Malchus said, looking through the seam under Evaratus's seat. He and Zara inched as close to the front seam as they could. Without the wagon moving, they had an excellent view.

The three guards took on the challenge. They pushed and pulled, maneuvered and pried at the stuck wagon, all under the watchful eyes of the cheering crowds. After a while, when it was apparent that the guards were not getting anything accomplished, Evaratus summoned his hulking slaves.

"Go over there and act as if you're trying to help. Turn that wagon sideways, just enough so that it can be passed, but allow it to remain stuck on the embankment."

Malchus smiled as he watched his slaves approach the struggling guards. The crowd also watched. The sheer size of the men caused a lull in the cheering. The guards looked like boys in comparison to the slaves. They stood aside and let the two slaves have a turn at moving the ditched wagon. The two strong men grabbed hold of the front of the wagon and easily moved it sideways so it could be passed. Then, pretending not to be able to move it any farther, they shrugged as if to say, "Oh well," and returned to Evaratus.

The traffic began to slowly move around the wagon.

Sweating profusely and still struggling in the dirt, the guards looked up as the wagon with a star carved into its side slowly rolled by.

"Thank you! God bless you! Thank you very much!" Evaratus said as they rolled past. He bowed his head in thanks, and the guards smiled appreciatively, having earned the accolades by their efforts.

THIRTY-EIGHT

Jonathan's horse slowed cautiously after coming upon the stopped traffic. "Keep moving, you fool beast!" he growled at his horse, his anticipation peaked. He could think of only one reason why the pilgrims should not be moving. The fugitives had been found and arrested. They had probably put up a fight. If only he had been there for that. *If only,* he seethed.

"How much farther?" he said aloud after coming around another bend only to find the traffic halted to the next turn. He wanted to whip the horse into a gallop, but the crowded, narrow road made that impossible. If only he could scream without dagger-stabbing pain. He had only enough control to keep himself from running the pilgrims over. He studied the landscape off to the left, hoping to find an opening where the beast could run, but he had to admit the terrain was too rocky. He would only waste more time and risk crippling his means of transportation, not that he cared for the animal.

Hearing a disturbance around the next corner, he knew he was finally getting close. Traffic was starting to move, albeit slowly. There were probably busybodies staring at the captured slaves in irons. He had trained his men well. He might even allow them to administer some of the punishment—but only after he had them first. His fantasies were becoming more vivid every second. Before taking them back to Jerusalem, he would have to detour them off the main road for some initial payback. A taste of what was to come.

He felt for his whip, then remembered having given it to the other guards to use to punish Japhet. No problem, they would be along soon enough. A good flogging off the road and away from the crowd would cover up any evidence of the prior lashing the slaves had received in the dungeon. Caiaphas would have no objection to his administering hard punishment to captured escapees who believed the Nazarene was the Messiah. The traitors. Simple death would be too good for them. And if he got back early enough, he would be able to pick up where he left off with the girl. "Move!" he yelled as he dug his heels into the horse's ribs again.

The road widened on the curve, and Jonathan took advantage of the space to quickly pass around the curve on the outside. He saw the guards and was thrilled his anticipation had not been disappointed. He raced on, but the closer he came to them, the stronger the frown on his brow became. What was going on here, and where were the manacled criminals?

Jonathan pulled back on the reins momentarily to witness what his mind would never have considered. His trained guards were right now diligently at work untying the prestigious temple stallions from some pilgrim's dirty old wagon. And if he could believe what his eyes were seeing, the guards were smiling while being congratulated by travelers passing them by.

Whatever the source of the sorcery, Jonathan was determined to crush it and get back to the task at hand. He snapped the reins and was upon his men a moment later.

"What, may I ask, are you doing?"

The three guards turned around, breathing heavily and sweating, with smiles still on their faces. Upon eye contact, however, their expressions turned to stone.

"Well?" Jonathan said.

"The wagon was blocking the traffic—" one of the guards said.

"We had already inspected every caravan and wagon when we—" a second guard quickly interrupted.

"The pilgrims expected us to help, and it seemed—" the first guard nervously interjected.

"Except for the big man and his two slaves, there was really no one else to—" said the third.

"The biggest men I ever saw."

"Huge," a guard said, reaching both his hands upward as the other two nodded.

"They moved it, but then it became too heavy for them and it was still stuck on the—"

"They said they couldn't stay but that it was good of us to—"

"And everyone has been so appreciative of our help that—"

Jonathan shook his head and put both his hands over his ears. "Silence!" he shouted, then, grimacing terribly, he clenched his fists and stomped his right foot several times on the dusty road.

The guards froze to attention.

"I don't care how this happened," he said in hushed tones, with one hand still on his throat. "We have to find those runaway slaves—and we have to find them soon. Now finish untying those horses," he said, and then noticed the other two guards approaching. "Wait!" he said, drawing his sword as they turned to leave.

The guards' eyes bulged at the sight of the sword.

"Did you see anything that looked like this on any of the wagons?" he said, drawing with the point of his sword in the dirt an oversize version of Japhet's star.

The three guards did not flinch. They just stared at the star without looking at each other or saying a word.

THIRTY-NINE

Malchus looked through the seam in the wood to help stay his sanity. The sun was beating down hard, and the vegetation along the road to Jericho was all but gone. The road was no longer narrow and treacherous. The farther away from Jerusalem they traveled, the farther they descended into the Judean Desert, a baron wasteland known for its mysterious nomads, ambushing thieves, and fanatical prophets, but more than anything else, its suffocating heat. Soon they would level out at the bottom near the Dead Sea, known to be the lowest place in the world and, consequently, the hottest.

Malchus had never realized he had a fear of tight places, but then again he had never been in such a tight place as this, barely able to breath from the stuffy heat and the dust coming in through the hole. With the wagon pitched downhill, his head throbbed and he felt nauseous.

Malchus found the pointy knife Evaratus had supplied to make the first hole in the floor and decided to dig out a second hole in the far more conspicuous front wall. At the moment he did not care about the risk of a visible hole. He was losing his mind and wanted to scream.

Zara looked ill, lying still in a pool of sweat with her eyes closed. He pulled the water sack's plug, took a sip and squeezed the remaining drops onto Zara's lips. If only he could hold the skin over her, he might be able to get a little more out of it.

"Thank you," she whispered without opening her eyes. "I feel like I'm being baked."

He rapped hard on the front wall with the butt of the knife to get Evaratus's attention.

"Shhh!" Evaratus said.

"Never mind that," Malchus yelled. "Find a place off the road to hide. We need to get out of here before we die. Besides, we need more water."

With no immediate response, Malchus rapped again.

"I'm looking," Evaratus said. There are some boulders coming up on the right. We could hide behind them for a while."

"Hurry," Malchus said. He didn't like the way Zara looked, with her thick black hair stuck to her face, her skin blistered with sweat, her lips chapped, body limp.

Suddenly, from behind the wagon, the slave on the mule whistled loudly. The slave on the horse quickly turned around, then motioned for Evaratus to look.

Malchus looked through the seam and cursed under his breath. Jonathan and five guards were speedily weaving through the pilgrims. Malchus did not like the way they were not taking the time to closely inspect the pilgrims with the same thoroughness they had earlier.

"Here they come. There are six of them. Six altogether," Evaratus said, speaking toward the covered pile of cargo behind him loud enough for Malchus and Zara to hear. "Lord help us.

Five guards. The man is possessed. He's lost his mind. Lost his mind completely."

One of the horsemen caught up to Jonathan, who was in the lead, and pointed out the wagon.

"Zara!" Malchus said as he struggled to turn to her. "Wake up! We've been spotted."

"What?" Zara said groggily.

"Jonathan's here!"

"Jesus," she whispered, awaking.

Jonathan led the charge, then signaled for three of the guards to close rank along the left side of the wagon, and two followed him along the right. The horses flanked the wagon on both sides. Six pairs of eyes stared at the covered cargo area. Jonathan gave his horse a slight kick and rode directly next to the driver.

"Evaratus!" Jonathan said, genuine surprise in his voice.

Malchus felt Zara's hand slip into his. He did not have to tell her how important it was to remain perfectly silent.

"Jonathan!" Evaratus said, as if astonished.

"As I remember, you were brought in on an escort," Jonathan said, "but now you're returning with a wagon."

"And a good one too. More comfortable than my horse, and it allows me to bring more gifts and supplies back to Cos."

Malchus had to remind himself that this was part of the plan. He wanted to say something to encourage Zara, but all he dared to do was hold her hand tightly and watch Jonathan and the guards through the wagon's seams.

Jonathan nodded as he momentarily dropped back a step or two and surveyed the wagon.

Malchus watched Jonathan's eyes, hoping to God that he was not familiar with Japhet's signature star. Just then the wagon wheel hit a bump and Malchus got his chin smacked. He winced but absorbed the pain without a sound.

"What brings you so far into the desert?" Evaratus asked.

"We are looking for two people. The man who escorted you from Bethany to Jerusalem and his female companion, a Nabataean slave girl. Do you remember them?" he asked, staring at the cover tarp.

"Yes, indeed I do," Evaratus said, clearing his throat. "Malchus and Zara. In fact, they're the ones who got me this wagon."

Good thinking, Malchus thought. *That could explain why Evaratus had Japhet's wagon.*

Jonathan frowned. "They sold it to you?"

"Traded for it, actually. They told me it had been a gift to them from the old man. Japhet, I believe his name is?"

Good, Malchus thought, weighing every word. Without the slightest glitch of conscience, Malchus prayed fervently God would help Evaratus with this stretching of the truth.

"Yes, yes, Japhet. But what did you give them in return?"

"Err, my horse," Evaratus said, but not as convincingly as Malchus would have liked.

Jonathan tilted his head slightly and frowned in a way Caiaphas would when asking Jonathan to explain himself. Malchus had seen it a hundred times, but with Jonathan on the receiving end. This was the first time he did not find it amusing.

"You traded your horse?" Jonathan said. "And they gave you a wagon and a horse? Why would they do that? You seemed to have gotten the better deal."

"Better for both parties," Evaratus was quick to add. "My horse was a magnificent stallion, the prize of our stables, and they seemed to feel it would be an excellent addition to the temple's already brilliant stock. As for me, though this workhorse has not the speed of mine, he is better suited for towing this wagon, which allows me to bring back gifts from holy Jerusalem."

"They wanted to give this prize horse of yours to Caiaphas?"

"Yes, and very excited too. They were quick to mount up and rush off to Jerusalem."

"Jerusalem?"

"Of course. Where else would they go? I'm surprised you didn't see them. Maybe they took the Hinnom Valley. Two people of exceptionally high character, in my opinion."

"Really? Well, I have a list of wanted criminals, and they're both on it. In fact, you'd be surprised who else is on it," Jonathan said sharply, one eyebrow arching high on his forehead.

Malchus wondered if Jonathan had not realized the list was gone.

"Criminals? Surely you jest?" Evaratus laughed.

"You think I would come out here for amusement?"

"But what could they possibly have done wrong that you would come after them with such a show of force? Are they murderers?"

"Their crimes are numerous and serious. They're on the run," Jonathan said. "When brought to justice, they will pay dearly. At the moment they are wanted fugitives, which is all you need to know," Jonathan said harshly, his temper beginning to show.

"Then I'm truly sorry to tell you you're heading in the wrong direction," Evaratus said, looking at the guards who completely surrounded the wagon, slowing it almost to a stop. He turned to the one closest to him. "So, were you able to get that wagon out?"

The guard stared back at him without answering, his face flushed.

Jonathan shot an angry glare at the guard, then returned his attention to Evaratus.

"Somehow I don't think they would risk heading back toward Jerusalem," Jonathan said as the guard in front of the wagon stopped his horse, forcing the wagon to come to a halt. The wagons behind him also stopped.

"Well, we haven't seen them this way. Why are you stopping us?"

Through the hole, Malchus could see sweat dripping from Evaratus and onto the ground. *Poor Evaratus,* Malchus thought. He was trying to stay calm, but the pressure was getting to him. From behind, Malchus could hear pilgrims in the stalled traffic getting very impatient. Shouts of protest began to be heard in the distance, then closer, but Jonathan was ignoring them.

"You seem nervous, Evaratus," Jonathan said, leaning toward him. "Is there anything wrong?"

"Nothing. It's just very hot sitting here in the blazing sun chatting with you."

"But I feel we have so much more to talk about."

"Frankly, I think we've talked long enough! I would like to be on my way now if you are through. My journey is a long one, and we've stopped the traffic."

"Yes, of course. We wouldn't want to inconvenience the pilgrims. We can talk better behind that group of boulders," Jonathan said.

"I must protest. If you don't want this action reported back to the high priest, then—"

"Silence! You have aided the escape of two fugitives and have stolen a wagon and horse from a local stable. Maybe we should start back to Jerusalem and begin the report to Caiaphas with that."

"How dare you accuse me of stealing this wagon," Evaratus bellowed. "Yes, let's go see Caiaphas now. We'll see what he has to say when he's found out how I've been detained and accused."

Malchus closed his eyes in despair. Going behind the boulders was tantamount to going down into the dungeon, but the alternative of going back to Jerusalem was more than he could physically bear in this heat. He would sooner disclose himself and Zara to their captors than have the life drained out of them like figs laid out to dry.

"No! Over there!" Jonathan ordered, giving a nod to the guards who immediately took hold of Julius's lead and led the wagon off the road.

Evaratus became unusually silent, and his slaves followed the wagon without incident. The way to the boulders was bumpy and painful. Finally, Malchus watched the rocks cut off the public view, and the wagon stopped.

"What's in the wagon?" Jonathan suddenly demanded angrily, not taking his eyes off Evaratus but motioning to the cargo with his head. "Because of your past reputation, I will show you mercy if you are honest with me. This is your last chance."

Zara was squeezing Malchus's hand, nearly cutting off the circulation. He wished there was something he could do to still her fears, and his own, but he had all he could do to keep his own composure.

"I've already told you. Supplies for the journey and gifts for my people," Evaratus said, indicating with a wave of his hand. "Did you take me out of view to rob me?"

Jonathan said nothing but looked at one of the guards on the opposite side of the wagon and nodded. The guard drew his sword and sliced downward along the side of the wagon, the razor edge sliding along Malchus's viewing seam and cutting through the taut straps holding the tarp in place.

"Have you lost your mind, or have you never learned how to untie a knot?" Evaratus yelled.

The guards immediately drew their swords in answer to Evaratus's outburst. They pointed them at the hulking Cos slaves and ordered them off their animals. The slaves looked to Evaratus, who immediately nodded for them to obey. Meanwhile, the guard who had sliced off the straps used his sword to pull back the burlap tarp that covered the cargo.

"And what do we have in here?" Jonathan said confidently, pointing to the two long, irregular, white stow bags.

"I really must protest the way you're treating me. It is you who is acting like a common bandit," he said loudly. "But if you must know, the bags are filled with sheepskins," Evaratus said.

"Open the bag," Jonathan ordered the guard.

Malchus felt the springs give slightly with the weight of the guard climbing on board, and he could hear his movement above. The guard was close enough to hear a stomach growl.

"Wait" Jonathan ordered. "I'll do it myself." He pulled his sword while still on his horse. He raised it up as if he was about to cut into the bags, then looked to Evaratus for a reaction.

"Go ahead," Evaratus said. "But I swear you'll pay for every damaged fleece."

Jonathan frowned, and then suddenly, he turned his wrist and threw the weapon like a spear as hard as he could at the white bags, startling the guard in the wagon. It struck the floor with a *thud* at the end of the stow bag closest to the front of the wagon and right behind Evaratus. The razor-sharp sword tore clean through the stow bag and through the weathered wooden floor of the wagon and the shallow ceiling below. The shiny steel end of the sword just missed Malchus's right eye, sending dust and splinters into his face.

Zara gasped.

"I told you. Sheepskins!" Evaratus said immediately.

Jonathan furrowed his brow, staring at his sword.

Zara stared at Malchus without blinking or breathing. Malchus broke eye contact only to look at the sword's point, then back to Zara.

Jonathan dismounted and climbed into the wagon. Everyone's gaze was upon him. He nudged one of the stow bags with his foot. Then the other. The bags moved easily, without the weight or bloodshed he was apparently looking for.

"Are we finished?" Evaratus said.

Jonathan said nothing, still staring at the bags.

"Look," Evaratus said consolingly. "You're on a mission, and you're zealous to accomplish it. I can understand that. Why don't you continue on before it gets any later, and we'll clean up this mess."

Jonathan looked at Evaratus, but still had nothing to say.

"You go your way, I'll go mine," Evaratus continued. "What happened here stays here."

Jonathan nodded but was still silent and frowning. He grabbed the handle of his sword and pulled, but it would not come out. He looked at Evaratus, almost apologetically, and then worked the sword back and forth.

Malchus backed his head slowly away from the moving blade.

Finally Jonathan's sword came free and was instantly replaced by a shaft of sunlight stabbing brightly into the secret compartment. Malchus backed away from the sunbeam, and Jonathan climbed humbly off the wagon.

Malchus watched Jonathan walk back to his horse. His muscles were still cramping tense, but at least he was able to breathe again. Zara was still as rigid as a board, but that would soon pass also. Jonathan would be gone, and they could get out of this oven.

"We'll take care of that. Just go." Evaratus said to the remaining guard who was trying to tidy up the fleece-filled stow bags.

Malchus watched the dust particles dancing and shimmering in the solid sunbeam. The light flickered on and off with the movement above. Some of the wool that had been in the stow bag before it had been ripped by the sword was dropping through the gash in the floor as the guard worked. Malchus heard what he thought were Evaratus's impatient fingers drumming on the seat.

The guard seemed to have finished, but Malchus still had not heard the now-familiar spring adjustment that occurred when someone climbed on or off the wagon. Malchus stopped breathing again. He wanted to look up through the gash to see what was happening, but he imagined there might be an eyeball staring back at him.

Suddenly, a sword plunged through the gash and hit the floor of the hideaway, just missing the hole Malchus had carved. The sword was yanked out and sent in again with the same result.

"Sir. I think you should look at this," the guard on the wagon said.

Jonathan's head snapped around like a hawk's.

FORTY

Get everything out," Jonathan yelled, once again reaching for his throat in pain. He quickly climbed back onto the wagon. He and the only guard not holding someone at sword point proceeded to attack the cargo, throwing everything out of the wagon until it was completely empty.

Again, swords were drawn on the Cos slaves, who looked to Evaratus for how they should respond. As before, he motioned for them to submit. A sword knows not size.

"How does it open?" Jonathan demanded, his weapon pointing at Evaratus. "Tell me now, or I'll begin driving my sword into it and figure it out myself."

"Don't!" Evaratus yelled. "I'll open it. You must get out first." Evaratus then spoke to the cargo area of the wagon. "Time to come out, my friends."

"God will not forsake us, Zara," Malchus said to her. The words flowed easily, when he saw the fear on her face, but he did not feel nearly as confident as he wanted her to believe. The floorboards of the wagon began to rise upward, then flipped over. The sunlight was blinding, but the air felt wonderful compared to the no longer secret compartment. At least he no longer had to choose which was a better place to die.

Malchus slowly got to his knees and helped Zara to hers. The heat had drained much of his energy.

"Well, look at what we have here," Jonathan said proudly. "Come on, we don't have all day."

Malchus crawled to the back of the wagon, wearily climbed over, then helped Zara off.

"You, too, fat man. Get off. And if one of your slaves has anything to say about that, we'll kill you first," Jonathan said as Evaratus was marched by. "Just so you know, you're in as much trouble now as they are. How nice that you weren't going to report me to Caiaphas. What did you say? What happened here stays here? How prophetic."

Malchus did not like that they were behind the boulders, hidden from public view. Zara was having a hard time standing, so there was little chance of escape without her falling victim to a temple sword, though a quick death might be preferable to Jonathan's verbal strut.

"Get those two slaves and bring them over here. I want everyone in one place where I can see them," he ordered.

The temple guards made Evaratus's slaves dismount at sword point and herded them together with Malchus, Zara, and Evaratus.

Julius, who had been a model of compliance, was acting strangely, moving about, snorting, and jerking his head.

"What's wrong with that horse?" Jonathan said to Malchus.

"I don't know. Maybe your horse is in heat."

"My—I would not ride a—Oh, never mind," he said abruptly, and then turned to the guard who had discovered the secret compartment. "Hold that beast still, or I'll feed it to the vultures."

"Yes, sir."

Jonathan took a moment to survey his prisoners and then shifted his gaze to the guards. "I must say, I did not expect to have so much company on my way back to Jerusalem." He massaged his beard. "We will split into three parties. Evaratus, since you are so fond of this wagon, you and your two slaves will be once again escorted to Jerusalem, but this time the attention you receive will not be as envious. You will be tied, and three of my men will make your situation plain to all. You should have weighed your decisions more carefully, but it's too late for that now, isn't it?"

"I regret nothing," Evaratus said boldly, meeting Jonathan eye to eye.

"You will. You will," Jonathan said as he moved on to Malchus.

Malchus had to squint as Jonathan eclipsed the sunlight and stood before him.

"We have a score to settle, don't we. Maybe you won't make it back to Jerusalem. Maybe I'll take care of you myself, right here and now. Then you can join your friend, Japhet."

Malchus narrowed his eyes. "Japhet?"

"Ah! Did I forget to mention?" Jonathan looked at a guard and snapped his fingers. "My whip," he ordered, and then caught it from the guard's toss. "Poor old man. He tried to play the hero for the boy who saw you leave with the horse and wagon. I must admit, he was stronger than I gave him credit for. He survived thirty-eight lashes, but, I'm sorry to report, the thirty-ninth was more than he could stand." Jonathan was smiling like a perverse lunatic again.

Malchus could not believe it. His old friend, Japhet, killed at the hands of this madman. If not for Zara, he would throw another elbow into his throat and die, as long as Jonathan died with him.

Jonathan cracked the whip, but Malchus did not flinch. "Unfortunately, I don't have the time to drag you back. You will ride that donkey with a guard at each side. But not before you are flogged in the presence of your friends. By me. I want your journey back to be a memorable one.

Suddenly, Malchus could think of only one thing. He did not like the way the math was adding up. He watched Jonathan's perverted gaze shift to Zara.

"So, my dear," Jonathan said, smiling at Zara. He grabbed her face in his hand. "We have some unfinished business to attend to." Zara quickly yanked her head away from his grip and turned away in disgust.

"The last time you were alone with her you wound up unconscious in the dungeon," Malchus shouted. "Send her with the two guards, and you'll have all the time in the world to drag me or anything else your sick little mind conjures up. Or are you afraid to take me alone?"

Jonathan's eyes widened for a moment, but then, taking another glance at Zara, he looked back at Malchus and smiled. "Bind their hands behind their backs," he said to the guard holding a sword to Evaratus. "But first, Malchus," Jonathan said, walking past Zara, "there's something I'd like you to have since you're so brave." Jonathan turned slightly to his right and appeared to be reaching for something in his robe, then, with all his might, he turned his body left and followed through with his right fist, blindsiding Malchus hard on the jaw, knocking him to the ground. He then kicked him in the side.

Malchus gasped and curled in pain, his face in the dirt. He could not breathe. By the end of the day he knew that either he or Zara or both would be dead. Like Japhet.

"Get used to it, the day is young," Jonathan said as he opened and closed his own hand to shake off the pain from hitting him.

"You're an animal!" Zara screamed as she hurried to Malchus. No one stopped her.

"No!" Malchus yelled, spitting sand mixed with blood. "Leave me alo–"

The whip cracked, and Zara stiffened.

Swords were instantly pressed against vital organs as Evaratus and his slaves reflexively jerked toward Jonathan.

"This is just the type of behavior that got you both in trouble earlier," Jonathan said, looping the whip around Zara's neck and pulling her away from Malchus.

Malchus struggled to his feet and lurched after her but was immediately knocked back down by another guard. He lay motionless, fighting for consciousness, his only strength emanating from extreme hate and love. He raised his head to see both Jonathan and Zara looking at him. Jonathan was smiling, and Zara still had the whip around her neck, but her eyes were trying to say something that Jonathan could not see. She was widening her eyes, staring at the ground before Malchus.

Malchus almost frowned at her but then saw it. It looked quite natural to the uneducated eye. Nothing more than a broken twig in the sand or a wood chip that had ripped off the wagon in all the turmoil. But Zara knew exactly what it was and had apparently dropped it there for Malchus.

FORTY-ONE

Japhet's whistle.

Malchus put his hand on the whistle as if to support himself, then hid it in the palm of his hand. He might have the logic, but she definitely had the nerve—and the imagination. But why not? What was there to lose? What was a little more pain if it meant a chance for freedom? By the day's end he would either be dead or in prison awaiting death. And Zara would, well, he would rather not think of what her portion would be in Jonathan's custody. A fate worse than death in her eyes.

"Hiding behind a girl, Jonathan? You're always hiding behind someone. I'll never forget how you hid behind the traitor in the Garden of Gethsemane when Jesus came. A good thing you had Roman soldiers there to protect you with Annas not there. Has your father always been overprotective? Is that how you got this way?"

The immediate look on Jonathan's face told Malchus he had hit a nerve.

"What are you saying? How dare you speak my father's name."

"I'm not saying anything your men here don't already know, as well as the rest of Jerusalem."

"I'll cut your lying tongue out."

"And everyone else's too? Your insecurities have been common street knowledge for years. Don't tell me you haven't heard? Why do you think your own father passed over you for Caiaphas to inherit the high priesthood?" Malchus said, then swallowed hard.

Jonathan's face flushed red as the veins on his forehead swelled. His dark eyes would not blink. Then, as if the ultimate final authority on his own life, he said, "You—You know nothing."

"I know everything," Malchus quickly responded. "Though I'm sure you've never noticed, I've been there for it all. Every pompous moment. And after you leave, I see the laughter and frustration you've left behind. What do you want to know? Caiaphas thinks you are an idiot but tolerates you for the sake of your father, who sees you as an incompetent child and a constant embarrassment. His greatest fear is that if Caiaphas dies, you'll become high priest and destroy Jerusalem before the Sanhedrin can dump you," Malchus said, struggling to his feet.

The guard was about to knock Malchus back down, but Jonathan sharply ordered him to halt with his outstretched hand. Malchus pretended not to notice as he continued.

"And what was my crime, knocking you unconscious with one punch while trying to protect Zara? Are you afraid I'll do it again? Humiliate you twice in the same day?"

Jonathan threw Zara to the ground, the whip still around her neck.

"Is that how your father taught you to be a man?" Malchus said, pointing at Zara. "A coward born of a coward?"

Jonathan smiled while massaging his hands. "I'm going to enjoy this more than I thought. When I am done with you I will leave your beaten body here for the vultures and drop your head in Japhet's watering hole when I pass by. That I promise you."

Malchus swallowed at the thought, but still persisted. "Then don't forget to tie me up first. You wouldn't want your men to see me do what I did to you in the dungeon." Malchus continued moving closer to Jonathan.

Zara struggled to her knees and reached her hand out to one of Evaratus's slaves. Ignoring the guard's sword pricking the small of his back, the slave bent over to help her. She wrapped her arm around his neck and brought her mouth to his ear as he set her on her feet.

"If you're a man, prove it," Malchus said, then spit in Jonathan's face.

Jonathan screamed. His oncoming fist was readable enough that Malchus could have avoided it had he wanted to. And Uncle Laben would have salivated at such a clear opportunity to plant another elbow bash into the Adam's apple. But as it was, Jonathan's punch landed hard on the left cheekbone and sent Malchus back to the feet of the guard who had knocked him down. The guard promptly kicked dirt in his face and laughed.

"Don't interfere yet," Jonathan scolded. "When he can no longer stand, cut his head off. Until then, he's mine."

The guard obediently took a step back and drew his sword.

Malchus could not see with the dirt stinging his eyes, but he could hear, and he did not like the new rules or how quickly he heard the sword being drawn behind him. His escape plan had become an excellent method of torturous execution. He somehow needed to lead Jonathan to where the others were, some twenty feet away, without his realizing that he was being led. He needed to be close. Really close. The problem now would be keeping his head.

"Get up!" Jonathan ordered, primed to punish.

Malchus shakily stood up, wiping the dirt from his eyes with the sleeve of his tunic while trying to position himself between Jonathan and the others, but the instant he opened his eyes Jonathan's fist drove him in the opposite direction and again his face plowed the earth.

Dazed, he found himself at Julius's hooves, not at all where he wanted to be. Next to Julius, the guard had Julius's reins tightly wrapped several times around his hand and wrist.

The guard who had been ordered to remove Malchus's head when he could no longer stand had moved into position next to him. He had apparently discovered sunlight reflecting off his highly polished sword and maneuvered the hot beam into Malchus's eyes. When Malchus turned his head away, he could feel the heat now on the back of his neck.

Jonathan and the other guards roared with laughter as Malchus managed to his knees, the reflection of the sword following his neck. Behind Jonathan he could see that one of Evaratus's slaves, the one who had helped Zara, was saying something to the other slave. Only once before had he heard the slaves speak, and it was in their native language. Whatever he was saying, it did not seem to concern the guard who was assigned to him, whether because of the foreign tongue or because he was too caught up in the entertainment.

"Come on, Malchus," Jonathan said, waving him over.

Malchus felt faint. The heat of the sun, the beating, and what was now a desperate thirst seemed to be winning the battle. The landscape seemed to be moving strangely, and even the sound of laughter started to fade. If only he had some water.

The heat on the back of his neck was replaced with the cold blade of the sword. Jonathan shrugged as if to answer the guards' desire to end it now.

Behind Jonathan he could see Zara was crying and pleading with him to get up, but he could not hear her.

"Free in you," Malchus whimpered as he reached up and found a piece of leather harness hanging from Julius. Pulling on it, Malchus fought his way to his feet.

Jonathan and the guards cheered derisively.

"Very good, very good. You have me now," Jonathan mocked.

Standing upright may have momentarily saved him from the sword, but it did nothing for his dizziness. If anything, he felt more stable on his knees. He took one step toward Jonathan and then another, each time to applause.

"Free in you," he repeated to himself as he stumbled forward.

"Just so you don't die thinking I have no compassion, I will grant you a last request. I feel you should have some say as to where your head should be buried. After all, you've provided us with such rich entertainment," Jonathan said, then looked about to his guards to confirm his obvious superiority, which, of course, they did with their continued laughter.

When Malchus got close enough, Jonathan stuck his chin out as a target. Malchus, half falling forward anyway, lunged and took a swing. Jonathan stepped to the side and tripped Malchus who again found himself facedown in the dirt.

"Malchus, get up," Zara cried. She was much closer.

Jonathan took a moment to observe Zara, then walked to Malchus. "I grow bored with you, slave. The time has come to end this charade and get on to better things," he said, looking at Zara.

Malchus grabbed the sand and pulled himself toward Zara and Evaratus's slave on his stomach. When he came close enough to touch her sandal, Jonathan's foot came down hard on his hand. As Malchus cried out in pain, he was kicked in the ribs.

The guard with the sword stepped up, but Jonathan motioned him away and drew his own sword. "I've earned the pleasure," he said with a smile.

Malchus was coughing, aching, and completely exhausted. He tried to get to his knees but could not move. If not for Zara, he would welcome the sword. He barely could breathe, and soon he would not even have to worry about that. Whatever was going to happen would happen with him on the ground where he lay. He was done.

"Turn over, slave," Jonathan said, pushing his foot into Malchus's side. "I want you to see the one who beat you."

Malchus turned over to see Jonathan raising his sword. He was wearing that perverse smile, but just as he was about to bring down the sword he paused and frowned.

"What's that in your mouth?" Jonathan said.

Malchus blew Japhet's whistle as hard as he could.

The shrill cry of the whistle pierced the air. Upon hearing it, Julius furiously reared upright on his powerful hind legs, pulling the guard who was holding him completely off his feet and into the air with him. The guard screamed for his life. The spectacle instantly stole everyone's attention . . . including Jonathan's. His brief shift of focus to the towering animal balancing on his hind legs, doing just what Japhet had taught him to do, was all that was needed.

Evaratus's slave shot his powerful hand forward and grabbed Jonathan by the neck. Jonathan's eyes bulged and immediately teared as the slave squeezed his injured throat. The sword fell, just missing Malchus as Jonathan reached for his neck with both hands. The slave then pulled him firmly against his own chest. Jonathan was pinned to the wall of a man bigger than himself, his back to the slave's front, the slave's right hand firmly clamped around Jonathan's neck like a vice. Jonathan clutched helplessly at the slave's fingers.

"If anyone moves, I'll have him snap his head off like a twig," Evaratus roared, the threat in his voice unmistakable. "Tell them to step away, Jonathan, or you're dead," Evaratus ordered, nodding to the slave, who immediately tightened his grip.

Jonathan quickly motioned with his hands to the guards. They immediately obeyed and backed away.

Julius finally came down, the guard still screaming. The man untied his arm and hurried to the other guards in obvious pain.

Zara dropped to her knees and cradled Malchus's head.

"Water," he said.

Evaratus's other slave, apparently hearing Malchus's plea, grabbed Jonathan's sword and went to the wagon to retrieve some water. None of the guards made the slightest move toward him.

"Jonathan," Evaratus said quietly, looking directly into his bulging eyes. "Order them back to Jerusalem. All except one, who will travel back with you if and when we say so. I wouldn't want to see you mugged. And if we see any sign of their trying to follow us, you'll answer to him," he said, motioning to the slave who held him fast. "Understand?"

Jonathan nodded, barely able to move his head or speak, air itself being rationed by the slave's hand.

Evaratus ordered the slave to loosen his grip, but just enough for Jonathan to give the orders and select the guard that was allowed to stay. Not one of the guards left with a protest, nor did any offer Jonathan any reassurance. They simply obeyed, mounting their horses and riding back the way they had come, never once looking back.

Malchus figured they would hurry away before Jonathan was allowed to have another guard with him. There was nothing else they could do with Jonathan at the complete mercy of Evaratus and his slave. The guard who remained watched his comrades disappear. He appeared depressed.

Evaratus's slave gently dripped water onto Malchus's forehead, then Zara helped his head up so he could drink.

"Easy," Zara said as Malchus grabbed the water sack.

FORTY-TWO

A full moon dominated the night sky and lit up the mountains of the Judean Desert plain as day. The nearby Dead Sea gave the air a scent of saltiness. Jericho, the oldest city in the world, was directly ahead. The old wooden wagon, traveling alone in the moonlight, pulled over to the side of the ancient road.

Evaratus's slaves removed the cargo from the bed of the wagon and lifted the floor planks, revealing Jonathan and the remaining guard, wedged into the tight space, with their hands tied behind them, lying on their backs, and looking up. Their faces were filthy from Malchus's ventilation hole. The slave pulled both men upright by their robes.

"What are you planning to do to me?" Jonathan asked, making no mention of the guard beside him.

"Let you go," Malchus said. "I'm not going to haunt the rest of my life by killing you, which is what you deserve for what you did to Japhet."

"I've done nothing to be ashamed of."

"God will be your judge, Jonathan. Though I think you should know we sent written word back to Caiaphas of your crimes."

"Crimes? Jonathan said incredulously. "Look at me. I'm the one tied up here. How dare you treat me this way. I was only following orders. You're the criminals."

Malchus shook his head. "The only crime I'm committing is sending you back to Jerusalem. I'm sure Caiaphas will be thrilled to see you survived."

"You're just jealous!" Jonathan snapped. "Without me, the temple guard would fall apart, and Caiaphas would have no reliable successor. And without me, the Romans would not think twice about turning us all into slaves like you." He sputtered in anger. "Why are you smiling?"

"Because I'll never hear your voice again. Listen, we're no longer *letting* you go. Now we're *telling* you to go. We'll give you water and the donkey to ride back to Jerusalem with," he said, feeling as if he owed the donkey an apology.

"The donkey?" Jonathan asked indignantly. "You want me to ride into Jerusalem on a donkey?"

Malchus smiled and shook his head. "Don't worry, you won't be mistaken for the Messiah. He's already come."

Jonathan and the guard climbed out of the wagon. The slaves untied their hands. Malchus found himself hoping that Jonathan would try something heroic with Evaratus's slaves. He didn't. Instead he reluctantly climbed upon the donkey.

The guard stood next to the donkey, obviously waiting for Jonathan to make room for him.

"What do you want?" Jonathan said to the guard.

"I—"

"That's right. You lead," Jonathan said. The guard stared at the long road before them, then began to walk, taking the donkey by the reins.

"Aren't you afraid they will turn around and follow us?" Evaratus quietly asked Malchus.

"No," Malchus answered. "I know him. He has only one guard, who is ready to ask us to take him anywhere that Jonathan won't be. Bravery has never been his strength. And when Caiaphas gets a hold of him . . ." Malchus thought for a moment what that scene would be like. He would love to see Jonathan's explanation of what really happened and how Caiaphas would react knowing the other side of the story. That moment was the only thing he would miss in Jerusalem . . . and Judah. But maybe he would see him again someday.

All the cargo had been loaded into the false bottom of the old wagon, except for the two sheepskin-filled stow bags that were propped up as cushions for Malchus, Zara, and Evaratus. The three of them lay back, heads resting comfortably against their pillows, looking up at the stars and drinking from one of several wineskins Evaratus had purchased in Jericho a few hours before. Malchus's arm was around Zara's shoulders, her head resting against his chest. Evaratus appeared to be in deep thought, stroking the hair on his chin.

For Malchus, the day's events seemed distant in the peace of the moment, almost dreamlike. Yet they were events that would be spoken of for years to come in both Cos and Jerusalem.

The two slaves were at the reins and on the watch. As for Julius, he plowed along with "no quit in him," just as Japhet said he would.

"Where will you go now?" Evaratus asked, still staring at the heavens.

"To be honest, before we left Jerusalem this morning, we didn't even know we were going. Our only plan now is to put distance between us and them."

"I was hoping you'd say that." Evaratus said. "You two would honor me greatly by accompanying me to Cos. You would be a tremendous help. You were witnesses. My people need to know who Jesus is and what he has done. They need to hear about him. If you come, I will give you work and pay you a good wage. And maybe I can even arrange a place for you to live—a place you can call home for as long as you wish."

"Cos," Malchus said as he mulled over the idea. Cos was within Roman jurisdiction, but they had committed no crime against Rome. Caiaphas would not dare ask Pilate to arrest them, not with all the favors he had used up trying to stop Jesus. And even if Caiaphas did ask, Pilate would tell him to have the temple guard take care of it. And Caiaphas would certainly have more important uses for them in Jerusalem. In fact, if he thought they were in Cos, he would probably be glad that they were far away from him, with their newfound beliefs.

Malchus looked at Zara and squeezed her close. "Well?" he asked.

Zara's eyes glistened in the moonlight. A tear formed, reflecting light like a crystal. "I love you," she said.

"And I love you."

"Well, I love both of you!" Evaratus bellowed up through the quiet of the moonlit night.

The two giants smiled, and one snapped the reins. Julius looked over his shoulder at the wagon, then broke into a slow trot.

FORTY-THREE

Malchus stood in an open Greek ruin on the hilltop, waiting for the ceremony to begin. There were still a few hours of sunlight, which, at the moment, was drenching spectacular vistas at every turn. Cos was truly beautiful. Malchus had never seen such green hills and meadows. He took in a deep breath of the salty air blowing up the hillside from the pristine coast below and stared dreamily at the ocean, watching the waves break on the sandy shore. He had never seen such large waves on such a pleasant day.

As gorgeous as the countryside looked, however, his mind was on the night to come when he would finally be alone with Zara.

Amid the sound of crashing waves, he could hear people busy at work, the hustle and activity of people building. When they came ashore yesterday, Evaratus told him how Cos was still recovering from an earthquake years earlier that had turned the ancient Greek buildings all over the island into so many piles of rubble. Malchus recalled the earthquake at Caiaphas's house when Jesus died, but had trouble imagining a force that could crumble such timeless and seemingly indestructible structures.

Evaratus remembered it well and was among the fortunate survivors. His account of its magnitude was unbelievable, except for the evidence of the rebuilding still under way. Regardless, Malchus was hardly concerned.

The deep-blue Mediterranean surrounded him like the desert sand once had. The desert had a beauty all its own, but it could not compare to this. Like life past and life present. The sea was dotted with islands big and small, randomly scattered. His gaze chased along the horizon. Sailboats of which he had only heard stories over warm fires were cutting through silver eddies, trailing wakes that pointed them out like arrows.

And the birds. He had never seen such exotic wild life. White and loud and very large, diving in and out of the sea with a hunter's determination, then riding wind currents up the hillside as if at play.

Malchus followed one of the birds over his head and inland above rolling hills that stretched half the length of the long island, interrupted only by a large mountain in the middle of the range. Malchus wanted to climb that mountain with Zara so they could see all of their new world together. A world lush in living colors and smells. A world very different than the one he had known.

Seated on the temple ruins surrounding Malchus were dozens of his new neighbors. He remembered some of the faces from the night before when Evaratus convened a meeting in the center of town to share with everyone that their long-awaited Messiah had finally come and to tell them what he had seen. The news was received enthusiastically, and praise and worship spontaneously broke out. People sang and danced for hours, celebrating the Messiah's arrival with wild abandon. There were no pretenses. No religious overtones. No vying for power. None of what had become the norm in Jerusalem. There was no competition with God. No contest. God was the welcome winner, and everyone wanted to know what to do to be a part of the Messiah's kingdom that Evaratus had heard Jesus speak of.

Evaratus had spoken for hours. Then he had interpreted for Malchus, who told the story of his ear being restored in a faraway olive grove. When he was done, those who heard wanted to hear it again. So he told it again. And again. Until virtually everyone had heard it and was retelling it with the same excitement and detail with which Malchus remembered it. These people seemed as different from Caiaphas and the priests as the green hills of Cos were from the dust of Jerusalem.

Suddenly, a booming deep voice seized the crowd's attention. It was Evaratus. He motioned for Malchus to come to him. The surrounding crowd stirred with confirming smiles and nods as he walked forward. Malchus could not believe the love these people had for him. Here, he was anything but the invisible slave. Then, when he neared Evaratus, the big man put his hand on Malchus's shoulder, smiled, and looked approvingly at him as if he were his own son. Smiling from behind Evaratus, and standing a head above the crowd, were his two bodyguards, both showing the first sign of any emotion since Malchus had met them.

"Well, what do you think so far?" Evaratus asked.

"This place is spectacular. More beautiful than you had described."

"What would you say if I told you that I could show you beauty even beyond what you've seen so far?"

Malchus could not answer. His heart was pounding. He knew the time had come.

"Behold," Evaratus said as he gestured grandly with his right hand for Malchus to turn around.

Zara approached in her wedding dress. She was flanked by two young girls on either side who were dropping white flower pedals at her feet as they walked. She was radiant. Like an angel. Like she herself was sent from Heaven just for him. Malchus could not stop smiling as he stared into her beautiful face. Her eyes searched his. Her hair was covered in flowers that danced in the breeze. Her white dress swept from her left shoulder and was followed by a floral train that the ocean winds lifted and billowed, making her look as if she were floating toward him on a field of lilies.

She *was* the most beautiful woman he had ever seen, and he could not believe God had brought them together. They stared at each other, their joy touching the entire assembly. Malchus took her hands in his. He squeezed them tight, as if he would never let them go, looked up, and spoke so only the two of them could hear. "Free in You."

Zara was not so subtle. Looking up to heaven, she shouted for all to hear, *"Free in You!"* and threw her arms around the man she was about to marry.

ABOUT THE AUTHOR

W. G. Griffiths was born and raised on Long Island and currently lives there and in New Hampshire with his wife, Cindy, and children. When not writing, researching or building, he can usually be found exploring mountain paths in America and abroad, hunting the lower Arctic or riding a horse. He has written several other books, including *Driven* and *The Road to Forgiveness* and is currently finishing the sequel to *Driven*.

Readers may learn more about
W. G. Griffiths and e-mail him at his
website, *www.wggriffiths.com*.

Additional copies of this book and other book titles by RiverOak Publishing are available from your local bookstore.

If you have enjoyed this book, or if it has impacted your life, we would like to hear from you.

Please contact us at:

RiverOak Publishing

Department E

P.O Box 700143

Tulsa, OK 74170-0143

Or by email at: info@riveroakpublishing.com

Visit our website at:

www.riveroakpublishing.com